COME FLY WITH ME

INVERTARY TOO, BOOK 1

JANET ELIZABETH HENDERSON

ABOUT COME FLY WITH ME

They married in their teens.

They haven't seen each other in ten years.

And now they have to fake a relationship to keep their land.

At seventeen, Katya Savage eloped with her lifelong best friend, Brodie MacGregor. Everything was perfect for two glorious years—until Katya became obsessed with her great-grandmother's legacy. To be fair, who wouldn't get excited about having a female bomber pilot in the family tree? Brodie, that's who. Because when Katya asked him to help her find a plane exactly like the one her great-gran flew during World War Two, he had a hissy fit and gave her an ultimatum—him or the plane. Yeah, that was a dumb move...

Anyway, now Katya's back. With her plane. And all she wants to do is set up a scenic flight business on the land gifted to them both. Unfortunately, there are a few teeny tiny problems with her plan: 1. Brodie has his own ideas for the land that don't involve her or her plane. 2. The family who gifted the land to them wants it back. 3. The only way to keep the land is to convince their families, the town, and a bunch of lawyers that they're back together again.

Now, if they could just stop fighting long enough to act like they're in love...

A NOTE FROM JANET

Welcome to Invertary Too - the second season of my Scottish romantic comedies. Thank you so much for buying *Come Fly With Me*. I hope you enjoy reading it as much as I enjoyed writing it. Invertary Too is set in the same small Highland town as the first series, but with a whole new set of characters. Although, the old ones do pop up now and then too, so keep an eye out for them!

I'd also like to give a shout out to, April McBride, who won the competition to have a character named after her. Your name fits in perfectly, April!

In the meantime, I look forward to hearing what you think of *Come Fly With me*. Happy reading!

Janet x

1

———

It wasn't every day you watched a World War Two Soviet fighter plane make its way up the main street of a small Highland town. To be fair, it *was* wingless and secured to a flatbed lorry at the time, not flying over the cobblestone road. Still, the sight was definitely out of place in among the crooked old white houses that made up the high street. Nor did it blend in with the green hills and blue loch that gave the town of Invertary its picturesque setting. In fact, the aircraft was such an oddity—in a town where oddities were commonplace—that it'd brought everyone out to watch the spectacle.

"So, she's really come home then?"

At his younger brother Darach's words, Brodie MacGregor grimaced. "It would appear so."

"And she has the plane she went off to find."

"Aye." The self-same plane that was responsible for ending his marriage.

"I hear tell she's a rocket in the sky. Can fly pretty much anything you put in front of her."

Brodie cocked an eyebrow at his brother. "Where exactly did you hear that?"

"A wee bird told me." The dickhead grinned. "Must make you feel like a complete arse, seeing as you told her she'd never make it as a pilot or find one of the planes her granny used to fly. In fact, some might say you had egg on your face from being so bloody arrogant in the first place."

"If *some* were to say that within my hearing, it would be the last words they uttered."

From the mocking smile on Darach's face, it was clear he wasn't intimidated by his brother's threat. Idiot. Even though Darach had a couple of inches on Brodie, and some army training under his belt, the numpty still thought he could take him in a fight. Brodie knew better. Unlike Darach, *he* never pulled his punches with his brothers. It was the only way he'd managed to survive growing up as the middle child of seven boys.

"Did she give you a heads-up she was coming back?" Darach asked, lifting his chin toward the cab of the truck, where Brodie's ex-wife sat behind the wheel.

"A letter from her lawyer."

"So, she's still pissed at you, then."

"You could say that. I was charged for the postage."

Darach burst out laughing. "I always liked that girl."

Aye, and so had Brodie. Liking Katya was never the problem—living with her was.

When the truck sped past, he caught sight of Katya's face as she stared straight ahead. And just like that, his jeans became uncomfortably tight while his stomach did a backward somersault. Almost ten years since they'd parted ways, and all it took was one glimpse to make him want to bed her. It came as a brutal blow to his ego to discover his Katya addiction hadn't waned. And he'd just bet she would laugh her head off if she ever found out.

Darach elbowed Brodie to get his attention. "Does it bother you that she's still calling herself MacGregor?"

"No."

Sure, it'd been a slap in the face when she'd kept the name and dumped the man, but he could hardly blame her. MacGregor was preferable to Savage any day of the week. In fact, he'd often wondered if one of the reasons she'd been so eager to marry, despite them both being barely legal, was just to get rid of her family name.

But then, there were easier ways to achieve that than taking on a MacGregor.

"Do you think she heard about your plans?" Darach mused as they watched the plane disappear over the crest of the hill at the top of town.

"I'd be surprised. Her family doesn't exactly live on this planet most of the time. Even if they heard the gossip, it probably didn't register."

Darach grinned widely. "Have to say, I kinda miss the family dinners we had when you two were together."

Yeah, it was hard not to smile at those memories. Brodie caught his brother's eye, and they both said, "Delia Savage's dramatic monologues!" And burst into fits of laughter.

"But seriously." Darach wiped at his eyes as he sobered. "What are you going to do if she has plans for your land?"

And just like that, all the humor in the situation was sucked right out. "I'll do what I have to." Both their names might be on the title, but he'd been the one tending the land for the past decade. Katya hadn't set foot on it since she'd walked out on him.

"Eh, I hate to point this out, big brother, but you don't

exactly have a lot of options. Unless you split the land down the middle."

Aye, that wasn't going to work. Their plot of land was a long, narrow rectangle, with the best views lying on one of the shorter sides. Even if they halved it, neither of them would take the back section with the crappy views. And you couldn't split it lengthwise, because they'd both end up with a strip that was too narrow to be of any decent use.

"She'll just have to see reason." Brodie folded his arms over his faded blue plaid shirt.

Darach nodded. "Because Katya's well known for her ability to see reason. Like when you told her to do exactly that, right before she left you."

"This is different." It had to be. "We've both grown up since then. Surely now, we can act with civility toward each other?"

"The letter from her lawyer seemed really civil."

Brodie glared at Darach as he wondered for the millionth time why he'd been cursed with six smart-arsed morons for brothers. "Are you trying to help here?"

"Mainly, I'm trying to ensure I get a ringside seat for whatever happens next. I know it's going tae be helluva entertaining." He mimed an explosion, with sound effects.

"Dickhead."

"*Entertained* dickhead. One whose sister-in-law has returned to town and is about to drive my brother insane."

"*Ex*-sister-in-law," Brodie corrected.

Darach slapped a hand down on his shoulder. "If you'd wanted her to be my ex-sister-in-law, you should have divorced her. Calling her your ex-wife doesn't make it so in the eyes of the law. Although, I'll admit, saying she's your estranged wife is kind of a mouthful."

"I couldn't divorce her. You know that." As did Katya.

If he wanted his dream house, he needed the land Ben Baxter gifted them on their wedding day. And the only way to keep it was to stay married. The gift came with the stipulation that if they divorced, the land reverted to the Baxter Family Trust. Out of his grasp forever.

Along with all the dreams attached to it. Because there was no way in hell he could afford to buy a piece of land like the one they'd been given *and* build his dream house on it too.

So, no, he couldn't divorce Katya. Not without giving up on *all* of his dreams. And seeing as one of those dreams had walked out on him a decade earlier, all he had left was his house.

"I'd better get going," he said as he straightened away from the wall he'd been leaning on. "I want to be there when she gets to the property."

"I might as well come along." Darach tried not to look eager but failed miserably. "Once Katya sees what you've done, she'll kill you, and someone will have to cart your body back to Ma and Da."

"Your support brings a tear to my eye."

"Always happy to help," Darach said with a grin.

"The place has changed," Katya told her best friend as they drove slowly through her hometown.

"Really?" Denise Abebe looked skeptical. "I feel like I've fallen into some sort of time warp. There's an old milk van back there delivering glass bottles to doorsteps. I didn't realize people still did that. And what's with the fashion? That's the third woman I've seen in a shapeless polyester coat and nylon headscarf."

Katya grinned at her fashion-obsessed friend. "You could have stayed in London, you know."

"And miss the fireworks? I think not." Denise angled the rearview mirror to check her hair, then patted her glorious Afro until it met her satisfaction. "I need a trim. Is there anyone in this backwoods town who can style black hair?"

"How would I know? It's been ten years since I've been home."

Ten years filled with travel, adventure, hard work, and sometimes hardship. But in the end, she'd done what she'd set out to do. She'd found and bought a plane exactly like her great-grandmother used to fly in the Second World War, and she'd learned to fly so she could pilot it.

This was the last leg of her journey to restore Natasha Klimova's forgotten history and establish her legacy in the country that'd become her home. Katya intended to use the classic plane to give something back to the community that had given her great-grandmother a second chance at life. She wanted everyone to be as proud of Natasha as she was. Unfortunately, she had to get past her ex-husband to make it happen.

"Is it only me," Denise said, "or is there an unusual number of good-looking men wandering around this town? Dear Lord! Is that Josh McInnes?" She twisted in her seat to stare out the back window.

"Who?" Katya kept her eyes on the road.

"*Who?* I despair of you sometimes. Josh McInnes. American singer. Does stuff like Sinatra. He's gorgeous and sings like sex on a stick."

"I wasn't aware sex on a stick could sing."

"Once you hear him, you'll understand what I'm talking about." Denise flopped back into her seat. "What's he doing in the Highlands?"

"Again, I wouldn't know because *I've been gone ten years*," Katya said, enunciating each word slowly.

"Being back makes you bitchy," Denise grumbled.

But it didn't. It made her soul sing. Katya felt able to breathe for the first time in years. The tension in her shoulders eased, and she found herself sinking into her seat with a smile on her face.

Of all the places she'd seen on her travels, nothing compared to Scotland. To home. The glow of the afternoon sun warmed the emerald and violet of the hills around the town. The loch's surface danced with sparkles, and the crooked white houses that made up the shops lining the high street were awash with golden light.

She opened her window wide and took a deep breath. It was the scent that really made it home. Warmed heather and peaty soil, cut grass and pine, and the bite of crisp air after it skimmed across the surface of the loch. Nowhere on the planet had the same scent.

Nowhere but home.

Denise's voice stirred her from her thoughts. "I've seen a bakery, a sweet shop, an ice cream café, and a fish and chip shop advertising deep-fried curry. Apart from the fact I don't even know how you'd deep fry a curry, I'm wondering if there's anywhere in town that sells vegetables."

Katya couldn't help but laugh. "Don't worry, I'm sure we can dig up a carrot or two for you."

"Yay," Denise said drolly. "So, will you point out your ex if you spot him?"

"I won't have to. I'm sure Brodie will crawl out of the woodwork soon enough."

Katya wasn't about to admit she'd already spotted him in the crowd lining the cobblestone road. A split-second glimpse out of the corner of her eye had been enough to make her palms sweat and her heart race.

Conditioning. At least, that's what she was telling herself. It made sense her body would react to the sight of him. It'd been doing exactly that since she'd turned fourteen.

Denise smacked Katya's arm to regain her attention. "You've already seen him, haven't you? Where is he?" She craned to see out of all the windows. "Which one is he?"

"We've passed him."

"Why didn't you say something?"

Uh, because she'd been physically unable to speak? Katya cleared her throat and shrugged. "It wasn't important."

"You are such a liar. And a bad one at that. Now tell me, how did he look?"

"Like Brodie." *Only more so.* Katya's cheeks burned.

He'd filled out—broader shoulders, leaner face, more compact muscle. The boy stripped away to reveal the honed man. Part of her, the part that wanted to feel justified in what she did, had hoped he'd gone to seed. She'd imagined him with a beer belly and receding hairline, but it wasn't to be. The boy she'd married had been beautiful, but the man he'd become was sex personified.

And he could have been hers.

If she'd stayed.

"You can't fool me," Denise said. "I know you too well. It's normal for your ex to affect you, especially physically. Call it muscle memory. The body's used to doing what the body does around them." She waggled her eyebrows, making Katya laugh.

"Don't worry, any residual *muscle memory* connected to Brodie will evaporate as soon as he starts talking." Katya remembered well how his negativity dampened her libido.

"Uh." Denise pointed down the road. "Are you seeing what I'm seeing, or is sleep deprivation making me hallucinate? I knew we shouldn't have driven all night."

Katya lifted her gaze and groaned. "I told them not to do this."

But, as usual, her family hadn't listened to a word she'd said. Instead, they'd decided to welcome her home in their own special way—which involved everyone in the local amateur dramatics club.

"I don't know what I'm looking at here." Denise was wide-eyed with bewilderment. "You'll need to translate, because my fine English backside doesn't get this at all."

Katya slumped in her seat. "See the banner?"

"How could I miss it?"

She had a point. Strung right across the street, it was wide enough to make Katya worry the plane might get tangled in it when they drove underneath.

"It says, 'Katya MacGregor—Saved from the Fairies,'" Denise said. "In glitter."

"My mother loves glitter. I think she got a bulk deal on it at some point, and now it goes on everything."

"Focus." Denise pointed at the banner. "Explain."

"Okay, so there's a Scottish folk tale about a man, Rory MacGillivray, who the fairies seduced into partying, and he couldn't escape. His intrepid family saved him by literally dragging him out of his yearlong party." She cast Denise a droll look. "Mum came to London last month and told me not to let the big city suck me in. Said it was all just smoke and mirrors, and it was time to come home."

"Oh!" Denise burst out laughing.

"Yeah, oh." She pointed at the little round ball of a woman barreling toward them and waving dramatically.

"You've already met my mother. I think she's playing the part of a fairy."

"You think? She has wings."

"In my family, wearing wings could mean anything."

"And the guy dressed in traditional Scottish gear, looking like he's just stepped out of wardrobe for *The Highlander*? I suppose he's playing the father."

"No, that is my dad. And that's how he dresses every day. He says trousers are bad for his parts because they cut off the circulation." Katya paused. "He's an artist." Really, that was the only explanation she had for him.

"Who's the old man with the goat?" Denise gestured to an older man sitting on a deck chair at the side of the road.

"My grandfather. That's his pet goat, Isla."

"Any idea why Isla's wearing a tutu?"

"She's supposed to be a fairy?" Katya guessed as she slowed the truck to a halt.

Her mother plastered herself to the driver's door, arms outstretched as though trying to embrace the truck. "My darling, my baby, my long-lost daughter has come home at last!" she called to the crowd before looking up at Katya, who peered down from the window at her mother. "Come, child, we have prepared a feast for your return. It has been far too long since I've seen your beautiful face."

"Hi, Mum." Katya didn't bother pointing out they'd spent the weekend together in London not a month earlier. Delia Savage, who'd once played a corpse in an episode of *Taggart* and was in the middle of another grand performance, was rarely swayed by logic. "You do know that the fairies took Rory? If you're welcoming me home, you should be dressed as my mother."

"What kind of costume would that be?" her mother hissed. "This one is much more fun. And later, once we've all had some dinner, the group and I are going to perform fairy dances. Just like the jig Rory was forced to dance when he was taken." She pointed at the rest of the amateur dramatics club, who waved excitedly.

"How do you know what dance he did?" Denise called, squishing into Katya's space to grin down at Delia.

Delia winked up at her. "A fairy told me."

"Don't encourage her." Katya pushed Denise back into the passenger seat.

Denise opened her mouth to speak, but whatever she was about to say was lost in the wail of an electric guitar.

Katya hung her head. "That's my brother and his band."

In her eagerness to get back to Invertary, she'd conveniently forgotten that her family still lived there. Was it too late to turn the truck around and return to London? She'd be more than happy for the fairies to seduce her there if it meant not having to suffer another Savage-family performance.

As the crowd started to sing, Denise grinned. "Is that…?"

"Aye. They're murdering John Denver's 'Take Me Home, Country Roads.'"

"I'll admit, I'm not familiar with Scottish folklore, but I'm pretty sure none of the stories would include a John Denver song."

"Welcome to Invertary," Katya said as Isla the goat escaped and took off down the high street toward the loch, her sparkly blue tutu bouncing as she ran.

2

There was a brand-new, shiny, and very large padlock on the gate to Katya's property. Her shoulders turned to solid rock. Of course there was. Because nothing in life was ever easy—especially when it came to the MacGregors. One of whom was leaning against the post beside the locked gate looking nauseatingly smug.

"Holy Hotness, Batman," Denise muttered as the truck came to a halt beside the man. "Is that your ex-husband? It is, isn't it? Hubba-hubba."

"What does that even mean? Hubba-hubba? And no, there is no hotness here." Katya glared at Brodie. "Arseholes who lock people out of their own property are *not* hot."

"The padlock isn't hot. But whoa, baby, look at the man."

"The man is responsible for the bloody padlock."

Denise shrugged, and Katya was almost certain a little drool was coming out the corner of her mouth. "His actions don't detract from his hotness. I could do a bad boy. Yes, I could." She nodded as though agreeing with herself.

"You're not *doing* my ex-husband. And I'm *not* arguing

with *you* anymore because I need to get out of the truck and argue with *him*."

"I'm coming too." Denise scrambled for the door. "If he smells like a forest, all bets are off because I'll have to get me some of that."

Katya didn't bother answering. Instead, she slammed the truck door and strode over to face off against Brodie MacGregor. The glimpse she'd gotten of him on the way through town hadn't done him nearly enough justice. Age had taken the soft, raw material that'd made up the boy and honed it until he was all lean muscle and defined features. A brush of stubble emphasized his angular jaw, and his sharper cheekbones only drew attention to his dark blue eyes.

His lashes were still too thick and long for him, but the unruly cap of hair he'd sported in his teens had been given the short-back-and-sides treatment.

Katya hated to admit it, but Denise was right: Brodie was hotness personified.

She stopped with a few short feet between them. Folding her arms to hide her suddenly sweaty palms, she glared at her ex. "You have crow's feet around your eyes."

His eyes widened for a second, before he frowned. "Great to see you too, Kat. The extra pounds look good on you."

Oh, now he was just being mean. One look at her would make it clear she was still the same size she'd been when she left him... Okay, well, maybe slightly curvier. It wasn't that she'd gained weight; it was more a case of the weight she already had moving around until it decided her hips and boobs were the best places to settle.

She made a point of staring at his thick almost-but-not-quite black hair. "I know a tattoo artist in London who can fill in the gaps of a receding hairline. I could give you her number if you'd like."

His hand twitched as though he wanted to run his fingers through his hair to be certain everything was where it should be. "Since we're being so helpful, you might want to stop by the loch while you're here. My granny always swore the water could clear up almost any skin condition."

Skin condition? She had one teeny tiny pimple on her chin. You could barely see the thing!

"Okay." Denise walked into the gap between Katya and Brodie and held up her hands. "Do you think we could stop this before the scratching and pulling hair starts?"

Brodie didn't even glance at Denise as he answered her. "I don't know what you're talking about. We're just two people exchanging pleasantries after years of not seeing each other." He glared at Katya.

"If that's what you call pleasant, I don't want to see mean," Denise muttered.

Brodie shifted his gaze from Katya, allowing her to breathe again, and flashed a smile at Denise. Katya did *not* like the gleam of appreciation in his eyes when they landed on her gorgeous friend. Nor did she like the way Denise cocked her hip and stuck out her chest.

"Well now," Brodie drawled. "I don't believe we've met. I'm sure I would never have forgotten if we had."

Denise bloody giggled as she held out her hand. "Denise Abebe, the best friend."

"Oh, you're definitely the best." Brodie held on to her hand a tad longer than was polite, making Katya want to smack both of them.

"I'm going to vomit," she announced, and it wasn't a lie. They were making her sick. "Don't even pretend you have charm. Denise knows otherwise—when she isn't thinking with her libido. And seriously, ten years as a single man, and your pick-up lines are that corny? I'm embarrassed for you."

Brodie's eyes turned flint hard. "Well, I've no' exactly been single these past ten years, have I?"

Katya felt like a bucket of cold water had been dumped over her head. "You're in a relationship?" Her cheeks burned at the stupidity of the question. Of course he was. It wasn't like he'd been in limbo since she left. Yet, it had never occurred to her there might be another woman in his life.

"I can see your travels haven't made you any smarter." Brodie dropped Denise's hand. "When I said I've no' been single, I meant I'm still shackled to you."

His words barely registered, as Katya was too busy biting her tongue to keep from asking if he was in a relationship.

"Oh." Denise sounded sympathetic. "I've just realized how difficult that must have made dating. It's kinda hard to get serious with someone who's still married." She glanced between them. "You two really should have dealt with that years ago."

"Now, why didn't we think of that?" Katya said, still staring down Brodie. "Maybe because we couldn't without losing the land. Which is why I'm here. I want access, Brodie. Take off the padlock."

"You've shown no interest in the land for a decade. I assumed you didn't want it, so I've made my own plans. And wouldn't you know it? Those plans don't include letting my estranged wife dump her relic of a plane on *my* land."

"It isn't *your* land. It's *ours*."

"Really?" He lifted an eyebrow at her, a vision of cocky arrogance. "I seem to remember Old Ben Baxter saying we should use the land to put down roots in Invertary. That he wanted to give us a future in this town. You can't put down roots if you aren't around to do it, now, can you?"

"I didn't leave for good. I was only gone a few years. And now I'm back and ready to put down my own bloody roots."

"Aye, well, you're too late. There's no space for your roots because I've already planted mine all over the land. Every square inch has been claimed by my roots."

Denise raised her hand. "I'm confused. That sounds like you've been scent marking your territory. Please tell me you haven't been peeing out there for the past decade. Have you?"

"He means," Katya ground out, her gaze locked on Brodie, "that he's already started implementing his plan for the land. What have you done?"

"What we'd intended to do before you ran off to play pilot. I'm building a house. The crew starts this week, and there's nothing on the architect's drawings that even remotely resembles a hangar for your plane."

Fire coursed through her veins, searing her. "You can't do this."

"According to my lawyer, I can. As long as we're still married, the land won't revert to the Baxter Trust. But nothing in the stipulations of the gift says both of us have to agree on what to do with the land. Anyway, it wasn't like you were here to discuss plans. It's pure dumb luck you came back before the house was already built. But don't worry, Kat. I'm sure you'll find a parking spot for your plane somewhere." Brodie grinned. "I hear they've got space at the dump."

Oh, that was it. Now she was going to kill him. It didn't matter that there was a witness. Denise was her best friend and would help her bury the body.

On. The. Land. She. Owned.

She managed one step toward him before the coward turned and vaulted over the gate. "See those little flames in her eyes?" he asked Denise. "They're a sure sign you're about to be on the receiving end of Kat's right hook. Isn't that right, darling?" He winked at Katya.

"I am not your darling." Her words were a growl as she grabbed the gate, ready to launch herself over it and chase Brodie down to wipe that damn grin off his face.

"Are you seriously going to climb the gate?" Denise asked. "Am I supposed to stand here and watch you chase him around the paddock?"

"Don't worry," Brodie said. "She won't catch me. Her legs are too short."

Katya could barely see straight as she started to climb. Brodie MacGregor was the devil. Nobody could make her angry like he could.

She had one leg slung over the gate, when her phone rang with her mother's ringtone—Bette Midler's "Diva."

Brodie burst out laughing. "You're still using that ringtone for her? You'd better answer, or Delia will hunt you down. Guess chasing me around the paddock will have to wait."

To hell with that. Her mother could wait. Katya jumped down into the paddock.

"Short legs?" she asked.

"Oh, crap," Brodie said.

There was an ear-piercing whistle, and Katya turned to find Denise waving her phone before speaking into it. "She's right here," Denise, the traitor, said. "Wait and I'll get her. Of course, it's no problem." She thrust the phone over the fence to Katya. "Stop acting like a preschooler," she hissed.

"I can't help it," Katya said. "He makes me regress." She reluctantly took the phone. "I'm a bit busy, Mum. What's up?"

"Dinner's in twenty minutes. I don't want it getting cold while we wait for you."

"We'll be there," Katya said on a groan. "I just have to deal with a little problem first."

"Hi, Delia," Brodie shouted.

Katya wasn't fast enough to cover the phone.

"Is that Brodie?" Her mother sounded delighted. "Tell him he has to come to dinner too."

"I will not!"

"Katya Jane Savage MacGregor, that man is still family, and unless you want to divorce him, it looks like he'll always be family. Now, tell him I invited him to dinner."

"No."

Her phone went dead. A few seconds later, Brodie's phone rang. He tugged it out of his jeans pocket. "Hi, Delia." His eyes danced, and his smile was filled with evil delight. "I'm sorry, but I don't think it's a good idea to come to dinner tonight. Katya's in a murdering mood. Aye, some things never change. Next Sunday? Of course I'll come for lunch. See you then."

He hung up and grinned that smug grin of his that made Katya want to strip him naked, tie him up, and leave him for the midges to feast on.

"You're plotting something evil, aren't you?" He took another backward step away from her. "You have that same look on your face you had when you were thirteen and told me you'd help me gel my hair so I could impress Mary Cameron. But it wasn't gel, it was glue, and I had to get my head shaved to be done with it."

Ah, good times.

But Katya was more interested in the present. "Take off the padlock so we can unload the plane," she ordered.

"Sorry, Kitten." Brodie shrugged. "Darach has the key,

and he went home already. Looks like you'll have to drive it to your mother's."

"There's no way I'm moving it further from *my* land." Her jaw hurt from tensing continually, making it difficult to get the words out. "Call Darach and get him to bring the key."

"No can do," the fool said. "It's his night to watch *The Bachelor*, and nothing gets between my brother and his sad reality TV addiction."

Katya clenched her fists, let her head fall back, and screamed at the sky.

"I think that means she plans on leaving the truck here," Denise translated. "And I'm hoping she means to leave it after she's given me a lift to her parents' house. Because these shoes weren't meant for walking across town. They're vintage McQueen, and let me tell you, that man sure knew how to design a sexy shoe. Impossible to walk in, but sexy."

Brodie looked bewildered. "He made shoes? I mean, each to their own, but making ladies' shoes doesn't really go with the man's man image or his motor-racing obsession."

"Not Steve McQueen, the actor," Denise said with disgust. "Alexander McQueen, the fashion designer."

"I want to be on my land!" Katya shouted at the top of her lungs.

"Aye, well, we can't always get what we want, can we? I wanted a wife who meant it when she vowed till death do us part."

"Right, that's it. I'm going to drive through the bloody gate." She stalked back to the truck, only to be blocked by Denise.

"You can't." Denise held out her hands. "The truck's borrowed, remember?"

"Tell you what," Brodie said. "Since I'm a gentleman—"

"Ha!" Katya barked.

He blithely carried on. "How about you leave your plane here, and I'll give you a lift to your mother's? See? There's no reason why this has to be uncivilized."

Katya took a deep breath. It didn't help, so she took another. Nope. Still not calm.

"Before she rejects your offer," Denise rushed to say, "I accept for both of us." When Katya started to object, Denise talked over her. "Don't mess with me. These shoes might look fabulous, but my feet are killing me. We're taking the ride."

"One condition, though," Brodie said, making Katya want to scream again. "No punching me in the face."

"That seems reasonable," Denise said. "Doesn't that seem reasonable?"

"I need to hear the words, Kat." Brodie appeared to be enjoying himself far too much. "Do you promise you won't punch me in the face?"

A million different ways she could murder the man and be done with him flashed in front of her eyes. "Yes," she bit out.

"Then we're good to go." He pulled his keys out of his pocket and ambled toward her. "After you." He motioned to the gate.

Katya smothered a growl as she climbed, then stood watching as Brodie vaulted over. As soon as he landed on his feet, she socked him in the stomach. With a groan, he bent double, and Katya snatched his keys. "I promised no punching in the face."

"That's just mean," he groaned.

"Can we go now?" Denise demanded. "I can't watch this anymore. I'm embarrassed for both of you. And I'm hungry." She turned away and looked over her shoulder at them.

"You see this backside? It doesn't come naturally. It needs regular meals and chocolate cake to keep it looking this good."

"It's very impressive." Brodie rubbed his stomach while putting some distance between himself and Katya.

Katya stalked past her friend. "Let's go. And I'm driving." She glared back at Brodie.

Denise didn't have to be told twice. She rushed to the car, obviously worried there would be another delay with dinner. Brodie took his time, clearly wanting to stay out of Katya's punching range. The coward. But it did mean she was able to get in the car and lock the doors before he could join them.

He tugged at the handle. "This isn't funny. Unlock the car."

She opened the passenger window a crack. "Maybe when you're calling one of your brothers for a lift back into town, you could ask them to bring the key for the padlock." She started the engine.

"Katya, I'm serious." And to be fair, he did look it. "Get out of my car, or I'll call the cops."

"Go ahead." Matt Donaldson would most likely give her a medal for pissing a MacGregor off.

As she drove away, Brodie shouted after her. "You can't leave me here."

Katya wound down her window and shouted back. "Watch me."

3

"Well, that went better than I thought it would," Brodie muttered as he watched his SUV disappear around a bend in the road.

He put his hands on his hips and hung his head, disgusted with himself. Five minutes in each other's presence, and they were re-enacting their childhood. But then, lifelong habits were hard to break—even after ten years apart.

As far back as he could remember, Katya had been by his side, arguing and getting into mischief right along with him. Even as a child, he'd known Katya was his. His to fight with, to play with, and to love. Never even noticing other girls—unless it was to wind Katya up—he'd known that one day he'd marry his best friend, and they'd never have to be apart.

A sharp pain jabbed inside his chest, and he absently rubbed it. Never, in all the time he'd spent planning out their lives, had he thought he'd have to live without her. When she left, he'd been lost, and a part of him had mourned her ever since.

It had taken years to get his life back on track and to come to terms with the fact his future didn't include Katya.

And now she'd come home.

Brodie folded to sit at the side of the road and drew up his knees to rest his arms on them. What had he been telling his brothers? That he'd moved on from Katya, that she was in his past? He snorted. What a load of bull. When she left, she'd ripped out a part of him, leaving behind a gaping hole. One he'd thought he'd managed to fill with other things, but seeing her again made him realize how wrong he'd been. The hole was still there. It had just scabbed over.

In reality, he was still the same broken man she'd left in her wake.

All. Over. A. Plane.

His gaze turned to the beast in question. It looked so innocuous—de-winged and strapped to the back of the truck. You would never have guessed it was capable of derailing a man's life. And making a mockery of him with everyone who heard his pathetic tale.

And Brodie could do nothing about it. Legally, the land belonged to both of them, and unless they wanted to lose it, they'd eventually have to share. Which meant that even if he did manage to build his house, he'd still have to look out at the plane every day. A huge, ugly reminder of everything he'd lost.

With a frustrated sigh, he picked up a stone and tossed it at a tree, contemplating his current predicament. Since Katya had stolen his car, it was either a long walk to town— and the house he shared with two of his brothers—or call one of them to come get him. And he'd rather cuddle up to Katya's plane than listen to his brothers ribbing him about his stolen car. Wearily, he got to his feet. Looked like he was walking. As he scowled at the truck, another idea began to form in his mind...

What if he drove himself back to town? And if he should happen to leave Katya's precious plane somewhere that wasn't his land, then that was only an added bonus.

Aye, he liked that idea best.

At last his youthful transgressions came in handy, because all it took was his Swiss Army knife and a little know-how to start the engine of the old truck that Katya had, helpfully, left unlocked for him. As he put the truck in gear, his mood brightened. He'd stood by while Katya left, but he sure as hell wasn't going to idly stand by while she returned. He'd changed in the time she'd been gone. Katya had no idea who she was dealing with now, and he couldn't wait to introduce her to *this* Brodie.

Whistling a jaunty tune, he headed down the hill and into town.

KATYA'S FAMILY home hadn't changed one iota in the past ten years—and nor had her family. Well, except for her younger brother, Stephen. He'd shot up and was now a good head taller than her.

"Oops!" she said when he opened the door, using the family nickname that irritated him.

"Don't call me that," he mumbled as she wrapped him in a hug that had him squirming to get free.

"What else would I call the family accident?" She held on tighter. It was, after all, a big sister's duty to drive her younger brother nuts. "You know we love you, Oops."

"Let go," he complained. "I don't do public affection."

That had her grinning into his chest. "You're growing like a tree."

"I'm fifteen," he grumbled. "I grow. Are you done yet? This is embarrassing."

"At least your sunny attitude hasn't changed." She released his lanky frame but ruffled his hair instead, making him scowl at her. "Aw," she teased. "You look sad. Come here and I'll hug it away."

"Just for the record," he said. "I didn't miss you while you were gone."

"Liar."

"Hey, Stevo," Denise said as she came through the door behind Katya. She stopped abruptly and gaped at him. "Holy crap, you've grown."

Stephen's whole head turned red as he muttered something unintelligible and backed away from them. After tripping over nothing, he scurried down the hallway to his bedroom.

"What'd I say?" Denise watched him go.

"Nothing. But you said it using a *girl's* mouth. One that's attached to an *attractive girl's* body."

"Oh!" Denise was sympathetic. "I would rather have my toenails removed with pliers than live through my teen years again. I remember this phase, only I didn't run when a boy spoke to me. No, I giggled uncontrollably and looked like a total dork."

Katya patted her friend's arm. "You're still a dork."

"Thanks."

"You came!" Her arms wide, Katya's mother rushed from the kitchen and made a beeline for her daughter.

"Mum, you called five minutes ago and told me to get here. Why are you surprised I made it?" She hugged her mother tight, breathing in the scent of rose petals that seemed to follow her around.

Delia took a step back before patting Katya's cheek. "I'm never quite sure what you'll do. After all, you did wander off all those years ago and haven't been home since."

"I didn't 'wander off.' I left to train as a pilot. And I saw you and the family whenever I could."

"You mean whenever we could visit you." Her mother pursed her lips. "I don't recall you coming back to visit us."

"You know why I didn't want to return to Invertary." This ongoing argument was one of the reasons.

"Yes." Delia stuck her nose in the air. "I know exactly why you didn't come home. Cowardice. You were afraid to face your husband."

"Mum," Katya groaned.

But, now done with her, her mother turned her attention to Denise, giving her an enthusiastic hug and compliments on her outfit instead of a reprimand. Typical.

Denise pointed to Delia's full-skirted dress and pinafore apron. "I'm loving the 1950s vibe you've got going there, Mrs. S."

Suck up, Katya mouthed at her friend.

"One must make an effort for dinner," her mother said in an over-the-top English accent.

Her mother tucked her hands into the crook of Katya's and Denise's arms and led them around the eclectic mix of furniture that made up their living room.

There was the old vinyl sofa her father found in a skip when Katya was a child. Her mum had re-covered the cushions in a crazy multicolored floral pattern that clashed with the burnt orange of the faux leather frame. The coffee table was made out of empty glass bottles her father had melted and fused together. And every inch of the walls was crammed with his paintings. Some of the huge canvases depicted realistic scenes from Scottish history, while others were a mixture of shapes and dreamlike images.

Four mismatched armchairs of various shades, bookcases that overflowed with art texts and plays, and an old stereo surrounded by a vinyl album collection dating back decades took up the rest of the room. Odd little mementos, childhood artworks, and small sculptures filled every other spare bit of space.

It looked like a gallery and a second-hand shop got together and had a child they'd abandoned to a colony of monkeys.

The kitchen/dining room was more of the same. Except the huge wooden table that once dominated the room had disappeared, replaced by three different-colored Formica tables that sat edge-to-edge in a row forming a large rectangle.

Her father sat at one end studying an art journal with a glare.

"Where's the old table?" Katya asked.

"Your father turned it into a sculpture," her mother said as she took a pot off the stove.

"Needs must," her dad muttered.

"Hi, Mr. Savage," Denise said with a wide grin, clearly enjoying the insanity of Katya's family.

"Denise." Her father nodded. "Name's Fraser. Use it."

Katya rolled her eyes at Denise. "You can see where Stephen gets his charm."

That earned her a brief, amused smile from her dad.

"Sit anywhere," her mother ordered while carrying a large casserole dish to the table. "I made your favorite." She placed it in the middle of the table and lifted the lid with a flourish. "Sausage and tomato surprise."

Katya didn't bother telling her that the dish was Brodie's favorite, not hers. She'd always preferred her mum's macaroni cheese.

"Yum," she said instead.

Looking pleased with herself, Delia went off to fetch the potatoes.

Denise leaned over to Katya and whispered, "What's the surprise?" She nodded toward the dish.

"There isn't one. The surprise part was added when Mum made it one time without the sausages. She forgot to put them in. Surprise—no sausages."

Denise laughed. "I love your family."

"They're yours. My gift to you."

"I heard that," her dad grumbled, his eyes still on the journal.

Katya lowered her voice further, hoping he wouldn't hear what she had to say next. "FYI, if you drop anything on the floor, don't look under the table when you retrieve it. Dad's a traditionalist, which means there's nothing under his kilt. You might catch a glimpse of more than the family tartan."

"That's a joke, right?" Denise's eyes widened.

"No," her dad barked. "Underwear was created by the English to stop trousers from rubbing their wherewithal. Real men wear kilts and let their bits air, as nature intended."

"I'm curious," Denise said. "How does Mother Nature feel about bras?"

Katya answered, before her father could. "She'd rather we let everything hang loose and enjoy the freedom."

Denise was still laughing when Stephen slunk into the room.

"Hey, Stevo," Denise said mischievously.

He promptly tripped over his feet and fell onto their father.

"If you pulled your jeans up, you wouldn't trip," her dad told him. "Or better yet, wear that kilt I got you. You have fine legs for a lad your age. Might as well show them off. Maybe you'll attract a nice lassie."

"Somebody kill me now," Stephen muttered as he took a seat far away from Denise.

"Welcome home." Her mother set a big bowl of mashed potato on the table. "I added cheese, just the way you like it."

Or the way Brodie liked it, as Katya preferred her mashed potato plain.

She caught Stephen's eye and saw his amusement. "Aye," he said. "Welcome home. Better eat up fast, because Mum made your favorite pudding too."

"Don't say it," Katya begged, knowing what was coming.

"Rhubarb crumble." He burst into fits of laughter.

"I don't know why that's so funny." Her mother took a seat facing Katya.

"Neither do I." Katya glared at her brother, who knew she hated rhubarb and Brodie loved it.

"Dig in," her mother said with an unmistakable sparkle of mischief in her eyes. "There's nothing like food to bring back good memories."

That's when Katya realized her mother knew full well whose favorite dishes she'd prepared. And that meant Katya had to make a fuss over every mouthful, because no way would she give her mother the satisfaction of winning this round. So, she loaded up her plate with sausage surprise and tried not to think of Brodie while she ate.

4

———

"I'm going to kill him," Katya snarled the following morning as she glared at the place where her plane and truck should be.

"Is it an invisible plane?" her brother asked. "Like the one Wonder Woman flies?"

"You think you're funny." Katya scowled at him. "But you're not."

"He kind of is," Denise said, making Stephen blush again.

Katya clutched the coffee beaker they'd filled at the pub, as though it were gold. Dougal Jamieson, the owner of the town's pub and hotel, still made the best coffee in Invertary. But even that didn't brighten her mood.

She pointed her mug at the giggling fools. "I thought you two came along to help me. This isn't helping."

"Um, hello?" Denise pointed at nothing because that's all she could point at. "We came to help you unload the plane. The plane isn't here, so now we're improvising."

"If it isn't invisible," Stephen mused, "then it must be the rise of the machines. The plane came alive and flew off on its own."

Denise shook her head. "It couldn't. It doesn't have an onboard computer. It doesn't have much of anything. It's basically balsa wood and canvas."

"Good point," her brother said. "Then it could only have been Brodie."

"You think?" Katya snapped. "Gimme his number. I need to call him."

"I don't have it." Stephen grinned widely. "But Mum does."

"I hate everyone in Invertary." Katya pulled her phone out of the back pocket of her Levi 501s and tapped her mother's number.

"Hey." Stephen was still grinning. "Nobody forced you to come back."

"I came back to preserve Great-granny's legacy. This is the town she made her home after the war, and this is the place that should remember everything she did."

Stephen rolled his eyes and sat on the grass.

"Hello, darling." Her mother's voice spoke in her ear. "I don't have long to talk because we're in rehearsals for *Macbeth*. I'm playing Lady Macbeth again."

"Haven't you already done that about a million times?"

"Yes, but this time we're doing a modern interpretation of the text. We're all going to wear potato sacks and throw red paint at each other during the fight scenes."

Katya took a deep breath and reminded herself it had been her choice to return to Invertary. "I need Brodie's phone number."

"About time! This is wonderful news. You two should never have separated in the first place." There were muffled noises in the background, and someone called for Lady Macbeth to get a move on.

"We're not getting back together. I need to find out what he did with my plane. Could you text me his number?"

"Of course, dear. Whatever you say, dear. Anyway, got to go—my muse is calling." And with that, she hung up. A few seconds later, Katya's phone pinged with Brodie's number.

"I shouldn't have left the keys in his car," Katya grumbled as she dialed. She'd done that so he could pick it up without disturbing her or her family. "I should have hidden the car and held it hostage, just in case he did something moronic—like this."

"Brothers Construction," the voice said in her ear. "Brodie MacGregor speaking."

"What have you done with my plane?" Katya imagined the phone was Brodie's neck and tightened her hold on it.

"Well, good morning, Kat." Brodie's voice dropped into an amused drawl. "Sleep well?"

She ignored the way his deep brogue sent shivers racing down her spine. "Where's my plane?"

"I've no idea what you're talking about." It sounded like he was grinning while he spoke.

"This isn't funny, Brodie. Where did you put her?"

"Her? Does she have a name then? Are you two besties? Do you snuggle up together on cold winter nights?"

"Tell me where my plane is," she snapped.

"Temper, temper," the idiot said. "I assume it's where you left it."

"Stop lying to me. You know full well it isn't here, because you moved it. I swear, if anything's happened to that plane, I will tie you to a barbed wire fence, before I reach down your throat and turn you inside out. Then I'll chop off your head and play football with it."

"Ew!" Denise grimaced. "Graphic. And, I suspect, impossible."

Katya ignored her best friend as Brodie chuckled.

"That sounds interesting." His tone made it clear he was unaffected by her threat. "But I'm at a loss to understand how it will get you your plane back."

"Damn it, Brodie. I returned your SUV, so stop being bloody immature and tell me what you've done with my plane."

"You didn't return my car. You abandoned it on the road outside your parents' house where anybody could have taken it."

She scoffed. "Who? Nobody drives out that way."

"Things have changed in the Highlands since you've been gone. There are a lot more people wandering about doing nefarious stuff."

She wanted to scream, but she kicked a tree instead, grateful for her steel toe cap boots. "Is that your word of the day? Nefarious? I'm impressed. Now, where is my plane?"

"Sorry." Brodie made pathetic rustling noises. "You're breaking up. Must be a tunnel." And then he hung up.

Katya let out a strangled cry of frustration.

"Don't throw your phone," Denise cautioned. "You can't afford to replace it."

Katya hung her head, closed her eyes, and took several deep breaths.

"People talk about their relationship," Stephen said to Denise. "The way they were always fighting, or playing tricks on each other, or making out in doorways. Mum says they were Invertary's Romeo and Juliet."

"Romeo and Juliet killed themselves," Denise pointed out.

"Huh," Stephen said. "Sometimes Mum says they were like Bonnie and Clyde."

"Also, dead. Killed by the police."

"Rose and Jack?"

"Rose let Jack die to save herself."

Stephen grunted. "Yeah, sounds like Mum was on the money with that one."

"Enough," Katya said. "We've more important things to deal with than Mum's imagination." She reached up to tighten the ponytail high on the back of her head, then tugged down the faded T-shirt she'd gotten free at an airshow in Germany years ago. Right. She was ready. "Where would Brodie hide a truck?"

A moment's silence while they considered the options, and then, as one, they slowly turned to face the loch at the bottom of the hill.

"He wouldn't...." Katya whispered.

"He *did* seem pretty pissed at you last night." Denise came to stand beside her. Her lavender capri pants and bright yellow off-the-shoulder sweater served as a beacon to fashion in an otherwise green expanse.

"No." Katya shook her head. "He wouldn't...."

She honestly couldn't think of anything else to say. Did Brodie hate her so much that he'd drown her plane? The one that had taken her eight years to find and ten years to save enough to buy? No. Surely he didn't hate her that much.

Stephen sauntered over to stand at her other side. "If I was married to you, and you left me, only to come back to take my land, I totally would have dumped your plane in the loch."

As the world blurred for a second, Katya grabbed hold of Denise's arm to stay upright.

"Everybody in the car," she ordered when she could talk again. "We need to get to the loch."

Feeling nauseous, she climbed into the driver's seat of her father's antique Citroën 2CV. A car barely big enough for one person, let alone three. But even though her father had to drive hunched over with his knees at his chest, he deemed it an acceptable inconvenience, seeing as the car was French not English. As he'd told Katya many a time, a man couldn't sell out his principles for a wee bit of comfort. And Fraser Savage intended to suffer in his Citroën until Scotland was independent and the English had to pay for the privilege of trading with them.

A noble argument—if a little nutty—but Katya suspected the real reason he held on to the ancient car was he was a cheap Scot who never let anything go. Which would probably explain why he hadn't just traded the car in for a Japanese model. As far as she knew, he didn't have a beef with the Japanese.

"The plane is insured, right?" Denise said as they sped down the winding road to town and the loch.

"With what? Every penny I had went into buying it and getting it here. I didn't even have enough left over to hire a truck, remember? I'll have to sell a kidney to pay Big Davy enough to replace his."

Denise patted Katya's arm. "I'm sure it's fine. We're probably overreacting and thinking the worst. Right?"

Nobody replied.

～

"You know she's going to kill you, don't you?" Darach said once Brodie hung up on Katya. "Or, at the very least, make you suffer the agony of her wrath."

Brodie swung his feet off his desk and pulled in his chair. Their office was small, which meant four desks were crammed into a space designed for two.

"Aye." He grinned, feeling pleased with himself. "But it's worth the pain."

"You sure about that? Remember that time you spray painted her bike pink because she was a girl?"

Brodie chuckled at the memory. He'd been twelve at the time and more than a little annoyed Katya could do more tricks on her bike than he could. The jealousy had soon passed, and he'd been proud of her skills, but while it lasted, he'd struck out—with pink paint.

"Remember what she did in return?" Darach broke into his reminiscing.

"How could I forget?" He'd rushed out of school, ready to cycle over to Katya's to check on her because she'd been off sick that day. His bike had still been chained to the fence, where he'd left it, but the wheels were no longer round; they were square. "Still not sure how she pulled that off."

"Well, Katya loves that plane way more than she loved her bike. If I were you, I'd be hiring bodyguards or running for the hills."

"Good job I'm no' as pathetic and cowardly as you then, isn't it? She doesn't scare me."

Darach just laughed.

"Anyway, I didn't damage her precious plane. I moved it."

Darach shook his head slowly. "Aye, but you moved it into Kitty Baxter's tractor shed—without her permission."

Brodie couldn't help but feel chuffed at his genius. "She'll never think to look there."

Especially seeing as nothing but bad blood had existed between the Baxters and the Savages for decades. Something that hadn't been helped by Ben Baxter gifting Brodie and Katya a parcel of land for their wedding. Catherine "Kitty" Baxter had been none too pleased with her father's bewildering decision.

Conall, their youngest brother, strolled in from the back room, a mug of tea in his hand. "We still talking about the plane?" He sat at the other desk across from Brodie and helped himself to a custard cream from the tin of biscuits sitting on top of it.

"What else would we be talking about? Heaven forbid it might be work." Darach frowned at Brodie. "The Patels are coming in to talk about their house plans again this morning. You two have to be charming and accommodating. We need the work."

Brodie and Conall groaned in unison. Along with their black hair, blue eyes, and an inability to walk away from a fight, their frustration over the Patels' ever-changing plans was something else they had in common.

"I'm sick of drawing up plans for those two," Conall said. "Years I trained as an architect, only to spend my time moving a wall in the Patel house, then putting it back again two days later. This is agony."

"Aw, is the little baby architect upset?" Darach drawled. At twenty-six, Conall hadn't been qualified long, and his brothers never let him forget it. "With the amount of money they're paying us, the least we can do is let them fart around with their house plans. It will eventually stop, and if we can get those plans signed off today, we can start scheduling the work."

As project manager for their building company, Darach was keen to have everything written down and pinned to his noticeboard, in neat rows of colored paper. The brothers suspected Darach had a fetish for post-it notes.

Brodie was proud of their company. Without intending it, most of his brothers had chosen careers that fit seamlessly into a business they could all work at together. Darach was the organizational brain and the muscle. Conall was the architect and creative center. Brodie was the electrician, Bain the building and demolitions expert, and Kade was their carpenter. Only their two eldest brothers weren't part of the business, mainly because they didn't live in Invertary.

Even their dad, who'd worked as an electrician all his life, came out of retirement to help when needed—much to their mother's relief, because she considered their father's retirement punishment for her wild youth.

"Pass me the Patel file." Brodie held out his hand to Conall. "Might as well go through it again before they g—"

Just then, the door slammed open, and Katya stalked in, flanked by her best friend and her brother.

And she did *not* look happy.

5

"Hello, Conall. Darach." Katya gave them a nod before turning her laser-like attention to Brodie. "Hello, Satan's Minion. Do you want to hand over my airplane before or after I beat you to death?"

"Just an observation, Kat," Brodie said. "But it would be hard to turn it over when I'm dead."

The only warning Brodie got before Katya flew into a Berserker rage was the strangled scream she emitted before launching herself at him. She knocked him off his chair, sending them both crashing to the floor. His shoulder struck the corner of the desk. The back of his head hit the carpet. There might have been pain, but Brodie was too busy fending off Katya's frenzied attack to notice. If he wasn't mistaken, she was attempting to give him a noogie. Next, she'd be twisting his nipples or trying to give him a wedgie. It was official—he was back in primary school.

"Stop it," he snapped, struggling to capture her wrists. "This isnae fair. You know I won't hit back."

Apparently, Katya didn't care how unfair it was, as she kept on wrestling him.

"You're embarrassing yourself," he told her.

"You're embarrassing all of us," Denise said.

"I'm fifteen, and even I'm mortified," Stephen added. "I'm supposed to be the kid here."

He had a point, but unfortunately, his sister didn't want to hear it.

"I want my plane!" Katya's voice was a roar against his ear. "Give me my plane!"

They rolled across the floor, and suddenly Brodie found himself on his back with Katya underneath him. With her legs wrapped tight around his waist, she had his throat in a choke hold. Or at least he assumed that was what she was trying to do. Mainly, she was squishing his jaw and shoulder while digging her heels into his abs.

With little chance of him choking to death anytime soon, he focused his attention on keeping her boots away from his groin.

"Give me my plane!" she yelled, making his head ring.

"I don't have your plane." It was like trying to reason with a toddler. Brodie caught Darach's eye. "A little help would be nice."

His younger brother sat perched against the edge of the desk, his arms folded. "Seems to me like you've got this whole acting-like-a-child thing down pat. Not sure how I could help improve it for you."

"That's no' what I mean." Brodie glared at his brothers. "One of you get her off me."

Her arm tightened, squishing his face further into his shoulder. "Not until you tell me what you've done with my plane." As she trembled beneath him, he wasn't sure if it was from rage or something else. "Is it in the loch?"

"What the hell?" Brodie bellowed. "You think I'm capable of doing something like that?"

"I know full well what you're capable of," Katya hissed. "You're capable of stomping all over your wife's dreams because they don't fit in with yours. And you're capable of trying to snatch her land right out from under her nose." Her heels pounded against his stomach. "Did you drive the truck into the loch?"

"No!" He tried to turn to look at her, but it was impossible. "Hell no. Darach, Conall, tell her."

Darach ran a hand through his hair, looking worried. "Kat, you know Brodie. He can be a self-centered idiot, but he isn't malicious. Do you really think he'd do something like that? To you of all people?"

"Aye," Conall said solemnly. "I might have been a boy when you left, but even I could tell how much he loved you. He'd never do something like that. Especially to you."

"People change," Katya said, and it was scarcely a whisper.

Brodie's hands tightened on her ankles. "Not in the ways that matter, they don't. I swear to you, the plane isn't in the loch. It's safe and sound in Kitty Baxter's tractor barn."

Her breath hitched, and he stilled as panic surged through him. Was Katya going to cry? She never cried. Not even when she'd left him. His stomach clenched as he realized what that meant—she couldn't cry for him, for their relationship, but she'd cry for her plane.

"You know where it is. Now let me go." Brodie tugged at her legs. "This isn't funny anymore. I'm damned insulted you'd think I'd drown your plane."

At the sound of a throat clearing at the doorway, Brodie, along with everyone else in the room, looked over to see Mr. and Mrs. Patel staring at them, dumbfounded.

"Are we interrupting something?" Mr. Patel made a show

of checking his watch. "We were meeting at ten, weren't we?"

Darach was on his feet and crossing the room to the couple before Mr. Patel had finished talking. "You're right on time." His smile looked more terrifying than reassuring. "Come in, please. Don't mind them. They're...playing." He made bug eyes at Brodie, obviously expecting him to come up with a better explanation for them wrestling on the floor.

Katya's arms and legs fell away, releasing him. Brodie leaped to his feet before extending his hand to help her up. Thankfully, she took it without making a fuss.

Her hand felt warm in his but different from how it used to feel. Gone was the smooth, perfect skin of her youth. Now he felt the odd callus. It was the hand of a woman who worked hard and wasn't afraid of the damage that came with it.

When she would have pulled away, he tightened his hold and tugged her closer. "Sorry about that." Brodie smiled at the Patels. "We were messing around, entertaining my brothers. Not exactly work behavior, I know, but I'm just so excited to have my wife back home." He wrapped an arm around her shoulders and tucked her board-stiff body into his side. "She travels for work, and this last trip was a long one, wasn't it, honey?"

As he smiled down at her, he couldn't miss the anger flashing in her eyes.

"Yes," Conall said, distracting the Patels. "We hope this won't put you off working with us. We can assure you that we're professionals with extremely high standards...usually."

Darach stared pointedly at Katya. "We don't fool around like this on the building site. Isn't that right, Kat?"

She glanced up at Brodie, her eyes narrowed, and for a split second, he thought she would ruin things for them purely to make him suffer. But when he realized what he was thinking, it brought him up short—Kat would never do that, just as he'd never destroy something she loved.

Guess they'd forgotten a whole lot about each other in the years they'd been apart. Or they'd learned not to trust what was right in front of them.

Katya relaxed into him, her arm curling around his waist as she smiled at their clients. The move was familiar. There had been times when he'd thought they were joined at the hip, and he'd always marveled at how perfect she felt against him. Two halves of a whole, fitting together seamlessly.

An ache throbbed deep within his body. Not two halves. Not a whole. Simply two people forced together again by circumstance.

"I must apologize," she said smoothly to the Patels. "This is all my fault. I surprised Brodie this morning by sneaking up on him and launching a tickle attack that got out of hand." She poked him in the side, where she knew he was particularly ticklish, to illustrate her point. And, no doubt, to piss him off further. "I know I shouldn't have been playing like that at his workplace, but"—she shrugged—"I couldn't help myself. I do hope you understand and won't think less of Brothers Construction because of my behavior."

Katya sounded so sincere that he would have believed her himself if his jaw wasn't still aching from her badly executed choke hold.

The Patels shared a knowing smile.

"We were young once," Mrs. Patel said, a mischievous glint in her eye. "We know what it's like to get carried away with love, don't we, dear?"

As Mr. Patel's face turned an interesting shade of pink, Katya stiffened in Brodie's hold, and his hand flexed on her waist. Both of them reacting to the same unintentional barb. *Love.* The Patels thought them in love—and it couldn't be further from the truth.

Brodie took a deep breath and stepped away from Katya, suddenly needing to put some distance between them. "You should get going," he said to her, carefully keeping his face blank lest she realize how much of an effect she had on him. "You need to pick up your plane, don't you?"

"Plane?" Mr. Patel asked.

"Aye." Brodie tore his eyes away from Kat. "She's found a genuine World War Two Soviet night raid biplane and brought it home. Her plan is to give tourists rides over the loch."

Katya appeared shocked that he knew what she was doing, but she quickly recovered. Part of him wanted to tell her he'd listened to every word of her plans all those years ago. Her dreams were embedded in his soul: a stain of regret for all time.

She visibly swallowed. "I'm hoping to open a little museum to showcase my family history." Her shoulders going back, she stood a little taller. "My great-grandmother was part of an all-female combat squadron run by the Soviet Union."

Mr. Patel's jaw dropped before he composed himself. "Your great-grandmother was a Night Witch?"

Katya sucked in a breath. "Yes, she was. She flew with them for three years, right up until they were on the cusp of invading Berlin."

With clear awe on his face, Mr. Patel took a step toward Katya. "My grandfather was an officer in the Indian Air Force. He mainly flew missions in the Middle East and North Africa, but even he'd heard about the Night Witches. They were legendary among their fellow airmen for being relentless and fearless. We owe them much." He took another hesitant step forward and offered Katya his hand. "This is a good thing you're doing. It's important we remember the sacrifices that allowed us to live freely."

"Thank you," Katya whispered.

Mr. Patel beamed at Brodie. "You must be so proud."

Brodie cleared his throat, keeping his gaze from Katya. He was proud of Kat. He'd always been proud of her and always would be. No matter how much he might disagree with her or struggle to understand her choices, he'd never stopped being proud of her. "Yes," he said a little hoarsely, "I am."

Mrs. Patel rested her hand on her husband's back. "You know, dear, Mrs. MacGregor is probably looking for sponsors. What's a museum without patron support?"

Enthusiastically nodding, Kat beamed at them. "I'd love to talk to you about sponsorship, but no pressure, honestly. I'm still at the beginning stage of setting everything up."

"We'll call you." Mrs. Patel wove her arm through her husband's. "Now, let's discuss these house plans, shall we?"

"Absolutely," Darach said. "We're eager to help you build the house you want. Brodie, why don't you go with Katya to get the plane?"

"I think she's fine on her own." Brodie took a step away from her.

"No." Darach narrowed his eyes at Brodie. "We can do this without you, and we all know how much you want to help her pick up that plane."

"Especially seeing as you were the one to 'help' store it at Kitty Baxter's in the first place," Denise said sweetly.

"Aye," Conall added. "And it might be best if you're the one talking to Catherine Baxter anyway." Left unsaid was the fact the old woman wouldn't help a Savage even if her life depended on it.

"I don't need his help," Katya said. "I can get the plane on my own. Denise and Stephen will help." She waved a hand at them.

Denise was already shaking her head. "Nuh-uh, Stevo and I have a thing we need to do." She flung an arm around Stephen's shoulders, and for a second, Katya's brother looked like he might pass out. "Don't we have that thing?"

He nodded furiously.

"In fact," Denise said, walking Stephen to the door, "we'd better get going, or we'll be late. Have fun picking up the plane."

"But—" Brodie and Katya said at the same time.

"No buts," Conall said with a feral smile. "There's nothing urgent you have to do here at the office, and Katya obviously needs help. You're fine to go."

"In fact," Darach said darkly, "we insist."

Brodie had no option but to acquiesce.

Dragging their feet, Katya and Brodie followed Denise and Stephen out of the office. As soon as they were out on the high street, and the door shut behind them, Katya whooped and pulled her friend into a tight hug.

"Did you hear, Denise? They were talking about sponsorship!" She swung her equally excited friend around before releasing her just as quickly and yanking her brother into a fierce hug. "Sponsorship! Even if it's ten lousy pounds, it will still be more than anyone else has ever invested in my dream."

Her words sliced right through Brodie.

"PDA," Stephen squeezed out. "You're killing my rep with the PDA."

Katya set him free with a grin. "What rep?" She ruffled his hair before spinning toward Brodie.

And stopping cold.

He watched as the joy drained from her, like a balloon rapidly deflating. They both knew there would be no congratulations from him. Even if he'd wanted to give it, he wouldn't be a hypocrite. Suddenly, he became brutally aware of the chasm that had started opening between them the moment Katya discovered her great-grandmother was a war hero. Back then, it had been a crack. Now it was the Grand Canyon of separation.

Brodie cleared his throat. "Let's go get the plane then."

"Yeah," Katya said. "And you two don't have *a thing*, so you're coming too."

Denise shook her head. "Don't take this the wrong way, but after witnessing that wrestling match in there, I really don't want to be stuck in a car with you both. One disagreement, and we'll end up wrapped around a tree."

"Aye," Stephen said. "You can get the plane without us." He held up his phone. "Text me if you crash."

"Wimps," Katya grumped. She straightened her shoulders before turning her attention to Brodie, and he could almost feel the tension emanating from her as she girded herself for spending time alone with him.

That ache inside of him expanded. Once upon a time, he'd been the last person Katya needed to defend herself against.

"We'll take your car," she said. "I'll drive the truck back anyway." She tossed the keys to Denise. "If you manage to total Dad's car without getting hurt, I'll buy you cake. You'll be doing us all a favor."

Denise caught the keys with one hand. "Ten-four. Get rid of the tiny toy car. Gotcha."

"Okay," Katya said to him. "Where are you parked?"

"Up the street."

Without uttering another word, she started walking up the high street, and all Brodie could do was follow. Memories of the countless other times they'd walked up that street together filled his mind: images of them laughing, holding hands, stealing kisses. Now he walked behind Katya staring at her tight posture, aware his would look identical to anyone who noticed them. How far their relationship had sunk.

And all because a dead woman had come between them years earlier.

6

May 6th 1945

Two days before the end of World War Two in Europe.

Germany, close to the Polish border.

It seemed strange to describe flying in an open cockpit as claustrophobic, but that's how Natasha Klimova felt. The blackness of the night, broken only by moonlight peeking between the low-lying clouds, was oppressive. With the lack of visual markers, it was all too easy to become disoriented, and the loud chugging of the plane's engine didn't help with staying focused. The noise was almost hypnotic, and Natasha had been surviving on very little sleep for months. The four hours she'd managed that day, lying on the rough ground under the wing of her plane, hadn't even made a dent in her exhaustion.

There wasn't a lot of space to move in the cockpit, and what there was had been taken up by her heavy coat and oversized boots. Both were designed for men, with their much larger frames. The bulky clothing hampered her movements, making her feel trapped, but she was still grateful for every piece of it, especially her well-worn leather gloves. The thick layers had saved her from frostbite and hypothermia during more than one long winter of flying into enemy territory.

The sliver of material she'd used to pad her goggles, to keep them from rubbing, was long gone, and they now pinched her skin, leaving marks that would bleed if they weren't dealt with as soon as she landed. But the hunger pains that made her stomach spasm were the irritation she found hardest to ignore. Rations had been scarce these past few weeks, and she found herself daydreaming of the apricots gifted to them by some grateful Polish villagers months earlier. Oh, how she would have loved to have even one juicy piece of fruit right then. Just one...

"Ten minutes to target." The navigator's voice sounded in her ear, and a pang of embarrassment washed over her that she couldn't remember the woman's name. She was new. Although younger and less experienced than the rest of their squadron, most of whom felt like they'd been fighting decades instead of a few short years, the navigator still knew what she was doing. This was their ninth sortie of the night, and using only a map and compass, she'd found their target without fault each time.

"Copy that," Natasha shouted through the rubber hose that connected their masks.

Like everything else about their Polikarpov Po-2 biplane, their mode of communication was about as basic as you could get. The plane itself was little more than canvas stretched over wood and easily set alight by the tracer bullets of their enemies. And the aircraft was slow; so much so that its lack of speed had become an advantage over their enemy. When German planes slowed to follow them, the Germans stalled and fell out of the sky. Their biplanes were also quiet and easily maneuverable—advantages the so-called "Night Witches" used to their fullest.

Up ahead, a flare fell from one of their squadron's planes. It illuminated the target area below long enough for them to get their bearings. A German stronghold this time. One of the few left between the wave of Soviet forces and Berlin.

At the sight of the flare, Natasha dropped altitude to a dangerously low thirteen hundred feet and cut her engine, ready to glide in and drop their two bombs on the designated target. This close to the ground, anyone with a gun could take down the plane.

For a split second, she was flying a mission several months earlier.

A plane in front of her catching alight. Fire burning through it as if it were made of paper. Debris falling from the sky... followed by people...

"Get ready," her navigator shouted, dragging her back to the present. Marina! That was her name.

A familiar stillness washed over Natasha as she kept the plane steady. A stillness that had become second nature after three years spent piloting bombers for her all-female squadron. One that had kept her alive more than once, enabling her to react calmly when things went wrong.

As they so often did.

"Bombs ready," the navigator said.

The other women were right on schedule. With no communication between the planes and no way to see the bombs fall in the blackness of the night sky, they had only the confidence that everyone would do their job when the time came.

"Bombs away," Marina shouted as she released the mechanism. "No, wait. One's stuck. I'm going out."

It wasn't the first time, and probably wouldn't be the last, that they'd had to shove a bomb from its rigging. Natasha fought to hold the plane steady while Marina climbed out onto the wing. Lying flat on her stomach, she thumped at the jammed mechanism, and the bomb fell. As she scrambled back inside, Natasha wished, yet again, they had the space to carry parachutes.

Resounding booms shook the earth, one after the other, and sent shock waves through the air. Natasha's plane danced around like a puppet on strings. Orange, gold, and red bloomed up from each target site, painting the black night in streaks of bright light. For a few short seconds, the deadly sight was breathtaking in its ominous beauty, luminous color bleeding into the black, before being swallowed by billowing clouds of smoke.

It always took Natasha a moment to shake off the sight and its deadly implications. A moment too long when her aircraft had become a silhouette in the suddenly bright sky. The whole squadron were black targets for the searchlights to follow and weapons to find.

As the blast wave rocked Natasha's plane, she switched the engine back on and kept her eyes glued to the ground. Holding her breath tight to her, she scanned for the first flash from a searchlight. A beam of light piercing the smoke and aimed at the sky. At her comrades. Her friends. Her family.

There!

"Guns to the ready," she ordered into the tube connecting her to her navigator.

Natasha banked left and swooped down toward the

light. She took care to stay out of its swinging beam, not wanting to make herself a target too.

"Fire!" she shouted.

As the plane headed toward the light, the *rat-a-tat-tat* of their machine gun sounded, and the light blinked out. Knocked out by Marina's expert aim.

"Coming up on another one," she called, taking the plane into a sharp downward turn.

The cool spring air was a slap to her face. Still, it was nothing like the winters they'd endured on their way to Germany. No one was in danger of losing a finger or toe at this temperature. And for that, she was grateful.

"Get ready." She fought with the controls, aware that several more searchlights had replaced the ones they'd knocked out. "Fire!"

Without waiting to see if they'd taken out the light, Natasha moved on to the next one. Cutting through clouds of smoke, she darted out of the path of stray gunfire while making sure she didn't hinder her sisters' return to base.

"Last one," she said.

The other women had managed to take out the rest of the lights and were heading back to base to refuel and reload their bombs and ammunitions, ready for their tenth sortie.

"Get ready to fire." She took the plane into a sharp dive. "Fi—"

Something struck their left wing. The plane careened to the side, losing altitude fast.

Heart racing but hands steady, Natasha gripped the controls and fought to keep them aloft. Through the communications unit, Marina repeated a rosary—an action that would have seen her arrested under different circumstances. Religion of any kind was strictly forbidden in Stalin's Soviet Union.

Black soot covered her goggles, obscuring her view. Natasha wrenched a hand off the controls long enough to wipe an area clear. And what she saw made bile rise in her throat.

Their wing was on fire. Pieces floating away into the night. The flames rushed toward them. Eating up the canvas and wood as though it were dry, brittle kindling.

"I'm taking her down!" They had no other choice.

It was either land in enemy territory or burn in the sky above it.

NATASHA CAME to in a haze of confusion and pain.

"Marina?" The word came out as a croak.

No reply.

Feeling hard earth beneath her and the prickle of bushes against her exposed skin, Natasha tried to make sense of her surroundings. Her vision was obstructed, and she rubbed at her eyes—only to encounter her forgotten goggles. She tugged them off and threw them away, all the while groaning from the pain in her side.

The surrounding darkness was aglow with flickering flames, and shadows danced in a macabre performance that made little sense. Above her head, treetops obscured her view, but in the distance, beams of white light cut through the smoke as they aimed at the clouds.

Searchlights.

Her heart stuttered as the memories flooded back.

Gunfire. Burning. Falling.

"Marina?" Her voice was stronger this time. Was that a whine in reply? Hard to be sure.

The noise surrounding her was overwhelming—gunfire, bomb blasts, screams, and the roar of the fire. Struggling to shake off a feeling of disorientation, she dragged herself into a sitting position and leaned back against the tree behind her. Their plane was nothing more than a black outline within the flames in front of her—what was left of it anyway.

The fire had set the vegetation around it ablaze, reminding Natasha that she'd aimed for a small copse of trees in an attempt to break their descent.

"Marina?" she called louder now.

A pain-filled moan emerged from the bushes a few feet in front of the blazing plane, and Natasha caught sight of a boot-clad foot.

Marina!

Don't be burned. Don't be burned.

Memories of another time, another friend, made her head spin and her stomach lurch. Burned flesh. The smell. Oh, dear God, the smell. Not here. Not Marina. That was another time. Another place.

Not here.

Mustering what little strength she could and gritting her teeth at the pain radiating throughout her body, she crawled toward her navigator. Her right side felt as though it had been ripped open, and she had to fight the urge to scream. A scream would let the Nazis know she was still alive. Instead, she cautiously touched the painful area. No blood.

Broken ribs then.

She could cope with that.

Her head spun violently as she started to crawl again. Nausea assaulted her, and she retched. Everything around her zoomed in and out of focus. A detached, rational voice in the back of her mind told her she had a head injury. Most likely a concussion.

Fighting through the pain and nausea, she finished her crawl to the navigator and knelt by her side. Overgrowth covered the top half of Marina's body. No, not her body. Just Marina. She had to be alive. She just had to.

Natasha shoved foliage out of the way until she could see her navigator. Each movement sent blinding pain coursing through her body. With a shaky breath, she wiped the leaves and dirt from Marina's face and ran her fingers down her throat to check for a pulse.

A faint beat had relief sweeping through her, swiftly followed by the hopeless horror of their situation. Marina was unconscious, and Natasha was in no condition to carry her to safety. There was no way to radio their squadron for help or to signal for aid—even if their plane had been equipped with such things, the rest of the women would be long gone by now. They were on their own, behind enemy lines and very far from home.

Slowly, she moved her hands down Marina's still form, checking her for injuries. And it didn't take her long to find one—Marina was impaled on a branch. A deadly chill swept through Natasha as she tried to make sense of what she was seeing. Blood bubbled up and overflowed from the wound in Marina's stomach, despite the branch still being embedded in her body.

There was no way she would survive.

Natasha's breath hitched, a small whine of sound escaping her dry lips. She frantically swiped at her face, blinking back tears that would do more harm than good when her focus needed to be crystal clear. There was no time to cry, to mourn, to weep and wail.

Taking Marina's ice-cold hand in hers, Natasha held it tight. "Find peace in a better place, sister," she whispered.

Barely a second later, Marina breathed her last.

Carefully, reverently, with a heart so heavy it weighed her down—pressing her deep into the ground—Natasha pushed Marina's jacket aside and reached under the collar of her shirt. Tucked away and hidden on a plain gold chain was the religious medallion Marina had often rubbed as she whispered her illegal prayers.

She tugged it from her navigator's throat. "I will make sure your family gets this," she whispered. "I only wish I could do more."

Then, with one last look at her fallen comrade, Natasha hauled herself to her feet. Swallowing groans of agony, she dragged herself away from the blaze and into the darkness. She needed to find somewhere to hide. To heal. Some way to communicate with her squadron.

Hysteria bubbled inside at the thought of everything stacked against her survival. That voice in her head, the one that seemed to come from a part of her watching her predicament with an air of detachment, told her to give up. To sit down. To die. Anything else was hopeless.

With a clench of her jaw, she fought to shut out the voice.

Instead, she focused on placing one foot in front of the other, knowing she had to put as much distance as possible between herself and the plane. She had no other choice.

She'd made it no more than a scant few feet before someone stepped out from behind a tree to her left. Natasha gasped and clutched her side. This was it. The end. Either she'd die here at the hands of the Nazis, or they'd send her home to the Soviet Union to die. Everyone knew Stalin interrogated those who were captured or ended up behind enemy lines. Anyone lucky enough to survive the interrogation ended up in Siberia—merely another death sentence.

As she started to raise her hands in surrender, she heard it: a whisper of sound in a language she recognized as Lithuanian. "Night Witch. Come quickly. You are not safe here."

Relief sent Natasha to her knees.

7

"Why did you have to stash the plane on Baxter land?" Katya asked as she climbed out of the SUV Brodie had parked outside the barn.

"Because I knew it would piss you off." Brodie shrugged.

Katya wasn't even upset—she'd have done the same thing. "It doesn't exactly make life easier."

"Kat," he drawled, "just being *you* doesn't make life easier."

He had a point. She did tend to create her own problems. "Let's get this over with."

It had been a short, awkward trip to the farm, during which they'd barely said two words to each other. Now all she wanted to do was sneak in, retrieve her plane and get home to a nice warm bath, in the hope she could soak away the tension caused by breathing the same air as Brodie.

But, as usual, the universe was against her.

Because as soon as she set foot inside the barn, she found Catherine—never Kitty, at least not to her face—Baxter standing in front of the truck, with her arms folded and a scowl on her face.

A sneer curled Catherine's lip at the sight of Katya. "I knew it was only a matter of time before you came crawling up here to retrieve this." She inclined her head toward the truck behind her. "Imagine my surprise when the morning crew informed me there was an airplane parked in my barn. You're back in town five minutes, and already you're disrupting everyone's life. But then, disrespecting everyone around them is the Savage trademark."

Even though Katya had been raised to respect her elders, she was almost certain that didn't apply to the Baxter witch. "I see you're still the same delightful person you were ten years ago. When are you going to poop out whatever it is that crawled up your backside, unclench, and get on with your life?"

Brodie made a choking sound as Catherine hissed her displeasure. "And you are still the embodiment of the Savage name. I knew you'd never amount to anything, and I was right."

Katya didn't have the energy for a run-in with the Baxter matriarch. It was no wonder the Baxter cousins, who owned stock in the farm, were little more than silent partners. Spending five minutes around Catherine was enough for anyone.

"Get out of the way, *Kitty*," Katya said. "I'm taking my truck, and I *will* run over you if you don't move."

She could have sworn steam came out of Catherine's ears at being addressed by the despised nickname. It was well known around town that if you didn't want your business boycotted or your social gathering to fail, you didn't call Catherine Baxter Kitty.

It never ceased to amaze Katya that someone as elegant as Catherine could spew such nastiness. With her lithe figure, long white hair twisted into a neat French knot at the back of her head, and smooth skin a woman half her age would kill for, Catherine looked like one of those late-in-life models who walked the catwalks of the world. Even dressed in jeans and a blue tartan shirt, she appeared ready to have her photo taken.

"This"—Catherine pointed to the truck—"is on my property, which makes it mine. You are also on my property, which makes you a trespasser."

"I don't have the energy for this crap," Katya muttered before turning to Brodie. "Will my keys still work or did you trash the ignition when you stole it?"

"They'll work. But maybe we should talk this out, and you shouldn't do anything rash," he told her.

"Like marry my boyfriend on my seventeenth birthday?"

"Fair point. Just don't run over Catherine. It's not her fault the truck's here."

She dug the truck keys out of her pocket. "No. That would be your fault. So how about I leave you two to sort that out while I unload my plane? The padlock?"

"Is another issue."

In other words, it was still on the gate. Katya swallowed a scream of frustration and, leaving him to deal with the fallout of his own dumb idea, walked around Catherine to the truck. But, of course, it wasn't going to be that easy. The bitter, stubborn woman moved to block Katya's path.

"You, young lady, are going to wait here until the police arrive to sort this out." She pointed at Katya. "I will be prose-cuting you for trespassing."

"Well, at least we agree that one of us is a lady." Katya made another attempt to get around the woman, but Catherine blocked her again.

After dealing with drug lords who'd wanted her to fly their product and hadn't liked being told no, Catherine Baxter's attempts at intimidation had no impact on Katya. "You don't want to do this, *Kitty*. I've dealt with much bigger obstacles, and I have a mean right hook."

Before Catherine could say anything else that might piss Katya off further, Brodie stepped between them.

"Get in the truck, Kat," he said as he faced off against Catherine. "I'll deal with this."

With a sigh, Katya rounded both of them, climbed into the truck and started the engine. As far as she was concerned, Brodie and Catherine could beat each other to a pulp. They both deserved it. But, as she drove out of the shed, she couldn't help glancing over to make sure Kitty's claws hadn't taken out Brodie's eyes.

As soon as Katya cleared the shed doors, Brodie moved away from Catherine. "I'm sorry about stashing the plane here."

"As you should be." She dusted off her jeans as though being in the presence of a Savage had somehow sullied her. "We'll see what Officer Donaldson has to say about you assaulting me when he arrives. I called him as soon as my men told me you were heading up my driveway."

Tension turned Brodie's neck solid and rubbing at it had no effect. "Don't play it this way, Catherine. It won't do anyone any good, especially you. You don't have a whole lot of goodwill left in town, so don't throw what you do have away over some stupid prank I played on Katya."

Drawing Catherine into his argument with his ex-wife hadn't been his best decision ever, and it wasn't lost on him how immature and pathetic his actions were. He blamed Katya. She made him nuts.

"This is the second time you've trespassed on my property, Brodie MacGregor. If I were you, I'd save my conversation for the police." Disdain dripped from her every word.

"We don't need the police. I've already apologized about trespassing and hiding the plane in your barn. It was dumb, and I'll own it, but don't make this worse for all of us."

"Oh." She folded her arms and tapped short bare nails on her shirt. "I intend to make it as difficult as possible for both of you. It's time you made that separation of yours permanent and returned *my* land to the family estate—where it belongs. It should never have been gifted to you in the first place. My father wasn't in his right mind when he did it."

"We both know that's crap." Brodie was fast losing patience. "You tried to prove it at the time, and Ben's lawyers squashed the idea flat. What is your problem? Seriously? Why are you this desperate to get that land back? Is it sitting on an oil reserve? Does it have sentimental value? Is not owning it blocking your plans for the farm? Tell me what the problem is because I'm at a loss here."

"The problem?" Catherine barked out a nasty, mocking laugh. "The problem is the Savages. I don't want even one inch of this land in their possession. They don't deserve it. None of them. Not after what they did to my family."

"Nobody knows what they did to your family. Not even them," Brodie said with exasperation. "Maybe if you actually spelled it out for a change, somebody could do something about it." He had enough on his plate with Katya's return; he didn't need the cryptic, passive-aggressive accusations of Catherine Baxter.

Her eyes flashed with fury. "Do you really want to know? Or are you just trying to make me back off?"

"I'm serious—I want to know."

"Then come with me." She stalked past him, and he followed her up to the house.

He'd never been inside the Baxter farmhouse, and he had to admit, he was curious. The home had been in their family for generations, and they'd had the money to keep it in good condition. With its whitewashed walls, gray slate roof, and black-trimmed windows, the two-story building was a Highlands' icon. But, unlike other grand homes, this one wasn't open to the public.

Catherine led Brodie into the reception hall, and he was immediately captivated. A peach and blue Persian rug lay in the middle of the polished stone floor. Antique wooden chairs, their overstuffed cushions designed for comfort, sat before a large open fireplace with baskets of wood beside it. To the left, a blue-carpeted staircase wound up to the second floor. However, Catherine headed for the far doorway leading toward the back of the house.

As he followed her along the hallway, Brodie eyed the landscape paintings adorning the walls. He wasn't an artist and knew nothing about paintings, but they looked expensive. They passed an open door that revealed what must have been the living room. Although the walls were painted a strange shade of salmon pink, the cornices and oversized white marble fireplace had him salivating. It was also strange to note that all of Catherine's sofas were large, overstuffed, and appeared inviting. For some reason, Brodie had always pictured her perched on the edge of a stiff wooden chair—a voodoo doll clutched her in hands...

When she pushed through a door at the end of the hallway and disappeared, Brodie assumed she meant for him to follow, so he did. It was an office, and apart from the huge wooden executive desk and the stuffed stag head mounted on the wall, it was nothing out of the ordinary.

"Turn your back," she barked as she took a painting off the wall to reveal a safe.

Shaking his head, he did as she instructed. "Do you really think I have the knowledge to crack your safe? Or that I'd even want to?"

"A woman living alone can't be too careful."

"Aye, especially when that woman's a crack shot with a rifle, has guard dogs wandering the property, and cousins living on the adjoining land." A thief would have to have a screw loose—or a death wish—to take on Catherine Baxter.

While listening to the safe open and then Catherine rummaging around inside it, Brodie studied the photos arranged on the bookcase beside him. They showed Catherine with her parents: Ben and Anne Baxter. They weren't like the casual shots his family stuffed into frames and stuck haphazardly around the house. Instead, each was a formal portrait. A very young Catherine sat on Anne's knee, both females smiling at the camera, while a solemn Ben stood to one side. A cold rigidity to the images didn't speak of a close-knit family. But then, what did he know about portrait photography? Maybe these were normal.

"Here," Catherine snapped.

Brodie took that as her giving him the okay to turn back around. She stood on the far side of the desk, an envelope in her outstretched hand.

"Take this." A spiteful smile curved her lips. "I'd planned on donating it to the Savage Museum when it opens. Or perhaps I should say *if* it opens. Goodness knows it will probably go the same route as everything else they plan. That family's all talk and no action. Who knows, though.

Now that Katya's returned with that relic, maybe this idea will take off after all."

"You want me to take an old letter?"

"Yes, Brodie, and I want you to read every last word in the envelope. That way, you can fully appreciate what the Savages did to my family. And when you're done, you can hand it over to your wife. Let's see if she's as eager to set up a monument to Natasha Klimova once she's read it."

He took the envelope. It felt radioactive in his hand. "What's in the letter, Catherine?"

Her answering laugh was brittle and anything but humorous. She crossed to the window and gazed out over her land to the small private loch at the end of the glen. "My lawyer will be in touch about the land." Obviously, she wasn't going to answer his question about the letter. "I won't have it in the hands of a Savage. You can see yourself out."

Realizing he'd been dismissed, Brodie did as instructed. When he stepped out into the hallway, he found William McManus, the farm manager, leaning against the wall halfway down the corridor.

The older man straightened as Brodie approached. "I hope you didnae upset her."

"I'm no' exactly sure that's possible."

Brodie had a lot of respect for William; he was a man who knew his job and never hesitated to help out a neighbor in need, but for some bizarre reason, he was fond of Catherine.

"You'd be surprised, lad." William clasped him on the shoulder as he passed, heading toward the office. "You'd be surprised."

As Brodie walked away from the elegant farmhouse, a sense of foreboding settled over him. Kitty had threatened them with her lawyers too many times to count, but the way she'd said it this time had felt different. It was as though she'd finally figured out how to get the land back.

Seated inside his SUV, he considered the envelope resting like a bomb on the seat beside him. Part of him wondered if he shouldn't just hand it over to the Savages and step away from the whole situation all together. Really, Catherine Baxter's problem with their family was none of his business. He wasn't part of it anymore—even though Delia would very much like it to be otherwise.

But, in the end, curiosity won out over self-preservation.

For twelve years, Brodie had wondered why Ben Baxter would gift an expensive piece of land to a couple of newlywed seventeen-year-olds, one of them from a family the other Baxters hated. They'd barely known the man, yet he'd turned up on their doorstep less than a week after their wedding.

When he'd handed over the deed, all he'd said was, "This comes with conditions. Don't screw things up, boy." And then he'd left.

Now, why would a man do something like that for strangers? For a Savage?

Parked in the clearing at Lookout Point, high above the town, Brodie sent a text to Darach to tell him he wouldn't be in anytime soon. He then switched his phone to silent. With some hesitancy, he picked up the envelope and pulled out its contents.

In addition to a thick wad of paper, folded several times, there was a photograph. He studied the photo first. It was black and white, and someone had scrawled *Invertary 1946* on the front left-hand corner. In it, two men and a woman sat on the rock wall beside the loch. The old pub hotel, now called the Scottie Dog, sat in the background—looking exactly as it did now. Brodie turned it over and read the back: *Ben Baxter, Tom Savage, and Natasha Klimova*—Katya's great-grandmother. He looked at the photo again. They were laughing together, leaning into one another as friends do. The photo was interesting for sure, but it was Natasha who held his attention.

It was the first time he'd set eyes on the woman who'd derailed his life from beyond the grave.

8

———

May 7th 1945

The day before the end of World War Two in Europe

East Germany

Natasha lay on a bare cot in the corner of a stone-floored kitchen. The windows were boarded up, as the glass had been blown out at some point, and despite the chill in the air, there was no fire in the hearth—because the smoke would attract attention.

An overwhelming urge to use the bathroom had her struggling to sit despite the pain in her side. A low moan escaped her gritted teeth as her feet struck the cold stone floor, and she wondered how such an ordinary movement could cause her to break out in a sweat.

Her hand shaking, she wiped her hair from her face and realized she no longer wore her uniform. Instead, she was dressed in a long gray skirt, mended in places, and a faded pink blouse beneath a threadbare cardigan. Glancing around the clean and orderly room, she couldn't see her own clothes anywhere, not even her boots.

There was a wooden cabinet containing mismatched dishes, laundry hanging from a rail suspended from the ceiling, and a hutch with canisters labeled *Coffee* and *Sugar* —although Natasha knew without checking they would be empty. In the middle of the room stood a table, scrubbed spotless, with three chairs.

"Good," a voice said from a doorway that led further into the house. "You are awake."

A middle-aged woman, drawn and gaunt, entered the room and crossed straight to the cot. Natasha stiffened as a hand came out to press against her forehead.

"Your fever has broken." The woman continued to speak Lithuanian with a nervous smile. "This is good news. I'll get you some soup." She turned toward the wood-burning stove, which had a battered old pot sitting on top of it. She lifted the lid and stirred its contents with a wooden spoon.

"Toilet?" Natasha asked in rusty Lithuanian through a dry throat.

The woman put down the spoon and hurried back to her. "It's outside. Here, let me help."

Given that being upright made her head swim, Natasha wasn't about to try walking without aid. "Thank you."

She wrapped an arm around the smaller woman's shoulders, and together they slowly made their way through the kitchen door. Once outside, Natasha couldn't help but look around. All she saw was a variation on the same thing she'd seen since the war began: rubble, with discarded belongings strewn among it, and smoke rising from smoldering piles of ash.

Her carer's house was one of only three still standing in

the street, and even then, it was clear they'd all taken damage.

The outhouse had lost its roof and part of the wall that faced a tree. The toilet was still there, and a bucket containing some dirty water sat beside the seat, waiting for her to finish and empty it into the toilet. Small scraps of faded newspaper hung from a nail on the wall.

After doing her business, Natasha tipped water down the toilet and opened the door to her savior.

"I'm sorry," she said, as she didn't know what else to say. She was a burden, a danger to anyone who sheltered her. "I'll leave as soon as I can." She had to find her squadron and hope they didn't hand her over to Stalin's interrogators instead of welcoming her back into the fold. It was well known that anyone who fell behind enemy lines, or was captured, was considered a traitor. Rumors out of Russia said they ended up dead or in the Gulag, which was as good as dead.

"There's nowhere to go, child," the woman whispered as she helped Natasha back to the house. "If you wander out there, they'll get you." She spat on the ground in disgust. "Nazis." The word was a hiss of breath. "And there's nothing to be sorry about. You fight for us." Her eyes welling, she slapped a hand to her chest. "You fight for us when we've been abandoned. We've lost so many, seen too much, and then...your planes..." The woman blinked rapidly. "Your people have moved on. My neighbor saw them fly away. You can't go after them now."

Natasha said nothing as the woman helped her sit at the old table. A bowl was placed in front of her.

"I'm sorry, it isn't very warm. I can't heat the stove during the day...the smoke..." The woman's face reddened.

"I understand." Natasha's hand shook as she lifted the

spoon and took a sip. It tasted tangy and slightly of spinach. Green pieces floated in the cloudy liquid, and it had an earthy undertone. "Thank you."

"It's nettles," the woman said. "We have a couple of potatoes for this evening's meal, and my neighbor will hunt in the woods tonight. He might find something to fill our bellies tomorrow. Last week, he caught a rabbit." Her brow furrowed. "It's too dangerous to hunt in the daytime. The Germans are picking up anyone they can get their hands on to help with the fight. Even the elderly aren't safe now."

"This is good," Natasha assured her. "Just what I needed." She swallowed another spoonful. "I'm Natasha. What's your name?"

"Lina Juska." She looked around as though a little lost. "We came here for a better life. We were afraid when Stalin came to power. There were rumors about him wanting to take back everything lost in the revolution—including Lithuania. We lived in Vilnius. My father was a doctor and very smart. He saw the future coming and knew life would become harder in our home country. So, we moved to Poland, and that's where I met my husband. He was German, so we moved here." Lina wiped at her eyes as she turned her back to Natasha. "My husband disappeared when he criticized Hitler. This was before the war—when we still thought we had a voice. When we thought we could have a say who led us."

Natasha placed a hand on Lina's arm. "I'm so sorry." How many times had she said that since the war started? How many more times would she have to say it before it ended?

"It was a long time ago now." Lina lifted the apron tied around her waist and wiped at her face. "We might get some meat tonight," she repeated. "Pieter will go hunting once it's dark. We had rabbit last week...or maybe the week before...."

Natasha's throat became too tight to swallow, but she forced down the last few spoonfuls of soup. Food was not to be wasted.

"My clothes?" she asked as Lina carried her bowl over to the sink.

In a basin with a small amount of water in the bottom, Lina cleaned the bowl before drying it and returning it to the shelf. "I burned them." She spoke quietly, hesitantly, as though afraid of Natasha's reaction.

"That's good," Natasha reassured her. "We'd both die if they found a Soviet uniform in your house."

Lina peered through a crack in the boarded-up window. "If anyone asks, you must say you're Lithuanian. My cousin. The neighbors won't tell anyone anything different. There's no love for the Nazis around here." She looked back over her shoulder at Natasha. "You've always lived here but have been away at school in Poland. You can keep your given name, but you must call yourself Juska now."

Seeing fear in Lina's eyes, Natasha didn't object—she knew they'd both be in danger if it was discovered Lina had rescued a Russian pilot. "Once I'm stronger, I'll try to find my squadron."

Lina's eyes darkened. "If you want to live, you can't go back. You know that."

She swallowed hard. "The Soviet Union is my home."

"If you go back, Stalin will kill you. If you try to find your squadron, the Nazis will kill you." Bleak eyes held Natasha's gaze. "None of us have a home anymore. The war took them from us. All we can do is survive, day by day, praying the fighting will end and that we might somehow know what to do next." Lina turned to Natasha and forced a smile. "We might get meat tonight. Pieter is hunting. Last week, we had rabbit."

"Rabbit would be good," Natasha said gently.

"Then it's settled." Lina nodded. "Cousin Natasha wants rabbit too. I must tell Pieter he has to find us a nice plump one." She took Natasha's arm and helped her back to the cot. "Rest and get better. I'll return soon."

The door closed softly behind Lina as she left to tell her neighbor to hunt for a rabbit.

That was the last time Natasha saw her.

And in the weeks spent in Lina's tiny house, she never met a Pieter among the people hiding within the town's ruins.

9

———

Katya texted Denise and Stephen to meet her at her land, then she drove straight there to offload the plane. Only, when she arrived, she didn't find her helpers. Instead, she found a whole lot of workmen. Builders, to be precise. And if she wasn't mistaken, they were marking out foundation boundaries to prepare for digging. Tiny little posts, some with bright orange string stretched between them, made up a grid on the ground.

Bloody Brodie still planned to build his house.

On her land.

Without permission.

Oh, hell no!

There was no need for the bolt cutters she'd picked up at her parents' house on the way over because the gate stood open. Katya drove the truck through and parked right in front of the other vehicles—so they couldn't miss her arrival—and was pleased to note that all work stopped at the sight of her.

She climbed out of the truck, slammed the door, and stalked toward the men, easily identifying who was in charge because it was another MacGregor. Of course. And the coward had his phone in his hand, no doubt texting the back-stabbing moron she'd married to snitch that she was on site.

"Pack it up," Katya called out to Bain, one of Brodie's older brothers, as she stalked toward him.

His smile oozed MacGregor charm. "Good to see you too, Katya. You look well. I like the long hair—it suits you."

"Don't try to charm me, Bain MacGregor. Unlike every other woman in Scotland, I won't fall for it. To me, you'll always be the boy who actually enjoyed eating worms."

His lips twitched. "You'd be surprised how good they taste with curry sauce."

Hands on hips, feet apart, she glared at him. "I'm serious. You guys don't have permission to build on *my* land, so you can pack everything up and go on back to the office."

At under six foot, Bain was one of the shorter MacGregors, but what he lacked in height, he made up for in muscle and attitude. Those muscles flexed now as he folded his arms across his blue T-shirt. "Well, here's the thing. I have a brother who would argue that we don't need *your* permission to build *his* house on *his* land."

"You know full well Brodie and I own this land together. He can't do anything without me signing off on it first. And I didn't sign off on this." Katya waved a hand to indicate the lines marked out on the grass. "He shouldn't even have started. What the hell was he thinking?"

"That it would be more convenient to ask forgiveness than permission?"

Was Bain trying to wind her up? "Please tell me you don't find this situation funny."

All humor was wiped from his face. "The alternative is to get pissed. And when it comes right down to it, I like you,

Katya, always have. But you walked out on my brother, leaving him devastated, and now, just when he's got his life back on track, you turn up, ready to screw with him all over again. So, seeing as I don't find any of that funny, I'm looking for humor where I can find it."

"I didn't screw with Brodie before I left, and I have no intention of starting now. I want you and your work crew off our land."

"We'll go this time, Katya, but you need to know we have his back. The brothers aren't going to let you pull any crap this time."

She cocked an eyebrow. "And how exactly would you stop me?"

"A lot has changed since you left. We have skills and resources we never had last time. It would be unwise to mess with us."

"Did you get that line from an action movie? For the record, I'm unimpressed with the threat. The last time one of you lot intimidated me, I was still in nappies." She turned to the work crew, put her finger and thumb to her mouth, and blew a shrill whistle. "Pack it up, boys. There won't be any building today or any other day. I own this land too. If anyone needs further clarification, they can contact my lawyers. I'm sure they'll be more than happy to explain."

To her disgust, the men still looked to Bain for permission before they cleared out.

As they slunk off, Bain eyed her with open curiosity. "Why are you back, really?"

Katya pointed at the plane with a "duh" look on her face.

"No." He shook his head. "Why did you come back *here*? You could have set up your tourist business in a place that actually attracts tourists. They're not exactly queuing up in Invertary looking for something to fill their downtime. So why here? Your great-gran was Russian. Shouldn't you be over there reminding them of what she did for them? Or even East Germany or Poland, where I'm sure people would be grateful to know all about her. But you're not. You're here. In Nowhere, Scotland. That makes a man wonder."

"Give me a break." Katya rolled her eyes. "All you wonder about is who you can bed next."

"People change."

She stared at him.

"Fine, not me, but other people. Now tell me why you're back here."

"Because this is where Natasha lived for the majority of her life. It's where she had a family and a home, which makes it the best place to commemorate everything she did."

Bain clearly didn't believe her. "Aye, right. And I suppose snatching the land out from under Brodie's nose is just the icing. Why else would you be here?"

"You're forgetting that Invertary's my home too."

"Not for the past ten years, it hasn't been. While you've been off gallivanting, Brodie's been here, living his life, making friends, and helping to build the town up. He has more right to this land, to his dream, than you."

His words were an arrow that hit true. "We all have the right to our dreams, Bain."

He closed the distance between them until he stood beside her and turned his face to stare at her. "Let him be, Kat. He's finally over you. If you still care about him, even a little, let him get on with his life in peace. Doesn't he deserve that much?"

"That and more," she answered honestly.

Bain's smile was the one she remembered from when

they'd hung out together as a family; it made her feel like she belonged. "You're looking good, Kat."

With that, he sauntered across the field to his pickup truck and climbed inside.

As Katya sighed, her gaze came to rest on the pegs in the ground, and a sense of recognition made her spine tingle. Before she could question her reasoning, she found herself walking the perimeter of the house, gauging the rooms, assessing the layout.

The more she visualized it in her mind's eye, the more her heart raced. This wasn't any old house. This was the house she'd planned with Brodie. The one with a spacious living room that had angled windows overlooking the town to the loch. The one with the curving staircase and a TV room located in the back corner, where a fireplace would roar.

Everything they'd discussed as they sat in the exact same spot where these pegs were laid out was marked on the ground. This wasn't Brodie's house. It was *their* house.

The bastard had stolen their house and claimed it as his own.

BRODIE JUMPED at a knock on his car window. He looked up to see a grim-faced Bain glaring down at him.

He lowered the window. "What?"

"Didn't you get my text? Your wife closed down your build."

"Ex-wife. And no, my phone's off."

"Aye, let's focus on whether I call her your wife or your ex. That's the most important part of what I just said." Bain shook his head in clear disgust. "Did you hear me? You've been cockblocked over your house."

"Cockblocked?"

"That house has been your main romantic interest since Katya left." His brother studied him. "You don't seem all that upset over the news your build's been postponed."

"I was expecting it." Brodie pinched the bridge of his nose. "If I won't let her set up an airport, she sure as hell won't let me build my house. Only problem is, we now have a crew who're expecting work and wages."

"Don't worry; they're covered. As of this morning, the Patel build is a go, which means we can move the crew over to their site until you get your crap sorted with your *ex-wife*."

Brodie frowned at his brother. "You know that Katya coming back has made everything more complicated for me, don't you? You could be a little more understanding."

"Aye. I could." Bain grinned. "But where's the fun in that? Anyway, what are you doing sitting out here instead of working in the office—where you should be? You hiding from Darach?"

"No." There were times when he wondered what went on in Bain's head.

His brother shrugged. "It's a reasonable question. I hide from him all the time. A man can only take so many lists and deadlines before he needs some peace."

"How did you know I was out at the lookout point anyway?"

"It's on your top ten list of places to come when you mope. I figured Katya coming back would be reason to mope, and here I am."

Brodie stared at him. "You're seriously weird."

"I know. Now, are you going to tell me what you're doing out here then, or do I have to guess?"

The last thing he wanted was to endure Bain's favorite game of twenty guesses. Instead, he handed over the sheet of paper he'd just read.

"What's this?" Bain looked unimpressed.

"Kitty Baxter says it's the reason she hates the Savages."

"A marriage certificate?" Bain paused as he read. "Well, damn, I did *not* see that coming. So, Natasha was married to Ben too? The Savages won't like this."

Bain MacGregor—master of understatement.

"No kidding. From the date, I suspect this marriage happened shortly before Natasha married Tom Savage. But if that's the case, why didn't Kitty hand over the divorce papers too?"

"You think she was married to both of them at the same time?" Bain grinned. "I *like* this girl."

Brodie gave him the photo he'd found in the envelope. "This was with it."

"Two best friends with the woman they both loved. It's a romance novel." His brother's eyes went wide. "Or a porn movie. Holy crap, do you think it was one of those poly relationships?"

"I don't know what to think." Brodie reached out the window and took the items back before Bain could drool all over them. "I also can't figure out why this would explain the Baxters' hatred for the Savages. Is it because Tom stole Natasha from Ben? Or because she broke his heart when she left him and ended their marriage? Or was it because she was a bigamist?"

"She's hot, but I don't get why they were fighting over her," Bain said helpfully. "I mean, if one woman becomes hard work, you move on to the next. There are literally billions to choose from."

"It's a miracle you're still single," Brodie said, genuinely awestruck by his brother's logic.

"Hey, don't knock it. Look how marriage worked out for you. I'm not dumb—I learn from my brothers' mistakes."

"Katya wasn't a mistake." Now his brother was pissing him off. Again. It was one of Bain's natural talents.

The smile on Bain's face was pure devilment. "You know, your Katya looks better than she did ten years ago. I mean, she was bonny back then, but now"—he let out a low whistle—"she's sexy and confident. Her figure has filled out too, did you notice? And you know what they say about women when they hit their thirties—they're working their way up to their sexual peak. When is that again? Thirty-five? Aye, I bet she's up for all sorts of stuff now that she never was then. Seeing as you're no' interested in her anymore, would you mind if I made a play for her?"

Brodie's fist shot out, and he punched his brother right on the nose. Then, leaving Bain to clutch his face and whine like a wee baby, Brodie rolled up the window and went back to trying to figure out what to do with the items Kitty Baxter had given him.

10

———

Straight after Katya pulled the plug on Brodie's building plans, she'd made an appointment with her solicitor. At eleven o'clock the next morning, she sat in his office reception area waiting to discuss what they could do to stop Brodie's build permanently. So much for working things out in a civilized manner—a hope she'd harbored before coming home. Now her main concern was whether her credit card would cover her legal costs.

Lawrence Mayburn had spent most of his adult life working as a barrister in England, but when his wife decided she wanted to be closer to their daughter and grandkids, he'd relicensed as a Scottish solicitor. Although Katya had never met him in person, she'd enjoyed dealing with him over the phone. Before Lawrence, she'd been represented by a firm in Glasgow who'd treated her as yet another number in their vast legion of clients. It had worked fine, but as soon as her mother told her that Invertary had its own law firm, she'd swapped to Lawrence. When it came to the MacGregors, it was always best to have someone nearby to keep an eye on them.

"Mr. Mayburn will see you now," the receptionist said from behind her sleek wooden desk.

"Thanks." Katya stood, dusted off her jeans, and headed through to Lawrence's office. She supposed she should have worn something more appropriate for seeing a solicitor, but apart from several pairs of jeans, the only other thing in her suitcase was a pair of shorts. She figured the jeans were more respectable.

As soon as she entered his office—located at the back of one of the many narrow buildings along the main street—Lawrence Mayburn stood and held out his hand. A distinguished man in his early sixties, he had pristinely styled gray hair and wore an elegant, tailored suit. His warm eyes and genuine, welcoming smile were in keeping with her impression of him from their interactions over the phone, and she found herself relaxing.

"Katya." He shook her hand. "We meet at last. Please, take a seat." He sat in his black leather executive chair behind his mahogany desk and pulled a notepad toward him.

"Thanks for fitting me in at such short notice." Katya sank into one of the brown leather armchairs facing his desk. "As I told your receptionist on the phone yesterday, I need to find a legal way to stop Brodie from building because I don't think shouting at him and his brothers will work for much longer."

"Yes, she passed on your message. Unfortunately, there's been another development in your situation this morning. Given that you were coming in to see me, I refrained from contacting you until we could discuss it in person."

Katya sank back into her chair. "What's Brodie done now?"

Lawrence adjusted his computer monitor, swiveling it

out of their line of sight, then clasped his hands on the desk. "I'm afraid this isn't about Mr. MacGregor. It's about Catherine Baxter."

That had Katya jerking up straight. "For the record, I wasn't trespassing. I was merely retrieving stolen goods Brodie hid on her farm. I got out of there as soon as I could, and I didn't even carry out the threat I made against her. Honestly, I was on my best behavior."

Lawrence seemed to be fighting the urge to laugh. "That's good to know, but Ms. Baxter's solicitor didn't mention trespassing during our call this morning. It seems Ms. Baxter is insisting that you and Mr. MacGregor have violated the conditions set down for ownership of the land her father gifted to you."

Okay, now she was perched on the edge of her chair. "I don't see how. Brodie and I are still married. Ben's only condition was that the land would revert to the family trust if we divorced."

Lawrence consulted the notepad in front of him. "According to her solicitor, you and Mr. MacGregor are attempting to defraud the trust by adhering to the letter of the condition while flaunting the spirit of it. In other words, you are no longer husband and wife in any way other than your marriage certificate. You both live as single, divorced people, which is in direct breach of the conditions of the gift."

"But, but..." Katya blustered as she looked around the room, searching for inspiration in the conservative décor. "Legally, we're still married."

"Yes, but they claim that Mr. Baxter's intention when he made the gift was that you would live happily together and 'use the land for your joint future. Ms. Baxter is arguing that you and Mr. MacGregor have done neither. You went your separate ways and only remain legally married in an effort to defraud the Baxter Trust out of a piece of its land."

Katya opened and shut her mouth several times before words eventually came out. "Can she do this?"

"I'm afraid that, under Scottish law, she has quite a strong case." He leaned forward, looking eager. "You see, unlike English law, Scottish law is based on a mixed system, which means the laws governing property and land owner-ship are—"

"Lawrence," Katya said, "we both know there isn't a snowball's chance in hell I'll understand anything you say next, so please just tell me, is this serious? Could Catherine take the land from us?"

Lawrence sat back in his chair, compassion on his face. "The short answer to both questions is yes."

Deflated, Katya sank into her chair as Lawrence's computer pinged. He tapped on his keyboard.

"I hope you don't mind," he said gently. "I spoke to Mr. MacGregor's solicitor this morning, and we discussed this new issue. As I'm in Invertary, we've agreed it would be best for me to speak with both of you. Because of this, I've taken the liberty of inviting Mr. MacGregor to our meeting, as I knew you'd want this resolved as quickly as possible."

Before Katya could even process that information, the door opened, and Brodie walked in. Shrewd eyes took in Lawrence's demeanor and Katya's slumped body language.

"Hey, Lawrence," he said as he shut the door behind him. "What's Katya done now?"

"Typical." She rolled her eyes at Brodie. "You always assume I'm the root of all your problems."

"That's because you usually are." He sat in the seat beside her. "Rough night? Are those dark circles under your eyes? Were you tossing and turning because you couldn't get me out of your mind?"

"Yes. I spent hours plotting ways to murder you and hide your body." She turned to Lawrence. "Is it still a crime if there's no body?"

"Yes. Please don't murder Brodie. I'm close to retirement and trying to reduce my workload. A murder case would interfere with my golf game."

"Well, we wouldn't want that." Katya smiled at her lawyer. "It can wait until after you've retired."

"That's most appreciated." Lawrence was clearly amused.

"As entertaining as I find listening to Kat plot my demise, I'd really like to know why I'm here." Brodie lounged in his seat, clearly unbothered by Katya's threat. She really needed to come up with a new one.

"Old Woman Baxter thinks she's found a way to take the land off us," Katya said.

That had Brodie's full attention. "How?"

"As I explained to Katya," Lawrence said, "you may have a marriage certificate, but you don't live as husband and wife. Ms. Baxter is arguing that you're only staying legally married in order to defraud her family and that your relationship is a sham."

Brodie seemed a little nonplussed. "Well, that's all true."

Katya let her head thump back against the chair, closed her eyes, and groaned. "Please don't put him on the witness stand."

"What?" Brodie demanded. "It's not like we've hidden the fact you've been gone for ten years. Hell, I've even had other relationships in that time. It wouldn't take a genius to figure out our marriage is a sham."

She opened one eye and glared at him. "You've had other relationships? In town?"

"Did you think I was a monk while you were gone?"

Now she considered it, a part of her had thought exactly that. "No. And in case you were wondering, I wasn't a nun either."

"I wasn't wondering," he snapped.

"Katya, Brodie." Lawrence held up his hands as though asking for peace. "We need to deal with the issue at hand. Ms. Baxter plans to take you to court to prove your marriage is a sham, so we must come up with a strategy to foil her plans. I'm assuming you both want to keep the land?"

They nodded—while frowning at each other.

"Good," Lawrence said. "Then we need a plan of action." He turned to a new page in his notepad and picked up a pen.

"You mean you want us to lie," Brodie said. "Because that's the only thing I can think of, and I'm not sure anyone would believe us. We can hardly tell everybody we were still a couple over the past ten years when there are plenty of witnesses and evidence that says otherwise."

"Wow, big sentences," Katya said. "Does your brain hurt?"

"Katya, please," Lawrence said, making her mumble an apology. "As far as I can see, there's no way to rewrite history. You have clearly been separated for years, and everyone knows it. All we can do now is address Ms. Baxter's concern that you are currently married in name only. I feel..." he hesitated, "that the only way to fight this is to convince everyone your marriage is back on track in every way possible. In other words, Invertary has to believe you are a loving, committed married couple. You must understand that, as your solicitor, I'm not advocating you deceive anyone. That isn't something someone in my position could or should do." It was clear from his protestations that pretending was exactly what he was asking them to do. "I'm merely suggesting you live together and work at reconciliation, so we can present the case that you're trying to fix your marriage."

There was a beat of silence, as if the whole world had paused to suck in a deep breath, and then the shouting began.

~

BRODIE WAS on his feet in an instant. "You have got to be kidding me! You want us to fake being together? Have you met us?" This was the craziest plan he'd ever heard, and he had six brothers who specialized in crazy plans. Hell, Kat's family was famous for coming up with dumb ideas, and this one beat them all.

Lawrence held up his hands. "I would never suggest such a thing. I'm asking you to work at your marriage."

"Aye, we know what you *have* to tell us, and we know what we're hearing," Brodie growled. Bloody lawyers, always covering their own backs, but Lawrence definitely meant for them to fake it until he could get the Baxter objection thrown out of court.

"I can't live with him. I can barely stand being in the same room." Katya, who'd jumped out of her chair too, was now pacing the room. "No one's going to believe we took one look at each other after ten years apart and suddenly fell in love all over again. For Pete's sake, we were rolling around wrestling in his office just yesterday. That story's already all over town."

"So's the one about me locking her out of her land,

stealing her plane, and hiding it on the property of her family's arch-nemesis."

"When I had tea with the Knit or Die ladies this morning, I was very vocal about how much Brodie annoys me. I may have also told them he's moonlighting as a stripper and looking for work, which was before they helped me sign him up to every website I could find that supplies mail-order brides."

"You did what?" Brodie shouted.

Katya glared at him. "You know you deserve it. Plus, you always wanted a nice obedient, boring wife, so now you can pick one from a catalog."

"That is completely deranged." Brodie had to clench his fists to keep from strangling her. "I can't believe you roped in the local knitting club to help you."

"I didn't rope them in—they were eager to volunteer. They said that a scaredy-cat who gave up on his wife because he didn't want to step outside his comfortable wee box deserved everything he got."

He leaned into her until they were practically nose to nose. "I didn't want to go on a wild-goose chase, wasting time on something that didn't bloody matter. That isn't fear, it's sanity."

A finger poked his pec. "My great-grandmother matters. If it wasn't for people like her, we'd be living under Nazi rule right now. She risked her life to save all of us."

"And I suppose that justifies you upending our lives to go chasing after her memory?"

"She was a war hero. An honorable woman. She deserves to be remembered."

"Aye." Brodie saw red. "So honorable that she was married to two men at the same time!"

Katya sucked in a breath. "What?"

Brodie cursed, wanting to kick the walls in frustration. "I didn't mean to tell you like that." To be fair, he hadn't even decided whether he wanted to tell her at all. He'd been leaning toward leaving the envelope in the Savage mailbox and washing his hands of the whole matter.

Fingers curled around his forearm. "Brodie? What did you mean?"

He let out a sigh. "Damn it, Kat. You make me nuts, and then I blurt stuff."

Her fingernails bit into his skin. "Not like this, you don't. You need to explain."

"Fine." He shrugged out of her hold, ran a hand through his hair, and plopped back into his seat. For a second, he was surprised to see Lawrence. He'd forgotten they were in the man's office. "After you drove your plane away from the Baxters' farm, Kitty gave me an envelope. She told me it would explain the grudge-fest between your families."

Katya slowly sat back down, keeping her eyes glued to him.

"There was a photo in the envelope and a marriage certificate. The photo was of Tom, Ben, and Natasha, all laughing together. The marriage certificate was for Natasha and Ben."

Wide eyes glanced between Brodie and the solicitor. "I don't understand," she said.

"Join the club," Brodie muttered.

"If there's a marriage certificate, there must be divorce papers," Katya said.

"I was curious and did a search of the national database. Nothing came up."

"No," Katya whispered. "She couldn't have been married to both men at the same time."

Lawrence cleared his throat. "I realize this is disturbing news, but we have more urgent matters to attend to, Katya."

She nodded, looking defeated as she slumped into the chair, and Brodie had to fight the urge to fall back into old habits and comfort her. The need was so powerful that his fingers tingled to reach out to her. But instead of giving in and having her reject him, he folded his arms tight against his chest.

"Okay," Katya said to Lawrence, her voice flat. "What do you need us to do?"

Lawrence gave Brodie a pointed look.

"Fine." Brodie pinched the bridge of his nose as a headache formed. "We'll do what we have to do to keep the land."

"Good." The solicitor picked up his pen again. "Then let's discuss what form your reconciliation will take."

11

Five weeks after VE day, 1945

A village east of Berlin, Germany

With no radio in the village, there was no way of telling what was happening with the war. It was only when the gunfire became less frequent, and the bombing ceased entirely, that Natasha realized something had changed. The question was what exactly.

She wasn't sure how much time had passed since Lina rescued her. The days had begun to blend as the hunger gnawing at her insides grew. All that mattered now was the search for food—a rarely successful endeavor. She'd lost so much weight she scarcely recognized herself, but she didn't care about that. All she cared about was the agony of starvation. Some days, the only way to cope with it was to sleep, shivering on the cot in Lina's kitchen, too weak to generate enough body heat to stop shaking.

The locals hiding along with her in the rubble were as kind as their fear would allow. It had become second nature to regard each other with suspicion, especially with someone like her, who couldn't speak their language. Remaining silent was a blessing. It meant she couldn't accidentally tell someone who she was. One slip, and her life would be over. Either the Nazis would capture her and send her to an internment camp, or the Soviet Army would sweep her up and send her to Stalin. She was no longer certain which fate was worse.

Subsisting on a thin broth made from roots she found in the forest and hoped wouldn't poison her, Natasha spent her time wondering why she hadn't died in the plane crash. No one would have missed her if she'd died. She had no family to go home to in Russia—her parents were long gone, and the conflict had already claimed her brothers. All her friends were caught up in the war, and she didn't know their fates. Even if Stalin didn't execute her for supposedly deserting his army, she had no reason to return home. No reason to be alive.

Yet, here she was, clinging to life when the odds were stacked against her.

At night, when the hunger became a monster that consumed her, she wondered what her fate would be. Would she die on the thin mattress of the creaky cot in Lina's barren home? Would she somehow forge a new life in Germany after the war? Would the side that won allow her to? When exhaustion eventually overcame her worries, she dreamed of fire. Of seeing Marina in the wreckage. Of breathing burning flesh.

And then she'd wake to wonder, yet again, why she'd been given one more day.

One more endless day filled with hunger and fear.

Until it wasn't.

On a bright afternoon, when the sun sat high in the sky, motor vehicles rolled down what was left of the village's main road. There were several of them—more than enough to make a noise that jarred the landscape and drove Natasha to scream inside her head.

As they made their way down the street in a convoy, a voice called out in German over a speaker with words she couldn't understand. And with Lina gone, she had no one to translate.

All Natasha could do was hide in the tiny house and peek through a crack in the boarded-up windows. Her heart racing and breathing shallow, she scanned the street, searching for a clue as to what she'd have to endure next. That's when it registered—the symbols on the cars weren't Nazi. Instead, one lone white star was emblazoned on the side of each vehicle.

The Allies had arrived.

Relief was a tidal wave that knocked Natasha off her feet. Hunger and exhaustion overwhelmed her as she fell, and she was unconscious before she hit the floor.

When she came to, she found herself surrounded by soldiers speaking in languages she didn't understand. Gathering what little strength she had left, Natasha scrambled away from them and into the corner beside the empty cupboard. Her starved brain struggled to understand something, anything, about what was happening. Was the war over? Were the Allies fighting nearby?

Natasha kept her lips clamped tight for fear she'd blurt out information that would get her sent to Stalin. No one could learn she was Soviet. Not ever. The men held up their hands in a gesture of peace, their smiles hesitant in a way that signaled their intent to reassure. But all she saw was a group of soldiers she didn't understand and the risk of being exposed.

From the back of the room, near the door, someone shouted in German. The only words she understood were 'Lina' and 'Lithuanian,' and then, as though the Red Sea parted before him, a man made his way toward her.

He crouched on his haunches in front of her, his smile gentle. "Are you Lithuanian?" he asked in the language.

Natasha didn't trust that her accent wouldn't betray her, so instead of replying, she nodded.

"We're with the Allied forces," he said. "The war is over, the fascists defeated, and we're here to help. Can you tell me how you came to be here?"

She jerked back, her head striking the wooden shelf, but she barely felt it. The war was over? Could it be true?

The man seemed to know what she was thinking and addressed her concern. "The Nazis surrendered weeks ago. We"—he gestured to his colleagues—"are trying to deal with the mess they left behind. I swear to you. This isn't a joke. The war truly is over."

Natasha hardly dared believe him. She tried to wet her dry, cracked lips, to ask him to explain again, but it was impossible. The man turned to the men beside him and spoke in another language.

A few seconds later, one of them handed him a water canteen, which he offered to her. "Please," he said. "Drink."

Unable to look away from the impossibly blue eyes that had captured hers, she took the canteen with shaking hands. The water was heaven on her dry tongue, and she wanted to gulp it down, but she didn't. Instead, she sipped at it, aware that others might need some too.

They had no water pump in the village, and the pipes were damaged, so rainwater collected in empty pots was their only water supply. Everyone in the village had suffered from the clear blue skies of the past week as their water rations ran out. Fearing she'd drink too much if she kept it, Natasha offered the bottle back to the man.

He shook his head. "You need more, and we have plenty. Drink your fill."

It was a gift that would have made her weep—if she'd had any fluid to spare for tears. The man waited patiently while she drank, waving at his fellow soldiers to tell them they could leave. By the time she'd finished every last drop of water in the canteen, only the man who spoke Lithuanian and another, with a white armband emblazoned with a red cross, remained.

She handed him the empty bottle with a whispered thank you in Lithuanian.

"We have food outside," the man said. "When you're ready, we can get some. It's only bread and soup, but it will help."

He might as well have offered her manna from heaven, and Natasha found she could cry after all. Hastily, she swiped at the stray tear on her cheek.

"Can you tell me how you came to be in Germany?" he asked again. "It's a long way from Lithuania."

Panic almost stole her breath. She didn't want to lie to the man who'd been so kind to her, but she couldn't tell the truth. All she could do was give him Lina's story. "When my village was wiped out in the war, I had nowhere to go but to my cousin Lina."

A subtle shift in his expression that she couldn't identify made her suspect he didn't quite believe her. "Then you have no home to return to?" he asked.

Natasha stared into those clear blue eyes and gave him the truth, hoping her accent wouldn't set off alarm bells for him. "There's nothing left for me in my country. If I return, it will only be to danger and death."

"We have a place you can go until we find you a new home. We've set up housing for everybody we find displaced by the war. Once you're there, we can look into sending you back to another part of Lithuania. Everything will be fine, I promise."

No. No, it wouldn't. The Soviet Union controlled Lithuania. It would only be a matter of time before someone discovered she'd been a bomber pilot shot down during the war. They would brand her a traitor and send her to Stalin. She'd be tortured to find out what, if anything, she'd told the enemy, and then, if she was lucky, they'd send her to the Gulag. If not, they'd execute her.

"Can you stand?" the man asked, rising to his feet. "Here, let me help. We'll get you some food and take down your details before we assign you to a camp." He held out his hand to her.

Natasha grasped it as if it were a lifeline. When he would have led her out of the room after the red cross man, she used what meager strength she possessed to hold him back. Understanding eyes met hers.

"I can't go back. They'll kill me. Please, don't send me back." It was only after she'd spoken and registered the shock on his face that she realized she'd used Russian instead of Lithuanian. *Stupid, stupid, stupid.* The lack of food had dimmed her mind, making it difficult to think straight.

"You're Soviet."

There seemed no point in denying it now—all she could do was nod.

He lowered his voice and spoke in perfect Russian. "There are no women in the Red Army. Were you spying?"

"I flew bombers."

He blinked as though surprised. "I've heard about the female squadrons. You were a Night Witch?"

She nodded again, her hand tightening on his. "I was shot down, and that's considered traitorous in the Kremlin. I won't survive an interrogation."

His jaw clenched and unclenched as anger flashed in his eyes. She feared he thought her a coward.

Natasha flinched. "Please, I can be useful. I'm an engineer. I'll go anywhere except the Soviet Union. I'll do anything." Her stomach spasmed at the knowledge of what she was offering. What she would do to remain out of Stalin's clutches.

"No," he said. "You won't."

The man raised his voice and called to someone outside the building. Natasha didn't understand what he'd said, but she suspected he was about to hand her over to the Soviets. Why would he do otherwise? She was nothing to him, merely another displaced person in a war that'd displaced millions.

"Let's get you some food," he said in Lithuanian as he led her over to the door.

"Why aren't you speaking Russian?" she asked, confused.

"Why would I speak Russian to a Lithuanian?" His smile almost took her back to the floor. He must have felt her knees give way because he wrapped an arm around her waist to hold her up. "We've been searching for an engineer. You'd better eat up and regain your strength—there's a need in one of the camps. From there, we can find you a new home." He paused, as though thinking something through.

"A lot of Lithuanian refugees are relocating to Scotland. Maybe that would suit you too."

Natasha clung to him as they stepped out into the dazzling afternoon sunlight. "Thank you," she whispered in Lithuanian. "Thank you, Mr...."

"Baxter." His blue eyes twinkled. "Ben Baxter."

12

"This is wonderful," Delia gushed as she took the clothes out of the suitcase Katya had just put them into, refolded them, and put them back. "I knew if you and Brodie spent some time together, you'd want to patch things up."

"It's not like that, Mum." Unfortunately, she couldn't tell her mother they were faking their reconciliation, because Delia couldn't keep a secret if her life depended on it.

Her mother threw a T-shirt at Katya's head while practically dancing on the spot. "Then what do you call this? You're moving in with him! If that isn't a sign you're getting back together, I don't know what is." She picked up the T-shirt from where it'd landed on the floor and folded it again. "I can't wait to tell everyone at amateur dramatics. They'll be over the moon too. They all agree that you two shouldn't have split up in the first place."

"*All* of them?" Katya cocked an eyebrow at her mother, knowing full well she was exaggerating for dramatic effect. It was what she did best.

Delia waved a hand. "Away with you. Nothing you say could ruin my mood today."

"This is a bloody stupid idea." Her scowling father stood in the doorway as if planning to physically block her exit. "I have nothing against Brodie as a person, but he made a terrible husband. Why would you go back to someone who doesn't support your dreams? I didn't raise an idiot."

"You didn't raise her at all," her mother said. "You were too busy painting."

One look at her father and Katya knew there was no point in trying to reason with him—he was wearing his mourning tartan, the Black Watch.

"Everything's going to be okay," she assured him. "If it isn't, *I'll* go after Brodie with a shotgun."

"Promise?" he demanded gruffly. "And not with that sissy buckshot—real bullets this time."

"I promise." She gave him a hug, breathing in that combination of turpentine and oil that had followed her through her childhood.

"Don't worry, Mr. S," Denise said as she sneaked past Fraser and into the room, where she opened the cupboard door in the corner and pulled out *three* suitcases. "I'll be there to watch over them."

Katya pointed at the cases. "Didn't you arrive with two?"

"Didn't you promise me you'd throw out all the shirts you own that have oil smudges?"

"I only said that to shut you up. If I didn't have these shirts, what would I wear?" Honestly, Katya didn't see what the big deal was with her wardrobe—it worked. It was functional, and none of her bits were hanging out. What more was there?

"Oh!" her mother said. "You're right, Denise. How did I

miss that? This won't do. You can't move in with Brodie without some pretty clothes and sexy nighties."

"Woman!" Her dad's head turned beetroot red. As far as he was concerned, his daughter couldn't even spell the word sex, and that was how it would always be.

"It's okay." Delia patted Katya's arm in reassurance. "I'll go to the lingerie shop to pick you up something nice, and then I'll drop it off later."

Great. Her mother had already found a reason to come visit her at Brodie's, and it'd only been twenty minutes since she'd informed her parents she was moving.

"Maybe you could pick her up something to wear that didn't come free with a keg of beer," Denise, the traitor, said to her mother.

The two women considered Katya, shaking their heads.

"I wish she had your dress sense," Delia told Denise. "Honestly, I don't know where I went wrong. By the way, I love that jumpsuit you're wearing; that ruby color really brings out your skin tone marvelously. Wherever did you get it?"

"Right, that's it." Katya herded everyone toward her childhood bedroom door. "Everybody out. I need peace to finish packing."

"Maybe we could shop now," Delia said to Denise.

"I'm leaving in five minutes," Katya called after them. "With or without you, Denise!"

Her dad lingered after the others had gone down the stairs. "Are you sure you know what you're doing?"

It was awful to see him so worried. "I'm doing the only thing I can do right now. Trust me, it will all work out."

With an unconvinced shake of his head, he left Katya to her packing. She closed the door behind him and sat on the edge of her bed, letting out a long breath. Her visit to the solicitor had been one hit after another. First, the news that Catherine Baxter wasn't done coming after the Savage family and the land Ben gifted Brodie and her. Then, the "suggestion" that she and Brodie reconcile—when they all knew Lawrence meant "fake being properly married." And finally, the news that her great-grandmother—the war hero and woman Katya believed would bring respectability to their family name—was potentially a bigamist.

Any one of the things she'd learned in that office would send her parents into a tailspin they'd never come out of, but *three bombshells?* If they found out about all of them, her dad would lock himself in his studio and only surface to eat. And her mother, well, she'd probably write a one-woman show about the scandals that rocked the Savage family and then take it on the road.

"What am I doing?" she whispered to the ceiling.

Unsurprisingly, no wisdom was forthcoming.

With a sigh, she mentally reviewed Lawrence's plan. A private hearing between the various lawyers and their clients would take place the following week. By then, Katya and Brodie had to be able to fool everyone into thinking they'd rekindled their relationship.

She'd have more chance of convincing everyone she could fly just by flapping her arms.

With a groan, Katya pulled her phone out of her pocket, opened her banking app, and checked her balances. Yep, she was still pretty much broke. If she couldn't set up her business on that land, she wouldn't be able to afford anywhere else for years. Which meant going off again to take jobs flying anything and anyone until she'd made enough money to return to Invertary and buy another piece of land—if there was even one available by then.

It had taken her years to scrape together enough to buy

the Soviet bomber. Longer than it probably should have, but Katya had also been searching for other memorabilia to put in her museum, and that took cash too. Even then, when she'd finally managed to get her hands on a plane, the only one she'd been able to afford had been in such a state it'd taken a year to restore it. And that had included calling in every favor owed to her.

All she had left was a small amount of savings. Barely enough to cover the cost of building a shed large enough to house the collection of war memorabilia she'd built up over the years—and keep her plane out of the harsh Scottish weather.

Man, she needed to find a job. One flexible enough to allow her to run her museum and fly any tourists prepared to take a chance on a plane made of balsa wood.

She threw herself back onto the bed and groaned loudly. "What am I doing?" she asked the empty room.

"I don't know," her brother replied through the wall. "Women are a mystery. Even when you're related to them."

Katya was still laughing hysterically when Denise came to see what was holding her up.

"I don't quite understand why you think having you and Katya living with two of your brothers will convince Kitty Baxter you're back together." Bain leaned in the doorway, watching Brodie change his bedsheets.

"It's here or Katya's parents' house. It's no' like we can go out and rent a place to share for the duration." Brodie smoothed down his duvet. That was as good as it was going to get. "This is Invertary; there are no houses for rent right now, and unless we want to hole up in the hotel above the pub, this is the best we can do." He gathered up his bedding and faced his brother. "You and Darach could always go live with Ma and Da until this is over."

Bain was laughing too hard to answer, so Brodie pushed past him and headed back downstairs to shove his laundry in the machine.

When he walked into the kitchen, it was to find three more of his brothers seated at the table. He was fairly certain that if his oldest brothers had been able to get away from work, they would have made the trip to Invertary to be there too.

"If this is an intervention, you can take it elsewhere. Pretending our marriage is on the mend is the only play we have to keep the land." Brodie crossed the room and stuffed his sheets into the front-loading washing machine under the counter.

"This isn't an intervention," Darach said. "It's an audience."

"Aye." Kade, Darach's fraternal twin, grinned. "We've got to see this."

"We thought we'd act as judges," Conall added. "Let you know how your performance is going and whether people will believe it."

"I plan to make scorecards," Kade added.

Brodie pointed at Conall and Kade. "Out. Now. You two don't even live here. There's no need for you to hang around."

"Oh, I don't know," Kade said. "I have a great need to watch you and Katya try to act like you don't hate each other's guts."

"I don't hate Katya." Brodie glared at all of them. It had no effect. "I feel nothing for her but irritation."

"And yet," Bain said as he sauntered into the room, "he

tries to break his brother's nose when that brother suggests Brodie step aside and let someone else have a run at his *ex-wife*."

"Brothers don't hit on their brothers' wives." Brodie paused before correcting himself. "Ex-wives. If we weren't related, I'd have told you to go for it."

Kade elbowed his twin. "You were right, Dar. This is priceless."

"Shut up, carrot top," Brodie snapped. As Kade was the only one of the seven brothers with rust-colored hair, it was an easy target.

"Is that the best you've got? You're off your game." Kade elbowed Darach. "He must be distracted; I wonder what's causing it."

"Aye, he's distracted all right," Conall said. "And it smells like he went overboard with the deodorant while he was busy thinking about other things. What happened? Did you forget to stop spraying? Or could you be trying to impress a certain girl with your spicy bouquet?"

His brothers thought that was hilarious.

Brodie patiently waited for them to calm down. "I used the normal amount of deodorant. You lot aren't nearly as funny as you think you are."

"Hey, don't lump me in with them," Bain said drolly. "I'm hilarious."

Darach held up his hand. "A question. Even if you do manage to pull this off, you two still need to divide the land. Have you thought about how you're going to do that, genius?"

"One thing at a time," Brodie said, because the answer was no, he hadn't a clue how they'd divide the land so they'd both get what they wanted out of it.

The doorbell rang, saving Brodie from answering any

further dumb questions. "Right. She's here. Everybody behave, and remember, not a word about this to anyone outside of the brothers—especially not Ma and Da."

"Do we look like idiots?" Conall asked, earning himself a smack on the back of the head from Kade.

"Never ask a question you already know the answer to," Kade told him. "And never set yourself up for an insult. Have we taught you nothing?"

Leaving them to their grumbling, Brodie made his way along the narrow hallway, past the living room and the steep staircase leading to the three small bedrooms and bathroom upstairs.

He threw open the front door to find Katya standing with a tight smile on her face. She spoke through her teeth. "People are watching."

Brodie glanced down the street, and sure enough, a good number of his neighbors had suddenly found things to do out on their front stoops. At the end of the road, parked beside the little play area, was Katya's truck. And it looked like Denise was struggling to remove a suitcase from it.

His eyebrows shot up. "Denise is moving in too?"

Tension radiated from her, but she kept that damn smile on her face. "Don't even think about arguing."

If nothing else, in the ten years Katya had been gone, Brodie had learned the wisdom of picking your battles. Instead of objecting, he turned and yelled into the house, "Katya's friend needs help with her suitcases."

Three burly men ran out of the kitchen, shoved Brodie aside, and fought to get out the door to reach Denise first.

"I call dibs," Conall shouted.

"You can't call dibs on a woman," Kade objected.

"You two don't stand a chance with me around, so you might as well give up now," Bain said.

"I see they haven't changed at all." Katya watched them descend on Denise.

"What's going on, Brodie?" Old Man Shepherd shouted from over the street.

Katya's spine snapped straight, and for a second, Brodie worried she'd break a bone from all that tension.

"Can't you tell?" Brodie called back, making sure his voice carried down the street to the rest of his neighbors. "Katya's moving in with me. We're getting back together."

"The hell you are!" The old man snorted.

"I don't think they believe us," Brodie drawled, suddenly feeling very wicked. "There's only one thing for it—we need to put on a show. Pucker up, buttercup. I'm coming in."

Katya tried to glare holes in his head, all the while keeping that fake smile firmly in place. "Don't even think about it. There are other ways of convincing the natives we're a couple again."

"Ah, but we're past the thinking stage. And seeing as no other ideas are popping up for us, I'd say now is the time for action." With a wicked grin, he wrapped an arm around her waist and tugged her flush against him. "Let's see if acting's in your genes because we need to sell this."

"Brodie, I swear, I will make you pay f—"

He quashed the rest of her objection with his lips.

13

———

Katya bit his bottom lip. Hard.

"Ow! If you draw blood," he whispered against her lips, "I'll retaliate."

"Like you scare me." There wasn't a play in his game-book she hadn't seen before. She could handle Brodie MacGregor.

"Admit it," he said between tiny kisses, "I might not scare you, but I definitely tempt you."

"Yes, you do tempt me—to violence."

"Liar." He angled his head and attempted to deepen the kiss.

Katya used her tongue to push his out of her mouth, and the world's dumbest duel commenced. It wasn't so much a kiss as a battle to keep the other person's tongue in their own mouth.

At last, Brodie's lips moved away from hers.

"That's how to do it!" Old Man Shepherd shouted as someone down the street whooped.

"You could use some mouthwash," Katya said as Brodie held her tight. He did smell like the forest—something she'd never admit to Denise—and she couldn't help inhaling him deeply. His strong arms around her and his firm chest against her cheek were sensations she'd missed almost as much as that forest fragrance.

Little about their situation was positive, but being able to indulge herself in aspects of Brodie she'd missed was something she'd happily accept—so long as they had to keep up the charade anyway.

So, she rubbed her cheek against his chest and said, "Time to let me go. That's enough of a show for the neighbors."

"Can't let go until you tell me whether it was good for you," he whispered, a smile in his voice.

Dickhead.

"I hate you," Katya said sweetly as she snuggled into him for their audience. She slipped her hand underneath his open plaid shirt to smooth over the cotton of his T-shirt until it rested over his chest—where she twisted his nipple.

"Right back atcha." He moved away quickly and took her hand.

"You really want to rub your nipple, don't you?" she taunted as he led her into the house.

"That was underhanded." Dark eyes met hers when he glanced back over his shoulder. "Just remember, turnabout is fair play. You got to play with my nipples, so I get to play with yours."

"Try it and lose a finger." But her traitorous body, conditioned to respond to him, had already melted at the thought of Brodie's hands on her breasts. Honestly, some days she completely despaired of herself.

As soon as they were in Brodie's living room, out of sight of his neighbors, she snatched her hand from his and put some distance between them. She made a show of wiping her mouth with the back of her hand.

"Have you had your shots?" Katya frowned at him. "I don't want to catch anything, and who knows where your mouth has been this past decade."

He waggled his eyebrows. "Only the good places. Anyway, I could say the same about yours."

"Unlike you, I use mouthwash." She looked around the room.

There were three mismatched sofas, all in a state of disrepair, with sagging seats and faded cushions. The biggest TV she'd ever seen filled the wall facing the sofas, and she counted three different game consoles plugged into it, with an assortment of controllers scattered around.

"Nice to see you've grown up while I've been gone."

"I thought I was grown up." Brodie perched on the arm of a sofa. "I had a wife, a plan for the future. Then she left me, and I thought, what the hell. Why save for a new couch when I can have the latest Xbox? It's not like I have to think about the wife and kids or building a family."

"Well, I hope you and your Xbox are very happy."

A commotion sounded behind them before Denise strode into the room, followed by the three brothers, each carrying a suitcase.

Denise grinned widely. "Aren't they charming?"

"They're something all right," Brodie said.

"I was going to go with mortifying." Katya shook her head at the sight of the brothers all jostling for Denise's favor.

"Aye, mortifying is the word for them," Brodie said, and Katya realized it was the first thing they'd agreed on since she'd come home.

"Let me take this upstairs for you." Kade snatched the

largest suitcase out of Conall's hand. He gave Brodie a quizzical look. "Where's she sleeping?"

"With me," Bain said.

"Nice try," Denise told him. "But I don't think so."

"You don't sound certain. Want me to help you make up your mind?"

To Katya's shock, Denise actually blushed. Bloody MacGregors; they could charm the pants off anyone.

"She can have Darach's room," Brodie said. "I was expecting Katya on her own, so I only changed our bed. But Darach can bunk with Bain, he's got the biggest room. I'll get him to change his bedding."

"Just in case you were wondering," Bain drawled, "I've got the biggest *everything*."

"I would excuse myself to vomit." Katya watched Denise giggle. *Giggle!* "But did you say *our bed*?" she asked Brodie.

"We're supposed to pretend we're in a real marriage, so where else would you sleep but with me?"

It astonished her that he seemed genuinely perplexed by her question.

"I'm not sleeping with you, Brodie. Everybody in this house knows the truth about our situation, so there's no need to keep up pretenses when the door is shut. Denise and I will take your room, and you can bunk with Bain."

He looked horrified. "I don't want to bunk with Bain."

Bain nodded as he pointed at Brodie. "I like his plan better. In fact, why bother Darach? Why not move Denise into my room, and you can bunk with Brodie?"

"So, Brodie's room for the girls it is then." Kade lifted the heavy suitcase. "Come on, Conall, we'll help Denise unpack."

They headed up the stairs, followed by an amused Denise.

"I notice no one's clamoring to carry my case." Katya watched them go.

"If we'd been sharing a room, I'd have made the effort. But seeing as you had no problem carrying it when you left in the first place, I'm sure you'll cope with getting it up the stairs." Brodie headed for the door. "Beer, Bain?"

"Don't mind if I do." Bain followed his brother.

Katya picked up her case and made it as far as the bottom of the stairs before Darach appeared.

"Come on, I'll take that for you," he said.

"At least there's one gentleman in the family." Katya smiled at him.

"Don't get too excited. Brodie told me if I didn't help you, he'd bunk with me instead of Bain."

She glanced toward the kitchen, curious, but there was no sign of Brodie.

"This is your room." Darach carried her case into the room on the right at the top of the stairs.

"Thanks." She smiled as she caught sight of Denise. Her friend sat on the edge of the bed directing Kade and Conall as they unpacked one of her cases and hung the contents in the space Brodie had cleared in his closet.

Denise patted the bed beside her. "Looks like we're sharing."

At the sight of the silver metal bed frame, Katya felt the blood drain from her face. It was the bed Brodie's folks had given them as a wedding present. She spun around, ready to head back downstairs and claim a sofa.

Darach stood in her way. "What's up, little sis?" He'd always called her that, despite her being two years older than him.

And because it was Darach, who'd always looked out for

her, she gave him the truth. "I don't want to sleep in that bed."

Understanding softened his face. "He couldn't get rid of it, said there were too many good memories associated with it."

Katya's throat tightened, making it impossible to get any words out.

Darach laid a hand on her shoulder, his touch gentle. "No other woman has stayed the night in that bed," he said quietly. "We moved in here not long after you left, and he's never had a woman stay overnight. Not that he hasn't seen anyone...."

"It's okay, you don't need to explain." She straightened her shoulders, pulled up her big girl panties, and turned back to Denise. "I hope you don't hog the blankets."

"It could be worse," Kade said with a sly sideways glance at Conall. "Bain farts in his sleep."

"Some things never change," Katya told Darach.

"Aye, I'm still the only sensible MacGregor," he said.

THERE WERE tea and biscuits on the living room coffee table because, apparently, Darach had confused a strategy meeting with afternoon tea. Brodie swallowed a sigh and sat as far away from Katya as he could while still remaining in the same room.

Darach had hooked his laptop up to the TV and set himself up beside it. The only thing missing was a lectern. Meanwhile, Brodie and Bain sat on the left-hand sofa, Katya was on the right-hand one, nearest the door, and Denise sat wedged between Kade and Conall on the middle sofa.

"Okay," Darach said. "As you all know, we have one week

to make these two look like they're in love." He pointed at Brodie then Katya before clicking the trackpad on his laptop.

The TV screen filled with the words "Operation Wedded Bliss."

As the laughter tapered off, Darach frowned at all of them. "Aye, laugh while you can, but this is serious. We've got one week to convince Invertary, in its entirety, that they're married in every sense of the word."

That sobered everyone up fast.

The screen changed, and a weekly calendar appeared. Darach produced a laser pointer and used it to indicate the sections he wanted to draw their attention to. "I've filled in all the main events and places that will attract the most attention. You two need to turn up to all of them and make a spectacle of yourselves."

"For the record," Bain said, "when he says spectacle, he means PDAs, not wrestling on the floor."

"Is this necessary?" By the sounds of it, Katya had already lost patience with the presentation. "Brodie and I know what to do. We've done it before."

"No offense, Katya." Darach was solemn. "You know how to be in a relationship with each other, you don't know how to *fake* being in one."

"I don't see the difference." Brodie had to agree with Kat on this one. They weren't idiots; they could fake a relationship.

"The difference," Darach said slowly, as though the speed of his words would help them understand, "is that when you're in a real relationship, you aren't paying any attention to anything that goes on around you. You have no idea how you look to other people. Whereas you two are *only* focused on everyone else. Without proper planning and support"—he indicated everyone else in the room—"this won't work."

"Think of it this way," Bain said. "Describe what it was like when you were together for real."

Brodie and Katya shared a look, and for a second, he could have sworn something zapped between them, as if the air had become electrified.

"We talked a lot," Katya said, her gaze still on him.

"Snuck into corners to kiss," Brodie added.

"We just wanted to be alone."

He couldn't argue with that.

"See?" Bain said. "That sounds inoffensive and private, which wasn't anything like the relationship the rest of us saw. Was it, boys?"

"Hell no," Kade groaned. "You had your hands all over each other and didn't care who saw. I was tempted to bleach my eyes on more than one occasion."

"You ignored everybody," Darach said. "Sometimes, you'd look at each other and then leave the room—mid-conversation. It was really annoying."

"Then there were the in-jokes," Conall said wistfully. "I never got any of those."

"The secret language," Bain added. "One of you would say something weird, like 'the coffee table,' and then you'd both burst out laughing."

"Or start kissing again." Kade shook his head. "I've seen more of Katya than I've seen of some of my girlfriends."

"Oi," Katya snapped. "I've seen all of you naked. Don't make me describe it to Denise."

"Oh," Denise practically purred. "Please do, and then you can also explain how you managed to see all the MacGregor brothers naked, because I don't know whether to go *ew* or *oo*."

"We were kids," Kade hurried to say. "We all ran around naked, but we grew up."

"Some of us grew more than others." Bain waggled his eyebrows at Denise.

"No way," Kade objected. "I grew way bigger than you."

"You're all wrong." Conall preened. "The parents saved the best for last."

"Okay." Brodie held up his hands before his brothers started whipping out their dicks to measure them and see who'd "grown" the most. "We get it—Katya and I were inconsiderate morons when we were dating. But we weren't that bad once we were married. We used to have you lot around for dinner all the time."

"Exactly." Katya pointed at him. "We were domesticated."

"Aye," Bain said. "I remember that domestication. You decided to make chicken curry for us, then you got distracted halfway through and disappeared into the bedroom. Darach finished the cooking, and we all sat around eating it while we listened to the sound effects coming through the door."

"What the hell?" Brodie shouted. "I thought you'd left."

"And waste a perfectly good curry?" Bain asked.

Katya stared at the ceiling. "Just when you thought life couldn't get any more humiliating...."

"If it's any consolation," Bain said, "you sounded good."

"Ew, no." Katya shuddered.

Brodie glared at Bain. "I should punch you again for hanging around to listen to us."

"You'd have to punch all of us," Bain pointed out cheerfully. "Start with Darach *if* you can reach his face."

Darach was not amused. "We've gotten off track here.

The point is, we need to plan your romance to ensure it comes across as real enough to fool Kitty and her lawyers."

Denise grinned at Darach. "This family is funny, but I *like* you. You're focused."

"I can be focused," Kade and Conall said at the same time.

Bain just laughed.

14

"Okay, smart-arse," Brodie said to Darach while Katya was still trying to get the image of his brothers listening to them having sex out of her head. "What do you have in mind for Operation Wedded Bliss?"

"I'm glad you asked." Darach got to his feet and pointed to the TV. "We've got a couple of events happening this week that will bring out the whole town." He shone his laser pointer on the first. "The women of Knit or Die are staging a knit-in on the lochside road during rush hour tomorrow morning."

"Wait," Denise interrupted. "Rush hour? As in an hour of rushing? In Invertary?"

"He means the ten minutes in the morning when there's more than half a dozen cars on the road," Bain helpfully explained.

"I love this town," Denise said.

"Anyway," Darach continued. "They plan to protest every week until the council agrees to put in a zebra crossing for the old folk. One of them was injured by a bus full of tourists while walking from the pub to the loch."

"Who was hurt?" Katya asked. "Are they okay?"

Brodie's eyes danced as he answered her. "The bus knocked Archie McPherson's warm chips out of his hands and ran over his flask of Glenfiddich. He suffered from shock. Nobody's sure if it was from the near miss or the waste of good whisky."

Denise almost choked on her tea when she tried to laugh and swallow at the same time. Both Kade and Conall patted her on the back. "Wait. Tourists stop here?" she managed to say once she was able.

"Only when they have to." Darach clearly didn't see anything funny in the situation. "But the same tour company bus comes through town, on its way to Fort William, at eight in the morning every Monday, Wednesday and Friday for the duration of the tourist season."

"Which is roughly two weeks in August," Bain said with a wink.

Denise was clearly delighted. "This is priceless. Why does your calendar say they're only protesting on Fridays? What about the other days?"

"The women go to Fort William to do aqua aerobics on Mondays and Wednesdays," Darach said.

At that point, they lost Denise, who was laughing too hard to be of any use, so she left the room to get control of herself.

"Don't mind her," Katya said as Denise left. "She doesn't get out much."

"Anyway." Darach waved his laser pointer. "As I was saying, the whole town will be out to watch the protest. Morag's shutting her bakery for the morning and setting up a pie stall, and I know Dougal will have a special at the pub to attract customers. It will be crowded, which means it's a good place to flaunt your new romance." He moved the pointer. "Then there's a council meeting coming up. Everybody will be there. And all you two need to do is sit at the back and hold hands. That'll be enough to cause the gossip-mongers to talk."

"Will the great Ms. Baxter be there?" Katya wasn't sure whether she wanted her to witness their act.

"Aye." Darach gave her a reassuring smile. "She's got an item on the agenda, so she'll be there to argue it."

"Great." Katya slumped down into the lumpy sofa.

"On top of that"—Darach pointed again—"there's the football match on Saturday between Invertary and Aberfoyle. Brodie's playing, so you need to be on the sideline, cheering him on."

Katya was surprised. "You're back playing football?"

"Have been for a while."

"I thought you didn't have time for it." He'd been a good soccer player when he was a kid but hadn't had the passion that would turn it into a profession. Unlike Flynn Boyle, Invertary's famous ex-footballer.

"That was when I thought I was starting a family and working hard to save for a house. Turns out, when your wife leaves, you have plenty of time to pick up new hobbies. Or, in this case, old ones."

"Right, that's it." Katya sat forward in her seat. "Enough with the passive-aggressive crap. Yeah, I left you. Yeah, it upended your life. Yeah, you're still upset about it. I get it. Everybody gets it. But you weren't the only one hurting back then, and you sure as hell aren't blameless. I don't need you to keep making digs about the past. It doesn't solve anything, and this situation's difficult enough without having to deal with the grudge you're lugging along with you every minute of every day."

There was a heavy pause before Brodie nodded. "You're right. I apologize, and I'll stop."

Katya's breath left her at his words. He'd always done that to her, taken the air from her lungs when he was man enough to admit his mistakes, apologize, and move on. It had been one of the reasons she'd loved him. Once he was called on something and saw it needed changing, he went out of his way to make it happen. No fuss, no complaining, just admission and change.

She blinked several times before sinking back into her seat. "Thanks."

"Good," Darach said. "Now that we've got that sorted, we need to deal with the romance side of things."

"I thought that's what we were doing," Katya said.

"That was the public side. You also need to be spotted out and about doing"—he made air quotes with his fingers—"private things."

"Dinner at the spa restaurant," Conall suggested.

"That's what I mean." Darach typed it into the Friday evening slot on the calendar. "Keep it coming."

There was silence.

Denise came back into the room and sat beside Katya. "What are we doing?"

"Apparently, we're watching five grown men try to come up with ideas for a romantic date. So far, we've got one suggestion."

Brodie cocked an eyebrow at her. "Like you're any better in the romance department."

He had a point.

"Oh, for Pete's sake," Denise said. "How about a romantic evening stroll around the loch?"

"Too many midges," Bain said.

Denise was undeterred. "A breakfast picnic?"

"Brodie and Kat on a picnic?" Kade said, as though announcing aliens had landed in Edinburgh.

"I'll admit," Katya said gently, not wanting to dampen Denise's enthusiasm, "it is a little out of character."

"An intimate breakfast at the pub." Denise's eyes went wide. "*After* you've spent the night there. I mean, everyone knows you're in here with half a rugby team, so they'd think it was romantic you'd booked a room just for the two of you."

"I like it." Darach added it to the calendar for Saturday night.

"Do we get a say?" Brodie asked.

"No!" everyone but Katya answered.

"Brodie could help Kat work on her plane after the football match on Saturday," Bain said with a wicked grin. "There's no way he'd do that if they weren't back together."

"I swear." Katya warned Brodie. "If you damage it, I will drown you in the loch."

"I won't damage it." He sighed with disgust.

"Oh," Kade said, "they need to attend family dinners. No way anyone would believe they're faking it if they sat down to eat with the two sets of parents. Hell, if Fraser even suspected it, he'd shoot Brodie."

"Great." Brodie looked about as happy as Katya felt at the latest suggestion. "That sounds like hours of fun."

"Brodie was invited to the Savage house for Sunday lunch," Denise piped up. The traitor.

Darach was already typing it into the calendar. "Okay, I think that's enough to be going on with. Now we need to practice kissing."

"I choose Denise!" Conall shouted.

"Not you, you div," Darach said. "Brodie and Kat."

"I knew that." Conall blushed as he sat back on the sofa.

"Um, excuse me." Katya was insulted. "We know how to kiss; we don't need any practice."

"What she said." Brodie gestured to her.

"Bain," Darach said with a note of long-suffering in his voice, "tell them what you told me."

"What? That their kiss on the doorstep looked more like a grudge match than a passionate reunion? The only person it fooled was Old Man Shepherd, and he's half blind. From where I stood, it looked like Brodie was about to strangle Kat, and she was planning to stab him in the gut. Listen to Megamind over there—you two need practice."

"That's utter rubbish," Katya told Bain. "We kiss fine." She turned to Denise. "Tell him. You saw us, right? We were kissing like normal people."

"Sorry, boo." Denise folded her arms. "I'm with Mr. Tactless on this. The kiss looked painful—as in, you were hurting each other."

"No, that happened later." Brodie rubbed his nipple through his shirt.

"You need to get used to touching and kissing in front of people, so it looks natural." Darach was earnest. "If you kiss here, it will help."

"Wait a minute," Brodie said as Katya's jaw dropped. "You want us to stand in the middle of the room and kiss while you grade us?"

"Well...aye."

"This meeting is over." Katya stood.

Denise grabbed her wrist. "Darach is right; you need the practice and the audience. Trust me on this, we aren't joking or messing with you. If you want to keep the land—both of you—you need to do this."

If it were anyone else trying to convince her, especially a MacGregor, Katya wouldn't have believed them. But this was her best friend, and although Denise had a wicked sense of humor, she would never do anything to hurt Katya.

"Fine." Katya sighed at Brodie. "Let's get this over with."

"And they say romance is dead," Bain muttered.

BRODIE HAD DONE a lot of strange things in his time, most of them because of Katya's prompting, but he'd never once thought he'd take part in a kissing assessment.

"If anyone laughs, I will hurt them," he warned his brothers.

"I won't hurt them...now," Kat added. "But they have to sleep, and I'm a patient woman."

Someone pushed the coffee table out of the way, and they met in the middle of the bright orange rug that someone must have bought in a sale.

"This is weird," Brodie complained.

"I feel like a performing monkey," Katya agreed.

"Would it help if we turned down the lights?" Denise asked.

"Then how would we see what they're doing wrong?" Darach said.

"Not helping, Dar," Brodie told him. He took a deep breath. This was no big deal; he'd kissed Kat countless times —although he'd liked her a helluva lot more back then, which made it easier. Now he found he wasn't quite sure how to place his hands or start the kiss so it looked natural.

"You're overthinking this," Bain said. "Just kiss her."

"Stop rushing me," Brodie snapped.

"And what makes you think he should kiss me? Why

can't I kiss him?" Of course, Katya would take the women's rights route in the situation.

"I wish one of you would get on with it," Bain said. "This is worse than watching that TV show with the two chicks that only talk and drink coffee. It's great when you can't sleep. Put it on, and ten minutes later, you're out."

"You mean *Gilmore Girls*?" Conall said. "I caught you sleeping through that last week."

"What'd I say?" Bain shrugged. "Better than sleeping pills."

Conall nodded. "Chick TV is mind-numbing."

"If we kiss," Katya said to Brodie, "will they all go away?"

Brodie couldn't help smiling at her. "Unfortunately, Bain and Darach live here."

As the tip of her tongue peeked out to wet her lips, Brodie realized she was as nervous as he felt. Maybe it was the scrutiny, or maybe it was kissing his ex-wife for the first time in ten years and making it look convincing. The kiss on the stoop didn't count. That had been to torment her, which had backfired because it'd tormented him too.

"Are we doing this?" she said quietly.

For a second, he wasn't sure if she meant the kiss or the whole pretending to be a couple thing. "Aye, we're doing it."

Slowly, he closed the distance between them. A strange but familiar sensation flowed through him as he neared her. It was as though he'd pushed through an invisible barrier and was now tucked inside Katya's personal magnetic field. Brodie remembered that feeling well.

"Hey," he whispered as his hands came up to cup her face, his thumb stroking along the line of her jaw.

"Hey," she whispered back, and her hands settled on his waist.

That's when he felt it. Her touch completed the electrical circuit, and now it fired between them. The sensation at once familiar and new. This was the Katya from his youth, only it wasn't. She was different, someone to discover.

Slowly, his eyes locked with Katya's as he lowered his mouth to brush his lips against the fullness of hers. He felt, rather than heard, her quick intake of air. Fingers flexed on his waist.

Their eyes drifted closed as he angled their heads to the position he needed. Soft, gently teasing kisses. He sipped at her. Tasting her, learning her. Her tongue tentatively touched his lower lip.

Brodie sucked in a breath, taking her scent straight into his lungs. Dove soap. He smiled against her mouth before deepening their kiss, asking for permission with gentle teasing touches of his tongue against hers.

Katya slid her hands up his back, pulling him closer. Brodie went willingly. The soft length of her body against his was the purest of temptations. He slid a hand around to the back of her head, threading his fingers through her hair, cradling her to him as their tongues explored, tasted, danced together.

A tiny, soft moan passed over Katya's lips and into his mouth. He swallowed it down. Fought the urge to moan in return. Instead, gently, almost reverently, he slowed the kiss. Brought them both back to earth softly.

With one last gentle pressing of their lips together, he rested his forehead against hers for a second.

A throat cleared. "Well, I don't think we need to worry about them being convincing," a voice said.

Katya stiffened in his hold, and her hands dropped from his back. Brodie released her just as quickly, taking a step back as the room swam into focus. A glance at Katya told him she looked as discombobulated as he felt. The kiss was a reminder that chemistry had never been their problem.

"*Now* the meeting is over," Katya said with finality. "I need to get some boxes from my truck."

"I'll help." Denise stood quickly. When Conall made a move to stand too, she held up a hand. "We've got this."

"Aye," Darach said. "Let's call it a night. Somehow, I don't think you'll have a problem pulling off a fake marriage, so long as you don't forget why you're doing it and start fighting in public."

"A marriage of convenience." Katya's dark eyes met Brodie's. "We can do that."

"Aye," Brodie lied, because he didn't think anything about this situation was convenient, especially not the rabid attraction that still buzzed between them.

15

Seven months after VE day, 1945

West Germany

Days turned to weeks, which turned to months, in the West German camp for displaced people. The old army barracks was filled to capacity with victims of war instead of Nazi soldiers, and Natasha found herself sharing a room with eight other women—some of whom had survived the extermination camps.

Rumors and stories about those camps spread like wildfire. Each more horrific than the last. Natasha spent her days helping care for the women who'd suffered the most. She fed them soup, rebandaged open sores, and held their hands when they whimpered as they dozed. The number of people lost in those first few months after being freed from captivity was soul-destroying.

Nights at the camp were punctuated by the screams of those

suffering night terrors or the sobs of people who'd lost everyone they'd loved. Daytime brought the interruption of visitors from other camps—people searching for missing loved ones—and regular meals. Food wasn't plentiful, but it was enough to survive and still better than the situation she'd been in at Lina's house, and Natasha was grateful for every single mouthful.

When she wasn't helping where she could, Natasha spent time learning English from a Polish woman who'd been keen to have something to occupy her time while waiting to be rehomed. And whenever he could, Ben Baxter would visit. Natasha found herself looking forward to those visits more and more. She wasn't sure if it had to do with breaking the repetitive monotony of the camp or whether she clung to him because he was the only person who knew her secret. The only one she could speak to in Russian and share stories about her experiences.

When the weather was fine, they'd make tea and sit in a corner of the camp grounds, far away from the others. Backs against a tree, legs stretched out in front of them, they'd sip their tea and talk. Ben didn't do small talk. The conversation was always intense. Two scarred people whispering about all the things they'd seen and done in the name of war. They were accidental confidants who'd become fast friends through their shared experiences, and there were days when Natasha wondered if she'd go insane without Ben to confide in.

It was on one such visit—while sipping tea and eating some much-coveted chocolate Ben had managed to rustle up from somewhere—that he brought up the topic of where she'd be placed after the camp.

"They found another German soldier this week," he said, staring off into the distance beyond the buildings.

Seeing only ruins. "He tried to convince everyone he was Polish and had been forced into a German labor camp."

"What gave him away?" Natasha nibbled at her chocolate as though it were pure, edible gold.

"His accent and bearing." As blue eyes met hers, she wondered if there would ever be a time when the color didn't startle her. "That and he was too healthy for the Nazis to have worked him to the bone."

"What will happen to him?" Her stomach tightened, but her voice remained even. Ben wouldn't bring up a story like this unless he had a reason.

"You don't want to know, Tasha." It was the same answer he always gave her. "They kept him in a displaced persons camp until they got to the bottom of his story."

Ah, now it made sense. "I haven't been relocated because they think I'm lying." She turned toward him, searching his face for the truth she knew he'd give her. "That's what you're trying to tell me, isn't it?"

His gaze remained steady, just like the man. "Yes."

It was reflex to tighten her grip on the old tin mug of tea, but she forced herself to calmly take another sip of the weak brew. That was the thing about Ben: he didn't try to soften news for her or hide anything—he gave it to her straight, one warrior to another, believing she could handle whatever he told her.

"If that's the case, I have to tell the truth and take my chances in Russia," she said evenly.

Those chances had diminished with each day she'd spent evading the Soviet Armed Forces. If they hadn't thought she was a traitor before she'd hidden in the displacement camps, they would now. What else would explain a pilot making no effort to return to her motherland? It would never occur to the good Soviet soldiers that she didn't want to face Stalin's insanity. Natasha shuddered at the thought.

"You're cold." Ben shrugged out of his worn regulation jacket and draped it around her shoulders.

"Spasibo," she whispered her thanks.

"I fear we made a mistake in telling the intelligence team that you're an engineer and would be a valuable asset to whichever country you were sent." He lifted his mug again and flexed his left leg. She knew he lived in constant pain from the damage caused to his thigh by a piece of shrapnel. A pain that would never go away. Just one more reminder of the war that Ben would carry with him forever.

"They're wondering why a skilled engineer wasn't conscripted into the Nazi war machine. And they suspect I'm lying to cover my involvement with the enemy." She shrugged. "It's nothing more than I would think if I were in their place, and we both know I *am* lying to everyone."

"I think"—Ben paused, appearing to choose his words carefully—"our friendship has protected you so far, but it won't for much longer. There are murmurs about taking you in for questioning."

"Of course." Natasha tucked a lock of hair behind her ear to cover the shaking in her hand. "I won't make it through an interrogation, Ben. There are too many holes in my story, ones I'm uncertain how to fill. I've no background information on Lina or firsthand experience of Lithuania. I only speak the language because I studied it in school. It wouldn't take an interrogation expert to crack me."

"It won't come to that." There was steel in his voice.

She gently placed a hand on Ben's arm. They rarely touched, but on this occasion, she thought it warranted. "It's best if I come clean before that happens. Otherwise, they won't believe I'm telling the truth when I explain I'm a

Soviet pilot who didn't want to return to her homeland. And it's the only way I can protect you. If it came out under duress that you knew my secret, I couldn't live with myself. Telling them before they discover it for themselves means I can say you know nothing."

He shifted in place, an uncharacteristically nervous move on his part. "There is another solution."

She cocked her head, wondering how awful it was to make Ben squirm. "Tell me; it's okay."

He fixed his steady gaze on her. "We could get married."

Natasha honestly didn't know what to say.

Ben hesitantly put his hand over hers where it still lay on his arm. "My time is almost up, and I'm heading home soon. My leg is getting worse, and according to my CO, I need rest. You could come with me, to Scotland. Quite a few Lithuanians are being relocated there."

"I'm not Lithuanian." It was the silliest thing to say, really, given everything else he'd told her.

His smile was sweet. "According to the camp authorities, you are. Which means it would be natural to want to go where your fellow countrymen and women were headed."

"But married, Ben?"

"My wife would be expected to return home with me."

Natasha took a second as she thought how best to word her worries without hurting her only friend in the world.

He squeezed her hand. "It's all right. The marriage would only be for the sake of getting you out of here. You wouldn't be tied to me forever...not unless you wanted to be."

"Ben," she whispered.

He cleared his throat and got to his feet, where he dusted off his trousers. "That's a discussion for another time. Think it over, and I'll come back tomorrow. But, Tasha, I'm convinced this is the only way to get you out of here before they start asking questions you can't answer."

As she watched him walk away, Natasha's heart clenched. She hadn't seen Ben as anything other than a friend, someone she trusted. She'd been in no state, physically or mentally, to consider anything else with any man.

Marriage?

Could she do it? Could she enter into another lie to get out of the one she was living? And would she toy with Ben's heart if she did so?

As she stood, her gaze scanned a group of camp administrators standing by the office block, their attention focused on her as they talked quietly among themselves. Natasha bent to pick up Ben's empty mug before making her way back across the barren courtyard to the dormitory.

She feared the decision on whether to take Ben up on his offer would be taken from her hands. Because he was right—her time was running out.

16

Katya couldn't sleep, which explained why she was sitting at the dining table at one in the morning with a mug of hot tea in her hand. In front of her, spread across the table, was everything she'd managed to find out about her great-grandmother over the years. Some of it had been stored and forgotten in various family members' attics, while other items she'd come across on her travels.

Sitting on top of it all was the marriage certificate and photo Catherine Baxter had given Brodie. And beside that, the marriage certificate filed by her great-grandfather on his and Natasha's wedding day. They were dated barely months apart.

Using her laptop, she accessed one of the marriage and divorce database services on the internet and typed in the details for Ben and Natasha. The certificate stated that they'd married in Berlin in 1945, so she kept her fingers crossed as she searched, hoping official records of the marriage hadn't gone missing in the war.

It took three different websites before she found a record

of their marriage on a military site. Unfortunately, even after searching several more databases, she still couldn't find any mention of a divorce taking place.

"You should be asleep," Brodie said quietly as he padded into the kitchen. His feet bare, he wore an old gray T-shirt over a pair of blue tartan flannel pajama pants. The man shouldn't have looked sexy in the getup, but he did. There was no justice in the world at all.

"So should you." She reached for her mug of tea, only to find it empty.

"I will be as soon as I make up a bed on the couch." He filled the kettle and switched it on. "Bain wouldn't let me share his bed, and the floor's hard. I'd rather try my luck with a lumpy sofa." He gestured to her mug. "Want a refill?"

"Yeah, thanks." They lapsed into a silence that started to feel way too awkward when she caught him staring at her lips. Suddenly, memories of their earlier kiss had her squirming in her seat.

"So," he cleared his throat, "what're you doing?"

Grateful for something, *anything*, to take her mind off *that* kiss, Katya lifted Ben and Natasha's marriage certificate. "I've been looking for an official mention of this."

His eyebrows shot up toward his bed-mussed hair. "I take it, from the look on your face, you didn't find one. Does that mean it's a fake?"

"Oh, no, it's real all right. The look is because I couldn't find any divorce paperwork to accompany it, and I've searched everywhere I can think of."

Brodie turned to make tea for them, giving Katya an excellent view of his broad, muscular shoulders and firm behind. When he turned with a mug for her, she snapped her eyes back to the table, where they belonged. He put the mug of steaming tea on the table in front of her and took a seat beside her.

"You know, your parents are going to love the news that old Tom Savage was a bigamist." The sad part was that Brodie wasn't being sarcastic.

"Mum will probably write a play about the scandal, and dad will tell everyone it's proof his family were always on the fringe of proper society. It feeds into his whole rebellious-artist image." The scene was so familiar—the two of them up late, talking alone—that for a second, Katya forgot they were strangers now.

"At least they'll take it better than Kitty ever has. Do you think she's figured out that if the wedding was a sham she's illegitimate?" Brodie moved some of the papers toward him and started sifting through them.

"I'd say so." Katya cradled her tea and watched him scan the documents she'd collected. "It would explain her nasty attitude. People her age really care about crap like that."

"There are people of every age who care about crap like that." Brodie held up a piece of paper. "So, your great-granny was in a camp?"

"Not a concentration camp, if that's what you're thinking; it was a holding place for people who couldn't return to their own countries. She lived there until she moved to Scotland—apparently with Ben."

"Huh," Brodie muttered as he read. "I didn't know about these camps."

Katya didn't bother pointing out he would have known if he'd made an effort to pay attention to anything she told him before she left.

He slid another folded sheet of paper toward him. It was brown and faded, its creases testifying to how many times it'd been unfolded and refolded. "What's this?"

"A letter great-gran wrote to her navigator—the woman who died when their plane was shot down outside Berlin. I think it was her way of coping with the death. Great-gran tells her she's sorry she couldn't save her, that she wishes things were different, and promises she'll make sure her parents get the necklace she wore. I think she wrote it while she was hiding in a house in East Germany after they crashed. She talks about how hungry she is, how she can't find food, and how the Lithuanian woman who saved her has disappeared. But she can't ask anyone about her because she can only speak Russian and Lithuanian, not German."

"She was shot down?" Brodie's intense gaze focused on Katya. "You only told me she was a bomber pilot for the Soviet Union."

"I didn't know much more than that back then." She waved a hand to encompass the table. "This is almost everything I've managed to glean about her since...well, since I left."

"So, she hid out in Germany? Why didn't she go back to the Soviets? I mean, they were working with the Allies to get rid of Hitler, surely an Allied soldier would have helped her get back to her squadron."

"Stalin executed failures or saw them as traitors. And having your plane go down behind enemy lines would have been considered a failure. If she went home, she would have faced the firing squad or the Gulag, and besides, her family had already been lost to the war." She took a sip of her tea. "She had two older brothers who were both killed at Stalingrad."

"Hell." Brodie shuffled through the rest of the papers. "I'm guessing she pretended to be Lithuanian to avoid being sent back to Russia."

"That's how she met Ben. He was a translator, and they called him in when they found her unconscious in the house of the woman who'd saved her. He found out she was Soviet, and they became friends. I'd always thought it was their friendship that brought her to Invertary; I didn't realize it was their marriage."

Dark eyes caught hers. "But you knew they were friends?"

"I found letters from Ben in Aunty Patty's attic down in Glasgow." Katya reached into the box sitting on the floor and pulled out a bundle of envelopes tied together with string. "They wrote to each other about their experiences during the war. I believe they were confidants, because Ben wrote that he'd never tell anyone else the stuff he shared with her." She handed him the letters.

"Can I read them?" Brodie looked sheepish. "I'm curious."

"Sure, but you'll want the translation; those are in Russian." She plucked a blue folder out of the box and handed it to him.

"You had them translated?"

"When I first started out, I couldn't read Russian, so I had to have everything translated."

Brodie's jaw dropped as he sat back in his seat. "You speak Russian?"

"I do now."

They stared at each other for a long moment.

"I really don't know you at all now, do I?" Brodie said at last.

Katya sighed. "It's been ten years, Brodie. We're not the kids who ran off to Gretna to get married as soon as we were legal." She gestured to him. "You're running your own business and plan to build a house. I speak Russian, fly planes for anyone who'll hire me, and carry around boxes full of other people's memories." Her smile was rueful. "People change."

"Aye," he muttered, his mind obviously elsewhere. "I guess they do."

"Anyway, I'd better get some sleep." Katya took her mug to the sink. "In a few short hours, I have to explain to the Knit or Die crew that signing you up for a mail-order bride was really a joke. That conversation should be interesting."

Brodie turned in his seat to look at her. "Why did you come back, Kat? Really? You've been living a wild, adventurous life all over the planet. It doesn't make sense that you'd come back to sleepy Invertary."

"This is my home." Another answer bubbled up inside of her, but she squashed it down. Brodie had nothing to do with her returning to Invertary. It was the confusion of their situation talking because she had no intention of ever letting him hurt her again. "This is where Natasha spent most of her life. It's where Ben lived, and he saved her—no matter how he did it. Where else would be a better spot for a memorial?"

She moved to gather up the paperwork, but he placed a hand on top of it. "Do you mind if I read some of this? I don't feel like sleeping yet."

"Knock yourself out." Katya turned toward the stairs. "And, Brodie? Just because we've had one civilized conversation doesn't mean I'm about to hand over the land for you to build your house."

He flashed her a dazzling smile. "I know."

With that image seared into her brain, Katya returned to Brodie's bed to try to sleep.

MUCH TO BRODIE'S DISMAY, Darach had been right—the whole town had turned up to watch the Knit or Die women block the lochside road through town. And when they weren't watching the women knit, they were commenting on seeing Brodie and Katya glued to each other's sides.

"I'd forgotten how nosy people are in Invertary," Katya grumbled as the latest person to ask them if they were together again walked away. "I don't even know that guy."

"Sure you do. He used to deliver our mail," Brodie said as yet more folk looked at him as if he were clutching a bomb instead of Katya's hand.

"That's Murray? Wow, he used to be such a skinny wee thing."

"He hurt his hip and had to quit the post office. Now he watches daytime TV instead of walking all over Invertary."

"That's a cautionary tale," Katya said. "Margaret Campbell's giving me the evil eye again. At some point, we'll have to go over there and explain about the mail-order brides." She hesitated. "And probably set the record straight about you moonlighting as a stripper."

Brodie frowned at her. "Aye, we should definitely sort that out. And it's Margaret Jamieson now. She married Dougal a wee while ago."

"Stop frowning—we're supposed to be in love, so look happy. I keep forgetting she married Dougal. That's one weird pairing."

"Weirder than us right now?" He smiled at her as lovingly as he could manage, feeling his cheek muscles groan at the effort. "Can you get face strain from smiling too much?"

"I don't know. Why is your hand so clammy? I don't remember them being that way. It's like holding a fish," she whined through her smile, which was an impressive talent.

"My hand isn't clammy; it's your imagination. You have a clammy imagination."

Katya started to roll her eyes at him but obviously remembered she was supposed to be in love, so "playfully" smacked him on the chest instead, her hand leaving a stinging handprint in its wake. "You're so funny."

"If you hit me one more time, I'm throwing you in the loch and telling everyone it's a romantic gesture."

"Like they'll believe y—" Her eyes widened. "Oh!"

"Aye, oh."

He'd tossed her into the loch during their wedding reception—and then followed her straight in. The stars had been out overhead, and their families had strung up fairy lights around the small picnic area. The townsfolk had provided the food, with everyone bringing their favorite dish, and her grandfather had played his guitar while people sang.

After their wedding ceremony in Gretna Green, he'd thought it the most romantic event of his life.

"Should we get a pie?" Katya gestured to Morag's stand. "Then we can at least have a break from holding hands, and you can dry off your clammy palm."

"I thought we could go to the pub and get a couple of cold drinks. It looks like it's going to be a rare stinker of a sunny day."

As they spoke, they each headed in a different direction, only to be pulled up short by their joined hands.

"Fine," Katya gritted out. "We'll go to the pub."

"No, pies are okay by me."

They swapped directions—with the same result. As they stood there, glaring at each other, Darach and Denise appeared in front of them.

"What are you doing?" Denise said through a smile that

was all teeth. "You don't look like you're holding hands; you look like you're handcuffed to each other."

"This is weird," Brodie complained. Then, noticing people nearby watching them, he threw back his head and laughed loudly, as though they'd told him a great joke.

Of course, that forced the rest of them to fake their own laughter.

"Nobody in their right mind is ever going to believe this act," Darach said when they were done.

"Isn't acting supposed to be in your genes?" Denise quietly demanded of Katya. "The two of you are completely wooden."

"If you want a proper actress, get my mother to hold his hand," Katya hissed. "I don't want to do it anyway."

Brodie held up their joined hands and gave them a pointed look. "You think I want this?"

"Dear heavens above," Denise snapped. "It isn't difficult to pretend you're hot for someone. Watch." She turned to Darach, grabbed him by the back of the neck, pulled him down to her, and kissed the living daylights out of him.

While the crowd around them whooped and clapped, Brodie and Katya stood there, stunned.

When she was done, Denise patted a dazed Darach on the chest. "See?" she said to Brodie and Katya before looking up at Darach. "Did the earth move for you?"

"Uh, no," the idiot said honestly, shutting down any hopes of a repeat performance. Had Brodie taught him nothing?

"Exactly." Denise beamed at him. "We have no chemistry whatsoever, and yet, we managed to pull that off. Whereas you two have chemistry, and history, and experience with each other. So, make a bloody effort." She hooked her hand through Darach's arm. "You're buying me a coffee," she told him.

With a grin for Brodie, Darach let Denise lead him into the pub.

"She's right," Katya said with what could only be construed as grim determination. "We can do better. All we have to do is remember that the touching and kissing and sweet words mean nothing."

"Because they do."

"Exactly." She tossed her long ponytail and straightened her back with determination. "Put your arm around my shoulders, and we'll walk over to the knitting group."

"You know, this whole thing would go a lot better if you'd stop telling me what to do. I know how to behave like I'm hot for someone."

"Really?" She cocked an eyebrow at him.

"Aye, really."

They glared at each other.

"You are going to put your arm around my shoulders, aren't you?" she demanded.

"Aye." He let out a sigh and draped his arm around her.

Her hand slipped into the back pocket of his jeans. "Right, let's go deal with Knit or Die."

Three paces later, they tripped over each other and almost landed on top of the new vicar.

"Back to holding hands, it is." Brodie gripped her hand firmly before striding across the cobblestone road toward Margaret Jamieson, who was studying them with a mixture of skepticism and curiosity.

"Remember," Katya muttered, "you love me, all is forgiven, and we've realized we belong together. That's what we're going for and what we need to sell. We can do this."

As her words sank in, something ripped open within

Brodie, and it felt as though the world had tipped on its axis. Suddenly, putting one foot in front of the other proved to be much more difficult than it should have been, and despite being surrounded by the noise of a crowded street, all he could hear was Katya's voice.

You love me. All is forgiven. We belong together.

It was as if those words had found something inside of him. Something that had been lost for such a long time, and that something grasped at her words like a lifeline. And from the way his heart raced, Brodie wasn't sure it would be possible to ever let go of those words. Over and over, they repeated in his head like a mantra until they became embedded within his soul.

Could it be true? Was it even possible? Did he want it to be?

"Are you okay?" Katya whispered.

"Aye, aye, I'm fine. A wee bit lightheaded from lack of sleep."

"Do I need to find you some coffee?"

"No, it's okay."

"Good, because we have to focus on the mission. This is how we're going to save our land and our future. It's game time."

But all Brodie could hear were the words echoing in his mind.

You love me. All is forgiven. We belong together.

Dear God, he hoped it was just delusional thinking brought on by exhaustion.

17

———

"So, you're a couple again?" The leader of Invertary's knitting group was clearly skeptical. "But you *weren't* together yesterday, when we were trying to find him a mail-order bride? That was fast work."

"What can I say?" Katya was fed up with wearing a fake smile. Her face hurt. "The heart wants what the heart wants. It's destiny, and the stars aligned for us. It's as though we were meant to be together...again."

Shona McBride, who sat in the deckchair beside Margaret's, cupped a hand behind her ear. "Sorry, can you speak up? I think I might have missed one of the clichés you just spouted."

The row of retired women, all wearing matching T-shirts with the words Knit or Die across their chests, giggled like schoolgirls. They'd lined their deckchairs up right across the road, from the bottom of the high street to the lochside, and it looked like they were in it for the long haul. They had flasks at their feet, and plastic containers filled with home baking were doing the rounds. And the knitting needles were clacking busily.

"At least you've got the weather for your protest," Brodie said inanely.

"You want to discuss the weather now?" Margaret cocked her head at him in disgust.

Brodie was right, though—it was a perfect Scottish summer's day. The sky was blue, the sun was out, and the loch sparkled. The green hills that cradled Invertary seemed to almost gleam in the morning light. The only thing ruining the picturesque sight was the line of traffic backed up down the road.

Bus and truck drivers honked their horns and shouted, but the people in cars and the tourists on the buses happily abandoned their vehicles to go for a wander through town. There was plenty to keep them occupied while they waited for the road to clear because Invertary knew how to put on a protest. As well as the pie stall, a coffee stand, and a break-fast special at the pub, entrepreneurial artists were selling their work by the side of the loch. There was even a piper out on a boat, and Katya spotted a member of her brother's band busking on a corner.

"I've got to ask," Brodie said to Margaret. "Why are you knitting with wire instead of wool?"

"We're making a fence," she said. "A woman in the islands did it, and we thought it sounded like a great idea. We plan on stringing this across the road when we can't be here."

"Um," Brodie said. "You realize somebody could easily move it out of the way, right?"

"Not the way we'll fix it to the road, they won't." Margaret looked determined.

"What happens if you get the pedestrian crossing before you can use the fence you're knitting?"

"Don't worry." Margaret narrowed her eyes. "We'll find a

use for it. Ever since we started yarn bombing and took to protesting, we've discovered nothing is wasted. Last month, we protested the lack of services in town for pregnant women by sending all the booties we've knitted over the years to the regional health board. So, I'm sure we'll find a use for a wire fence."

The woman in the chair beside Shona elbowed her and jerked her head toward Brodie. "Is this the stripper?"

"I'm going to go with no," Shona said wryly. "This is my sister-in-law, April. She heads up the new chapter of Knit or Die in Fort William and was really looking forward to supporting Brodie's latest business venture."

April McBride leaned forward in her chair with an air of solemnity that made Katya think the woman was about to impart some great wisdom. "We're calling our group Knit or Die Harder." She beamed.

"I still strip." Brodie remained straight-faced. "But only for Katya."

"Anybody else feel like vomiting?" Margaret Jamieson said as she stood. She tucked her knitting into the chair behind her and pointed at Brodie and Katya. "You two, follow me." And then she marched over to the stone wall at the edge of the loch.

Once they reached the wall, Margaret turned her back on the town, folded her arms, and stared down Brodie and Katya. "Spill," she ordered.

"I don't know what you're talking about." Agitated, Katya shook off Brodie's hold to reach up and tighten her ponytail.

"I'm talking about you two hardly being able to look each other in the eye, let alone hold hands. If you're back together, then I'm the queen of Scotland."

Brodie leaned against the wall and smiled. "That's harsh, Margaret. Can't you see our love is eternal?"

"So's your bullshit." Margaret gave them a firm, motherly look that almost made Katya want to blurt out their secret.

Man, she was good. No wonder her daughter, Kirsty, never got away with anything when she was growing up. "You use that look on your grandkids too, don't you?" Katya said, impressed. "I bet you know everything that's going on in Kirsty's house."

Margaret's grin was broad. "Don't think you can distract me. I know a scheme when I see one, and you two are definitely up to something. If you tell me, we might be able to help."

Katya shared a look with Brodie, who shrugged. His hands were in the pockets of his jeans, his white T-shirt dazzling in the sun. If he was as tense as her, it didn't show. Which, for some utterly illogical reason, made her want to smack him.

With a sigh, Katya decided they could confide in Margaret. But as she opened her mouth to speak, she spotted Kitty Baxter's foreman loitering at the edge of the protest, his attention firmly focused on Brodie and Katya. The spies were out.

"I've no idea what you mean," Katya said. "You should be happy we're back together; you always said we were made for each other."

"Aye, I've been known to say a lot of things. So, I guess this new romance means you'll be turning your land into an airport, then." Margaret folded her arms over her shirt. Yep, there was no way of getting anything past the woman. "We couldn't exactly miss the plane Katya drove through town. Pity you'd already started on your house, Brodie. Seems such a shame to waste all that work."

Honestly, MI5 had nothing on the women of Knit or Die.

If there was a secret to unearth, they would find it. Then they'd cover it in multi-colored knitting and complain loudly about it at the next town council meeting.

Before Katya could say anything, Brodie answered, "Now, what makes you think we aren't building the house? We can't live with my brothers forever, you know. Anyway, Katya said she loved the architectural plans Conall drew up." His eyes sparkled at her, daring her to argue. The ass.

Katya gave him the evil eye before smiling at Margaret. "He's having you on. Of course, we're building a museum and runway on the land. Brodie doesn't want all the hard work I did while I was away—finding the plane and gathering info for the museum—to be put to waste. Do you, darling?"

He oozed charm as he spoke to Margaret. "Katya's only saying that because she's worried what people will think when they find out she's gone off the memorial museum idea. After spending ten years obsessing about all that crap, she's fed up with it and wants to set up home on our land, in our new house, and start popping out babies. I told her not to worry. I'm sure the council will put up a plaque somewhere to remember her great-granny."

Katya clenched her hands into fists as she fought to keep a smile on her face. One she was sure must have appeared utterly feral, but it was the best she could manage. "I think Brodie slept through part of our discussion about the future. I definitely want a plaque, but the museum and tourist flights are still going ahead. And our land is the perfect location for both."

"You're right; I don't remember agreeing to that. Plus, I don't think you're being realistic. It'll be a bit tricky to fit in the cockpit when you're heavily pregnant," Brodie mused. "Maybe Dougal could park your plane outside his new conference center, where everybody can admire it. Wait a minute, I know a guy who could dip it in bronze and turn it into a proper relic."

Now he was really pissing her off. "My plane isn't a relic. It's a piece of living history."

"It's a piece of barely functional history. I'm no' even sure you'd get insurance to cover flying it." Brodie shook his head as though amused. "Have you thought this out, Kat? It's good we're back together because you need a sensible influence in your life. Don't worry, I've got your back."

"Trust me, the insurance company won't have a problem with the plane. There's nothing wrong with it. It's perfectly safe. In fact, why don't I take you up in it to prove it?"

"I'll give that some consideration." He shared a bemused look with Margaret. "The Savages and their wild ideas... It sure keeps life interesting, I'll tell you."

A red haze spread across Katya's gaze. Brodie knew he was pushing one of her hot buttons. She'd spent her entire life listening to how irresponsible and weird her family was and how she'd grow up to be exactly like them. When he'd accused her of the same thing before she left, she'd been devastated. Now he was making her mad.

"I'm curious," he said, clearly oblivious to the rage bubbling inside her, "how you're planning to get this new business off the ground. Pun intended. Where's the startup money coming from?"

"I don't see what that's got to do with you," Katya growled.

"If he's going to be your husband again," Margaret said, reminding Katya that the knitting group leader was still there, "then I expect it has a lot to do with him."

Katya forced through gritted teeth, "The bank will snap up the opportunity to support a new business in Invertary—

one that not only attracts tourists but also honors a local war hero's legacy."

"The bank might ask how you'll make money out of the business once it's started." Brodie raised an eyebrow. "I don't know if you've noticed, but that plane of yours only seats two people, and one of them has to be the pilot. You plan to take all these tourists up there one at a time? Not very efficient business practice, is it?"

He looked so pleased with himself, so smug and superior, that Katya snapped. Before she'd even realized she was going to do it, she pushed hard in the middle of his chest and toppled him into the loch.

There was a loud splash accompanied by shocked gasps.

Katya's anger disappeared in a flash, and she swallowed a groan. So much for convincing the town they were in love.

The women of Knit or Die rushed to the wall and peered over to see if Brodie was okay.

"We're still working out a few kinks in our relationship," Katya told them as his head bobbed above the water.

BRODIE TRUDGED up the main street to his office, soaked jeans rubbing like sandpaper in places no sandpaper should ever touch. At least it was summer. The last time Kat shoved him into the loch, it'd been the middle of winter, and he'd almost died of hypothermia on the way home.

"You can tell that girl of yours is back," one of the old men who played dominoes at the pub called out to him as he passed. "Feels like old times, seeing you like that!" And then he cackled so hard it turned into a cough.

Brodie wasn't amused. All he wanted to do was get to his

office, change into his spare clothes, and mentally prepare himself for the next encounter with his loving wife.

"The first person to make a smart-arsed comment dies," Brodie said as he pushed through the door to their company office.

Fortunately, Darach was the only brother present. Unfortunately, he was having tea with their da.

His father, who was the shortest man in the family, barely topping five-foot-eight, looked him up and down over the rim of his mug. "Felt like an early morning swim, son?"

His entire family thought they were comedians. "Katya shoved me into the loch." Brodie opened the bottom drawer in his desk and pulled out some clothes. "I need to change before I lose all the skin off my balls." With that, he turned and headed for the bathroom at the back of the building.

He should have known he'd find his da waiting for him when he came out into the back office. The fact his chair blocked Brodie's path to the front office made it clear he wanted to talk.

"Why'd she dunk you this time?" his da asked casually.

Brodie wasn't fooled. The man had the senses of a shark when it came to blood in the water.

"I don't have time to talk," Brodie said. "I need to get some work done."

His da pointed at the chair opposite. "You've got five minutes for your old man."

Stifling his irritation, Brodie sat.

The astute eyes of a man who'd raised seven sons met his. "What did you do?"

There was no point in arguing his innocence, not when he already felt guilt eating at him. "I slagged off her plans for the museum and the plane rides. Then pretty much told her she was exactly like the rest of her wacky family."

His da took a sip of his tea while he mulled that over. "Now, why would you say something like that?"

"Because"—Brodie ran a hand through his damp hair—"she wants to use our land to start her business, and I'm trying to protect my future. I've spent ten years saving and planning for that house build. She's got no right to walk back in here and upend my life all over again."

It wasn't anything he hadn't said in the years since she'd left, but this time, it lacked conviction. Probably because he knew he'd deliberately poked the bear to get a reaction at the loch. Her throwaway words about love and forgiveness had affected him enough to make him lash out.

"You know," his da said, "out of all my boys, you're the one who worries me most."

"Knowing Bain, I find that hard to believe."

His father chuckled. "Aye, that boy definitely has his issues, but you're the one I fear is destined to live a life you don't really want."

"Da." Brodie leaned forward to rest his arms on his knees. "I'm knackered and in desperate need of some coffee. I'm also fairly certain I swallowed some loch water because now my stomach aches. If you have something to say, could you get to the point?"

"Okay." His father put his mug on the desk beside him. "You're the middle son. You've spent your life keeping the peace between your brothers. It's hardwired into your genes to go along with things for an easier life. You don't even notice you're doing it half the time."

"I didn't go along with Katya's idea to find a plane," Brodie pointed out, ruining his da's attempt at armchair psychology.

"No, you didn't." He ran a hand down his face. "And I think I'm to blame for that."

Now he was worrying Brodie. "Da, I've no idea what you're talking about here."

"That girl always made you take risks. The only time you went wild and got into any sort of trouble or tried anything out of the ordinary was with her. She pushed you, and it was good for you. But your natural instinct is to stick with what's familiar. I think that's why you never went with her. You were too busy holding on to a plan for your life that wasn't even yours." His father's face twisted with guilt.

"What do you mean, it isn't mine? I think I'd know if I was following someone else's plan."

"Would you?" He shook his head. "I pressured every single one of my boys to follow in my footsteps and become an electrician, and you're the only one who did it."

Brodie shrugged. "It was no big deal. It's a decent job."

"Aye, it is, but you never once considered any other path after you knew I wanted another electrician in the family. You were making me happy, keeping the peace. It was the same with your house. I spent hours telling you and your brothers that it'd been my dream to build my own place, but I could never afford to. Then, when Old Ben gave you the land, I laid it on thick about how lucky you were and how you couldn't waste it. That you needed to build the house of your dreams—just like I always wanted to do." He rubbed a hand over the spot where his heart lay. "Did you ever once consider an alternative use for the land?"

"Why would I? Building a house is a good idea."

"Until Katya had another one, and suddenly you freaked out because you actually needed to think about what you wanted instead of going with the flow. That's why you reacted the way you did. It wasn't that you were set on your plans; it was because Katya was the only one to challenge them and make you think about whether they were yours to begin with."

"Da, you're worrying me here." The conversation felt a lot like a confession from a dying parent. "You're feeling okay, aren't you?"

"Aye, I'm fine. It just seemed the right time to talk to you about this. Son, Katya's the only one who's ever made you think for yourself, but she was never known for her patience. If she'd given you a wee bit more time to consider her ideas for finding the plane, you might have gone with her. Instead, you panicked and told her she was as nutty as her family, so she stomped off in a huff."

Brodie sat back in his chair. "That's oversimplifying it a tad."

"Is it? Without her, you revert to the status quo. I mean, here you are, setting up a business with Darach. Did you think about whether you wanted to do this, or did you go along with it to please him? Then there was the job on the oil rigs. Katya encouraged you to take it, but as soon as she was gone, you gave up your place there and stayed home to work with me. Don't even get me started on the house. Son, seriously, why are you building a palace for one in Invertary? You don't even have a girlfriend because you're still married to Katya. Who's going to fill that big house?"

"I think you're making a fuss about nothing," Brodie told him. "I'm happy with my life."

"Are you really?" His da stood and picked up his mug, then turned toward the door into the front office. "Think about what I've said. I wouldn't want you making any more mistakes because of me."

18

The sewing group at the camp had managed to get their hands on a German airman's silk parachute to make Natasha the most beautiful wedding dress she'd ever seen. Unlike the other garments and material that made their way to the camp, there was an abundance of silk in the parachute, which meant the dress had puff sleeves and a full, voluptuous skirt. Wearing it made her feel like a princess.

It also made her feel guilty seeing everyone go to so much trouble for a wedding that wasn't even real.

"You shouldn't have done this," Natasha said to Rasa, the Lithuanian woman who'd organized the dressmaking sessions.

"Don't be silly." The older woman fussed with the hem of the dress, making sure it sat perfectly. "Weddings are to be celebrated. It's a sign life goes on and the Nazis didn't defeat us, that our spirit isn't broken. Every wedding and birth in this camp is a reason for us all to celebrate."

Natasha felt grateful to the generous woman who'd lost her own husband in an extermination camp. "With your skills, your wedding must have been very beautiful."

A bittersweet smile curved Rasa's lips. "My Jurgis could scarcely keep his hands off me. It was most inappropriate for the serious ceremony my parents arranged."

Natasha covered the woman's hands with hers. "I'm glad you had that."

"Yes, our memories are the gold the Nazis couldn't steal." Rasa turned her toward the mirror. "Now, what do you think?"

For a second, Natasha was breathless. "I don't deserve this," she whispered.

"None of that nonsense." Rasa patted Natasha's hair. "We all deserve whatever happiness we can find. Right. You're ready. Let's go see how handsome your gentleman is today."

Holding up the skirt of her dress, Natasha followed Rasa through the stark gray corridors of the former SS barracks. Each doorway they passed was filled with the smiling, hopeful faces of those who'd lived through the horrors of hell. They called out their blessings and well wishes to her, while behind them, the ones too weak and ill to leave their cots added their voices to her day.

As she picked her way through the rubble of a wall damaged in a blast, she thought of her parents and brothers. Of the people who should have been there to witness this day. Her father would have been disappointed in her. He'd planned a marriage between Natasha and the son of one of his doctor friends, to be held at the prestigious and luxurious Hotel Metropol in Moscow.

"Are you nervous?" Rasa whispered as they made their way across the debris-littered courtyard to what used to be the commanding officer's private dining room. As the only building in the complex with any semblance of style, it was used for all special events. "Your mother should have been here to explain about your wedding night. I'm happy to go over things with you if you're uncertain about fulfilling your marital obligations."

There were no blushes from Rasa at the topic, not after everything she'd witnessed during the war. After seeing young women paraded naked in front of soldiers or raped for amusement before their death, what happened between a married couple on their wedding night was far from shocking.

"Thank you, Rasa, but there's no need." Natasha didn't want to tell the kind woman there would be no wedding night. At least, not in the way she meant it.

As one of their fellow refugees held open the wood and glass door for them, Rasa took a peek inside. "He's there, and he's handsome as ever," she gushed, sounding like an excited schoolgirl. "This is wonderful, Natasha. You'll live a happy life with your man, far away from the damage of the war." Her smile looked self-conscious for a second. "I had to look up Scotland on a map because I wasn't sure where it was."

"So did I," Natasha confessed, and they laughed together.

Butterflies invaded her stomach as she walked into the officer's quarters. The ornately carved wooden fireplace had been strewn with wildflowers collected from the local forest floor. Beautiful garlands made from greenery hung around the walls, and the remainder of the parachute fabric used for her dress had been draped over a table in the center of the room. More flowers sat in the middle of it, along with a brown paper package tied with string.

Rasa nervously gestured to the package. "The women gathered what we could to help you start your new life. It isn't much, but it might be helpful."

Tears at the generosity of people who had almost nothing burned in Natasha's eyes. "Thank you, Rasa." She hugged her friend. "And please thank everyone who contributed. I will take good care of everything they've gifted me."

"You can thank us by living a wonderful life with your husband in Scotland." Rasa's whisper was ferocious against Natasha's ear. "This is our revenge—we will be happy."

"Yes," was all Natasha could say.

When she released Rasa, she took a deep breath and turned to the two men standing in front of the decorated fireplace. Ben smiled at her, looking as nervous as she felt.

The other man, Ben's commanding officer, gestured toward her.

"Please take your place beside your intended," he said in English.

Natasha had never been more grateful to the woman who'd taught her the language before being relocated to America. One of the few taken in by the US, who had strict quotas for refugees.

Smiling, she stood beside Ben.

"Ready?" he asked.

There was nothing else to do but nod.

19

"So, this is the spa restaurant." Katya looked around at the classy interior of the renovated old church. "Is the food good?"

Wishing he didn't feel like a goldfish in a bowl as the other diners stared at them, Brodie nodded. "The best food in Invertary."

As a waitress led them to their table by one of the large stained glass windows, Brodie placed his hand on the small of Katya's back, feeling her body move under the thin fabric of her dress. The urge to splay his hand wide in order to access more of her was almost overwhelming. He fought it off by reminding himself that this was Katya, and no good ever came from making things complicated between them.

Like him, Katya had dressed up for their date. While he wore charcoal jeans, an open-necked pale blue shirt and suit jacket, she wore a short black form-fitting dress with thin straps and a scoop neckline. On her feet were black four-inch heels with tiny gold bows at the back, which she seemed to be having trouble walking in.

When she'd almost twisted her ankle for the third time,

he slid his arm around her waist to hold her up. "Where did you get those shoes?" he whispered.

"Denise wouldn't let me wear my Doc Marten boots. These"—she glanced down at her shoes in disgust—"are Prada." She frowned up at him. "Apparently, she saved for a year to buy them, and if I damage them, I need to repay her with a life of servitude."

"She doesn't just want to be reimbursed?"

"No, because she knows I'm penniless. Plus, this way, she can make me suffer for a whole lot longer." Her gaze was pleading. "If you're going to retaliate for the loch, can you at least let me take my shoes off first?"

"Sit down, Katya," Brodie said with long-suffering as they reached their table.

He pulled out a seat for her at the linen-covered table and she sank down into with a grateful sigh.

As soon as they had menus in front of them and drinks ordered, Katya leaned toward him, her voice low. "I'm sorry for pushing you in the loch?"

Aye, he bet she was. "Why is it your apologies always sound like questions?"

She appeared to give this serious consideration. "Either because I'm not really sure I'm sorry, or I want to cover my bases in case an apology isn't needed, or I'm not sure the person even wants an apology."

"You've spent a lot of time thinking about this, haven't you?"

"I seem to spend a lot of time apologizing," she said ruefully.

"And yet, nothing changes."

"Are we going to fight or eat? People are watching, and I'd rather eat. I made the mistake of dropping by my parents' house for lunch and the lectures put me off my food. Dad wants to shoot you again, and Mum thinks we should renew our vows." She smiled with wicked amusement. "At the loch."

"I hope you hid your dad's shotgun." Brodie still had a scar on his backside from the last time.

"He got to it first, and I couldn't find it. Don't worry, I told Dad we've matured, and we know what we're doing this time." Katya grinned. "I think he bought it."

When the waitress returned with their drinks—a beer for him and a glass of white wine for Katya—they ordered their food. Once she left, they lapsed into a heavy silence. While Katya occupied herself with studying the décor, Brodie studied her.

Her waist-length hair fell in waves about her shoulders like a silken waterfall. The candlelight brought out the red hues in all that brown. The red hues in turn made her olive eyes appear emerald. Her skin was still as flawless as it had been ten years ago, and she wore minimal makeup. If memory served him right, it was probably just mascara, and lipstick—a soft pink shade that made her already plump lips appear fuller. Her short fingernails were varnish free, and her only jewelry was a gold chain around her neck.

"Why are you staring at me?" she said.

"I'd forgotten how beautiful you are." Brodie saw no point in lying. Katya had always been beautiful to him, and their time apart hadn't changed that.

"Brodie," she gently chided, her cheeks turning pink. "I don't want to spend the evening arguing. Can't we have a nice meal together?"

Brodie rested his forearms on the table. "How about we pretend we've only just met, and this is our first date?"

Her eyes narrowed. "Are you trying to pick me up? Because that ship has sailed."

"No, I'm trying to put on a show for everyone watching to make them believe we're back together. Remember? The plan. The reason we're here. The reason you were staggering around in Denise's shoes."

"Okay," she said slowly. "And you think pretending we don't know each other will help?"

"It can't make things worse. What do you say? Are you up for it?"

A mischievous sparkle appeared in her eyes, reminding him Katya loved to play. She picked up her drink and sat back in her seat. "So, Brodie MacGregor, do you come here often?"

"Now and then. One of my brothers fancies himself a pastry chef and likes to come here to critique the desserts. He often drags us along."

"*One* of your brothers? You have a few?" Her shoulders relaxed as she smiled at him, making it clear she was beginning to enjoy herself.

"Six brothers. None of them as handsome as me, of course." Brodie reached for his beer.

"Is that right? I guess I'd need to judge that for myself. Maybe we could arrange a lineup?"

"That sounds fair." He took a sip. "So, what about you? What do you do for a living?"

"I'm a pilot," she said almost defiantly. "Small aircraft."

"I thought people only flew small aircraft for fun. How does a pilot make a living from that?"

Katya cocked her head, considering him. Perhaps wondering if he was setting her up for a joke at her expense. But in the end, she must have decided he was only playing his part.

"I got my license at a flight school in South London. It was attached to a private airfield, where lots of companies and hobbyists kept their planes. It didn't take long to figure out these people sometimes needed a pilot, and word got around I was reliable. And that I'd pretty much fly anywhere at any time. From there, a series of connections led me to flying small commercial planes in Europe and North Africa."

Despite his intentions, Brodie found himself intrigued. "What if someone wanted you to fly something illegal?"

She stilled, her eyes turning dark. "How do I know you aren't an undercover cop?"

He spread his jacket wide. "No gun. No badge. And you're more than welcome to pat me down for a wire." Brodie couldn't remember the last time he'd had this much fun on a date.

"In that case, the answer is, if it was drugs or human trafficking, I said no. Firmly. Everything else, I upped my fee."

"Holy crap, Kat." Brodie dropped all pretense of them having just met. "Please tell me you didn't put yourself in danger. There's a whole lot of gray area that doesn't fall under the heading of drugs and human trafficking."

"I know, and I was careful. Mainly, I transported black-market goods into countries with limits on their imports/exports. Sometimes I flew someone with a metal case handcuffed to their wrist from Africa to Europe. I never asked what was inside, and they didn't tell. Once or twice, I helped people get out of a country when it became too difficult for them to stay there."

"You scare the crap out of me," he admitted.

"Don't worry, Brodie. I spent most of my time transporting wealthy executives to meetings."

The woman needed a keeper. Someone to stop her from jumping on every daft idea that popped into her head. Someone who could watch her back when she got in too deep—just like he'd done for her while they were growing up.

"I'm glad to hear you took every precaution," he said, stepping back into the role of first-date man. "What did you do when you weren't flying people around?"

"I was a treasure hunter." She clasped her hands in front of herself on the table, the white linen reflecting light onto her pale skin.

"Treasure?" Her arms were more muscular than he remembered, and she had calluses on her hands from hard manual work.

"The kind that's worth more than gold," she said with gentle teasing in her tone. "I went in search of information about my great-grandmother. She was a Soviet war hero who couldn't return to her country for fear of being killed. My family never talked much about her when I was growing up, so when I found out she'd been a bomber pilot, I went hunting for more information."

"A bomber pilot is impressive." To be honest, he was genuinely beginning to think there was much about Natasha Savage that was impressive. A night spent reading about her life—the things she'd seen, done, and endured— had ignited a curiosity within him. "Where did she bomb?"

"Are you sure you want to talk about this?" Katya said pointedly. "Some people find it boring."

"I don't see how that's possible. A beautiful woman talking about the war? That's two male interests in one go. Add a discussion on Scotland's chances in the next World Cup, and you might well be the perfect woman." The irony of the situation was, as Brodie spoke, he realized it was true. If anyone else had wanted to discuss the Second World War with him, he'd have been all over it, dredging up years of knowledge from books he'd read and films he'd watched.

But because Katya had been the one to develop an interest in the topic, Brodie's younger self had seen it as a betrayal of everything they'd built together.

Brodie was beginning to think his younger self had been a bit of an idiot.

DINNER WAS NOT GOING the way Katya had envisioned. For one, Brodie was actually good company, and their conversation was entertaining and amusing. Of course, pretending they didn't have a truckload of baggage from their shared past—baggage neither of them was anywhere near dropping off at lost and found— certainly helped.

She'd never thought for a minute she'd be able to share her passion for the war and her great-gran's part in it with him, but for once, he seemed genuinely interested.

"Okay," she said as the waitress served their meals. "I'm going to take you at your word and talk endlessly about the late, great Natasha Klimova."

"Go ahead." He gestured with his knife.

"Well, one of the most interesting things I learned during my hunt for information was about her involvement in liberating the first concentration camp discovered by the Allies."

Brodie let out a low whistle. "She helped free the people in Majdanek?

"You know your war." Katya was impressed. Most people only knew the names of the most famous camps—Auschwitz, Ravensbrück, Bergen-Belsen.

"I read." He shrugged, drawing her attention to the good, good things the cut of his jacket did for his shoulders. "Plus,

I think most young boys absorb war facts from the air around them. By the time we're ten, we think we're experts."

"True." She took a bite of her steak that cut like butter and groaned. "This is amazing."

"I know, right?" He gestured to his plate. "Try the salmon. It's perfect."

"Later." Katya nodded. "Save me a piece."

"So, your great-grandmother was involved in Majdanek?" Brodie prompted.

"Yep, she bombed the barracks and the roads around the camp, giving the ground forces time and space to get in and liberate it. She also helped provide emergency medical care for the people they found inside. The fleeing Nazis had cleared out most of the prisoners by then, but they'd left some behind. As far as I can tell, they were all in a bad way, and even though Natasha only had the medic training she'd received, she stepped in to help. All the women in her squadron did."

"I can't even imagine what that must have been like." Brodie speared a potato. "How did you find this out?"

"Those letters between Ben and Natasha. He mentioned it in one of his. I got the impression Natasha was trying to stop talking about the war because her letters didn't reveal much about it, but Ben's were filled with war stories. Like the fact he was part of the team that liberated Bergen-Belsen." She put down her cutlery and drank some water. This was a hard topic for dinner conversation.

"We can change the subject," Brodie offered, easily reading her actions.

"No, it's just that I've read those letters so often that they feel real to me now. I can see the images in my head when I think about them. The piles of bodies, the shallow mass graves, the starving people with wide, hopeless eyes. Damn." She blinked back her threatening tears.

Brodie's hand reached across the table to cover hers. "Let's talk about something else. You okay?"

Katya found herself turning her hand over to thread her fingers through his. "Yeah."

"Well, isn't this cozy?" a nearby voice sneered.

Together, they looked up to see a woman glaring down at them. It took Katya a moment to recognize her, and when she did, her jaw dropped.

"Mary? Mary Cameron?" Katya gaped at the woman she hadn't seen since high school, when—she winced—she'd threatened to shave her head if she didn't stop chasing Brodie.

"Yes. Mary Cameron." She cocked her hip, which appeared to be wrapped in a purple bandage doubling as a minidress. "You're sitting in my seat. Brodie and I had a date tonight."

Katya snatched her hand from Brodie's as though burned.

She stared between the man facing her, who looked like a deer caught in the headlights, and the woman in stripper heels, bleached hair falling in waves to her shoulders, and more makeup than Katya's face had seen in her whole life.

"A date?" Katya said. "Together? You two?"

"Yes." Mary spoke loud enough for everyone in the restaurant to hear. "Imagine my surprise when I heard he was back with his *ex-wife*."

"Oh, hell," Brodie muttered before pushing back his chair and standing. "I meant to cancel, and I forgot. I'm sorry, Mary."

"No matter." Mary's smile was saccharine sweet. "We can

start our date now. I'm sure Katya won't mind finishing her meal alone. No doubt they can find us another table."

"No need." Katya shot to her feet. "Take my place. I've lost my appetite."

At the table next to them, someone Katya didn't recognize had their phone out and was giving the person on the other end a blow-by-blow of their interaction. "Aye," the woman said. "I think the relationship is back off again because the girlfriend has turned up." There was a pause before she added, "I know. Complete man-whore."

Katya had heard enough. "I'm going home." She turned toward the front entrance, desperate to escape the gleeful scrutiny.

Only she'd forgotten about her damn borrowed shoes.

Her ankle turned as she rushed to get away, and she toppled forward, doing a belly flop into the middle of the phone-woman's table.

There were gasps, and shouts, and flashes going off as the phone-woman took pictures. And underneath it all was the unmistakable sound of spiteful giggling. Hands grasped hold of Katya to help her back to her feet. Once there, she assessed the damage.

She now wore what looked like chicken and mushroom pasta.

"Let me help." Brodie released her arm and reached for a napkin.

"No!" While holding up a hand to stop him, Katya kicked off her friend's shoes. Pasta falling from her body, she slowly bent down to pick up the shoes before aiming them at Brodie's head.

Of course, she missed.

One landed in someone's dessert.

The other went straight through a stained glass window.

"Call the police," Mary shouted. "Tell them another Savage has gone insane."

With what little dignity she could muster, Katya half walked, half limped to the door—dripping pasta as she went.

"Kat!" Brodie called after her.

"Let her go," Mary said loudly. "We don't need her."

As she passed the stunned hostess, Katya said, "Please bill Brodie MacGregor for any repairs."

The woman nodded, but as Katya let the door swing shut behind her, she remembered she'd left her bag, complete with phone and wallet, hanging on the back of her chair.

To hell with it.

She'd walk.

With one last growl at the building behind her, she set off down the road. Only to realize after a few steps that she had no idea where to go. She couldn't return to Brodie's house—she was so furious there was a good chance she'd smother him in his sleep. And unless she wanted to see her dad locked up for murder, she couldn't go to her parents' house.

That left only one option.

20

After peeling Mary off him, and collecting Katya's bag and Denise's shoes, Brodie stopped by the kitchen.

"I'll pay for the damage," he told a stony-faced Deke—the restaurant's owner and chef.

"Damn straight, you're paying, and you're banned until you sort things out with your ex. I've heard all about your wild relationship the first time around, and I don't want you back in here until you've both settled down."

"Seems fair." Brodie grimaced. "Sorry about the window, and the food."

Deke sighed. "Don't worry about it. The restaurant's all over social media already, but the main complaint is the diners hated having a great meal ruined. So, it's all good publicity." He lifted his chin toward the foyer, which could be seen easily from the open plan kitchen area. A furious Mary was glaring at them. "What about her?"

"She got herself here, so she can get herself home. You know what she's like," Brodie said to his soccer teammate.

"She harassed me for weeks to set up this date. I only did it to shut her up."

"And I remember telling you it was a stupid plan. It took you months to shake her off after the last time you dated."

Brodie pinched the bridge of his nose. "How was I supposed to get rid of her?"

"Just say no." Deke frowned.

"You don't prise off a limpet with a simple no."

"Well, you'd better think of something that will prise her off, because she's heading this way." Deke, the coward, exited stage left. At speed.

"Brodie," Mary whined. "You owe me an apology for going out on a date with your ex-wife when you should have been with me."

"Aye, I do." Brodie frowned down at her. "But that doesn't excuse you interrupting our meal. We both know we were meant to meet at the pub. You could have called when I didn't show, instead you turned up here. I'm guessing one of your friends saw Katya and me having dinner and called you. Who was it?" He scanned the room. "Never mind. I can see Janice in the corner. I told you last time, and I'll tell you again—you need to keep your friend out of my business."

"If I'd kept her out of it, I'd never have known you were standing me up to see *Katya*." She practically spat the name.

"I'm sorry I forgot about our dinner and didn't cancel, but I'm also sorry that I agreed to the date in the first place."

She gasped. Dramatically. "You don't mean that. We can't keep away from each other, even when we try."

Oh, he'd tried, all right, but Mary kept finding him. Maybe his da was right, and he was hardwired to keep the peace—even when it meant doing things he didn't want to do. If it hadn't been for Kat shaking up his life and making him stand up to the people around him, would he have ended up married to Mary? Would he have said yes to her many invitations to avoid rocking the boat? Was he that complacent? Judging by the sick dread in the pit of his stomach at the thought of what his life could have been, Brodie suspected the answer to all of those questions was yes.

It was time to stand up for what he wanted. Or, in this case, didn't want. "Mary, there's nothing between us. I'm sorry if you thought there was after we slept together years ago, and I'm sorry for letting you think I'd be happy to start things up again. Although we had a good time during our brief affair, I should have made it clear that I felt we weren't suited to each other. We never have been."

"Typical!" She stomped her glittery shoes. "Katya comes back into town, and no one else gets a look in. I *hate* that girl!" Then she promptly burst into tears.

"Okay. Good talk," Brodie said, backing away. "I'm sure you'll find another man who has nothing to do with Katya."

"Why does she always win?" Mary wailed.

Brodie took that as his cue to leave. Possibly never to return, as he suspected Deke would never let him set foot in this place again, no matter the outcome with Katya.

One thing was for certain, he needed to sort things with her. The look on her face when she realized he had plans with Mary had been a punch to his gut. Mary and Katya had been rivals all through school, with Mary never missing an opportunity to remind Katya that her family was laughed about all over town. In all honesty, Mary had been a bitch. Something that hadn't changed since their school days, but that Brodie had managed to overlook.

Which meant his da had been spot-on all along. He had reverted to not caring what he did after Katya left.

He needed to find her and make sure she was okay after

the chaos in the restaurant. She couldn't have gotten far without her keys and wallet, but that didn't mean she'd be easy to find. Katya didn't think like other people, which made her harder to predict. Something he'd always loved about her.

Brodie pulled out his phone and dialed Darach. "Is Katya at the house?" he said as soon as his brother answered.

"What do you mean, is she at the house? She's supposed to be at dinner—with you."

"Aye, it didn't quite go as planned, and she ran out of the restaurant without her bag. You don't think she'll have gone to her parents' house?" If she had, there was no way Brodie could get to her without suffering a backside full of buckshot.

"I'll get Denise to call Stephen. Hopefully, he can let us know if Katya's there without setting off their dad's radar. I'll call you when we know something."

"Good, I'll check our land. Maybe she's gone there to hang out with her plane. She left her shoes at the restaurant too." Brodie didn't see the point in telling Darach *how* she left them. "I'm worried her feet will get shredded if she takes it into her head to walk all over town. Plus, what if someone we don't know offers her a lift? If they try anything on, she won't be able to call for help because her phone's in her bag too. She could get hurt. We need to find her."

"On top of that, if your date was such a disaster, you need to find her fast so you can try to salvage this. Maybe take her to the pub and show everyone you're fine together now. Otherwise, you might as well give up on the charade of your new romance, along with the hope of keeping your land."

The air left Brodie's lungs in a rush as his heart raced.

He hadn't, even for one split second, thought about the land. Or even the damage this evening had done to the public perception of their fake relationship. All he'd thought about was getting to Katya, making sure she was okay, and trying to explain about Mary.

"You still there?" Darach said in his ear.

"Aye," Brodie squeezed out the word. "Got to go."

Before his brother could say anything more, he ended the call. As soon as he was alone inside his car, he took several deep breaths and admitted the truth to himself.

He wasn't pretending anymore.

He wanted Katya back.

"Thanks for taking me in." Katya accepted the mug of hot tea. "I didn't know where else to go, and I was worried I'd murder Brodie if I went back to his place."

"You know, this could all have been avoided if you'd accepted my offer of help in the first place." Margaret Jamieson settled into the armchair in the corner of the living room she shared with her new husband, Dougal. Fortunately, Dougal was still at his pub and hotel for a wee while longer because, unlike Margaret, Katya wasn't sure he could keep a secret.

"How would it have helped?" Katya said. "I would still have gone to dinner, still have had to deal with Mary, and still would have wanted to stab Brodie in the eye with my fork."

"Because," Margaret said with long-suffering, "I would have warned you that they had a date set up at the pub. At the very least, you could have reminded Brodie to cancel. It's typical. When that boy gets around you, he can't think about anything else. Which means now we have to figure out a way to do damage control."

"It's pointless." Katya tucked her feet up under her. "No one in their right mind will believe we're a couple now."

"The key," Margaret mused, "is to get everyone treating you like you're a couple. That way, Kitty Baxter will think we already believe it."

"You're talking in circles, and I'm too tired to follow."

"What if everyone was in on the secret except Kitty and her lawyer?"

"I don't see how that would work. Someone would tell her."

"Who?" Margaret looked excited. "Everybody hates her. Well, except for her farm manager, but we won't tell William. This is a brilliant plan, and I am a genius."

"I don't even understand the plan, so I'm not sure about the genius part." Katya reached for the chocolate biscuits, regretting she hadn't managed to finish her dinner before Mary arrived and ruined her appetite. "I'm not sure I can pretend with Brodie anymore. I feel sick even thinking about him going on a date with Mary. Not that I'm interested in him, you understand, but because it was Mary. *Mary?* He should probably get a rabies shot."

"Stop distracting yourself with the trivial stuff," Margaret said. "You waved goodbye to the man ten years ago. Who he takes to his bed is no business of yours."

"Bed?" The room began to spin. Or maybe it was her head on her shoulders. Because yuk! "I thought they only had dinner plans. But bed? I'm going to vomit."

Margaret waved a dismissive hand. "That was ages ago, and knowing Mary, I'm sure he regrets it. But you can console yourself with the old adage that if you sleep with a dog, you'll catch its fleas."

Katya's stomach lurched. Mary and Brodie? Yeah, she was definitely going to vomit.

"Who has fleas?" Dougal boomed as he came into the room. He stopped short when he spotted Katya. "You didn't tell me we had company."

"Brodie and Mary. He caught her fleas when they had sex." Katya gagged. "Where's the bathroom?"

Nonplussed, Dougal pointed to the hallway and Katya made a run for it. Fortunately, there was no puking. Unfortunately, her imagination was seared with images of Brodie and Mary together. Images she would *never* get out of her head. After splashing water on her face, she returned to the living room, wishing she was alone so she could process the news.

"Are you okay?" Margaret looked worried. "I shouldn't have told you like that."

"It's fine. It's all fine. As you pointed out, he doesn't belong to me. It's not my business who he takes to bed, or what he catches when he does it." She shuddered at the thought.

Dougal was sitting in the armchair beside his wife and leaned over to pat her hand. "Now then, this isn't anybody's fault."

Katya wasn't so sure about that. She was pretty certain Brodie was to blame for everything. But she smiled at the couple and feigned agreement.

As usual, Dougal was dressed head-to-toe in Elton-John chic, with a luminous green waistcoat, purple shirt, and green tartan trousers. Dougal's dress sense had long been a source of speculation around Invertary. There were those who thought he dressed ironically and those who thought he must be color-blind. Katya had always been of the opinion he just had bad taste.

"Now, what's brought you out to visit so late on a Friday night?" Dougal asked once settled.

While Katya was debating the merits of telling him about their fake relationship, Margaret went ahead and blurted it all out.

"Now, you see," she said. "They need to pretend to be in a real marriage until next week, that's when the hearing is, to stop Kitty Baxter from taking the land back."

"This is a secret, Dougal," Katya said.

"One I thought we'd share with the town," Margaret said mischievously. "Apart from Kitty's farm manager, who'd tell her it's all fake."

Dougal didn't hesitate. "Morag McKay. That woman hates everybody and she'd sell out Katya and Brodie in a heartbeat."

He wasn't wrong. If it weren't for Morag running the only bakery in town, no one would go near her.

"Our parents can't know either," Katya said. "There isn't one out of the four of them who wouldn't blow it for us. Or lose their mind over our relationship being fake."

"Our lips are sealed where they're concerned." Margaret did that thing where she pretended to zip up her mouth and throw away the key.

"Don't worry." Dougal winked at Katya. "We'll make sure all the right people know about your and Brodie's problem, and we'll make sure to keep your parents in the dark. You won't lose your land if we have our way. Ben Baxter was very clear when he gave it to you that he wanted you to have it. His daughter has no right to let her bitterness get in the way of his gift."

To be honest, Katya was beginning to think that Catherine had a right to her bitterness. If she'd found a wedding certificate that turned her father into a bigamist, she'd have been pretty mad too. "Thanks, Dougal, Margaret. We need all the help we can get right now."

"You can count on us." Margaret shared a smile with her husband.

And, for some reason, Katya wasn't reassured.

21

January 1946

Their journey to Scotland began in the belly of a tank. A friend of Ben's dropped them off a few miles west of Berlin, where they met up with another army vehicle that then took them a few miles more.

Natasha squeezed in beside her new husband, self-conscious whenever their bodies touched as the car bounced over damaged roads. Apart from Ben taking her hand to help her on and off their transportation, they'd barely touched. Even her wedding kiss had been a chaste peck on the cheek. It was nothing less than she'd expected and hoped for in a marriage that was only meant to rescue a friend. And that was all it was to Natasha. Unfortunately, she wasn't sure Ben was on the same page.

Before they'd started their journey, Ben pulled her aside and whispered in her ear, "I know you don't love me, and I don't expect you to. We've both been through a lot.

But I want you to know that I have feelings for you, Tasha, and if you wanted to try to make this marriage work, I wouldn't object. So please think about it." Then he'd pressed a kiss to her forehead and left her to say her goodbyes.

Now she sat beside him, a small battered suitcase clutched tight in her lap. It contained her beautiful wedding dress, the precious gifts from her fellow camp residents, and the necklace she'd removed from Marina after the crash. One day, when everything had settled and the world was more peaceful, Natasha would return the medallion to Marina's parents in Moscow. It was a silent promise she made to her navigator each night before sleep. During their trip, Natasha had a lot of time to think about her promise. And her future.

Transport through Germany and France was patchy at best. Tired Allied forces used what meager resources they had to help the people around them, and little was left over to assure the comfort of their soldiers. There was so much rebuilding to do. And as news filtered down to Natasha and Ben, they became aware of the scale of need in Europe and the rest of the world. The war had left millions homeless and traumatized. Countries were decimated, food was scarce, and winter had hit hard. Already, snow was making it difficult to help those who needed it most, and world leaders feared another famine like the one in Holland the winter before.

Given the magnitude of everything going on around them, it was easy to understand why transport home for one army translator and his new wife wasn't high on anyone's list of priorities.

At the border with France, Ben managed to scavenge some winter coats from American soldiers leaving for home.

It was the luckiest they'd been on their trip so far, as the snow had started falling in earnest the night before.

"There's a train leaving for the coast tomorrow," Ben said as they bedded down, fully dressed, on mats in the corner of one of the American tents. "If we get there early, we should be able to find a space." He didn't need to tell her there would be a lot of desperate people trying to board the same train.

Belly full, thanks to the generosity of the American forces, Natasha felt hopeful they would find a space. Things were finally looking up. They were warm, safe, and well-fed for the first time in weeks, so surely fate had decreed they'd get the transportation they needed.

"Come here," Ben said. "We'll be warmer if we stay close."

Natasha thought about it and nodded, leaning into his side as his arm went around her. It was the closest they'd ever been, and it felt...nice. Comfortable. Easy. She sighed and settled against him.

"You'll love Scotland," he whispered. "It's as green as you'll ever see. Invertary's a friendly place too. You'll have no trouble fitting in. I can't wait for you to see the loch, with the purple heather-covered hills surrounding it. There's no fairer sight in all of Europe."

"It sounds wonderful," she said honestly. It seemed like paradise.

"Our home is an old farmhouse, passed down through the generations. I'll admit it's in need of some modernizing, but it's warm and comfortable, and there's food aplenty."

Natasha hesitated, not wanting to upset him. "Will I live with you?"

His body tensed beneath the palm she had resting on his chest. "If you want to."

"Then we'd have to tell people we're married." She couldn't live with Ben without them knowing. A scandal wasn't how she wanted to start her new life.

"Like I said, it's all up to you, Tasha."

"I need time," she whispered. Time to get to know him as a man rather than her rescuer and confidant.

"That's fine."

He sounded a little strained, so she changed the subject. "I thought that farmers in Britain were allowed to stay home from the war." She'd heard some of the Allies talking about how necessary farmworkers were to their country, which made them exempt from conscription.

"Unfortunately, I wasn't the farmer. I inherited the land and didn't take much interest in it. I was too busy trying to learn every language under the sun." Ben chuckled. "Look where that got me. No, my best friend, Tom, runs the farm. He's the finest farmer in Scotland, although you'd never know it because he doesn't tend to take life too seriously. If there's a party, Tom will be the first one through the door, guitar in hand, ready to entertain the ladies."

She struggled to imagine somber, quiet Ben being best friends with a man such as Tom.

"Captain Baxter?" an American soldier whispered as he approached.

"Yes?" Ben sat up, taking Natasha with him.

"We have a situation and need someone fluent in German. Can you help?"

"Of course." He took his arm from around Natasha. "I'll be back soon; try to get some sleep."

"Be careful," she said as he left.

Natasha was dozing when a gunshot woke her. The sound of running feet and shouting followed the blast. It was strange how, after being used to daily gunfire, a single shot could render her wide awake. An hour later, Ben returned. His face drawn, he'd changed his clothes, and he held a gun in his hand.

"Why do you have a gun?" Natasha asked as he tucked it into his duffel bag.

"The German had it." His head fell forward as his eyes closed briefly. "He was a Nazi officer pretending to be Jewish to escape the Allies. He gave himself away when I was talking to him, and a search of his person revealed the gun and...and gold." Agony-filled eyes met hers. "Gold he'd taken from people's teeth."

Natasha's trembling hand covered her mouth.

"He tried to bribe us with the gold. To make us forget who he was and send him on his way." Ben sat on the mat beside hers. "There was a struggle, and I grabbed his gun from the table where the Americans had put it. I shouted for him to stop fighting. He wouldn't listen..."

"It's okay," Natasha soothed. "It's okay."

"I killed him," Ben said.

"You had to do it." She knew Ben, and she knew he wouldn't have done it if he'd had another option.

Ben looked down at his hands. "Do you think the blood will ever come off these?"

She wrapped a hand around one of his. "They're clean now. Look?"

Dark eyes met hers. "They'll never be clean, Tasha. I've lost count of how many men I've killed. My hands are soaked in their blood."

"Not only yours," she whispered. A bomber might not look their victim in the eye, but that didn't mean death wasn't left in their wake.

"When I'd changed out of my blood-stained clothes, the American handed me the German's gun. Told me to take it as a souvenir for a job well done. For saving his life." He seemed bewildered. "I couldn't refuse."

"I know," she whispered.

He stared at her, looking lost. "I can't get that gold out of my head. There was such a lot of it, Tasha."

"Come." She tugged at him. "Lie down beside me. If you can't sleep, then talk. You know I'll always listen, and I'll never judge."

He came to her side willingly, and as the silence of night fell over them like a blanket, he whispered the horrors of what he'd seen on the day he'd helped liberate Bergen-Belsen concentration camp.

"We looked everywhere for you," a frowning Darach told Katya when he opened the door to their house after Dougal dropped her home.

"Why?" Katya padded inside.

"Why?" Darach put a hand on her shoulder to stop her from walking down the hallway to the kitchen. "It's almost midnight. You've been gone for hours with no phone, no money, and no shoes. Everyone's been worried—especially Brodie. If I'd had to hear one more time about your feet getting cut up on your walk, or some guy abducting you from the side of the road, there would have been violence."

"Katya." Brodie stalked out of the kitchen. "Are you okay?"

She was definitely missing something because she couldn't figure out why the guys were overreacting. "I'm fine. What's going on? Why were you two worried about me being out alone in Invertary? Has Catherine put a hit out on me?"

They clearly weren't amused, and for a second, she thought Brodie was going to reach for her—the same way he used to pull her into a hug when they were together. Instead, he ran a hand through his hair.

"I was worried something had happened to you," he said gruffly.

"I wasn't," Denise called from the kitchen. "I told them if you could handle yourself with the London Mob, then you could handle a walk through a sleepy Highland town."

Oh crap. "You told them about the Mob?"

Denise's head popped around the doorway. "Purely to reassure them."

"They wanted you to run drugs?" From the color creeping up Brodie's neck, it looked like it was only a matter of time before his head exploded.

"I said no," she pointed out.

"To. The. Mob." Brodie forced the words through clenched teeth.

Darach had the same grim, almost angry, look on his face as Brodie. "People don't say no to the Mob."

"This isn't the movies." Honestly, it was far too late at night to be dealing with their outrage. "People say no to the Mob all the time."

"Aye, and do all of them have to leave the country until the Mob gets over it?" Brodie gritted out.

Katya turned to the kitchen. "Is there anything you *didn't* tell them?"

Denise was unrepentant. "I thought it'd reassure them."

Judging by the way Brodie and Darach were frowning at her, Katya would have to say Denise's plan had failed.

"I'm fine." Katya held up her hands. "Then and now. I can take care of myself."

"No," said a stony-faced Brodie. "You really can't. You scrape by on luck and bravado, and it's a miracle you're still alive."

The realization that he'd been genuinely scared for her made her soften. "Seriously, I'm okay."

"This time." His jaw firmed. "I should never have let you go off on your own. You need a keeper."

This again? "It's only Invertary."

"I'm not talking about tonight," he said with clear exasperation. "I meant ten years ago."

As Katya rocked back on her heels, she registered the same shock in Darach.

However, Brodie wasn't paying attention to their reactions. He was too busy ranting to himself. "If I hadn't been so concerned with myself, I'd have realized you attract trouble, and without me to watch your back, you could have gotten yourself killed."

"Clearly I didn't," she pointed out but refrained from adding that he wasn't making any sense.

"Aye," he said grimly. "But what about the next time you wander off? Who'll make sure you're fine then?"

"Brodie, I'm not going anywhere. I'm staying here in Invertary, remember?"

"Not only in Invertary." He pointed at the floor in front of his feet. "You're staying right by my side, so I can keep an eye on you. You hear me? Don't even think about wandering out of my sight." He turned back toward the kitchen, muttering about her giving him premature gray hairs.

"What's going on with him?" Katya asked Darach, genuinely confused.

Amused, he patted her shoulder. "I'll leave you to figure that out, little sis."

"Whatever." Katya was too tired to deal with MacGregor logic. "Come on, I need a cup of tea, and then I'll tell you what happened with Dougal and Margaret. They've got a plan to help us with the whole fake relationship thing."

"You told them?" Darach groaned. "What part of *secret operation* didn't you understand?" He took a deep breath and called toward the kitchen, "Brodie, she's roped in Dougal and Knit or Die."

Loud cursing emerged from the kitchen, before Brodie appeared in the doorway with the sleeves of his pale blue dress shirt rolled up. He had his arms folded. "What did I say about being out of my sight? Get in here and tell us what you've done now."

"I resent that." Katya squeezed past him and into the kitchen, where she took a seat at the dining table beside her traitorous best friend. "I was helping."

"Aye, those three words should be on every Savage-family gravestone. Along with 'I thrive on drama.'" He plonked a mug of tea and a sandwich in front of her. "Eat and talk. We need to know what trouble we have to get you out of now."

Denise elbowed her. "He's really sexy when he turns all commanding."

Ignoring her best friend, Katya reached for her sandwich. It was corned beef, cheese, and pickle—her favorite. When she glanced up, Brodie's dark, intense eyes were studying her as though she were some sort of science experiment. She crossed her eyes back at him.

And her heart skipped a beat when he smiled.

～

"Let me count the ways this could go wrong," Darach said once Katya had filled them in on Margaret's plan. "For a start, Kitty Baxter talks to more people than her farm manager and the baker. You know that, right?"

"I'm wondering what the chances are of a whole town keeping a secret." Denise's skepticism answered her own question. "Actually, forget I said that."

"It's going to be fine," Katya assured them as she finished her sandwich. "It might even help. Goodness knows, Brodie and I keep stuffing up this whole pretending we're together thing." She patted Denise's hand. "I'm sorry about your shoes."

She waved Katya off. "They're fine. Brodie brought them home. Next time, I'll let you wear your boots."

Brodie nursed a cup of tea. "Your handbag's over there." He nodded toward the counter.

"Thanks. I guess I need to talk to the restaurant owner about paying for the smashed window." She winced. "And probably about buying some folk another dinner."

"Smashed window?" Darach frowned at his brother. "You never told me about a smashed window."

"It's covered," he said as though it were nothing. "I told Deke to bill me."

"I'll pay you back." With what, Katya didn't know, but she mentally added it to her list of debts.

"You don't need to. It's my fault anyway," Brodie said evenly, his intense gaze still on her. "I'm the one who forgot about Mary. Hell, I'm the one who got involved with her in the first place."

Katya really did *not* want the details of that situation. "Who you date is none of my business."

"Aye, well, I don't want to know who you've spent time

with over the past ten years either, but I'm still sorry about Mary." He sat forward, resting his mug on the table. "Last night was the first I've spent any time with her in years. After you left, I...we...I..."

"You had revenge sex with my nemesis," she guessed, the words stones in her throat. "Like I said, it's none of my business."

"I need to know we can get past this," Brodie said softly.

"It means nothing." Except that Katya needed to have a shower from thinking about them together. "It doesn't affect my ability to be your fake wife."

"Technically, you're still my *real* wife."

"Technically," she agreed. "Until we can figure out a way to divorce without losing the land."

As Brodie's eyes captured hers, she found herself falling into their blue depths. He'd always had so much emotion in his gaze, and that hadn't changed.

"Let's call a truce," he said. "Start afresh. From now on, we're a couple. We're in love. And the past is forgiven and forgotten. Right?"

There was something in his tone—something heavy, something serious. Something that should have made her worry and run for the hills. Instead, the room contracted until only the two of them remained. The Brodie Bubble. That's what she'd called it when she was a teen. The place where only they existed—she'd thought it popped long ago.

"Truce," she whispered.

Someone cleared their throat, bursting the bubble. Katya blinked herself back to reality and found Denise grinning at her.

"Since there's nothing we can do until tomorrow," her friend said. "I'm heading to bed."

"I want to stay up a wee while longer," Katya said. "See if there are any clues in the stuff I've collected about Ben and Natasha's marriage. Something that would get Catherine to back off."

"Seriously? Haven't you been over those like a thousand times?" Denise pushed away from the table and carried her cup to the sink.

"Yeah, but I still think it's worth a look."

"Honey," Denise said. "If you haven't found anything by now, there's nothing to find. You'd be better off getting some shut eye."

"Later. I'll feel better if I read through what I can first."

"I'll help," Brodie said lazily. "I'm not tired anyway."

She should have told him she didn't need help, but an extra set of eyes would come in handy. "You sure?"

"Aye. Turns out Natasha's life was a whole lot more interesting than I thought it would be. Plus, I'd kind of like to know what went wrong between her and Ben."

"Well, you two have fun." Darach headed for the stairs after Denise.

"I'm sure we will," Brodie said, his gaze on Katya.

KATYA WOKE to find her legs stretched out under the coffee table in the living room and her cheek plastered to Brodie's chest. For a second, she froze, assessing their situation and trying to recall how she got there.

They'd been at the table in the kitchen when Brodie had suggested they might be more comfortable in the living room. Once they'd spread everything out on the coffee table and sat on the floor, Brodie had covered their legs with a blanket to keep out the nighttime chill.

And then they'd had the strangest time going through the notes Katya had collected over the years. Instead of the sarcastic comments she'd come to expect from him, he'd asked intelligent questions and offered some interesting ideas on what had become of Ben and Natasha's relationship. It'd been fun, sharing her theories and the tidbits she'd learned over the years, watching him react enthusiastically before coming up with his own theories. It'd felt like old times.

Around two, Brodie made them hot chocolate and offered biscuits while she read aloud the letters Natasha had written that hadn't been translated yet. The next thing she knew, she'd woken up on top of him. With his arm wrapped around her and his hand threaded through her hair, he was snoring softly.

She'd forgotten how warm he ran; it was like cuddling up to a furnace. *Cuddling.* Not something she should be doing with her ex. Things were complicated enough without them becoming too familiar with each other again. Still, seeing as they were alone, and he was asleep, she took the time to study the features that'd haunted her dreams over the past ten years.

His nose was on the large side and his lips a little thin, but she'd always thought his features made him more handsome because they weren't perfect. He had a dark shadow of stubble on his jaw, and his hair was in need of a trim. Dark eyelashes formed crescents on his cheeks, hiding the smokey blue of his eyes, and there was a scar at the corner of his eyebrow. One that hadn't been there when she left.

A familiar aching pain made her stomach lurch. He wasn't the boy she'd once known. He'd experienced things during their time apart that she knew nothing about. She was no longer the only woman he'd slept with, and his hands weren't the only ones that had explored her body.

The dull throb of grief was a yoke around her neck, pressing her down, keeping her there. This fake relationship of theirs—when they weren't screwing it up—was a dim reflection of what used to be between them. A reminder of all they'd lost, turned their backs on, left behind. They could never return to what they'd been, and Katya didn't want to, as the pain of his rejection was still a fresh wound on her soul. But maybe they could learn to be friends again.

They'd been friends long before they'd become lovers, and then husband and wife.

Yes, she was sure they could become friends. Perhaps not as close as they once were, but they'd been children back then, and now they were adults—with all the history and baggage that comes with age.

As he stirred beneath her, she wondered what being friends with an adult Brodie would be like. Would it involve watching him with other women? Watching him fall in love? Watching him start a family and live in the house they'd planned to build together?

Reality was a bucket of iced water. Friendship would never be part of their future.

As his eyelashes flickered, his arm tightened around her. "Hey," he said in that husky morning voice she'd once loved.

"Hey," she said back. "We fell asleep on the floor. I think I drooled on your shirt."

He chuckled. "It'll come out in the wash."

Unlike the stains of rejection, which went much deeper.

Katya eased herself out from under his arm and tugged down her dress, which had ridden up in her sleep. "I need to tidy this stuff away." She got to her feet and picked up the box from beside the coffee table. "And you need to get ready for your football match."

Brodie sat away from the couch edge that'd propped them up. "You okay?"

"Absolutely." Katya gave him a wide, wide smile. "Why wouldn't I be?" She lifted the boxful of papers. "I call dibs on the shower," she said as she hurried from the room.

Without once looking him in the eye.

23

Brodie could still play soccer. And watching him still made Katya horny as hell. Which was *not* a good reaction in any way.

"It's the shorts, isn't it?" Denise mused from beside Katya on the sidelines. "It has to be. I mean, I know nothing about this game or how it's played, and yet I find myself engrossed. It's got to be the shorts. Seriously, look at the way they hug the backside on number five. Do you think he's single?"

"Are you even looking at their faces?" Katya demanded. "Number five is Bain."

"Really?" Denise raised her line of sight, only to see Bain grinning over at both of them. "Would it be wrong if I took him to bed? Like, would it make me a traitor to the cause or something?"

Katya smacked the back of Denise's head to knock some sense into her. "You're not sleeping with Bain, and it has nothing to do with betraying any weird sense of loyalty you might feel; it's because it would be yucky."

"I'm thinking you might not be the best person to talk to

about this. You see him as a brother, whereas I see him as a hot backside in thin silken shorts."

A cheer went up, and they looked down the pitch to discover there'd been a goal.

"Which team scored?" Denise said. "Which goal is our team defending again? Is it that one? Do we cheer or boo?"

"It's too late now. The play has started again anyway. But, for the record, the other team scored."

"Oh, that's a shame. Are they nearly done yet?"

"No. They haven't even finished the first half."

Denise groaned at the sky. "Even fit men in tight shorts can't keep my attention for too much longer. We should have brought wine."

"To a game in the middle of the morning?" Katya was beginning to think Denise deserved Bain.

A whistle blew, and the players jogged to the sidelines. Bain headed straight for Denise.

"You were checking me out." He smirked. "You want some of this, you only have to ask."

Katya smacked her hand over Denise's mouth before she could answer. "She isn't asking." Denise licked her hand. "Gross!" Katya yelled as she rubbed her palm on her jeans. "Now I have to go wash my hands."

"Then maybe next time you'll let me speak for myself," Denise said, her eyes on Bain. "I have one question for you —do you really fart in your sleep?"

"I hate my brothers," Bain muttered before jogging off to get a drink.

"I'll take it that's yes," Denise called after him. "Pity. He definitely has the best rear on the field."

"I think I might vomit," Katya said.

"I hope not," Brodie said as he came up to them, "because I was planning on a kiss for good luck."

"What?" Katya blinked at him.

"Oh, you two!" Denise said loudly. "Get a room." She lowered her voice and hissed, "You're in love, remember?"

"Exactly." Brodie's eyes crinkled as he snuck a hand around Katya's waist and pulled her to him. "Make it look good, Kat."

And then he kissed her.

No, calling it a kiss was like calling Valrhona just chocolate. This wasn't a mere touching of lips; it was full-on sex using only their mouths.

His palm pressed against the small of her back while his other hand threaded through her hair at the nape. Katya could do nothing but wrap her arms around his shoulders and hold on tight, because his kiss didn't start slow—it hit full speed right out of the gate. Her last thought before her mind went blank was that she'd forgotten how good Brodie was at kissing. And how addictive those kisses could be.

He made love to her mouth with his tongue, lips, and teeth. Teasing and tormenting her in a confident dance that left her breathless and moaning into his mouth. It was only as he slowed the kiss, easing her back down to earth, that she became aware of the catcalling all around them.

Blinking her way out of a lust-induced daze, she glanced around, seeing spectators and players alike cheering them on.

"That's sure to bring us luck." Brodie pressed a kiss to her forehead. "Thanks, Kat."

And then he jogged back onto the pitch as though nothing had happened. Leaving Katya to sway in place while she watched him go.

~

"So," Bain said to Brodie once he was on the field, "you're going to play the rest of the match with a hard-on. Good move, bro."

"Shut up." It wasn't his best comeback, but Brodie was suffering. The situation's only saving grace was that he'd worn tight spandex training shorts under the looser team shorts; otherwise, it wouldn't have been his football skills drawing attention.

"Are you supposed to, ahem, react when this thing between you two is fake?" Bain jogged in place beside Brodie. "Are you sure it *is* still fake?"

"Are you sure you should be over here defending me when I'm on the same team as you?" Brodie pointed up the pitch. "You're needed up there."

His brother waved that off. "We're going to lose anyway. We always lose."

"And people say we have no team spirit."

"They say that because we spend more time fighting with each other than taking on the opposing team. That's what happens when you have five brothers playing on the same side."

He had a point. They really needed to spread the MacGregors out over other teams.

"Plus"—Bain looked disgusted—"our goalie sucks."

Aye, they never should have put Josh McInnes in goal, but the singer almost killed himself running up and down the pitch, which meant the goal was the safest place for him. They would have kicked him off the team altogether, but his wife wanted him to get exercise, and no one was prepared to argue with Caroline McInnes. That woman had single-handedly organized Invertary for years, and she was fierce when it came to fairness and consequences. Brodie had long thought Caroline's reign of terror was mainly due to the fact she treated everyone in town as though they were preschoolers who needed a firm, guiding hand.

Plus, the last time a team kicked Josh to the curb, they'd found themselves signed up for every volunteer activity Invertary ran for a whole year. None of the MacGregors had that kind of time to waste. Which meant Josh kept his goalie position, and their team lost every game.

"We shouldn't have taught an American how to play football," Bain said with a shake of his head. "That's where we went wrong. Americans should stick to their sissy version of rugby."

"Josh can't play American football either," Brodie pointed out. "I've seen him try."

A cheer sounded as Josh let in another goal, and Bain sighed. "I'd better get over there and goalie for our goalie. I can't live through the shame of another ten-nil loss."

As Bain sped off down the field, Brodie watched Kat. Her lips were still swollen and pink from their kiss, and her hair was mussed from where he'd held her. Damn, if she didn't look sexy as hell.

Now he'd admitted to himself he wanted Katya back for real, all he'd been able to think about was their booking at the hotel that evening. He'd finally have Kat all to himself, far away from prying eyes and interfering brothers. With her seduction all planned out, he'd already ordered strawberries and champagne for the room—much to Dougal's delight. The pub owner had tried to give Brodie romance advice, but he'd managed to shut that down sharply.

Aye, he couldn't wait to get her alone. He planned to wine and dine her, all the while reminding her how explosive they were together. Sex with Katya was on a whole other level than anything else he'd experienced, and they could be that for each other again. All he had to do was convince her he'd forgiven her for leaving him, and then everything could go back to the way it was supposed to be.

"Brodie!" someone shouted, dragging his attention from Katya.

The ball hit him square in the middle of his face, and he toppled like a tree. As Brodie stared up at the sky, he felt blood pouring down his cheeks and knew his nose was broken—again. Darach, who reached him first, ripped off his shirt and held it to Brodie's nose.

Kade appeared beside his twin. "How many fingers am I holding up?"

"Two. And I don't appreciate the gesture." Brodie's lips felt swollen, and he'd suddenly developed a lisp. "I think my nose is broken," he told them as the rest of the players arrived.

"Let me see," Darach said, removing his shirt from Brodie's face.

The crowd parted as someone pushed their way through, and Katya fell to her knees beside him. "What the hell, Brodie," she said. "The game's played with your feet, not your face."

That was the woman he loved: she oozed sympathy—and sarcasm.

She held his hand tight as he smiled up at her. "I'm okay. It's only a broken nose."

"Um, not only." Katya winced.

Brodie looked up at his brothers for answers.

Darach appeared horrified, while Kade and Conall were fighting not to laugh. Bain stuck his head over Darach's shoulder and burst into hysterics.

"What?" Brodie demanded.

"Let's just say, you're lucky there's a dentist in town," Bain said through his laughter.

"It's okay." Katya patted his hand. "The doctor can realign your nose, and the dentist can fix those teeth. You'll be fine in no time."

"Fix my teeth?" He felt for his front teeth with his tongue.

And tasted blood, then the sharp jagged edge of not one, but two, broken teeth. Brodie groaned. So much for his romantic night with Kat.

"I'll call the Patels," Conall said.

"I'll call the doctor," Kade said.

"I'm calling everybody I know." Bain pointed his phone at Brodie. "Say cheese."

SINCE THE PATELS hadn't yet set up a dental clinic in town, they'd called in a favor with colleagues in Fort William. So, after the doctor snapped Brodie's nose into place and strapped it with tape, Conall drove him to the dentist to have his teeth fixed.

By the time they arrived back in Invertary, early evening, Brodie had two black eyes, a taped red nose, and swollen lips. Oh, and thanks to an over-enthusiastic dentist, he also had no feeling in his cheeks and the inability to keep drool inside his mouth.

"This is a disaster," he told Conall, or at least tried to, as the words weren't coming out properly through his thick, numb lips.

"I wouldn't go that far," replied the overly chipper baby of the family. "Thanks to Dougal and Margaret letting everyone in on your secret, they all made a fuss about how upset Katya was, and how she cared for you, and how you could really see the love in her reaction to your injury."

"In other words, they went over the top in describing a fantasy couple who bear no resemblance to Katya and myself."

"Aye." Conall grinned.

Brodie groaned. "I had everything set up for a night of seduction. I'd planned on telling Kat I don't want to pretend, I want our marriage to be real...in reality." Maybe they'd given him more drugs than he'd realized because nothing was coming out right.

"Seriously?" Conall glanced at him before returning his attention to the road. "You want to get back together with her?"

"Aye, I was going to tell her I forgive her for leaving me and ask her to try again. I had it all worked out."

"Uh, so you planned to *graciously* forgive her and then try to seduce her?"

Brodie frowned then yelped with pain. "I don't like the way you put it, but that's exactly what I'd planned."

Conall shook his head. "That's exactly what you *shouldn't* do."

"What do you know? You're so young, you can barely grow a beard."

"Obviously, when it comes to women, I know a helluva lot more than you."

"You're single," Brodie pointed out. "I'm married. Who here knows more?"

"Um, the guy who hasn't had a woman walk out on him?"

"Why are we having this conversation? It doesn't even make any sense." Brodie closed his eyes, wishing his face didn't throb so much.

"Hey, Siri," Conall said to his phone, "call Darach."

"Calling Darach," the phone said through the car's dash.

"No, don't call Darach." Brodie's head was killing him, and he didn't need to have this conversation with even more people.

"What's up?" Their brother's voice filled the car.

"Nothing!" Brodie called. "Everything's fine. We're hanging up now. Siri? Hang up on Darach."

The phone obviously took orders only from Conall.

"Brodie plans on telling Katya he forgives her for leaving him, and he thinks it'll make her fall into bed with him when he's done."

"I didn't say that," Brodie objected, but he had to admit he'd been thinking it.

"Wait a minute," Darach said. "I'm putting you on speaker."

That had Brodie shooting straight up in his seat. "Is Kat there? She'd better not be listening."

"The women are out somewhere," Darach said. "Now repeat that again for the rest of us."

Conall, the rat bastard traitor, did what he was told, and when he was done, laughter poured from the dashboard.

"This is priceless," Bain said. "You think she'll be so grateful you've forgiven her that she'll have sex with you?"

"I didn't say that." Now his head was thumping.

"If you've had a fight with a girl and you want her to sleep with you," Kade said, "you *apologize*. You don't tell her she's forgiven."

"I'm with them," Darach added. "It's a bit condescending."

"You think?" Conall gave Brodie a pointed look.

"And what exactly am I supposed to apologize for?" Brodie demanded.

"For forcing her to choose between you and her dreams?" Darach said.

"For making her leave and not going with her?" Kade added.

"For being an arsehole," Bain chimed in.

"Look"—Brodie went to reach for the bridge of his nose, wanting to pinch away the tension, but caught himself before he caused any more damage—"I'll admit I'm not as blameless in how our marriage ended as I thought I was. I should have given Katya a chance to explain more about her great-grandmother, maybe asked her to give me a few months to consider things before I gave her an answer—"

"Maybe not have told her she was as crazy as the rest of the Savages," Bain interjected.

"I was going to say I probably shouldn't have given her an ultimatum." Brodie slumped in his seat as the magnitude of his predicament sank in. "I need to apologize, don't I?"

"You know," Conall said, "this is why guys get a bad name."

"You're a guy, dimwit," Kade said.

"An *enlightened* guy," Conall corrected. "I've learned from the caveman mistakes of my six older brothers. Women love me."

"In your dreams," Bain told him.

"Brodie," Darach said. "You need to apologize. You've been a complete dick to that girl. Anything you say that isn't an apology will only make things worse."

"Even then," Bain said, "it's highly unlikely she'll take you back. What's to say you won't do something that bloody stupid all over again? Anyway, for all you know, she's got some rich guy waiting in the wings, and you're ancient history."

"Thanks for the encouragement," Brodie said.

"I'm hanging up," Conall said. "We're outside the hotel."

There were grunts of goodbye from his brothers as Brodie eyed the town's pub and hotel.

"Why are we here?" He'd called off his night with Katya when he stopped a ball with his face.

"Because this is where I've been told to take you."

Brodie shook his head. "You've got your wires crossed. The night's off, and I'm going home." To a lumpy couch and a whole load of painkillers.

"Nope, the text definitely said to drop you off here." Conall grinned at him.

"What text?" Which of his brothers was messing with him now?

"The one Katya sent while you were having your teeth fixed." Conall leaned across him and threw open the door. "Off you go; your girl's waiting."

Feeling more than a little confused, Brodie climbed out of the car. It was only as Conall drove away he realized he still had on his blood-stained football kit from earlier. With a sigh, he let himself into the hotel. Who cared what he wore? His day wasn't likely to improve anyway.

"Hey, Brodie," the receptionist called out. "You're in room 302. Go on up. Katya's already here."

"Great," he grumbled. "I hope she's brought painkillers."

With a crippling sense of defeat, he trudged up the stairs.

24

As Katya opened the hotel room door to Brodie, she bit her lip to stop from laughing.

"It's fine, go ahead. Conall almost wet himself when I walked out of the dental office. I don't care if you point and take photos, as long as you have some painkillers in there."

Swinging the door wide, she stepped aside to let him in. "The doc dropped some pain meds off earlier. Then Dougal dropped off champagne and strawberries. Which do you want first?"

"That's funny. Watch me laugh." He slumped in the red tartan armchair. "Oh, wait, you can't because my face is frozen."

Katya took a glass from the minibar area, filled it with cold water, and handed it to him along with the pills.

Brodie appeared hopeless as he considered them. "If I try to swallow these, I'll end up dribbling all over my shirt." He glanced down. "My blood covered shirt."

"It's not the worst I've ever seen you." Katya perched on

the end of the bed. When he looked blank, she said, "That time you shaved off your eyebrows."

Brodie groaned. "I was a ten-year-old genius who looked like ET until they grew back."

"That's what happens when you accept a dare from a MacGregor." She felt no pity for him, as he'd made his brothers do much worse. "Now take the pills. I can cope with seeing you dribble."

"Great." He fumbled with the bottle cap before downing two tablets with some water. And yes, there was drool. "You should have canceled the room. One look at me, and nobody will believe we're holed up for a romantic night."

"I didn't keep it to fool the town. They're already eagerly drinking the Kool-Aid. Everywhere I've gone today, they've greeted me with a wink and hearty congratulations on our relationship. I thought you could use a night on a proper mattress instead of a lumpy couch."

He stared at her for a second before he closed his eyes and said, "Thank you, God."

"I'll take that as an enthusiastic yes to a decent night's sleep." Katya headed into the bathroom. "But first, and don't take this the wrong way, you need a bath."

"Shower," Brodie corrected. "I'd only fall asleep in the bath and wake up riddled with cramp. It's that kind of day."

"Shower it is then. I was going to run you a bath, but I think you can deal with a shower yourself."

"If I didn't look like I'd gone ten rounds with Rocky, I'd make some lewd suggestion about how you could help me in the shower."

Katya couldn't help grinning. This was Brodie at his best —self-deprecating and funny as hell.

"I don't suppose there are some clean clothes around here I can change into?" Brodie said.

"Never thought about clothes," she admitted.

"Ah, you wanted to keep me naked."

"It would be a distraction from the sight of your face."

"That's just mean," he said.

"Tell you what, I'll rustle up some clean clothes for you while you wash off all that blood."

"It's a deal." He pushed out of the chair. "I have to ask, though, why are you here? Why not send one of my brothers to settle me or even get Dougal to tell me I had the room to myself for the night?"

Katya shifted uncomfortably. She'd been asking herself that same question for hours, but the answer was staring straight at her, and she wasn't afraid of being honest—especially with herself. "I wanted to make sure you were okay."

Knowing information like that left her wide open, she braced for his comeback.

"I'll see you soon, then," he said softly. "I really need that shower. Before the smell knocks me out."

"Lovely." She smiled at him. "You want me to bring you up something to eat?"

He stared at her.

"Gotcha. Maybe later you could call down and ask Dougal to bring you up some soup...with a straw. Or baby food? You could have him blend his cottage pie into mush and serve it with a spoon."

"Enjoy this while you can, Kat. I'll be my handsome self again in no time."

"How many weeks did it take for your eyebrows to grow back again?" She slipped out the door before he could answer.

Still smiling, she made her way downstairs and into Brodie's car, which she'd helped herself to earlier. It was only a short drive to Brodie's house to pick up some clothes.

"I thought you were staying at the hotel for the night," Bain said when Katya let herself into the house.

"Why would I do that?" And why was he pretending to be interested? Bain wasn't famous for showing empathy for, or even interest in, the people around him. Basically, he was the human equivalent of an angry badger wearing a sandpaper suit—rough side facing out—and a tinfoil hat.

"Do the words 'fake marriage' ring a bell?" he grumbled at her.

"Brodie's in no fit state to fake anything right now, and everybody will tell Catherine Baxter we were locked away at the hotel all night anyway—even if neither of us was there. After I take him some clean clothes, I'll sleep here. If it makes you feel better, I'll go back to get him for breakfast. A nice public breakfast in Dougal's restaurant."

"That all sounds well and good, but I think you should stay there. What if he has a reaction to his pain meds? Somebody needs to be there to watch him."

Yep, Bain was definitely up to something because subtle, he was not.

"Fine, you can go then. Make sure you grab him some clothes first."

"Hell, no." He stepped back at the thought, then obviously remembered he was trying to be persuasive, so he flashed a smile. It reminded Katya of a crocodile she'd seen on her travels. All teeth and a blatant desire to bite. "I mean, what would Kitty Baxter think if anybody saw me coming and going from *your* hotel room? And you're better at dealing with him when he's in pain. You know what he's like. He'll take everything in sight to stop it, and those pain meds are dangerous."

"Right. It needs to be *me* who talks him out of downing all the pain pills. I wonder how Brodie coped for all those years while I was gone. It's a miracle he isn't addicted to aspirin."

"Aye, it is." Bain nodded solemnly. "You should have thought of that before you ran away."

Okay, she'd had enough of him now. "Brodie isn't going to have a reaction to the meds, and he isn't going to overdose on them either. I'm taking clothes to him, and then I'm coming straight back here. Now, stop driving me crazy, Bain. I won't stay away just so you can try to get Denise into bed."

He finally gave up all pretense of worrying about his brother. "For your information, I don't need to *try* to get women into bed." He turned and pointed to his backside. "This does all the work for me."

With a roll of her eyes, Katya stalked up the stairs to Brodie's room.

Denise was sitting on the bed, painting her toenails purple. "What are you doing here?"

"Brodie needs clean clothes." She opened the closet. "Did you know Bain's angling to get you into his bed tonight?"

"He can angle all he wants; Kade and Darach have been spilling his secrets all afternoon. Any mystery that man held for me is long gone." The nail-polish-loaded brush paused midair. "Although I wouldn't say no if he wanted to put on a tight pair of underpants and parade up and down in front of me for a while."

"You are deeply disturbed, and I wouldn't suggest that to Bain if I were you. He'd do it in a heartbeat, and then he'd expect detailed feedback on how he looked." After grabbing some jeans and a shirt, she turned to the dresser and rummaged for underwear. "I'll be back soon. Please don't do anything weird with Bain while I'm gone. I'd hate to have to bleach my eyeballs if I walked in on something I couldn't unsee."

"I'll make no promises. In a town this size, a girl has to find her own entertainment."

With a shake of her head, Katya left the room, and a few minutes later, she was back at the hotel above the pub. Instead of walking through the pub to get to the rooms, she entered the building by the hotel entrance.

The receptionist winked at her. "Don't worry, your secret's safe with me," she whispered before giving Katya a thumbs-up.

"I feel so much better knowing that," Katya said solemnly, and the woman beamed.

The hotel room was dark when she unlocked the door, with only a sliver of light coming from the bathroom. It took a second or two for her eyes to adjust, and when they did, she saw Brodie lying flat on his back in the middle of the bed, a towel wrapped around his waist. His feet were still on the floor, but he was sound asleep.

Amused, Katya tiptoed across the room to place his clothes on the armchair.

"Kat?" he mumbled. "Come to bed."

"I'm going back to your place, so you can have a good night's sleep."

He stirred then, raising himself to his elbows. "Stay with me, Kat." His words were slurred, making her frown at him.

"How many pain pills did you take?"

A loopy smile lit up his face. "Enough to make the pain stop." He pouted, or at least tried to. "But not the drool."

"Brodie," she grumbled. "They're strong pills. You're only supposed to take what the doctor recommends."

"I know, I know, but what harm can it do? And now I feel

gooooooood." He flopped back onto the bed before raising his head. "Do I look better?"

"No." But he did look cute. Like a big, slobbering, lost puppy.

"Ugh," he grumbled as his head fell back to the duvet. "Stay with me, Kat. The bed's too big without you."

The desire to agree struck her like a gust of wind, almost taking her off her feet. "I don't think that's a good idea."

"It's a great idea." He grinned at the ceiling. "It's only sleep. I'm in no condition to try anything else. Plus, what if I have a reaction to the pills? What if I'm dumb enough to overdose? What if I wake in pain and can't find the bottle?"

It was hard not to laugh at his earnest expression. "Bain called you, didn't he?"

"I think so. I remember someone whining about you cockblocking him, and he's the only person I know who uses that term. Too much American TV." Brodie lifted his head again. "Do you know what his favorite show is?"

"I dread to think," Katya said drolly.

"*Friends*! He still has a thing for Rachel." As he collapsed into giggles, Katya picked up the med bottle. It was a whole lot lighter than it'd been when she left.

With a sigh, she kicked off her shoes, ready to curl up in the armchair for the night and watch over the idiot she'd once married.

"The room's spinning," Brodie said. "I can't feel my face." He poked at his cheeks.

"Stop touching it. You're already bruised enough." Katya lifted the thick hand-knitted throw from the back of the chair and wrapped it around her knees.

"Remember that time you fell out of the tree and hit a bunch of rocks?" Brodie said softly. "We were what? Fourteen at the time? You had bruises all over, but it was the black eye that had us worried the most. We thought your dad would see it and come after me with his shotgun."

"But he didn't." She smiled at the memory. Like every other memory from her youth, Brodie stood front and center. There was so little of her childhood that didn't involve him one way or another.

"Not that time, anyway."

"No."

The episode seemed funny now, but when she was sixteen, she'd thought her dad was going to kill her boyfriend. If she closed her eyes, she could still see him, running down the hill toward the loch, jumping fences and cutting through fields as he chased after Brodie. In the end, he'd run out of breath and fired his gun anyway, not expecting to hit Brodie but hoping to scare the crap out of him. It was a sheer fluke that Brodie's backside became a target.

He lifted his head to grin at her. "He kept shouting about me stealing your innocence. I seem to recall it was you who'd talked me out of mine." His head flopped back down again. "Maybe I should have told him that at the time."

Katya burst out laughing. "Only if you'd wanted him to aim at your head."

They lapsed into silence, and Katya wondered if Brodie had fallen asleep. Snuggling under the mohair blanket, she marveled once again at the tasteful décor of Dougal's hotel. It stunned everyone who'd met the man before being shown to their room. They expected to be confronted with disco-Santa-themed décor, but instead, it was classically elegant— all creams and whites with the occasional rich red tartan accent. Katya planned to ask him for some tips when it came to decorating her forever home.

"Come to bed." Brodie sounded as though he was

already half asleep. "It feels weird having you over on the chair when there's a bed here big enough to share."

The faint glow coming from the bathroom cast soft shadows over the room. She really should turn off that light. "I'm okay here," she said.

Old buildings were infinitely better than new in Katya's opinion. She loved the high ceilings and tall windows of the hotel, delighted in the oddly shaped rooms—as if the architect had indulged in one too many whiskies while on the job. Old buildings had history. A sense of belonging. She'd missed that while she was away. For years, she'd wandered through countries and towns, feeling rootless, hunting for a reason to return to Invertary.

Hunting for a biplane like the one her great-gran flew.

"Well, I'm no' okay over here alone." Brodie's deep brogue was rough as he fought sleep. "I'm only asking that you lie beside me. I promise I'll no' cop a feel." She smiled at the teasing in his voice. "It's been too long since I slept beside someone...since I slept beside you. I'm tired of being lonely at night, Kat."

"Am I to believe that none of your many girlfriends ever spent the night? Or that you didn't sleep at their place?" They were questions she should never have asked if she cared as little about Brodie as she professed. But the darkness and his sleepy voice made her blurt out what she was thinking.

"Haven't spent the night with anyone since you." He paused. "It's weird that sleeping beside another woman felt like more of a betrayal than anything else I did."

"I know what you mean." Her nights had always belonged to Brodie, and the few relationships she'd managed to have over the years had never understood. Not that there were many, and the ones she'd started had never lasted too long.

"Lie beside me, Kat," he purred. "Promise I won't tell if you don't."

Brodie was just too much of a temptation to resist. "I'm going to regret this," she muttered as she took the blanket to the bed. "Move up, so your head's on the pillow. You're hanging off the end right now."

His smile was pure ambrosia as he shuffled up the bed, still wearing only a towel. As he made space for her, Katya climbed onto the bed beside him, pulling the soft throw over herself and holding it up as an offer to share.

"I don't need it," he said. "It's warm enough."

He rolled onto his side to face her, and they lay like that until they fell asleep. A sliver of space between them, their eyes on each other's faces.

25

The Highlands were as beautiful as Ben had promised—the hills as emerald-green, the water crystal blue, and the air as fresh as an alpine spring. Of course, Natasha was smart enough to realize she was looking at it through the eyes of a desperate woman. One hoping for a new beginning, a second chance that didn't involve death, starvation, and destruction. But even knowing her reaction was colored by her experiences, she still believed Scotland to be paradise.

Invertary, too, was as picturesque a town as she'd ever seen. Rows of whitewashed houses ran alongside cobble-stone roads, down from the hills to the wide expanse of water nestled in the valley. Scotland didn't have lakes, she'd learned, but lochs. And this loch dazzled in the midday sun as they traveled the last part of their long journey on the back of an old truck.

"Well, what do you think?" Ben asked as they bumped along the road into town.

She smiled at the note of anxiety in his tone. "I think it's wonderful."

His face relaxed for the first time in weeks. It seemed the farther they got from Germany, the more uneasy he'd become. They'd spent their days tense, alert for any sign of trouble, even though the last leg of their trip had been through Britain. His mood turned particularly sour during their time in the disembarkation camp on the Anglo-Scottish border, and it grew darker after they were processed by the military dispersal unit in Edinburgh.

Since their time at the demobilization centers, Ben had scarcely slept; instead, he spent his nights whispering to her in the dark, recounting stories about everything he'd seen and done. Asking questions about her darker experiences during her years spent fighting, obsessing over every new piece of information they learned on their journey to Scotland.

Ben rarely wanted to talk about anything but the war anymore. Stories of his childhood or plans for his future seemed long gone. Talking over the horrors seemed to be his way of coping now they weren't living day-to-day anymore. Natasha had noticed the adrenaline fade from her body too. But unlike Ben, in her, a sense of thankfulness and a need for joy had replaced it.

She wanted to bury the past and live her future to its fullest. Whereas Ben constantly wanted to analyze the past and come to some understanding about what it all meant. Natasha didn't believe that was something they'd ever discover. As he grew more inward-looking, she became more outward-focused, and all talk of possibly spending the rest of their lives together ceased. The silence caused Natasha to assume they would file for a quiet divorce as soon as they reached Invertary, but when she'd tried to bring up the topic with Ben, he'd given her a dark scowl and refused to discuss it.

Now she wasn't sure where she stood or what they would do.

As the truck came to a halt at the side of the road abutting the loch, a group of people lingering on the opposite corner let out a whoop of pure joy. A man broke away from the rest and ran toward their vehicle. He was big, wider in the shoulder than Ben, with wavy rust-colored hair that fell across his forehead. He wore a faded blue shirt, gray trousers fitted with braces to keep them up, and massive boots. And his smile was as dazzling as the water behind them.

"Ben, you old bastard," he shouted. "You didnae die!"

For the first time since the day she and Ben met, his face brightened considerably, and the years fell from him. "Tom Savage. Have you run my farm into the ground yet?"

"Technically, the ground is where you want a farm to be." Tom beamed at them. "Now get down here and let me welcome my best friend home."

Natasha sat there stunned as the two men embraced, slapped backs, and hurled amused insults at each other. Tom Savage's joy was contagious, and she found herself laughing along with them. Everyone in the group seemed to gravitate to Tom, and he, in turn, effortlessly pulled them into his fun. The best part of all was seeing Ben laugh with his friend. The sight made the knot of tension deep inside her stomach loosen ever so slightly.

"Now, who's this?" Tom said when his eyes fell on

Natasha. "Don't tell me you've brought me a present." He clapped Ben on the back. "Get down here, lassie, and say hello to Tommy." He spread his arms as though expecting her to jump from the back of the truck into his embrace.

"This is Natasha," Ben said, his smile fading. "A friend from Lithuania." As agreed, he was keeping their marriage a secret until they decided what they were going to do about it.

As she made her way to the edge of the truck, Tom beamed up at her, his warm brown eyes sparkling with secrets, and fun, and happiness.

"I don't know where this Lithuania is, but she's fair bonny," Tom said. Obviously, she wasn't moving fast enough for him because he reached into the bed of the truck to clasp her waist with huge hands and lifted her right off it. "Welcome to Scotland," he boomed before wrapping his arms around her and spinning until she laughed so hard her face ached.

Natasha couldn't remember the last time she'd felt so carefree.

When he stopped spinning at last, Tom grinned at Ben. "I like her," he said with a wink at Natasha. "Can I keep her?"

Her face burned at the thought, even though she knew it was a joke. As the crowd roared with laughter, she caught Ben's eye, and that knot in her stomach tightened again. He was staring at her and Tom with the same suspicious look he got when discussing the conspiracies of the war.

It was then she knew there was something deeply wrong with her friend.

26

The scent of springtime in a forest woke Katya, and she nuzzled into the source of the fragrance, inhaling deeply. There was a firm, warm expanse of skin under her palm.

Oooooh, it felt soooo good.

And familiar.

Through a sleep-induced haze, her fingers explored the indents and contours of the muscles beneath them. Oh yeah, that felt good. Wondering if it tasted good too, she ran the tip of her tongue over the skin resting against her nose. Delicious.

A deep moan rumbled from the playground pressed against her, vibrating through her body. A large hand slid up her back and under her T-shirt to caress her skin. The touch made Katya snuggle closer to the body beside her as her leg lifted over his thigh.

She was wearing jeans. *Why* was she wearing jeans?

With a groan of frustration, she ran her hand down the rippled abs of her bed partner—encountering no obstacle. Only decadently naked man.

With a smile against the corner of his stubble-covered jaw, she tripped her fingers over curled hair to find the smooth, satin length of him. Without hesitation, she wrapped her hand around him.

His back arched as he aimed a guttural noise at the ceiling.

Katya's mouth watered at the feeling of his firm erection in her hand. She needed more. She had to get out of her clothes. She had to—

"Kat," the voice growled.

And with that, she was wrenched straight out of the delightful gray area between sleep and wakefulness. Her eyes flew open—to find Brodie naked beside her.

Her hand wrapped around his dick.

With a squeal, she scrambled out of bed. "What the hell, Brodie? You're naked."

"Aye." His morning-rough voice sounded more than content with the situation as he turned his head to look at her. "Hey, Kat."

"Don't...don't you Kat me!" She pointed at his morning hard-on, which was saluting her. "Put that away."

"Oh, there are places I'd rather put it," he drawled.

Her eyes snapped from the offending member to his face. He was grinning at her. The dressing had fallen off the bridge of his nose during the night, but there was still purple and blue bruising around it and his eyes. He looked like a demented raccoon.

"This isn't funny." Katya tried to regain some semblance of composure. Which was almost impossible with him stretched out on the bed like a feast for a starving woman. How long had it been since she'd had sex? Scratch that, how long had it been since she'd had Brodie?

No. Don't think about it!

Holding up a hand to shield her view of his very impressive erection, she tried to reason with him. "I apologize for... uh...fondling you. It seems I wasn't properly awake."

Dark, tempting eyes danced at her. "I'm okay with the fondling. Feel free to carry on."

"Be serious, Brodie. We aren't doing this?" Damn it. The bloody words had come out as a question, and judging by the smile quirking the corner of his lips, he'd heard it too.

"Doing what?" His hand slid over his abs, moving oh so slowly, tempting her to follow its journey south.

"Stop it."

"Stop what?" His eyebrows lifted in a parody of innocence.

"You know what!" Tempting her. That was what.

"Not like it's anything you haven't seen before." His hand disappeared behind the section she'd blocked from her view. But she saw his arm move and his jaw clench, and she knew he was stroking himself.

She should have run from the room, but her feet remained rooted to the spot with want. Unadulterated, desperate longing.

Without warning, he swung his legs over the edge of the bed and sat facing her, making her adjust her outstretched hand to hide the full glory of his new position. Katya found it difficult to resist. To stand strong. They had a lifetime of familiarity between them, and her body had been suffering withdrawal from his for a decade.

"Come on, Kat, come back to bed," Brodie teased. "You know you want to."

Oh, yes, yes, she did.

"No. Sleeping together would only make things between us even more complicated." She sounded weak. Hell, she felt weak.

The expanse of his muscled shoulders was an enticement she longed to explore. Her fingers itched to compare how he felt now with how she remembered him. Oh, dear heavens above, those abs! He'd always had them, but now, they were more manly...

Yeah, she wasn't making any sense.

None.

"Kat," he said softly, still sounding amused, "nothing could make things more complicated between us. So, I'm going to say to you what you said to me all those years ago when you sweet-talked me out of my virginity—stop being such a big baby and get over here."

"Brodie," she whined as she stared up at the ceiling. "It isn't smart."

"When have we ever been smart?" His hand curled around hers, gently pulling her toward him.

Katya kept her eyes on the ceiling. "I should go before this gets out of hand."

"But you don't want to." He pressed a kiss to the middle of her palm, making what brain cells she had left cease to function. "You want to see how I've changed, the same way I want to see what's different about you."

She looked down at his eyes—no further. Mostly.

She shrugged. "I am a little curious," she admitted.

"Bet you want to know if it'd still be as good between us as you remember. I know I do." He tugged her closer until she stood between his spread legs. "I've been dying to get my hands on you since you first drove into town." His grin was both boyish and charming at the same time, his eyes dark with lust. "Your boobs are bigger, aren't they?"

Katya couldn't help the laugh that escaped. This was who they'd been when they were together. No shame—only open curiosity and a reckless disregard for propriety.

As though reading her mind, Brodie rested his hands on her waist, underneath her shirt. "You were always flashing your boobs at me when we were kids. Remember how mad you were when I wasn't impressed by your first bra?"

"It was really pretty, but you just rolled your eyes and asked if it would help me play football better because you reckoned I sucked at it."

"To be fair, I did hope it might streamline you and speed you up a bit." His hands glided to the underside of her breasts, and his thumbs stroked along their curve. "They are bigger, aren't they? Are you going to tell me, or let me find out for myself? I'm a fair man; I'll swap information if you like."

"Does your dick still curve toward your belly?" The words came out before she could censor them.

"You were staring at it a minute ago, so you tell me."

"It was only a glance." Mostly. "And it was the wrong angle."

Grinning, Brodie looked down. "I think it might have gotten worse. At this rate, it's going to make a circle by the time I'm seventy."

She couldn't help but glance down too. "You're lying," she said breathlessly. "It's exactly the same."

"You think?" Dark eyes met hers. "Maybe you should do a more thorough investigation, to make sure."

"This is crazy," she whispered, dragging her gaze back to his face.

"But you still want to, right?"

She groaned in defeat. "Yeah."

"Well, climb on board, Kat. This love train is ready to be ridden."

They were both laughing when their mouths found each other, their kiss teasing and slightly desperate.

"Are you sure?" Katya said against his lips. "I won't respect you in the morning if you just offer yourself up to the woman who left you without any conditions."

"Aye, well, maybe that woman didn't have much choice in the matter." His words barely registered as his hands cradled her breasts, thumbs rubbing over her nipples, making her shiver with the sensations his touch evoked. "Plus, nobody respects me around here, so why should you be different?"

"Fine, don't say I didn't give you a chance to escape." She reached around to unhook her bra.

Brodie's hands were under her bra as soon as the band loosened. "They're definitely heavier." He cocked his head to the side and frowned as though thinking hard as he tested their weight. Solemnly, he gazed up at her. "I can't make a definitive conclusion until I've considered all the evidence. You have to show me your boobs, Kat. Off with that T-shirt."

She faked a sigh as she gripped the bottom of her shirt. "I suppose it's only fair. I mean, I can see all of you."

"I look good, don't I?" He grinned down at himself—until her shirt was gone. Then his attention was firmly on her. "Damn," he whispered in reverence. "Age has made you even more beautiful."

Her heart stuttered at his words.

And then his mouth was on her breast, kissing, sucking, nibbling, and it felt like the room was spinning.

Katya's hands clasped the back of his head, holding him to her. Oh yeah. This was a bad idea. The *best* bad idea she'd ever had.

"You taste like Empire biscuits," he growled against her.

Only Brodie would compare her to his favorite baked treat. Katya was laughing when he sucked her nipple deep into his mouth. Her laughter turned into a gasp.

"Do the other one too," she demanded.

Her nipple still in his mouth, he nodded before releasing her with a pop. "Absolutely. No woman wants lopsided boobs." And then he devoured her other breast.

If her knees hadn't been locked in place, Katya would have crumpled at his feet. Brodie knew exactly how to touch her to turn her to mush. They'd learned those secrets together, practicing hard and often until their techniques became second nature. *Nothing* felt like Brodie's mouth on her body. *Nothing.*

It had been far too long since she'd felt the sensations only he could induce. Her body had been starved of him, and now it wanted to glut itself on Brodie's touch until it was drunk from it.

"Room service for the loving couple," came the call, accompanied by a loud knock.

Dougal. With breakfast.

Katya squeaked, scooped up her shirt from the floor, and ran into the bathroom, banging the door shut behind her.

"Hey, Dougal," she heard Brodie say once the door to their room opened and closed.

After a beat of silence, Dougal said, "You're paying for the dry cleaning for that cushion cover, son. I provide cushions for guests to use to sit comfortably, not for them to rub their...nether regions all over. What do you think my guests would say if they knew the cushions were being used like that? It's indecent; that's what it is."

Katya shoved her T-shirt into her mouth to keep from laughing hysterically, then decided it would be much better if she wore it.

"I wasn't rubbing my...*anything* on the cushion," Brodie said. "You came barging in, and I had to cover up."

"I didn't barge—I entered as agreed, expecting to find two fully dressed people barely talking to each other."

"If it makes you feel better, we're still barely talking. Now, if you hand me my jeans, I'll return the cushion."

"There's no hurry. I'll have one of the maids bring up a plastic sack for you to put it in before you check out." There was the sound of something being put on a hard surface. Probably the tray of food.

That's when Katya realized it would be easier to leave with a buffer between her and Brodie in the room. Throwing the bathroom door open, she beamed at a frowning Dougal.

"Good morning," she said chirpily. A glance at Brodie confirmed he still sat on the edge of the bed, one of Dougal's precious tartan cushions pressed to his lap. Her lips quivering, she swallowed another giggle as she pointed at Brodie. "This isn't what it looks like. It's still a fake relationship."

"Aye." Dougal cocked an eyebrow. "I suppose he's only fake naked as well."

"Oh, no, he's naked, but there's a reason for it."

"This, I've got to hear," Brodie muttered.

Katya ignored him. "He had a fever." She blurted the first thing that came to mind. "We had to cool him down to break it."

"Weak," Brodie muttered, shaking his head.

"I agree." Dougal stroked his white Santa beard. "Last I checked, a smack in the face with a ball didn't cause fever."

Good point. "Something else must have caused it. Are you sure you don't keep these rooms too warm?"

Dougal's face turned beetroot red with outrage at the mere suggestion his hotel was less than perfect.

"I've got to go." Katya rushed for the door. "Maybe Brodie can explain the room temperature issue with you, so it won't happen again. I don't think you need to tell anyone about what you walked in on. Trust me, nothing happened here. It was all a misunderstanding."

As she rushed out the door, Brodie called after her, "Like hell nothing happened, you little coward."

Katya was still laughing when she let herself into Brodie's car. She drove out of town, feeling the need to shop for something new to wear to lunch with her parents. And she felt no guilt whatsoever at having abandoned Brodie to suffer through one of Dougal's epic lectures.

27

Brodie didn't see Katya again until they met up outside her parents' house a few hours later for Sunday lunch. She climbed out of his SUV as if she owned it, wearing clothes that looked new—which would explain how she'd managed to change without bumping into him at home. The witch had obviously spent the morning shopping in Fort William.

"Coward," he said by way of hello.

Her grin was unrepentant. "How was the lecture?"

"Long." Dougal enjoyed the sound of his own voice. "That man knows a lot of euphemisms for penis."

Her laughter was like sunshine after a storm. "Well, you did have one of his precious cushions pressed to your *nether regions*."

As he held open the gate for her, he nodded to his car. "You do know that's mine, right?" He'd had to get a lift to the Savages from Bain, who'd whined the whole way about his brothers ruining his chances with Denise by telling her he farted in his sleep.

"We're still married, which means half of the car belongs to me."

Katya looked so pleased with herself that he didn't bother arguing. It would have been pointless anyway because she was right. Under Scottish law, everything they'd acquired during their marriage, even while apart, was owned by them both.

"You do realize the same rule also means I own half your plane?" he said.

She tripped over the crazy paving making up the path to the front door. Brodie's hands shot out to steady her. "Guess you didn't think about that after all."

She narrowed her eyes at him. "I hope that wasn't a veiled threat."

He held up his hands. "No threat. The plane's all yours. I'll sign whatever you want to make you believe me. Now, are you ready for this? We need to convince your parents we're back together. Otherwise, there's no knowing what they'll do before the meeting with the lawyers tomorrow."

Katya didn't argue. The potential for Savage chaos was a very real concern.

"I'm ready." She checked the buttons on the black shirt she wore with blue jeans.

"It could do with one more undone." He offered his opinion willingly. The memory of Katya's breasts in his hands made his mouth water and his jeans tighten.

Very slowly, eyes on him, she fastened all the buttons right up to her throat.

"Tease," he said as they approached the front door, which was currently painted bright yellow. The color changed depending on Delia's moods.

Like everything in their lives, the Savages had put their

own stamp on the bog-standard two-story brick house years earlier. Dotted throughout the garden were sculptures Fraser had made from found materials—mainly old tires and metal parts. A large cement gargoyle stood sentry at the gate, and there was a small, striped marquee in the middle of the lawn—where Delia rehearsed for her many roles in local productions. As for the house itself, their main addition had been the ceramic geckos clambering up and around the door and onto the roof. He noticed one of them held a tiny plastic person in its teeth.

"That's new." Brodie pointed out the offending lizard to Katya.

"Stephen. Got to be. Mum loves those lizards; she wouldn't add to them. She thinks they're the epitome of good taste."

He gestured to the blue one beside the doorbell. "That's the one we mail-ordered her for Christmas one year. Which reminds me, I'm still getting requests from women who want a Scottish husband. I thought you were going to delist me from those sites?"

"When have I had the time? I don't know if you've noticed, but we've been kind of busy since Lawrence told us we had to look genuinely married by tomorrow morning."

She had a point. Brodie tugged at the navy blazer he'd worn with his best jeans and a white tee. "You ready?"

"Yep." Katya reached for the door handle.

"Why am I nervous?" he asked. "I've eaten here countless times. Hell, I wasn't even this nervous when we first started dating."

"Probably because you'd practically lived here since you were a toddler. I don't know why you're nervous, but if it helps, I won't tell anyone you've been trying to get me into bed again." She was laughing at him.

"I wasn't trying. I was succeeding."

She threw open the door. "That's what you think."

His hand curled around her hip from behind as he leaned in to whisper against her ear. "Don't worry, you'll have another chance to seduce me later. I know how desperate you are to get your hands on me."

She twisted toward him, ready to argue, but Delia appeared in the hallway before she could.

"Wonderful, you're here!" Today, she wore a tweed skirt suit, obviously channeling the queen's "at home" look. Brodie half expected to see a rifle tucked under her arm. She hugged Katya before clasping Brodie's face in her hands and plastering a kiss to his lips. "Thank goodness you two have come to your senses at last. Now, come eat. I have a surprise for you."

They had no choice but to bustle after her to the kitchen/dining room. Where they stopped dead in the doorway because Brodie's parents sat at the table with Fraser.

"Ma, Da," Brodie said. "What are you doing here?"

"We're celebrating with the in-laws," his da said drolly.

"I'm so excited," his ma said. "Aren't we excited, Joseph?"

"Aye, we definitely are, Theresa." His da beamed at them. "It's good to know my sons still listen to my advice."

"What advice?" Katya whispered to him.

"I don't have a clue," he whispered back.

"Come give me a hug." Brodie's ma stood and held out her hands to Katya. "I'm glad we've got our daughter back again. Seven sons, and none of them married but Brodie. Although poor Knox did have Linda for a while, God rest her soul." She made the sign of the cross. "As for the rest of them, I don't know where I went wrong. At this rate, I'll be dead before I get grandbabies to fuss over."

Really, there was nothing to say to that, so Brodie kept his mouth shut.

As Katya hugged his parents, Brodie nodded to her dad. "Fraser."

His reply was a tight-lipped smile and a narrow-eyed glare.

"I see you're in a celebratory mood." Brodie indicated Fraser's mourning tartan. "Glad to see you're taking the news about us getting back together so well."

"Delia?" Fraser called, still staring at Brodie. "Where's my shotgun? I've a feeling I'll need it."

"Dad," Katya admonished. "That's not funny."

"Ah wasnae joking," her father said.

"Enough of that," Delia called from the kitchen area. "Katya, come give me a hand with these dishes. Brodie, take a seat."

Since Fraser was at one end of the table, and his ma and da took up a side of it, he sat on the other side with a space between him and Katya's dad. Fraser smirked at his choice of seats, but growing up with six brothers had taught Brodie to stay out of arm's reach of anyone bearing a grudge.

"Here you go." Delia placed the dishes on the table with a flourish. "I made your favorite, Brodie—sausage and tomato surprise."

Katya gave her mother a droll look. "I thought that was *my* favorite."

"Don't be daft," Delia said. "Everyone knows you love my macaroni cheese."

Katya shook her head, making Brodie wonder what he was missing.

"Where's Steven?" Katya asked as she placed a dish on the table.

"With friends." Delia waved a hand toward the town. "All I know is that when I told him we were having a big family dinner, he grabbed his skateboard and ran for the door."

"At least one of us has some sense," Katya muttered.

"Interesting dining table you've got here," his da said as Katya and her mum took their seats.

"Chopped the last one up for a sculpture," Fraser said.

"Of course you did." His da shot his ma a look that made it clear his opinion of Fraser Savage hadn't improved over the years.

"I like having three tables instead of one." Delia smiled as she passed the potatoes. "It's so versatile. Now Brodie and Katya are back together, we'll have lots of big family dinners, and we can arrange the tables to fit everyone."

Brodie's da looked around at the overstuffed room. "I'm sure you could," he said, convincing no one.

"So," Delia said to Katya and Brodie, scarcely containing her excitement, "Theresa and I had an idea we know you're going to love." As she covered Brodie's ma's hand with hers, Katya slapped her hand onto Brodie's thigh and held on tight. Waiting for the bomb to fall.

The two mothers grinned at one another.

"You tell them," Delia said.

His ma didn't need to be told twice. "We've booked the church for your wedding!"

There was an expectant silence as both sets of parents waited for their response.

"Uh," Katya said slowly, "we're still married. Right?" She looked up at Brodie.

"Definitely."

"We know, silly." Delia waved a dismissive hand. "The

last time, you two eloped to Gretna Green, and we all missed the ceremony. This time, we thought it would be good if we were all involved."

"This time?" Brodie said, bewildered.

"Um"—again, Katya spoke slowly—"we did that because you lot banned us from getting married."

"Aye," Fraser barked. "Because we thought it would be a disaster seeing as how you were so young. I can't tell you how thrilled I am that we were wrong."

His mother tucked her short black hair behind her ear. "Now, Fraser, this is no time for humor."

Katya's nails dug into Brodie's leg, reminding him her father had no sense of humor. Something Brodie was well aware of.

"We thought," his mother said, "you might like to renew your vows as a sign that you're committed to each other again."

"For however long it lasts this time," Fraser muttered.

Brodie's da glared at Fraser. "What your ma means is that she wants her son's marriage blessed by the church this time. Father McMurty is in town for a few weeks, and he could perform the ceremony."

"It's as though God himself planned it," his ma gushed. "The priest who baptized you will be able to marry you, and I'll be able to stop lighting candles for the two of you. Something I wouldn't have had to do if you'd just had a church wedding in the first place." She beamed at them. "Don't you think this is a great idea?"

What Brodie thought was that his ma was fed up lighting candles for her wayward son.

Before they could answer, Delia spoke up. "We thought we could have a reception in Dougal's new conference center. Nobody else is using it anyway."

A ringing endorsement if ever Brodie heard one.

"Your brother could make a cake for you," his ma added.

"And," Delia said, bursting with excitement, "you could wear your great-grandmother's wedding dress."

Katya's fork fell to her plate. "You found Granny Natasha's dress? The one made from a parachute?"

"I did." Delia bounced out of her seat and rushed from the room, only to return a moment later with an old leather suitcase. "Your Aunty Janice found it in their storage unit, along with a bunch of other stuff none of the family wanted."

Katya cleared a space on the table between her and Brodie for the case. The lid creaked with age as Delia opened it to reveal a whole lot of tissue paper. Carefully, she peeled back the layers to uncover cream silk fabric.

Brodie watched Katya's face as the dress was carefully removed from the case. She seemed awestruck, and her hands shook with nerves.

"Move those dishes further away," Delia ordered. "I don't want to get food on it."

Brodie pushed the plates into the middle of the table as Delia lifted the dress out of the suitcase.

As the long silken creation appeared, his ma gasped, placing her hands over her heart. But it was Katya's reaction that interested Brodie the most. If there was such a thing as love at first sight, he was watching it happen.

Slowly, she stood, wiping her hands on her jeans before reaching for the dress. Cheeks flushed, she held it against herself.

"It's gorgeous," Katya said in a hushed tone. "Isn't it, Brodie?"

He couldn't see the dress. All he could see was the woman holding it, the woman who was born to be his and that he'd somehow managed to drive from his life. Even though they'd both made mistakes, he knew his were the greater because he'd thrown who she was back in her face and told her it wasn't good enough for him.

"Brodie?" Wide eyes caught his.

"Aye, you're beautiful."

She chuckled. "You mean the dress."

No, he didn't. Not a dress on the planet could do her justice.

Katya grasped the full skirt and swished it about. "I can't believe this was a German parachute. Mum, I'm going to need this for my museum."

Delia Savage was no fool and she quickly pried the dress from Katya's hands, knowing her daughter would release it for fear of damaging it, and then she packed it back into the suitcase.

"You can have it after you're married in it," Delia said firmly.

Katya gaped at her. "Mum, I can't wear that to get married; it's a piece of history." She looked to Brodie for support.

"Katya's got a point," he said. "We wouldn't want anything to happen to it. Anyway, there's no rush to get a dress. We haven't even agreed to renew our vows." That was the wrong thing to say, and Brodie knew it as soon as the words left his mouth.

The mothers glared at him as Fraser muttered, "Well, there's a surprise."

"That's it!" Brodie's da slammed his cutlery down on the table. "What is your problem, Fraser? It's been snide comments, bad attitude, and not-so-subtle tartan messages ever since we got here. Don't think we don't know you wear that kilt to funerals. Why don't you stop beating around the bush and say what's on your mind?"

"Oh no," Katya hissed.

"Da," Brodie started, but his father was already on his feet.

"No." He pointed at Brodie. "This is between me and Katya's father. If you've got something to say, Fraser, say it."

Fraser pointed at Brodie too. "You heard him, same as me. He doesn't want to renew his vows, which means he's no more serious about their marriage this time round than he was the first."

"That's not true. Brodie wants things to work, don't you, son?"

"Sure he does," Fraser said with heavy sarcasm.

"This isn't about what Brodie said, is it?" His da rolled up his sleeves. "You think my son isn't good enough for your girl. That's what your problem is, isn't it?"

"Well, now that you mention it." Fraser pushed back his chair and stood, towering over Brodie's da. He slammed his palms down on the table. "That's exactly what I think. If he'd been good enough for her to begin with, he'd have gone with her when she left town."

"She didn't leave town," his da shouted. "She left him." He thrust an arm out to Brodie. "If you want to attribute blame, at least put it where it belongs."

"Who wants pudding?" Delia said gaily while gathering up the half-full dinner plates.

"We should go," Brodie's ma said as she stood. "Joseph, there will be no fighting today. We came here to celebrate our children sorting their lives out. This is a good thing. It isn't something to fight about."

"Aye," Fraser sneered at Brodie's da, "away you go home.

The MacGregors aren't welcome here anyway. Not until your boy apologizes to my daughter and vows to make up for all the years he forced her to spend alone, without a husband to look out for her. A married man doesn't desert his wife."

"No"—Brodie's father went face-to-mid-chest with Fraser—"in the Savage family, they stick by them no matter how crazy they are. But then, the Savage men have always been a few sandwiches short of a picnic themselves."

Delia gasped at being called crazy.

"It's only his anger talking," Brodie's ma said.

"I think you'd better go," Delia said softly.

"Let's all go." Katya stood, grabbed Brodie's hand, and headed for the door.

"You'd best apologize for upsetting my wife." Fraser puffed out his chest as he growled at Brodie's da. "At least she doesn't spend all her time at mass, praying her wild sons don't knock up one of the many girls that traipse through their bedrooms."

"Are you calling my sons sluts?"

"If the shoe fits!"

That's when Brodie's da let out a war cry that would have made any Highlander proud and launched his fist at Fraser's head. His father was small but mean, and he had rage on his side. His fist connected, and Fraser staggered before shaking it off. Then, with a roar, he rugby tackled Brodie's da and took them both down in the middle of the three Formica tables, which folded like paper.

Food flew everywhere, landing on the furniture and walls. Delia and Brodie's ma clung to each other as they screamed. And, of course, Katya threw herself into the fight to try to separate the men.

"Brodie! Do something!" his ma yelled.

He did the only thing he could think of—he grabbed Katya around the waist with one arm and hauled her away from the fight before she got hurt. Then he stalked out the kitchen door, grabbed the garden hose, went back inside, and hosed down their fathers—all while carrying a struggling Katya under his arm like a rugby ball.

The fighting ended with the cold blast. Both men lay on their backs, panting from being too unfit to fight in the first place. Delia tiptoed through the debris and adjusted Fraser's kilt, which had flipped up while he'd rolled around on the floor. The sight was not only disturbing but also a reminder to everyone in the room that you really shouldn't fight with your dangly bits flying around. That bruise would take a while to heal, and Fraser would be walking funny until it did.

"Can we go now?" Brodie asked Katya.

"Get the dress first," she said.

"No!" Delia ran for the suitcase. "No wedding. No dress."

"Let's go," Brodie said, knowing full well they didn't have a chance in hell of getting the dress out of Delia's grasp.

Still carrying Katya, he strode out the back door, thinking it was safer than trying to get past the mess on the kitchen floor.

"You can put me down now."

"I don't think so." He headed for his car. "You'll just go back in there and try to get the dress, which will start another fight. It's safer if I keep hold of you until we're far, far away from here."

"Brodie," she said with faux innocence that set off all his alarm bells, "since we're already in a fake relationship, do you think it would be terrible of us to have a fake wedding ceremony so I could get my hands on that dress?"

Brodie opened the passenger door of his SUV, put her

on the seat, and shut the door. Then he hung his head with a sigh. There was no denying the whole Savage family was batshit crazy.

Although, to be fair, the MacGregors weren't much better.

28

—————

For the first time in her life, Natasha was in love.

And it wasn't with her husband.

Although there had never been anything more than a piece of paper joining her to Ben, she still felt tremendous guilt over having feelings for another man. Especially since it wasn't just any other man; it was Ben's best friend.

As far as she knew, outside of herself, only Ben was aware of the marriage certificate he kept at the farm. To the folk of Invertary, she wasn't Mrs. Baxter; she was Natasha Klimova—a Lithuanian refugee Ben met in Germany and helped relocate to Scotland.

From the day they'd arrived in town and Ben's friends had welcomed him back over drinks at the pub, they'd gone their separate ways. Ben to his farm and Natasha to a boarding house in town, where she rented a room from a widow with two teenage girls.

If she saw Ben at all, it was after dark—when he sought her out to talk about the memories tormenting him. Although Natasha desperately wanted to put the war behind her, she would never have refused Ben's need for a confidant. Not when she owed him her life.

Ben would talk for hours during those nighttime visits, their conversation spiraling down into the dark, murky places of conflict. The only topic off-limits was Natasha's desire for a divorce. No matter when she brought up the subject, he'd stop talking, get up, and leave. She was in a no-man's-land, where Ben would neither acknowledge their marriage nor end it.

As the weeks passed, Natasha came to believe Ben saw no need for a divorce because, in his mind, their marriage wasn't real. That's when she stopped asking and, like Ben, pretended the piece of paper tying them together didn't exist.

Which is how she ended up spending more time than was sensible with an oversized Scot who never talked about anything serious and went out of his way to make her laugh.

"What are you thinking?" Tom lazed in the chair opposite her, beside the open fire in the pub.

It was Sunday afternoon and his day off. Although, if there was a problem at the Baxters' farm, everyone knew where to find him.

The dancing flames from the fire made his russet hair glow like a beacon against the backdrop of their wintry view of the loch. Snow painted the hills white, the water was gray, and a pale sky sat heavily over the town. Being from Russia, Natasha was used to the snow, but there it had meant freezing and fighting to survive. In Scotland, it was a thing of intimacy and beauty.

She smiled over at him as she sipped her hot toddy. "I was thinking how beautiful this place is."

"Well, that's disappointing," he teased. "Here I was, under the assumption you were thinking about me."

Natasha hid her smile behind her drink. "You're beautiful too."

It was hard not to laugh when he turned a little green. "Men aren't beautiful, Nat. They're handsome or dashing, never beautiful."

"What about pretty?" She fought to remain solemn, which was always difficult around Tom.

"Keep your voice down," he hissed, glancing around the pub. As usual, there was no true irritation in his tone. He was playing with her, and she loved every minute of it. "Are you trying to ruin my reputation, woman? If anyone asks, I'm going to tell them your words are getting lost in translation, and what you really meant to say was I'm rugged and masculine."

"Of course," she said pretending solemnity. "I often do mix up my words. Sometimes I forget them altogether. Right now, I can't remember the word I'd use to describe you. It means sweet, entertaining, delightful...."

"Charming." His smile was cocky.

"No," she said slowly. "I think it's...annoying! Yes, that's it." She beamed at him.

His eyes sparkled with merriment. "Annoying, am I? And here I'd brought you a surprise. I think I'll just keep it for myself now."

"Surprise?" Natasha looked around but saw nothing. Over the weeks they'd spent time together, he'd brought her several surprises. All of them wonderful. Sometimes he saved up his rations and delighted her with a special meal, while another time, he'd found a smooth, colorful pebble, which he presented to her with the same flare another man would use for diamonds.

She glanced down at her wrist and his last gift—a cuff bracelet he'd fashioned from an old silver fork he'd found at a market. One end was the ornate stem of the fork, and for the other, he'd curled the tines to form a flower-like design. It was unique and wonderful. For a big, physical man, he had the eye and talents of an artist.

"Aye, surprise," he said with amusement. "It's a shame I'll have to forget all about it now because annoying men don't give surprises to their girl."

Her stomach flipped over, doing somersaults inside of her. "Your girl?"

"Aye." His dark eyes dared her to disagree.

Natasha wet suddenly dry lips and changed the subject. "I fixed a broken generator today, and Mr. McPherson told me I was the best hire he'd ever made." She felt giddy at the memory. Who knew a degree in engineering would be more appreciated in a small-town repair shop than in the factories of Moscow?

"I told you he'd recognize an asset when he saw one." Pride shone in Tom's face and her heart melted even further.

"I misspoke earlier when I said annoying. I definitely meant charming." She batted her lashes at him, knowing he'd find her lack of acting ability funny.

Sure enough, he threw back his head and roared with laughter, making everyone around him grin and chuckle. That was Tom. He spread joy wherever he went.

"Well, seeing as you think I'm charming, I'd best put in some effort at being exactly that." He got out of his armchair. "Wait here," he ordered before heading to the bar.

Natasha watched eagerly as he whispered to the barman, who reached under the bar and pulled out a brown paper package. It was large and, judging by the way he carried it, soft.

They attracted curious looks as Tom sauntered back.

"There you go," he said gruffly as he handed it over. "The surprise I've been saving."

"Should I open it here?" She held the package with reverence. Without even knowing what was inside, it was already precious to her.

"There's nothing embarrassing in there, which means it's fine to open in public." He picked up his whisky glass from the low table between them and settled back into his chair. His suggestive gaze made her wonder exactly what kind of gifts he planned to give her in private. Over the past few weeks, it had become more difficult to resist the temptation of Tom's kisses and taking things further with him. Like everything else he did, Tom was gifted at making her melt with the merest touch.

Her cheeks burning, she untied the string, coiled it up and placed it on the table. Then, taking care not to damage the paper, she unwrapped the rest of his surprise. She gasped, her eyes shooting to Tom's as she whispered his name.

His features softening, he gestured with his drink. "Try it on."

Natasha's hands trembled as she lifted the blue tweed coat out of its wrapping. "It's new," she whispered. It must have taken the bulk of his clothing rations and some under-the-table dealings to get it.

"Aye, it is. Came all the way from Harris, an' all." She must have looked blank because he added, "That's an island off the west coast of Scotland. They make tweed."

"Oh, it's wonderful, Tom."

"Put it on, so we can see if it fits." His voice was low and husky.

Hesitantly, because she knew they'd drawn an audience, she unbuttoned the double row of buttons that ran down the front of the coat before standing to try it on.

Tom stood with her and took the coat from her hands. "Let me," he said, holding it out for her.

She turned her back to him and slipped her arms into the sleeves, feeling the comfort of his large frame behind her. Shielding her. Warming her right to the core of her being. The coat fit to perfection, buttoning up to her throat and hanging down to below her knees. As well as the double row of buttons, it nipped in at the waist with a matching belt. When she reached for it, Tom gently turned her to face him.

And right there, in front of everyone, he fastened her coat and tied the belt.

"I'd say it fits fine," he said once he was done, his eyes dark with unspoken emotion just for her.

"Thank you, Tom, I love it."

"I hope it's no' the only thing you love, Nat," he said softly.

"No." She blinked back tears as emotion overwhelmed her. "It's not the only thing. It's not even the thing I love most in the world."

He cupped her cheek. "I know exactly what you mean."

Oh, how she wished they were alone so she could walk into his arms and let his lips take hers.

Instead, his hand dropped away, and to stop herself from reaching for him, she thrust her hands into the pockets of her perfect new coat. Only to find something already in them. In one was a pair of woolen gloves—in the same shade of blue as her coat. And in the other...

"Tom." His name was a gasp as she stared down at the gold ring in her palm.

"It was my mother's," he said, suddenly very serious for a man who always laughed.

As the pub fell silent, Tom plucked the ring from her palm and went down on one knee in front of her.

Tears streamed down her face now, and no amount of blinking would make them stop.

"Shh, this won't hurt a bit." He winked at her, and she found herself laughing through the tears.

Tom cleared his throat and spoke with the confidence of a man who knew exactly what he wanted. "Natasha Klimova, would you do me the honor of becoming my wife?"

There were so many things she should have said, not least of all explaining she was already married and she'd been born in Russia, not Lithuania as he believed. If he wanted to marry her, he should know what he was getting— and she was no prize. However, as all those thoughts rushed through her mind, Natasha opened her mouth and said the only thing that truly mattered—"Yes."

And Tom slipped the ring onto her finger.

29

"I thought lunch went pretty well, all things considered." Katya relaxed back into the passenger seat of Brodie's SUV and let him drive her through town. Her mind was still on the wedding dress, but she figured he wasn't up to helping her liberate it from her parents' house, which made her keep quiet about it.

For now.

She was pretty sure she could talk him into a heist later.

"They were an embarrassment," Brodie grumbled.

He wasn't wrong, but seeing as they'd long ago agreed never to apologize for anything their families said or did, that embarrassment had nothing to do with them. If their parents wanted to behave like toddlers, it was on them.

"Honestly," Brodie carried on. "I'm surprised Fraser didn't squash my da like a bug."

"Ah, but Joseph is tenacious. It was kind of like a bad-tempered pug taking on a grumpy old collie."

"Your dad's a collie?"

"How about a Saint Bernard?" she asked.

"I was thinking more along the lines of a humorless Doberman."

"That's only because he never lets you scratch his soft underbelly." This was fun. Katya hadn't realized how much she'd missed their dynamic—their friendship. Especially when it came to dealing with family.

Brodie shuddered. "After seeing far more of Fraser's *underbelly* than I ever wanted to see, I'm truly grateful I'm not allowed anywhere near it."

"Your reaction was too slow. You need to learn to close your eyes as soon as the kilt starts flying."

"I'll keep that in mind," he said drolly.

"What bothers me most is the fact we never get to finish a meal," Katya complained.

"Aye, we're no' having much luck in that department. I'm also sorely disappointed we didn't make it to pudding. I bet your mum made rhubarb crumble."

Brodie grinned at Katya's loud gagging noises. "I'm *glad* we missed pudding, although I'm sorry we didn't get to finish lunch because now I'm starving."

He glanced over at her. "Want to pick up some hot chips at the pub?"

"I think, after this morning, we should probably keep out of Dougal's way."

"Well, the spa restaurant is out. We won't get anything there until we've paid for the repairs—and calmed down. Deke's words, not mine." He gave her a dark look. "You're barely back in town a week, and we're already personae non gratae at the two main restaurants."

Katya chuckled at his use of the plural of persona non grata. They'd once looked it up in high school after being banned from the summer fair. "A pity it's Sunday, or we could have hit up the bakery." Sometimes, living in a tiny town was seriously inconvenient—especially when running out of places to eat.

Brodie checked his watch. "The fish and chip shop opens in a couple of hours. If you can survive until then, we can get some deep-fried pizza."

"Now you're talking." Although... "Can we swing by the garage to pick up some chocolate to tide us over?"

"Your wish is my command." He took a left and headed for the petrol station.

"And after"—Katya knew she was chancing her luck on Brodie's good mood—"we could drive out to see my plane."

"Didn't you spend most of yesterday with it?"

"You mean when you were being patched up? Yeah, I did." She took a deep breath and went for it. "It's such a lovely afternoon that I thought we could go for a ride."

There was no reply. In fact, Brodie was quiet for such a long time that Katya wasn't sure he'd heard her.

"I said, why don't we go up in my plane this afternoon?" she repeated, louder this time.

"Aye, I know what you said." He grimaced. "I'm trying to figure out how to reply without starting a fight."

That had her zeroing in on him with precision-focused attention. "What exactly do you mean, Brodie?" Her tone made it clear he should be *very* careful how he answered.

"It means you can be a bit sensitive about your plane."

Obviously, he'd missed her tone. "Are you worried you might somehow damage it?"

"No," he said slowly.

"Then it's my skills as a pilot that bother you?" Surely he couldn't miss the sub-zero tone on that one.

Thankfully, he wasn't that dense. "Believe it or not, I

trust you fine. I know whatever you set your mind to, you'll work at it until you're the best."

Katya settled back in her seat, somewhat mollified. "Then what's the problem?"

He sighed. "I don't trust the plane. It's a flying fossil. Even Boeing decommission their aircraft after a few years because of wear and tear. That plane's decades past being decommissioned. *Decades.*"

"First, the plane isn't a fossil, it's a classic," she corrected. "You understand classic machines—you had an old motorbike, and you had no problem riding it."

"I still do, but that's a well-designed piece of engineering, not a Soviet craft project held together with glue and string."

Okay, now he was really pissing her off. "I'll have you know I rebuilt that plane myself. There's absolutely nothing wrong with it. I wouldn't go up in it if there was."

Brodie gave her the side-eye. "Don't take this the wrong way, but you aren't exactly unbiased."

"Why is it people always say 'don't take this the wrong way' when they know there's only one way to take what they're about to say—with offense?"

"I knew I should have kept my mouth shut," he mumbled. "Look, it isn't you; it's the plane." He gestured out the windscreen. "It's one of Scotland's rare, perfect summer days, and I don't want to ruin it by dropping from the sky and dying in a ball of flames."

"You're overreacting. These planes hardly ever crash." Katya didn't bother telling him their top speed was so slow that you could generally cut the engine and glide in for a landing if there was a problem. She was fairly sure Brodie wouldn't find the information comforting. Not to mention, the planes were designed to fly at really low altitudes, which made them great for sneaking under the radar or taking tourists on a look-see. In fact, they could fly so low she was fairly certain they could jump out if something serious happened, risking only broken legs.

Okay, maybe that was a stretch, but the plane was safe—damn it.

"Hardly ever?" His eyebrows shot up. "There are about a million stories of them crashing in among all that stuff you've collected. Your own great-granny barely made it out of a crash alive."

"A million's a massive exaggeration, and Natasha was shot down. Under normal circumstances, the plane would have been fine, and they would never have crashed. Which means, unless somebody's out gunning for you, I think we'll be fine."

His lips thinned, and he shook his head. "Nope. Not doing it."

"Stop being a big baby, Brodie."

"Say that ten times fast." He flashed a grin before turning serious again. "I'm okay with being a big baby. As long as I'm one on solid ground. Look at this body." He lifted his shirt to flash his abs. "Does that look soft to you? No. A man is not designed to bounce if he falls from a great height."

Katya rolled her eyes. "You're totally overreacting."

"Okay." He parked in front of the petrol station shop and climbed out.

She followed. "Okay? That's all you have to say?"

"Aye." He pushed open the door to the shop. "My ego's healthy enough to cope with being accused of overreacting—just so long as it keeps me out of an ancient plane."

"Come on, Brodie, don't be pathetic," Katya cajoled as she followed him inside.

An old school friend working the counter squealed when they walked in. "Look at this!" she called. "It's the terrible twosome!"

"Good to see you, Suzanne." Katya walked over to say hi, but almost tripped when she spotted her belly. "Wow. You're pregnant."

Suzanne patted her belly. "This is our fifth. We're hoping for a boy this time."

"We? Fifth?" She glanced at Brodie for confirmation.

"Suzanne married Brian Thompson from the year below us," he said as he picked up snacks.

"He's my toy boy." Suzanne giggled.

"Five kids?" Katya was still stuck on the number. "How is that possible? We're the same age, and I'm only..."

"Thirty." Brodie slung an arm around her shoulders and grinned at her. "You feel a whole lot older now, don't you?"

"We started early," Suzanne said with a laugh. "You know, I always wanted a big family. We think this will be the last one, though, even if it isn't a boy. Our eldest is eighteen months away from becoming a teenager, and we're not sure we can cope with that *and* another baby."

Yeah, Katya wasn't following her logic. She pointed at Suzanne's very pregnant belly. "Won't that one be a toddler when your eldest hits their teens? How's that better than having a baby and a teen?"

Suzanne shrugged. "We figure they can both act out together."

As Brodie paid for the chocolate, Katya stared at Suzanne in shock. They'd spent their teens following the same bands and complaining about boys—Brodie for Katya, the rest of the boys in their year group for Suzanne. They'd even gone through the same experimental hairstyle phase together. Now here they were: Suzanne happily married with four and a half kids, and Katya basically divorced and homeless with only an old plane to her name.

"I know what you're thinking," Brodie said as they walked back outside into the sunshine. "You're wondering if you or Suzanne made the better life choices."

She frowned at his smug smile and the reminder he knew her far too well. "No, I wasn't," she lied as her gaze skimmed over a wooden table and bench set, and an idea popped into her mind. "I was wondering if you were up to a bout of arm wrestling." She grinned at him. "If you win, we don't fly today. I win, you let me take you up in my plane. What do you say? You too chicken to take me on?"

It was almost cute, the way Katya thought she could beat him at arm wrestling. "No, I'm not chicken. In case you haven't noticed, I have a wee bit more muscle than the last time you beat me."

"I would hope so," she said. "You stopped wrestling me when we were twelve, and your delicate ego couldn't cope with losing."

"No, I just couldn't stand listening to you gloat anymore."

"Whatever." She waved a hand. "Are we wrestling or not?"

"This is dumb."

"Brodie." She turned his name into a complaint.

"Fine." He lumbered over to the table. "One match. None of this best-out-of-three crap."

"I only need one." Katya sat on the bench opposite him, the attached wooden table between them. "You ready?" She put her elbow in the middle of the table and held up her hand.

Brodie clasped it with a sigh. "You're only going to embarrass yourself; are you sure you want that?"

"I'll live," she said with a sweet smile that made him suddenly suspicious.

"You cheat, you forfeit." He reminded her of their lifelong rule, brought in after their escalating attempts at cheating had gotten out of hand.

"I have no intention of cheating." She tossed her long hair over her shoulder and tensed. "You ready?"

"Aye."

"Then go!"

He knew it wouldn't be easy. Katya was no wimp, which meant he wasn't surprised when she didn't go down straight away.

"Goodness," she said, "I don't know if it's the sun making me hot or watching all that muscle flex. I need to cool down before I overheat." She started unbuttoning her shirt with her free hand.

Damn it, there was nowhere else to look except at the exceptional cleavage being revealed, button by button.

"Katya," he warned.

"This isn't cheating. You don't want me to faint from the heat, do you?" Her shirt was fully unbuttoned now, a sliver of skin exposed between the two halves, revealing a red lacy bra.

He groaned.

She held the edge of her shirt and flapped it to fan herself, exposing heaven from her throat to the waistband of her jeans. "Ooo," she moaned. "The cool air feels *so* good on my skin. I wish I could strip everything off."

That's when Brodie lost the match.

As Katya rebuttoned her shirt with a smirk, Brodie registered laughter coming from nearby. He looked over to see Kade and Conall sitting at the other picnic table beside the building.

"How long have you two been here?" He glared at them.

"Long enough to see the show." Kade grinned. "Thank you, Kat."

"You're welcome." That was Kat—she didn't have one ounce of self-consciousness in her entire body.

"We called out to you," Conall said, still staring at Katya. "Obviously didn't hear us."

"Eyes on me," Brodie barked, earning a sheepish smile from his brother.

"I didn't notice you at all." Katya reached for the chocolate and unwrapped a bar. She looked so pleased with herself that if they'd been near the loch, he would have dunked her in to help "cool her off."

"Aye, we gathered," Kade said, clearly amused. "It brought back memories of being ignored by you both all through my youth."

"I don't remember that either," she said.

"What do you want?" Brodie was fed up with their double act and more than a little nervous about what he'd lost in the match with Katya. He eyed the sky. Still cloudless. Still no wind. How hard could it be for a wee plane to stay up there?

"We wanted to say hello and find out how lunch went." Kade popped open a can of soft drink, which made Brodie realize they'd been in the shop too. Huh, he'd missed that as well.

"I want to know what Katya gets for winning your arm-wrestling match," Conall added.

"Lunch ended with the dads fighting on the floor," Brodie said.

"And Brodie has to come flying with me this afternoon." Katya beamed at everyone as she stood. "I need a cola; anyone else want anything?" There was stunned silence at her announcement of their bet. "I'll take that as a no," she said as she headed into the shop.

Of course, as soon as she was out of earshot, their audience chimed in with unwanted opinions.

"You're going up in her plane?" Conall gaped at him. "Is that safe? Do planes need a certificate to say they've passed an airworthy test? I mean, cars get an MOT, so there must be something like that for a plane. Right?"

"I don't know. She says it's safe." Brodie ran a hand over his face, wincing when it struck his nose. Although the bruising around his eyes had gone down significantly, and his teeth looked like new, his nose still throbbed from the break.

"Of course, she'd say it's safe." Kade rolled his eyes. "Remember the old wall you two tried to climb, and it crumbled? She said that was safe too. And the rotting tree whose branches kept falling off while you were up it? Perfectly safe, according to her. Are you sure you want to take her word for the plane?"

"There's a difference." Katya sat back down, drink in hand. "I'm a certified airplane mechanic. I wasn't qualified to assess the wall or the tree—and I was a kid."

"You won't crash and die, then?" Conall asked in all seriousness.

Brodie pointed at him. "See? It isn't only me."

"MacGregors." She shook her head. "Nobody's going to crash and die. Okay?"

"Well"—Conall shared a look with Kade—"in that case, where are you flying, and where's the best place to watch?"

"Can we rig up a camera on the plane?" Kade added with a grin. "We'd only aim it at Brodie."

"Aye, we'll take bets on whether he'll puke or scream like a baby." Conall had his phone out, his thumbs dancing over the screen, no doubt informing the rest of their brothers about Brodie's afternoon flight.

"We need evidence of what he does," Kade said.

"No camera," Brodie decreed, hoping Katya would back him up. She just kept drinking from her can, which wasn't a disagreement but wasn't a reassuring agreement either.

"Brodie." Conall pointed at him. "Darach says to turn on your phone and call us, so we can listen in during the flight. That way, we don't need a camera; we'll hear if he screams or pukes."

"I don't get why it's such a big deal." Katya tossed the empty can into the bin behind her. "You've flown before, haven't you?"

There'd been no need to fly when they were together. They couldn't afford to holiday abroad, and everyone he knew lived in Invertary. Plus, exotic holidays weren't exactly a staple for the MacGregors. They were lucky if they went camping up Ben Nevis for a week in July. That's why his first—and last—flight had taken place after Katya left. Unfortunately, he hadn't been alone. He'd gone on a trip to Spain with all six of his brothers.

"I've flown," he gritted out.

"Aye." Conall laughed. "He hyperventilated and had to breathe into a paper bag. We thought he was going to pass out, and we'd need to carry him from the plane."

"It was a dangerous flight," Brodie reminded them.

"No, it wasn't," Kade said.

Brodie shook his head. "There was a thunderstorm. The plane was bouncing around like a ball in a bingo machine. People were screaming."

"You were the only one screaming," Conall said. "Plus, there was no storm, just rain."

"He kept demanding to get off the plane," Kade continued their story. "Said the pilot was trying to kill us, and it was his legal right to be allowed onto the ground. There was no reasoning with him, so Knox faked talking to the pilot and told Brodie we were about to land and he might like a wee dram to calm his nerves while they did."

"He downed half a bottle of whisky and spent the rest of the flight passed out and drooling," Conall said.

"As soon as we landed, he puked all over Bain."

Brodie's two brothers were laughing so hard their faces had turned purple.

"They're exaggerating," he told Katya.

"We have the photos and video to prove it," Kade, the traitor, told her.

To her credit, Katya wasn't laughing along with his soon-to-be-dead brothers, although her eyes *were* dancing. "How did you get home?"

"I'd planned on taking the train through the Chunnel, but they spiked my coffee with sleeping pills and dragged me onto the plane. I don't remember much else."

"They almost didn't let him fly," Kade said. "It was touch and go whether we'd have to leave him alone in the airport to sleep it off."

"Well." Katya reached over the table and threaded her fingers through his, flashing him a sympathetic smile. "If you puke on the back of my head while I'm flying, I will flip the plane and dump you in the loch."

"And there's the caring, understanding girl I fell in love with."

Katya grinned.

30

"This is a bad idea," Brodie said as Katya strapped him into the rear cockpit. "This plane didn't even have wings a week ago."

"It did have wings." She grinned, clearly enjoying herself. "They just weren't attached."

"I don't like the idea that the wings come off. What if they aren't secure? What if they fall off mid-flight?" Damn it, his palms were clammy, and it felt like his heart wanted to break out through the wall of his chest.

"They won't fall off. I know what I'm doing. Here, you need goggles." She thrust a pair at him. "Put them on, Brodie. It's an open cockpit, and without them, your eyes will water. Besides, if you get hit by a bug, you want to be able to wipe its mashed body off the goggles instead of your eyeball."

"You're enjoying this far too much," he complained as he hastily put them on.

"Yes, I am. Now, put this on too." She shoved a headset at him.

Brodie stared at it as if it were alien technology. "I

thought we were supposed to shout through tubes on these planes."

"Welcome to the modern era, Brodie. The plane's now fitted with up-to-date communication equipment."

"Does that mean we'll be easier to find if we crash?" He pulled on his headset as Katya did the same with hers.

"No. It means I'll be able to hear you scream like a baby when we take off."

The plane looked different from his new position. It didn't seem as big as it had before he climbed in. The drab olive canvas that made up the body had some rust-colored paint on it, where a logo of some kind had once been. Brodie thought it a bad choice of color for a warplane seeing as it looked like blood.

Unless it *was* blood?

He shook his head and tried to focus on something else. The wooden struts holding the wings apart obstructed their view around the plane, making Brodie wonder how Katya's great-gran had coped with blind spots on those night flights of hers.

Great. Now he was thinking about random crap in an attempt to forget he was strapped to a decades-old machine made of wood and canvas. And fitted with dials that didn't look anywhere near as reliable as a computer screen. Not to mention the levers that moved metal bars running the length of the plane.

Hi-tech, it was not.

It belonged in a museum. Not in the air. Especially not with people in it.

Brodie shifted in his seat, trying to find a comfortable spot. There was hardly any space to move, and for some reason, the designers had thought positioning a lever between his legs was a great idea.

"I can't move. This plane's too small. It must have been built for short Russian guys."

"Stop whining," Katya said through the headset as she jumped down off the wing and disappeared around the front of the plane. "I told you, you're going to love this. It isn't anything like going up in a commercial aircraft with hundreds of other people. For a start, you don't have a tiny oval window. On this plane, you can look in every direction as you breathe in fresh air."

"Which is only another way of saying there's nothing between my head and the sky...or the ground."

Katya climbed up onto the wing and into the front cockpit. "I remember you being a whole lot braver than this."

"I remember when you made me help you take your bed apart because you wanted the mattress to sit on the floor, so the monster couldn't hide under it anymore." Brodie could still hear Fraser shouting when he'd found out what they'd done. Because not only had they taken the wooden frame apart, they'd also hidden it in the garden, to ensure Katya's dad couldn't put it back together again.

"I was seven, and I got over my irrational fear." She fastened her over-the-shoulder harness. "Exactly the same way you'll get over yours."

"By dismantling the plane and hiding it where no one can find it?"

"By trusting I'll give you a good experience up there."

"Why does that sound dirty?"

"Because you're a MacGregor?"

She appeared to pull some levers to her left then press various buttons. The dials attached to the back of Katya's seat moved, and Brodie gripped the rim of the cockpit until his knuckles turned white. "The dials back here are doing stuff. What does that mean? Do I have to do something?"

"No." Katya sounded amused over his headset. "They mirror what's happening up here. They were used by the navigator to keep them apprised of the plane's progress. Or so they could take over and fly from the back seat if the pilot became incapacitated."

Brodie was overcome with dizziness. "That's not funny, Kat. Not even a little."

"I'm sorry." She didn't sound sorry, she sounded entertained. "Nothing will happen to me. I'm starting the engine. Don't freak out, okay?"

Why did she have to say that? Now all he wanted to do was freak out.

Katya flicked a switch, and the engine sputtered then chugged as smoke billowed from the rotating blades on the nose of the craft.

"We're on fire," he whispered. "We're on fire!" he shouted.

"Bloody hell, Brodie! You nearly took out my eardrums. We're not on fire. That's just the engine burning off some fuel because I haven't primed her enough. I thought you'd rather see a little smoke than sit here while the engine turned over for ages."

"Kat," Brodie said in all seriousness, "you need to let me out. I'm not going to make it."

She twisted around in her seat. "Brodie, I promise you, this will be fun, and you will be fine."

"You keep saying that, but I feel like I'm having a heart attack here." He rubbed at his chest.

"Okay, if you really, seriously don't think you can do this, then we won't. But if you think you can, then once we're back on the ground, I'll give you a treat."

"I'm not going up there for a chocolate bar. This is serious. I wish it wasn't, but I'm genuinely freaking here."

"Tell you what, if you try one *very* short flight, when we're back on land, I'll let you kiss me...anywhere you like." Her lips curled with pure seduction.

"As in, I can kiss you in the car, or by the loch, or...?"

"No, Brodie, as in, I will strip naked and let you kiss me anywhere you'd like to—on my body."

His head fell forward as he let out a stream of curses. "You are an evil, evil woman."

"It's your choice," she said, her voice intimate in his ear over the headset. "I want you to come fly with me, what do you want?"

Brodie wrapped both hands around the rim of the cockpit again and held on tight. "I'm trusting you," he gritted out.

With a knowing smile, Katya turned back toward the front. "It'll be worth it."

Then the plane moved forward.

Okay, okay, I can do this. It's exactly like being in a car...in a field...with wings...

"The engine sounds weird," he said.

"Like a sewing machine?"

"Aye."

"That's just the sound it makes. Some people find it soothing."

They bumped along the short grass. *Short?* Brodie studied the ground. "Did you mow?"

"Had Stephen tidy up a strip, although this baby can take off on pretty much any terrain."

"Great," he muttered.

He probably should have objected to her taking liberties with their land, but he had more important things to focus on. Like the fact they weren't going very fast at all. It didn't feel like the last, and only, flight he'd taken. There, they'd suddenly sped up, pushing him back into the seat. "Are we going to take off? Or ride around the paddocks?"

"Eager. I like it." There was a grin in Katya's voice. "This plane takes off at a much lower speed than the one you flew on." There was a gentle bump, and the ground wasn't beneath their wheels anymore. "See? Smooth and easy."

Okay, Brodie, you can do this. That wasn't so bad, was it?

His fingers held on tight as they gained altitude, although, it wasn't too high. Nothing like the flight to Spain, where he'd seen only clouds. This time, the ground was close by, and he could see every detail of the town below.

Despite everything he'd feared about the flight, Brodie found his panic receding a tiny bit at a time.

"It's nice to be able to see all around you, isn't it? You really feel like you're in the air." Her love for the experience was in her tone as she practically purred the words. "How are you doing back there?"

He licked his lips. "I don't know," he answered honestly.

All he did know was that he didn't have the same sense of desperation he'd felt the last time he flew. In fact, he found himself distracted by the scenery beneath them and realized that Katya was keeping the plane as steady as possible.

"Look over there." Katya stretched out an arm to point, and a spike of terror shot through him that her hands weren't on the controls. Then he remembered this wasn't like driving a car. They weren't about to make any sharp turns, and no one else was in the sky with them, which meant no collisions.

Dragging his eyes from the horizon, he looked to where she pointed. "Is that...?"

"Half the town? Yeah." Her laughter was bubbles of joy against his skin.

A crowd of people stood on the lochside, filling the road in front of the pub. All of them staring up and waving at the plane.

"Do you want to go lower and wave back?" Katya asked.

To his surprise, Brodie found himself considering it. "No acrobatics?"

"No, I promise, only a lower pass."

"Okay then," he said, shocking himself with his answer.

"Okay then," she repeated with approval.

The plane moved out over the water, turning in a wide, slow loop, and Brodie reveled in the sensation of wind on his face. "In the other plane, I couldn't see who was flying or where we were going. Then there were all the people and those teeny wee windows."

Katya snorted. "That isn't flying. That's being cargo. This"—she threw her arms in the air—"this is flying."

He was grinning at her behavior before he realized it. Then, tentatively, he uncurled his fingers from the frame in front of him and raised his hands too. They shook as he stretched them into the sky. Air streamed through his fingers, and a rush of pure adrenaline hit his system.

"We're flying!" he shouted.

As Katya brought the plane in on a low swoop over the loch, in front of the crowd, everyone cheered and waved. Even though they were going slow, they were still too fast for him to pick out his brothers' faces. Which was a shame because he'd bet their jaws had hit the ground when they saw him.

"Want to do a flyby of Baxter Farm?" Katya asked, sounding mischievous.

"There aren't any bombs attached to this, are there?" he joked.

"Unfortunately, no."

"Can we pass over the loch again before we head for the hills?"

"Absolutely." Her voice curled around him.

Brodie craned his neck to see past the bars holding the two sets of wings apart. "Do people really walk out on the wings of these things?"

"I've done it." She sounded so blasé that he knew she must be winding him up.

Then again, it was Katya. "Seriously?"

She grinned at him over her shoulder. "I have the photos to prove it."

Damn, but she was gorgeous. Her eyes sparkling behind her goggles, the wind trying to tug her hair free from its braid, her cheeks flushed pink from the fresh air. It was more, though—she was brimming over with life, with excitement. It was contagious, and he couldn't help but grin back.

When her attention returned to her instruments, Brodie felt a strange peace settle over him. "I never knew it could be like this," he whispered.

When the plane turned toward the hills beyond town and Kitty Baxter's farm, Brodie closed his eyes and raised his face to the sun. "Next time, we need to bring flour. I could have easily opened a bag over my brothers."

"You think you can cope with a sharp turn or two?" Katya asked with pure devilment. "We could put on a show and scare the crap out of them instead."

"Hell, yes." Brodie laughed. "Just no turning upside down. I don't think I'm ready for that."

"Yet," she said. "Not ready *yet.*"

And then she headed back toward town.

31

Brodie seemed to have gotten over his fear of flying by the time they came in to land, although Katya still thought it best not to tell him the plane didn't actually have any brakes. Instead, it had a steerable tail skid that dragged along the ground to slow them.

While other aircraft won their pilots over with looks and fancy gadgets, the Polikarpov Po-2 did it through sheer flexibility. The plane could take off and land almost anywhere, easily fly under the radar, and dance around in the sky as if on strings. Plus, it was virtually impossible to stall and resisted going into a spin. It was a pilot's dream, which was why Katya loved it, and why she hoped Brodie's flight had shown him how awesome it could be.

After climbing down and placing the chucks under the two front wheels, she turned to ask Brodie how he felt about her plane now. As soon as she saw his face, all words died on her lips as a rush of pure, unadulterated lust slammed into her body.

He strode toward her, keeping her captured with his dark gaze. Intent written all over his face, he was a hurricane of need, and there was no stopping him—even if she'd wanted to. Hands grasped hold of her waist, and she was off her feet.

In one smooth move, he lifted and pinned her to the aircraft, his lips already on hers. It was a devouring. A desperate, needy kiss. The kind of kiss that stole your breath, your sense, and left you soaring.

Just as abruptly as the kiss had started, Brodie ripped his mouth from hers. "Am I hurting it?" he growled.

His question made no sense. "You're not hurting me." Her legs had drifted around his hips as she gripped him tightly to her, and her arms clung to his shoulders.

"Not you. The plane. Never mind."

She was flying again. This time, as Brodie took them both to the ground. Her shirt disappeared. Then his. Their mouths devoured as their hands fought to get at their jeans. Katya kicked off her shoes as they rolled until Brodie was beneath her.

"Argh," he snapped.

"What?" she sat up, straddling him, wearing only her jeans and bra.

"I think I'm lying on nettles." He held her tight while he sat up, pressing their chests together, turning her brain to mush all over again.

She nuzzled at his neck, kissing her way up to his ear where she tugged his earlobe into her mouth and purred when he moaned.

"Kat, check my back."

"Hmm?"

"My back. Something's sticking into me."

Reluctantly, she knelt up and peered over Brodie's shoulder. Sure enough, there was a clump of nettles attached to his lower back.

"Nettles." She cast about for her shirt, grabbed it from near Brodie's feet, and used it to protect her hand while she yanked them out.

He groaned. And not in a good way.

"We need to get off the ground. Stand up," he ordered.

Honestly, in the hope he'd quit stalling, she'd have hopped on one leg if he'd demanded it. She stood, took a step back, glanced up, and shouted a warning.

It was too late. Brodie's head struck the underside of the wing, and he sat back down with a thud—on the nettles. Loud cursing was closely followed by Katya picking yet more spiky leaves out of his backside.

"Do you have a concussion?" She felt Brodie's head as he leaned against the side of plane.

"No. What I have is a serious case of frustration." He pushed away from the plane and pointed at her. "Do. Not. Move."

Then he stalked over to his SUV, managing to step on something painful as he went. Katya stood, feeling helpless as she watched him cradle his foot and hop.

"I'm okay," he called back to her before opening the car.

For a second, she wondered if he might drive to town without her, instead he pulled some stuff out of the car and strode back—carefully—determination in every step.

"Get naked," he ordered while shaking out a blue tarpaulin and laying it on the ground underneath the wing.

"Don't you want me to put some antiseptic cream on your boo-boos first?"

"I swear, Kat, if you laugh, I will strangle you."

"Brodie"—she struggled to keep a straight face—"your foot's bleeding. There's a nettle rash starting on your back, and probably your bum. You still have a bruised nose and black eyes from football. And there's a lump the size of an egg on the top of your head... How can you possibly still have a hard-on?" There was no stopping it. She dissolved into laughter.

Brodie smoothed out a blue tartan blanket on top of the tarp before testing the whole area gingerly. When he was done, he nodded, then strode toward her with a look of maniacal determination. "You're still dressed."

"Brodie, I hate to say it, but the mood has passed." She wasn't lying either. For a second there, she'd been about to experience Nirvana and now, she mainly felt sorry for him.

"Is that right?" One hand clasped her nape, the other the small of her back, as his mouth covered hers.

And just like that, the mood returned.

With a vengeance.

IF THERE WAS one quality that defined Brodie, it was tenacity. A fact he was more than grateful for, considering how damn hard it was to get anywhere with the woman in his arms. It was as though the universe was out to sabotage him. Well, the universe didn't know who it was dealing with because nothing short of unconsciousness, or Katya herself, would get in his way this time.

"Jeans," he growled against her mouth before resuming their intimate duel.

"What?" she said on a gasp.

Taking matters into his own hands, he unfastened her jeans and pushed them down over her hips. "Kick them off."

"Stop moving your mouth away," she complained, looking more than a little dazed.

He undid the braid in her hair, setting her long, wavy

tresses free. "Don't you remember promising I could kiss you wherever I wanted?"

It took a second for his meaning to register. "I need help with my jeans." Katya leaned over to tug at them, lost her balance, and landed on the blanket in a tangled heap. "Maybe we should do this another time," she grumbled.

"Hell no, this is happening right now. I don't care if the sky falls on us, we aren't stopping for anything." He rolled her onto her back and tugged her jeans down her legs—taking her red lace panties with them.

"Nice." He twirled them around with a finger. "Girly."

"Well, I *am* a girl," she protested.

"Aye, so I see." His hands on the inside of her knees, he eased her legs apart, his eyes focused on the prize. "Now we're getting to the good stuff."

"Brodie!" Katya playfully smacked his shoulder.

"I'm going in," he told her solemnly. "I may be some time."

She was laughing when his mouth found its target, and then she released a breathless gasp.

Her perfume was heady, her taste divine. She was his own special treat or willing playmate to torture—depending on their mood. Right now, he was starving for her. Cradling her backside in his hands, he angled her closer to his mouth and lapped at her until she squirmed and begged for mercy.

Breathless, he lifted his head. "I'm sorry. Did you say something?"

"Brodie, stop being evil," she complained, her heels digging into his back.

"Evil would be slowing down or even taking a break." He ran the tip of his finger over her cute wee clit, delighting at the pink swollen sight in front of him. "I *can* be evil...if that's what you think I am."

"No. I'm sorry!" she wailed. "I didn't say anything. Not a word. Carry on."

"Thanks. I think I will." He lifted her back to his mouth and set about driving her straight up and over until she screamed out his name and clawed at his shoulders.

Suddenly desperate for her, Brodie shucked his jeans and stalked up her body. The sight of her flushed cheeks, swollen lips, and heavy lashes was almost enough to send him over the edge. But not until he was inside her.

Katya curled her leg around his hip. "Stop being such a big baby and get over here," she whispered.

"You always did know how to sweet-talk me." He surged inside her, finding her mouth to swallow her moan.

For a moment, the delight of being joined together, after so long, almost overwhelmed him. He wanted to lie there forever, feeling Katya surround him. Feeling her wet heat as it cradled his hard length. Knowing that was where he belonged.

She tore her mouth from his. "Move." Her heels bounced on his backside.

"If I move, this will be over a whole lot faster than I'd like."

"Then we'll just do it all over again." She tightened her inner muscles on his hard length.

"Damn it, Kat," he moaned as he buried his face in her neck.

The witch chuckled.

"Fine, have it your way," he complained.

And he moved.

IT WAS after the third time they'd made love, and were still lying on the ground under the wing of her plane, that something occurred to Katya. She rested her chin on Brodie's chest and stared up at him as she doodled on his skin with the tip of her finger. "Should we have used condoms?"

"I don't know, should we?"

"I'm on the pill. What about you?" She held her breath, waiting for his answer.

She was no fool—she knew he hadn't been celibate these past ten years—all she was asking was that he'd been responsible too.

"No, I'm not on the pill," the idiot teased.

Katya bit him.

"Fine, I'm clean and healthy, and apparently desperate, because I want to do that all over again."

Relief flooded through her, letting her relax back into him. "What are we? Sixteen? I need food. And a bed. The ground's getting cold now that the sun's fading." She pouted up at him. "Besides, you promised me deep-fried pizza."

"Well, as we've established, a promise is a promise." As he caressed her back, Brodie stilled beneath her, and her every instinct went on alert.

"Don't say anything," she warned. "Let's agree not to analyze this. It is what it is."

"Okay." He shifted slightly, putting his arm under his head to better see her. "I want to say one thing though—"

"No!" She slapped her hand over his mouth, knowing nothing good would come of a naked heart-to-heart.

Brodie gently clasped her wrist and removed her hand. "I regret not going with you all those years ago."

Her heart skipped a beat before it sank.

"Why did you have to say that? Didn't I tell you not to? Now you've ruined everything." Katya scrambled off him to search for her discarded clothes. Finding her jeans first, she shimmied into them. Almost rolling her eyes at Brodie's fascination with her bouncing boobs as she did so.

He cleared his throat when she pulled on her shirt, spoiling his view. "We need to talk. There's no point in pretending we don't have a history."

"Exactly." She pointed at him as she checked behind clumps of overgrown weeds for her shoes. "It's history. Which means it should stay in the past."

Brodie cocked an eyebrow at her and pointed upward— at her *historical* aircraft.

"That's different." She found one of his shoes and tossed it at him, possibly a little harder than necessary. "What good can come of us digging up old arguments?"

"I'm not arguing, Kat. I'm just saying I've started seeing things in a different light this past week, and I've realized I should have gone with you." He sat up and bent his legs, then rested his arms on them. "I was dumb. Young and dumb. I figured if you really loved me, you wouldn't completely change our lives purely because you'd found something more interesting than what we'd planned. That's why I gave you an ultimatum, never believing for one minute you'd actually leave. It was ego. Childish, pathetic ego mixed in with fear of the unknown. I'm sorry."

"No, you're not. You meant every word you said back then." *Where the hell was her other shoe?*

"I didn't. I wanted to make you hurt as much as you'd hurt me. I thought you were rejecting me, that's why I over-reacted."

"How could I reject you when I was asking you to come with me?" she snapped as she scooped up her underwear.

"Like I said, young and stupid."

Katya stuffed her underwear into the pockets of her

jeans. All she wanted was to run while shouting nonsense at the top of her lungs, her fingers stuffed in her ears. She didn't want to hear another word, didn't want to know he'd finally realized he should have come with her. That the ten years apart had been a mistake.

There was too much cruelty in thinking about all the time they'd wasted when they'd been apart.

She spun on him. "It's great you're having some sort of epiphany. Good for you. You can't rewrite history while you're doing it though. I remember every word you hurled at me back then, and you were right. I'm a Savage, through and through. I thought I was different, but it turns out I'm not. I'm just like every other member of my family who chases crazy ideas and plans weird schemes. I know that now."

There was her shoe!

She fell on it and tugged it on. Hopping on one foot to do so, desperate to escape.

"I didn't mean it, any of it," he said earnestly.

"It doesn't matter because it doesn't change the one thing that will always stand between us." Her heart throbbed with pain. "I left. Not you. Me. I took your ultimatum seriously and stopped believing you'd come around. How do you apologize for that, Brodie? How do I?"

She grabbed his jeans, removed his keys from the pocket, and proceeded to steal his car, yet again. Stranding Brodie with her plane, and hoping that this time, he'd leave it where she'd put it.

32

February 1946

Scotland

Word of Tom and Natasha's engagement quickly spread. Fearing Ben would hear from someone else before she could tell him, Natasha found someone who was going to be driving past the Baxters' farm and asked for a lift.

However, in her haste to get to Ben, she forgot one important thing. She was no longer wearing the American soldier's coat Ben had found for her; instead, she was still wearing Tom's gift. It was a slap in the face to the man who'd done so much for her, and she couldn't understand how she'd remembered to take off Tom's ring, but not his coat.

Thick snow coated the hills as her driver made his way up to the Baxter house. Even in her woolen coat, a shiver still ran through Natasha when she caught sight of Ben's family home. It always seemed so lifeless compared to the rest of Invertary, something others noticed too. Betty, one of her landlady's teens, believed the place to be haunted—by the victims of a mass-murdering Baxter who'd passed on his insanity to Ben. Betty McLeod had her own unique way of thinking about things that was often rather concerning.

"Are you sure you want to go in there?" asked Mr. MacCabe. "The laird has no' been in the best of moods lately." The old man's grey bushy eyebrows frowned as he considered the house.

"I'll be fine, thank you."

Mr. MacCabe appeared unconvinced. "You know, I could do with a cup of tea. I wonder if his housekeeper would mind making me one. Then, if I'm still here when you've finished your business with the Baxters, I'd be happy to give you a lift back into town."

"But you were on your way to somewhere."

"Aye." He looked worried. "It can wait."

It was a testament to the depths of Natasha's anxiety that she didn't turn down his offer. "Thank you. You're very kind," she said instead.

Together, they made their way up the snow-cleared path to the imposing front door.

"I don't see a chimney going," Mr. MacCabe said. "Maybe there's nobody here."

The door swung open, and Ben's young housekeeper smiled tightly at them.

"Hello, Anne." Natasha had always been friendly toward the woman, even though she was often short in return. "Is Ben home?"

Anne tightened the shawl around her shoulders. "Mr. Baxter's no' in the mood for company. It would be best if you came back another day." Her hand moved to the door.

"Please." Natasha took a step forward, blocking the

entrance and preventing the housekeeper from shutting them out. "It's urgent that I speak with him."

A flicker of uncertainty crossed Anne's face, reminding Natasha that the woman cared very much for her employer. "I haven't seen him for a couple of days. He's not left his rooms."

"Perhaps you wouldn't mind fixing Mr. MacCabe a nice cup of tea while I talk with Ben?" Natasha gestured for the man to go ahead of her into the house. "I can find my own way to Ben's rooms."

"Aye." Anne turned icy. "I'm sure you can." She turned on her heel, her back ramrod straight under the tight knot of hair at her nape. "Come with me, Mr. MacCabe. I've a teapot on the go in the kitchen."

With a worried glance at Natasha, he followed the housekeeper deeper into the house.

Natasha turned to the stairs that wound up from the entryway. With each step she took, her stomach lurched. A brittle laugh escaped as she registered the irony of being able to fly into a war zone in the dark, face off against the enemy, and return to base only to do it all over again, and yet the thought of speaking with Ben Baxter had her quaking in her shoes.

The house felt chilled as she walked along the corridor to the set of rooms Ben called his own. He had cousins who also considered the farm home, but none of them had yet returned to Invertary after the war. Their rooms were shut up and unused, making the house seem even more deserted. Natasha couldn't help but feel as though she were walking through a mausoleum rather than a grand farmhouse.

At the end of the corridor, she took a shaky breath and knocked on his door.

"Go away," Ben bellowed.

"Ben? It's Tasha," she called back, steeling herself for whatever came next.

The door flew open, and Ben stood there, looking haggard and unkempt. His gaunt face was unshaven, his shirt partially tucked into his trousers, and his hair obviously hadn't seen a comb in days.

"I'm glad you're here." He reached out, clasped her arm, and tugged her into the room. "I was going to come see you later because I've been thinking about the gold, you see." Unfocused eyes met hers as he leaned in closer. "I've figured out why the Nazis took it. You know, the gold from their victims. That gold." The stench of whisky coming from him was almost overwhelming.

"Maybe we could open a window and let in some fresh air," she suggested, gingerly stepping over the books and papers strewn across the floor.

"No." He rushed around her to block her path. "If you open them, they'll see in."

"Who'll see in, Ben?"

"The Nazis!" He thrust a hand through his hair. "Who else would we be talking about? We're in the middle of a war, Tasha. You, better than anyone, should know that."

Her heart physically ached as she gentled her voice. "The war's over, Ben."

He appeared disoriented for a second. "I know that. Don't you think I know that? It doesn't mean they aren't still out there planning something, though."

With a sweep of his hand, he cleared some books off an armchair and dropped into it.

Natasha, meanwhile, counted the empty bottles of whisky underneath the side table by his chair. "When did you last eat?"

"That doesn't matter." He abruptly leaned forward in his

seat. "I need you to get a message to the high command in London. I need you to tell them about the gold. I can't do it. I'm being watched."

"How about we see if Anne could bring up some soup first?" She rang for the housekeeper. "While we eat, we can make plans."

"Yes. Yes. That's a good idea."

"It will take a few minutes to talk to her and for her to return with the food," Natasha added. "Would you like to bathe and change while we wait? That way, you'll feel fresh when we have our discussion. For a conversation this important, we should both be in top form."

Ben shot to his feet, smiling at her. "I knew you were the right person to talk to about this. You always understand exactly what's needed. I won't be long." He paused at the door to his bedroom. "Don't bother her for hot water; the cold will do fine for bathing. And ask her to bring another bottle of whisky up with the soup, would you?"

Once the door closed behind him, Natasha let out a tense hiss of a breath and started clearing some of the mess. While putting books back on the built-in bookshelves on the far wall, she heard a knock on the door.

Anne's hopeful expression hardened when she realized Ben wasn't in the room. Then she noticed the mess and gasped, a hand fluttering to her mouth.

"I've managed to talk him into eating something," Natasha said. "Maybe soup?"

Anne nodded. "I have some on the stove."

Natasha gathered the empty whisky bottles and handed them to the housekeeper. "He also wants more whisky. I think it might be best if we forgot that request."

"Is he...is he well?" Anne's eyes strayed to the closed bedroom door.

Natasha sighed. "I don't think so. It may be an idea to send a message to Fort William and ask for a doctor to visit."

"Are you...?" Anne seemed to gather herself. "Will you be staying to look after him, then?"

"No, Anne, that's not my place." She tucked her hands into the pockets of the coat her fiancé had given her. It felt like she was wearing his embrace, and—heaven help her—she needed it.

The housekeeper took a step back as though struck. "Not your place? *Not your place?*" Her voice rose with each word.

"Please." Natasha cast a nervous glance at the bedroom door. "Keep your voice down. Ben's distressed enough."

"Aye, I can tell you're very concerned about him." Anne closed the distance between them. "Perhaps not as upset as a proper wife should be, though."

Natasha reeled.

"Aye," Anne sneered. "Your secret isn't as well hidden as you think. I know very well you married Ben just to get out of Germany. You took advantage of a good man's soft heart, and now here you are, flaunting your new lover in front of him. Have you no shame?"

"What?" Natasha whispered.

"Everybody's heard the news of Tom's proposal and his gift of a fine new coat. Does he know you're already married and you don't care one whit about your husband?"

The blood drained from Natasha's face—she felt every last drop of it go.

"I can see Tom doesn't know," Anne said. "Then perhaps somebody should tell him, before you con another man into looking after you." The housekeeper spun on her heel and headed for the door.

"No." Natasha grabbed her arm. "You don't understand,

and you can't tell anyone. Marrying Ben was to help me get out of the country."

Anne snorted. "Then I'd say I do understand."

"No, you don't. It was Ben's idea, and it was never meant to be anything more than a piece of paper."

Fury shone from the housekeeper's eyes. "Then why does he take that piece of paper out of his safe every night and stare at it? And why haven't you divorced him?" Her face twisted in pain. "Why can't you release him to find someone who does love him?"

"Someone like you?" Natasha whispered.

It was Anne's turn to pale. "I don't know what you mean."

"You have to believe me," Natasha said. "I've asked Ben for a divorce on several occasions, but he won't even talk about it. I came here this afternoon to try one more time."

"What happens if he says no? Will you go ahead and marry Tom anyway?" She shook her head in disgust. "Women like you belong in jail."

Anne tried to shake off Natasha's hold, but she couldn't let the woman go. Not when she didn't know what she would say or to whom.

"Please listen to me. I'm telling the truth. There's nothing between Ben and me but a barely legal piece of paper. It's Tom I love. Please don't ruin things for us. Please don't tell Tom about the marriage certificate. I don't think Ben even believes it to be real. He won't discuss it, and he won't divorce me. All he does is pretend it doesn't exist. What am I supposed to do?"

"How about honoring your legally wed husband?" Ben said. "Is that too much to ask?"

The two women spun to face him.

"Ben?" Natasha whispered.

"I'll get the soup." Anne turned and fled, leaving Natasha to the weight of Ben's glare.

"I came to tell you about Tom," she said as reasonably as she could.

"To tell me what? That he doesn't know you're already married?" For some reason, his clean-shaven face made him appear even more disturbed.

"We aren't married, Ben. Not in reality. It was all pretend, and you know it. Don't misunderstand me—I owe you my life, and you will always be a dear, dear friend, but I don't love you." She held out a hand in supplication. "You don't love me either."

"So, you can read my mind now too?"

"You don't acknowledge our marriage! I can't even get you to talk about it, so I'd say that was a strong indication of your feelings toward me."

"I was giving you time to fall in love with me," he roared, making Natasha cower from his rage.

The door burst open, and Mr. MacCabe rushed in. He glanced nervously between them before wetting his lips. "Are you all right, miss?"

"Yes, thank you." There was nothing else to say. "I think it's best that I leave now," she told Ben. "We'll talk about this another time." She stuffed her hands into her pockets to hide their shaking.

"Aye, we will," Ben said, and it sounded like a threat.

Without looking at her friend or saying goodbye, Natasha let Mr. MacCabe lead her from the room. For the first time since they'd met, Natasha was fearful of being alone with Ben.

As they made their way down the stairs, they passed the housekeeper returning with a tray of food.

Natasha placed a hand on the young woman's arm to stop her. "Be careful," she whispered. "He isn't himself."

Anne hesitated, then nodded. "I understand now," she said quietly before climbing the rest of the stairs.

Quietly, Natasha and Mr. MacCabe let themselves out of the Baxter farmhouse.

33

Brodie had been kicked out of his own house and told to wait by the car for Katya. Apparently, his pacing was annoying his brothers. Well, boo-bloody-hoo for them. They hadn't been locked out of their own bedrooms by their estranged wives and politely told to take it elsewhere by her best friend.

He'd spent a crappy night tossing and turning on a sofa with less padding than Paris Hilton's backside, and hardly an area on his body wasn't in pain. What the sofa hadn't bruised had already been bashed by either nature, stupidity, or an Aberfoyle cross kick.

His nose hurt, the bruises around his eyes had turned a fetching shade of puke-yellow, an itchy rash covered chunks of his back and bum, and his head throbbed from where he'd hit it on a plane. *A plane.* Even he knew that was a new kind of low. And on top of all his many aches and pains, Katya was now giving him the silent treatment—over an apology.

Aye, Brodie wasn't having a good day. And they hadn't even made it to the lawyer's office.

Leaning back against the driver's side of his SUV, he crossed his ankles and stuffed his hands into the pockets of his trousers. To add insult to injury, he was wearing his funeral suit. His charcoal-gray trousers and jacket, paired with a matching white shirt, was the best suit he owned, and he figured he needed all the help he could get to make a good impression at the lawyer's.

Not that it mattered when his face resembled a bag of plums, he had trouble sitting still for more than two minutes, and his feet were developing blisters in his rarely worn dress shoes.

"Katya," he roared at the house, losing patience with, well, everything. "Katya, get out here."

The door opened, and she stepped outside, glaring at him. "Keep your hair on."

Whatever irritation he'd felt melted away at the sight of her. Holy crap, she was gorgeous. She wore a form-fitting dress that came to just below her knees. It wasn't low cut, had sensible cap sleeves, and didn't cling to her like cellophane. And yet, it was the sexiest thing he'd ever seen. He didn't have a clue what it was made of, but it flowed with her every movement, skimming over her body in a blue wave that reminded him of water over pebbles.

"Shut your mouth, Brodie. With your luck, you'll swallow a fly and choke." Her hips swayed with every step she took toward him, and his gaze slid down her body to her feet.

"Matching high-heeled sandals?" With little crisscross buckles that begged to be undone.

"Denise dressed me." She folded her arms as she stopped in front of him, daring him to comment.

He swallowed hard. "What's in the teeny wee bag?"

"Mace."

Aye, that was his girl.

She tossed her hair over her shoulder, letting it flow down her back in a cascade of silken waves. "Are we going or what?"

That's when he noticed the ring on her left hand. The matching partner to the silver Celtic knot band he'd dug out of the box at the back of his underwear drawer and slipped on his finger that morning.

"You still have your ring?" The world seemed to wobble beneath his feet.

"So?" She planted her hands on her hips in challenge.

Brodie leaned away from the car. Suddenly, the day wasn't looking as bad as he'd feared. He'd just remembered something important about Katya—it wasn't what she said you needed to pay attention to, it was what she did.

"Where did you store the ring?" He took an oh-so-casual step toward her.

Her cheeks turned pink. "At my parents' house."

He took another step. "Whereabouts in your parents' house?"

Katya's eyes narrowed. "Why does it matter?"

"You can't remember?" he challenged, standing a hair's breadth away from her now.

"Of course, I can remember. It was in the...box." She couldn't look him in the eye.

"The box?"

"You know. The jewelry box."

"Kat," he teased, knowing she wouldn't answer him if he came across too heavy. "Have you been carrying my ring around with you? Did you hold it as you fell asleep and think of me?"

Her frown was adorable. "I took it with me in case I needed something else to sell."

"Aye, so you did." Brodie clasped her nape. "I'm going to kiss you now. Please do me a favor and don't knee me in the balls. It's one of the few places I have left that doesn't hurt."

His lips found hers before she could argue. For a split second, it was touch and go with his balls, but then she melted into him. Arms wrapped around his shoulders, and he couldn't resist turning to press her up against his car. Their kiss was slow, and sensual, and lingering...and tinged with desperation—well, on his part.

"You're going to be late for the lawyer," one of his brothers shouted.

Reluctantly, Brodie ended the kiss, pleased when Katya whined her displeasure. Darach was leaning out their living room window and Brodie shot him the one-fingered salute before walking Katya around to the passenger side and opening the door for her.

"The ring doesn't mean anything," she lied through kiss-swollen lips.

"I know," he said, humoring her before practically tap dancing around to the driver's seat.

CATHERINE BAXTER WORE a twinset and pearls to accompany the smug smile on her face. Her hair was in a pristine French knot, and she was bookended by two expensive-looking lawyers who wore matching black suits. The older woman should have seemed diminutive between the men, instead, she came across as queen to their knights.

"As you can see from the statements and evidence I've put together this past week," Lawrence Mayburn said from their side of the table in his small conference room, "Mr.

and Mrs. MacGregor are very much in a full, committed marriage."

The lawyer to Kitty's left slid the documents folder back to Lawrence. "It would certainly appear that's the case," he said.

Katya almost squealed with glee, but Brodie's hand on her knee stopped her. When she caught his eye, he didn't appear as convinced as she was that they'd won.

"However," his matching lawyer said, "I'm afraid it isn't this past week that's in question. It's the past ten years." He opened the much thicker folder on the table in front of him. "We have substantial proof that, although married in name, the MacGregors have not lived as a couple for almost a decade."

Lawrence didn't appear fazed, making Katya think he was worth every penny she'd paid him—on a monthly installment basis—to cover anything that came up while she'd been away. "Many modern couples spend substantial amounts of time apart. Mrs. MacGregor had to travel for work, and it took her away for long periods. Who are we to judge what does or doesn't constitute a stable marriage?"

"It isn't the stability of this marriage that's under question, it's the reality of it." The lawyer turned to a page close to the start of the folder. "In his notes about this gift, Mr. Benjamin Baxter made it crystal clear that it hinged on the couple remaining in a committed marital relationship. Mr. and Mrs. MacGregor have spent no time together in a decade." He passed Lawrence a sheet of paper. "This is a list of their acquaintances who've signed statements for our client on this account. Of course, if this case goes to court, we will call on closer friends and family to testify under oath as to the amount of time the couple has spent in each other's company."

To Katya's dismay, Lawrence said nothing to refute their argument.

"Further to this matter," lawyer two continued, "the MacGregors have separate bank accounts, emergency contacts, and home addresses." As he slid another piece of paper across the table, Catherine practically preened with glee.

"This isn't evidence of a complete breakdown in their marital relationship," Lawrence said. "Many couples maintain separate accounts and emergency contact details. Some even keep separate homes."

"True," lawyer one said. "Although, we also have sworn statements from women Mr. MacGregor has had relationships with over the past ten years. Documents that clearly state Mr. MacGregor referred to Mrs. MacGregor as his ex-wife and to their marriage as being over in all but name."

"We also have witness accounts of an argument between Fraser Savage and Joseph MacGregor in the Scottie Dog pub three years ago," lawyer two added. "Several witnesses recall both men shouting that their children were only staying legally tied together to keep the land."

Katya's hand covered Brodie's, and he turned his to thread their fingers together.

"Look," lawyer one said, "no one wants this to go to court. It would involve hefty costs for both of our clients. It would be best for all concerned if we could resolve this situation today to prevent that from happening."

"You can't win," lawyer two said with obviously fake sympathy. "You've openly flaunted the terms of the gift for ten years. Our client has lost patience with the situation and would like the deed to her land returned immediately. We all know that if this goes to court, you don't have a hope of proving the MacGregors haven't lived as a divorced couple for years."

"This past week—" Lawrence started.

"Is irrelevant," lawyer two finished.

Smiling like a cat about to devour a mouse, Catherine leaned forward. "If you don't mind, I'd like a word with Brodie in private."

"What?" Katya and Brodie said at the same time.

Brodie's hand tightened on hers as he faced off against Catherine. "Anything you want to say to me can be said in front of my *wife*."

Catherine chuckled dryly. "I'd prefer this was a private conversation. Are you sure you want to dismiss what I have to say without even hearing what it is first?"

"Our firm wishes to make it clear we have advised Ms. Baxter against this course of action," lawyer one said without emotion.

Katya didn't know what to think, and from the look on Brodie's face, neither did he. They turned to Lawrence.

"It's up to you," he said helpfully.

"I won't wait forever, Brodie." Catherine Baxter stood. "You have five minutes, and then I'm leaving. In the meantime, I'll let my lawyers deal with the details while you decide whether it's worth taking me on in court. Lawrence, may I wait in your office?"

Her question must have been rhetorical, because Kitty strode from the room without waiting for an answer.

34

___

There was a moment's silence after Catherine Baxter's exit before lawyer one addressed the room. "Shall we schedule a follow-up meeting for tomorrow?"

"Speak to my receptionist on your way out," Lawrence said. "She'll set something up."

Catherine's lawyers both stood and simultaneously buttoned their jackets.

"We'll refrain from filing papers with the Sheriff Court until we meet tomorrow," lawyer one said. "You have until then to decide whether you wish to contest this before a judge. Good afternoon." He nodded at them before they both let themselves out of the conference room.

"It doesn't feel like a good afternoon," Brodie muttered.

As the door closed behind them, Katya's hands began to shake. "We're going to lose our land, aren't we?" Her throat tightened, and she wasn't sure whether she wanted to burst into tears or kick the nearest wall. "The witch is going to take it from us."

"We don't know that for sure." Brodie ran a hand up and

down her arm in a caress meant to comfort. Unfortunately, he sounded about as optimistic as she felt.

"Lawrence?" Katya asked. "What do we do?"

"You have a couple of options." He stacked the papers in front of him. "You can fight this in a court, or you can give her the deed to the land. Only you can make that decision."

"But you have an opinion, right?" Katya said. "What would you advise?"

Lawrence rested his clasped hands on the table. "I'd advise you take time to discuss this before making a decision. It would be remiss of me to give you hope in this instance, which means I have to impress upon you both that your chances of winning this case are slim at best."

"Slim?" All Katya heard was that they had a chance. "That means there's a possibility we could win and keep our land?"

Lawrence ran a hand through his hair, leaving it remarkably unruffled. "I said there's a *slight* chance you'd win. The case would hinge on Ben's intent, which is difficult to prove. The wording in the conditions attached to the gift isn't as airtight as I would like, which means there's room for interpretation. They have a note, written in Ben's hand, that makes it clear he intended for you to use the land together, as a happily married couple. That won't help our case. Add to that, the slew of witnesses to both Ben's intention and your estrangement this past decade, and the pursuer has a solid case for you breaking the conditions of the gift."

"But we could win?" Katya asked again, a desperate sinking sensation in her gut. "If we fought? I mean, we could supply our own witnesses and bring up Catherine's unnatural hatred of all things Savage-family related. If we were anyone else, she wouldn't be doing this. I know of at least three other people Ben gifted parcels of land to, and she hasn't said a peep to them since."

"Yes, we could go that route." Lawrence was solemn. "Although, you need to take into consideration that it would be a lengthy and, most likely, costly course of action. With no guaranteed outcome."

"Lawrence," Brodie said, "friend to friend, what do you think?"

Their lawyer sat back in his seat and gave them a pitying smile. "Friend to friend? I'd have to say you're screwed. My best advice is to return the land and carry on with your lives, because Ms. Baxter is out for blood, and she won't stop until she gets it. She will bankrupt you both out of pure spite."

Katya couldn't sit still any longer. As she paced the length of the room, she tried to think of a way out of their situation. There had to be something they could do to make Catherine back off. When she stumbled over Lawrence's ancient rug for the third time, she kicked off her borrowed shoes, wishing she could do the same with the dress Denise made her wear. If she was about to lose her future, she'd rather be in her favorite comfortable jeans when it happened.

"What if we countersued her for persecuting my family? This isn't the only time she's gone after us." Even she knew she was grasping at straws.

"I'd have to repeat my earlier advice," Lawrence said. "It would be a difficult case to bring before the court, and it could be lengthy and expensive. Also, I'm uncertain what it would achieve. She would still carry on with her plans to take the land from you."

"Could we pay her to make her go away?" Brodie asked grimly.

Katya wanted to scream at the hopelessness of it all. "I

don't have anything to pay her. Pretty much everything I own is wrapped up in my plane."

"I have the money I set aside to build my house."

Katya gasped at the enormity of Brodie's offer. "Then you'd have the land but no money to build."

"Also," Lawrence added, "I suspect that even if you did have enough cash to cover the cost of the land, Ms. Baxter wouldn't take it. This is personal for her. It isn't about the money."

"No. It isn't. It's about the Savages." Katya let out an angry growl toward the ceiling. "I don't know how to fix this. I'm not even sure it's possible. The woman's held a grudge for such a long time. So long that everyone involved is dead."

"She doesn't want things fixed anyway," Brodie said. "Where's the fun in that when she can make a Savage's life miserable instead?"

"I feel," Lawrence said, "you both have to seriously consider returning the deed. It may be your only option to get out of this situation without sustaining too much damage."

"We need the land." Katya pressed a hand to her diaphragm, finding it increasingly difficult to breathe. "I can't afford another property. If I don't have the land, there will be no scenic flight business and no museum."

"Aye, and I'd quite like to build my house an' all," Brodie commented dryly.

Their lawyer heaved a sigh. "Listen to yourselves. You can't even agree on what to do with the land."

"No," Katya said slowly, her heart in her throat. "I know what to do with it. We're going to split it. Brodie can have the half with the best view for his house, and I'll have the back section for the museum and runway."

"That's not a lot of space, Kat." Brodie's expression softened at her offer.

"The plane doesn't need a lot to get off the ground. I can make it work. And we can plant trees along the boundary, so you don't have to stare at tourists all day long."

The intensity of his gaze made her cheeks burn. "You do realize your museum won't have a view from the back paddock."

She waved a dismissive hand, her heart racing. "They'll see plenty of view when they're up in the plane."

"A week ago, you wanted me off the land for good," Brodie said quietly.

"Yeah, well, I'm a pragmatist, and half of the land is better than none. Which is what we'll get if Kitty Baxter has her way."

"I think you're both getting ahead of yourselves," Lawrence said. "There's no point in discussing how to divvy up the land you'll likely lose. You need to deal with one issue at a time, and Ms. Baxter's lawsuit is the most pressing."

Katya glared up at the ceiling. "Is it too much to ask that this whole situation just goes away?" she prayed. Understandably, God wasn't interested in a prayer that told him off at the same time as asking for something. She looked back at Lawrence. "How big of a suspect would we be if the mighty Ms. Baxter were to go missing?"

"Don't even joke about that." Lawrence was serious.

"Do you have any other ideas?" Frustration made Katya want to strike out at anyone in her path. "Because I'm fresh out."

"I have an idea," Brodie said evenly. "Maybe I should go see what she has to say."

Katya immediately stopped pacing. "We don't negotiate

with terrorists, remember? We agreed on that when we were thirteen and your brothers tried to blackmail us when they caught us kissing after school."

"This is a little different." He leaned forward to rest his forearms on his knees. "They only wanted chocolate in return for not running to tell our parents. Catherine might have something to say that will help us keep our land."

"Like what?" Honestly, was he *trying* to infuriate her?

"I don't know, which is why I think I should talk to her, Kat. We have nothing to lose anyway, so I might as well."

Katya wanted to rage at the injustice of it all, because Brodie was right. "Fine. But I don't like it."

"Neither do I," Brodie said as he headed for the door.

Catherine Baxter stood at the window in Lawrence's office, looking out toward the hills.

"A minute to spare," she said without turning as Brodie entered the room. "I was beginning to wonder if you'd come at all."

Brodie closed the door behind him but didn't bother to take a seat. Instead, he stood in the middle of Lawrence's office, with its dark wood and brown leather décor, and got straight to the point. "What's this about then?"

When she turned to face him, her demeanor was positively gleeful. "It's about the land. I have an offer to make you."

"I'm listening." He pushed his suit jacket aside to shove his hands into the pockets of his trousers. Mainly to stop himself from giving in to the temptation to strangle her.

Kitty sauntered around the desk to lean against it. "I've

never had a problem with the MacGregors, which means I don't have a problem with you."

"Have to say"—Brodie rocked back on his heels—"it definitely doesn't look like that's the case."

"The truth of the matter is, I can't live with the knowledge that a Savage owns a piece of Baxter land. A MacGregor, on the other hand, *that* I wouldn't have an issue with."

A chill ran up Brodie's spine. "What are you saying, Catherine?"

"I'm willing to make you an offer." She picked a piece of lint from the sleeve of her lavender cardigan. "Divorce Katya, end the marriage for good, and the land will be yours." She held up a hand. "Before you think you can divorce her to keep the land, only to remarry once you have it, I'll need you to sign some paperwork I had my lawyers draw up." She tapped a finger on the folder lying on the desk beside her hip. "You must agree to have nothing to do with Katya or the Savages, otherwise the land will revert to my ownership."

A stillness came over Brodie as her offer sank in. He recognized his reaction as the intense focus brought on by a sudden rush of adrenaline. "The Baxters enjoy giving gifts that come with conditions, don't they?"

Her smile reminded him of a shark. "I did learn from the best. Although my father had the right idea, with the wrong execution. He made the mistake of believing you two wouldn't try to defraud him. However, I'm a wee bit more cautious. For you to gain my trust, I'll require a signature."

"Let me get this right." Brodie clenched his hands into tight fists within his pockets. "To have the land, without fear of you coming after it, I need to turn my back on my wife?"

She chuckled dryly. "It's not like I'm asking you to do something you haven't done before."

"And," he continued evenly, ignoring her mirth, "if I sign on the dotted line and agree to your conditions, I'll get to build my house and live happily ever after without having to hear another word from you?"

"We don't even need to acknowledge each other on the street." Catherine patted at her perfectly styled hair. "Let's face it, Brodie, it's not like you'd be sacrificing a whole lot to get what you really want. You haven't set eyes on your *wife* in years. Don't think for one second I believe the story you two have been shoveling all over town. Renewed romance?" She cocked an eyebrow. "You're back in love again and ready to set up home for real this time? Aye, and I have a tower in London I'd like to sell you."

Brodie didn't bother setting her straight on any of her misconceptions. After all, she wasn't the only one in town who believed his relationship with Katya was all for show. "What I'm wondering is why you'd make this offer in the first place. The land would still be gone, even if a Savage didn't live on it."

"Because"—her eyes glinted with malice—"knowing you still had the land would drive the Savages crazy."

"You hate them that much?"

"You saw the marriage certificate, Brodie. Tom Savage stole the love of my father's life out from under his nose, making bigamists of them all. Making me a *bastard*. Leaving my mother to suffer a loveless marriage because her husband's mind was always elsewhere—on the woman he truly loved." She scoffed. "You grew up in a happy family, which means you have no idea what it's like to live in one that's cold and distant. Did you know that right up until Natasha died she still had clandestine meetings with Ben? I saw them. Sitting by the loch in the dark, whispering to each other. Humiliating my mother while they did it.

Natasha Savage had no shame, and Tom Savage betrayed his best friend. So, yes, I do hate them that much."

"Bitterness will kill you, Catherine," Brodie said quietly, knowing the woman wouldn't listen.

And she didn't. She completely ignored his comment and pointed at the folder. "Take some time to look over the paperwork, but I'll require a decision by the end of the day. I'll be at the town meeting tonight if you'd like to talk in person. Remember, Brodie, this offer is for you only, and it disappears in the morning. If I were you, I'd jump on it while I had the chance."

With her jaw set and her head held high, Catherine Baxter swept out of the room, leaving him to stare at the folder—the contents of which could change his life forever.

Calmly, Brodie walked across the faded Persian carpet to the desk.

He picked up a pen.

Then he opened the folder.

35

February 1946

Scotland

I t was the monthly town meeting, and everyone would be present. Tom had insisted Natasha accompany him for the evening, saying it was the finest entertainment Invertary could provide. After her visit with Ben that afternoon, she didn't much feel like being around people, but spending time with Tom was too tempting to resist.

"We've no official town council," Tom told Natasha as he opened the door for her.

He'd already explained they held their meetings in the Presbyterian church at the top of the high street, as it was one of the few buildings in town big enough to seat everyone. It was also considered neutral territory because the vicar didn't have a business that would benefit from everyone meeting in his church—although he had been known to use the meetings to chase up lapsed parishioners.

"If there's no official town council, why is there a meeting?" Natasha asked as they settled on worn wooden seats at the front of the church hall, close to one of the iron radiators.

A glance around the large barren room, with its high ceilings and tall, thin windows, revealed all the attendees shared the same idea. Small groups huddled beside each radiator, while the center of the room had yet to fill.

"I said there's no *official* council, but we do have ourselves an *unofficial* one. The local government doesn't recognize the council, which doesn't stop them from running things." Tom took off his coat, folded it, and draped it over his knee, before pointing at the row of people sitting in the pulpit. "The old man who looks like a bulldog? That's our unofficial mayor, Angus McTavish, who runs the post office. Some say he got the job as mayor because he had access to the votes and counted himself in as the winner. I say it's because no one else wanted it."

Natasha's new fiancé had a way of making even the most mundane event seem like an adventure. She could have listened to him for hours.

Tom shifted in his seat until they sat pressed together from thigh to shoulder, smiling down at her as if she were the center of his universe. "That man in the clerical collar is Vicar MacDonald. He likes to consider himself neutral ground during discussions. The woman is Irene Shaw; she's a teacher at the local primary school and is really the one in charge. If you want anything done, you ask Irene."

"Why is there an empty seat on the platform?"

His smile dimmed. "That's Ben's. At one time, he was the voice of reason on the council. We're keeping it open for him until he feels up to coming back."

Natasha pressed a hand to her roiling stomach at the

thought of Ben and how disturbed he'd been that afternoon. It was clear he needed some professional help, and if his housekeeper didn't call a doctor by the morning, she intended to do it herself.

People slowly filed into the room, greeting Natasha and Tom with hearty handshakes and enthusiastic congratulations. Not to mention offers to help with their wedding.

"I'll do the cake," Mrs. McKay, who ran the bakery, said with obvious excitement.

A hand slapped down on Tom's shoulder. It was the owner of the local pub. "I've a cask of ale I've been saving in case the rationing became too much. Consider it a wedding gift for the reception. You're holding it at the pub, right?"

Tom thanked him heartily before looking at Natasha to check if the pub was okay for their party.

When she nodded, he answered for both of them, "The pub it is."

"We'll get everyone to bring something to eat." A woman Natasha had yet to meet joined their small group. "Some of us have been saving our rations for a special occasion, and what's a wedding if not a reason to splurge?"

"There's produce at the farm," Tom said. "I'm sure Ben wouldn't mind donating to the cause."

Natasha felt her cheeks burn with the knowledge Ben would very much mind having any involvement in their wedding.

"He'll be your best man, of course," the barman said.

Tom's laugh was carefree. "He'd kick my backside all the way to Edinburgh if I asked anyone else."

With each new conversation around the wedding, it became clearer to Natasha that she had to come clean with Tom. There was no way Ben wouldn't say something, not after his reaction during her visit, and Tom needed to hear the truth from her.

"We'll need a band," a young man said. "You playing, Tom?"

"When I'm not dancing with my bride." He took her hand. "If she lets me stray from her side, that is."

"Look at that," another man called out in amusement. "Who knew Tom Savage was a romantic?"

"I did." A woman at the back piped up and was quickly, and harshly, hushed by most of the room.

Tom's face turned the deepest red. "That was a long time ago," he told Natasha solemnly.

"What was?" She faked innocence.

"See why I love her?" he demanded of the crowd.

Just as things were getting a bit raucous, a gavel struck wood, calling the meeting to order.

As silence settled over the crowd, who were all wrapped up for winter in their warm coats and hats, the *unofficial* mayor raised his voice.

"First point of order," he said. "The Andersons had an accident with their cart the other day and broke the wheel. Anybody got a spare wheel or the fixings to repair theirs? Mind you, according to Old Anderson, there's no' much left to fix."

Hands went up from those who felt they could help, and Irene Shaw dutifully wrote their details in her notebook.

"Second agenda point," the mayor read from a piece of paper in his hand. "We need help with shoveling snow around town..." His attention shifted to the back of the hall, where the entrance was located. "Ben?"

Ben? Here?

Natasha twisted around in her seat. And there he was.

Standing in the shadow at the back of the room. The knot in her stomach tightened further.

"Ben!" Tom leaped to his feet, his face painted with delight. "There's a seat beside us if you don't want to sit with the council."

The joyous smiles of the townsfolk faded as Ben walked toward the front. And then the whispers started. They rushed through the room like a breeze through leaves: *Why's he wearing that old coat?... clothes are falling off him... awfy pale... heard he was injured in the war... A shot to the head... no' the same...*

Natasha tuned out the murmurs, her mouth becoming dry as she watched Ben walk stiffly down the center aisle toward his grinning best friend. His lips drawn in a tight line and his eyes dark with displeasure, he wore the stained and torn army coat he'd got from the Americans.

It didn't take a genius to see something was very wrong with Ben Baxter. As he passed each row of chairs, their occupants fell silent. It was almost as if the crowd as a whole feared breathing too loudly might lead to them missing something.

"Sit here." Tom appeared to be the only one in the room oblivious of the dangerous cloud surrounding Ben. "It's good to see you out of the house, brother." Tom's joy was clear as he stepped away from his seat, arms spread wide, ready to embrace his friend in welcome.

Ben removed his hand from his pocket.

And pointed a gun at his best friend's heart.

There was a collective gasp of horrified shock. Ben paid no attention to it or to the calls for him to put down the gun. His attention remained focused on the couple in front of him.

"Ben?" Tom said carefully. "What are you doing?"

"I'm taking control of a situation that needs it. Natasha," Ben snapped, "come over here, right now."

Confusion rippled around the room as Tom held out a hand to stop her. "Now, what do you want with Nat?"

"Don't call her that." Ben's eyes were deadly cold when they stared at Tom. "Natasha, come over here at once."

She had no choice but to do as he said. Palms sweating and heart pounding, she slowly got to her feet. All she could think about was calming Ben down enough to stop him aiming at Tom.

"It's okay, Ben," she said. "Put down the gun. We're all friends here, and you wouldn't want to hurt a friend, would you?"

"I don't intend to hurt anyone," he said. "I only want my wife to come home."

The ripple of shock made the air crackle.

"Wife?" the mayor asked hesitantly. "You're no' making any sense, lad."

"I'm making perfect sense. This is what I should have done as soon as we returned to Scotland; maybe then she wouldn't have taken to running around town with another man."

"It's fine." Natasha attempted to soothe. "I'm happy to go with Ben and talk. We're good friends, and I'm sure we can work this out."

As she tried to squeeze past Tom, he gently pushed her back behind him.

"You're confused, Ben." All amusement had evaporated from Tom's voice now. "Natasha isn't your wife, but she will be mine. I asked her to marry me, and she said yes. I was hoping you'd stand up for me as my best man."

The gun wavered in the air, making everyone freeze in place. "She's my wife, and I won't have you or anyone else take her from me. I'm the one who saved her and brought her here. She belongs to me."

"Ben, my man, Angus is right. You aren't making any sense." Tom took a step toward his friend. "We all know you were the one to get Natasha out of Germany, but that doesn't mean you own her." He took another small step.

"I have the paperwork to prove it," Ben declared, his aim back to being precisely focused on Tom. "There's a marriage certificate at home in my safe. Now move aside and allow me access to my wife."

"I can't do that," Tom said gently. "You're waving a gun around, and I've got to say, I'm a wee bit worried you'll lose control of it. We wouldn't want anyone to get hurt accidentally, now, would we?" He'd managed to get two steps closer to his friend as he talked.

"I'm serious," Ben told him. "I will shoot you if you don't get out of my way and leave my wife alone."

"Aye, I can see you're serious." Another step forward and Tom was almost within reaching distance of Ben.

"Don't do it," Natasha said softly, speaking to Tom.

"I don't want to do it," Ben snapped. "But he's forcing my hand by trying to take you. He betrayed me. They all did." His gun swept to the right as he gestured to the rest of the people in the room.

That's when Tom made a grab for the gun.

Screams rang out. Chairs crashed to the ground as people fled or hid. A child cried in its mother's arms.

And suddenly, Natasha was back on the Eastern Front.

As Ben and Tom wrestled for control of the weapon, she heard only machine-gun fire. Bombs fell, and the building rocked. The wailing and screaming grew louder, making her cover her ears. And smoke, so much smoke, burned her eyes and made her gasp desperately for air.

"Get down," she screeched the warning. "We're under attack. Take cover."

Tom.

She had to get to Tom.

A gunshot went off like a cannon beside her head. Natasha didn't think. She merely reacted, throwing herself at Tom and taking him to the ground.

"Where are you hurt?" To protect him, she tried to cover his huge body with her much smaller one. "Where's the wound? We must get help. Somebody help!"

"Nat." An arm wrapped around her, firm and tight. "Nat," the voice crooned. "It's okay. Everything's okay. You're in Scotland, and this isn't the war. The war's over; it's all over."

"Where are you shot?" Natasha frantically ran her hands over every inch of Tom she could reach, searching for blood.

"It wasn't me. I wasn't shot."

A hug smothered her so tightly it felt as if her bones might snap. A large body rocked her. Soothed her. Cooed to her.

And slowly, gradually, other sounds penetrated the fog of confusion and panic within her mind.

"He'll need the hospital." Fear sounded in the voice. "Bring the car around. We'll take him ourselves. Archie, you keep pressure on the wound."

All at once, the present came at her like a train through a tunnel, steamrolling right over the past.

"Ben?" she whispered.

"I'm sorry, love." Tom still held her tight, both of them lying on the cold church floor. "The gun went off."

"I need to see." She shoved away from him and scrambled across the floor to Ben.

He lay unconscious, blood pooling at his side.

"Move," she commanded. "I have medical training."

"Aye," a voice said. "We all got some training during the war; we know what we're doing."

"No." Natasha's military training took over. She was back in charge once again, and she would not tolerate insubordination. "You don't have my training for dealing with injuries sustained during combat situations. Move aside and let me do my job. *Now!*"

She shoved her way past the man blocking her and pulled aside Ben's coat and shirt to examine the wound. "It's gone through the flesh here. I don't think it's hit anything vital, but he's bleeding a lot."

A hand came to rest on her shoulder and squeezed. "What do you need?"

She relaxed at the sound of Tom's voice. "I'll need towels, a needle and some thread, a candle, bandages and dressings, and something to sterilize the wound."

"You heard her," Tom said, causing people to start running.

"I need you to apply pressure to his wound, front and back." She moved aside for Tom. "You're stronger than I am, and we need to stop the bleeding." Someone thrust a hand towel at her, and she grabbed it gratefully. "Tom, use this to help stem the flow."

As he took the towel from her, others dashed back into the room.

"I have the vodka," the barman said.

"Good." She took the bottle. "Move your hands while I disinfect the wound. We'll have to hold him down, this will hurt."

Tom secured Ben on his injured side while two burly men fell to their knees opposite her. One put a restraining arm across his chest, the other pinned his legs.

Natasha removed the towel and liberally doused the wound, front and back, with the alcohol.

Ben shot back to consciousness with a loud howl of agony, and the men had to fight to keep him down.

"Stay still," Natasha told him. "You've been shot, and we have to disinfect the wound."

"Tasha?" Ben seemed to have difficulty focusing on her. "I'm sorry, Tasha. I'm sorry."

"Shh," she soothed. "It's okay. We're going to get you help."

"I never meant..." His back arched from pain as she cleaned his wounds. "You, Tom, you're perfect for each other. I came... I came to give him the gun. A gift. Everything's all mixed up in my head. I think I'm here, and then I'm gone." Tears ran down the sides of his face, and the men looked away. Someone muffled a sob. "I'm sorry, Tasha."

"I know." She forced a smile for him. "We both do, don't we, Tom?"

"Aye." Tom gave his friend an emotion-filled grin. "To be honest, I'm a wee bit relieved to see you can be an idiot like the rest of us."

"I need to stitch these wounds," she told Ben. "This is going to hurt."

"Everything hurts." Ben rested his head back on the floor and closed his eyes, tears still rolling down his face, and Natasha knew he wasn't only talking about the gunshot wound. The war had torn Ben apart and he was suffering.

"Needle and thread." A young girl appeared beside Natasha.

"I have a candle." A boy held one out to her.

"Light the candle and pass the needle through the flame several times to sterilize it," Natasha ordered before lowering her voice to speak to Tom. "Hold him tight. This will be much worse than the vodka, and he can't move while I'm putting in stitches."

"You concentrate on fixing him up, and we'll take care of the rest." Tom leaned into her and placed a kiss on her forehead.

"Here's the needle." The young girl held it out to her.

"Spasibo." The word slipped out, and she stilled, hoping no one had noticed she'd spoken in Russian. It was a silly slipup brought on by the stress of the situation. One she couldn't afford to repeat. She wiped her forehead with her arm and took a deep breath. "I need more light."

"There's a lamp in my study," the vicar said.

"Ben," Natasha said. "I'm going to stitch your front first."

He nodded his head once to let her know he'd heard.

"I'll need more thread soon," she said to the crowd.

"We'll sort it," the mayor said. "You concentrate on what you're doing."

Natasha's hands remained steady despite a cold sweat breaking out on her forehead. As a lamp was moved into position beside her, she lifted the towel from the wound. Then, with one last glance at the men holding Ben to ensure they were ready, she started sewing his skin back together.

At the first prick of the needle, Ben's body turned wooden, and a strangled cry forced its way through his clenched jaw.

"You're doing great," Tom told him. "This won't take long, and you'll have a fine scar to show the lassies when we're done."

Blood ran over Natasha's fingers and hands, making her grip on the needle slip.

"Someone fetch a cloth," Tom called out. "Natasha needs to wipe her hands."

She dried off her hands using the offered cloth and

patted away the blood around the wound before carrying on. That rhythm continued—stitch, wipe, stitch—until she'd sealed both wounds with tight, precise stitches.

"How are you, Ben?" She reached for the bandages.

"Alive," he spat out, sweat dripping into his eyes from his forehead. His skin was a desperate shade of gray and he was shivering.

"Alive is good," Tom said, sounding relieved.

"Very good," Natasha agreed as she bandaged Ben's side. "We'll need blankets. We have to keep him warm."

Yet again, someone in the crowd went running at her words. Doing what little they could to help.

"You *have* done this before," Tom whispered with admiration as he watched her dress the wound. "Those stitches are perfect."

Swallowing down her anxiety, Natasha gazed deep into his beloved eyes and gave him the truth. "I had to sew up several of my comrades when they were injured during battle on the Eastern Front. I learned how to give emergency medical care from the Soviet military. It was compulsory training before they allowed us to take our places with our air squadrons. My job was to bomb the Nazis during the night. I was a pilot."

He reached out to brush her hair off her face, his hands far too gentle to belong to a man his size. "I always thought there was something special about you, Nat. Now I realize I was wrong. It's not only *something*. It's *everything*."

Natasha's heart melted into a puddle within her.

"Ben!" came a terrified shout from the doorway as his housekeeper dashed into the room. She fell to her knees beside Natasha and took Ben's hand. "What have you gone and done now?"

The relief at seeing Anne was clear on Ben's face. "I've made a right fool of myself," he said making Anne cry.

"It'll be all right, lass." The mayor awkwardly patted the housekeeper's shoulder. "We'll keep a close eye on him now Natasha's fixed him up. Irene? Set up a roster of volunteers to take turns watching over Ben until we can get the doctor out here."

Anne cleared her throat. "I've already called him, he's coming tomorrow." She kept a tight hold on Ben's hand as he drifted off to sleep. Exhausted from the pain and trauma.

"What did he mean about you being married?" the mayor asked Natasha.

She stilled, but Anne answered before she could. "Last week, he was convinced *I* was his wife. That's one of the reasons I called the doctor."

The mayor scratched his head. "He said there was a marriage certificate."

"Aye," Anne said. "And today, he thought the pigeons were spying on him for the Nazis."

With a bark of relieved laughter, the mayor wandered off to check on plans for taking care of Ben. The housekeeper caught Natasha's eye and gave her a smile, along with the slightest of nods, making it clear that their secret was safe with her.

"I want to go home," Natasha said, suddenly bone weary.

Tom stood and reached out a hand to her. "Come on then, I'll walk you."

As she got to her feet, she noticed her wonderful new coat was saturated with Ben's blood. It was one disappointment too many, and Natasha burst into tears. "My coat," she sobbed.

Tom enfolded her in his arms. "I'll get you another one."

"How?" It was hopeless, he'd used all his saved clothing rations on the one she wore.

"I'm resourceful." He kissed her head. "And motivated. Plus, I need to keep you safe and warm until our wedding."

"Only until then?" She snuggled into him, still crying but not caring who might be watching or what they thought.

"No," he whispered. "For the rest of our lives."

Then, right there, in front of everyone, Tom kissed her and made the world disappear.

36

———

Brodie had returned to the conference room, tight-lipped and furious after talking with Catherine. He'd tossed the keys of his SUV to Katya and tersely told her he was going for a walk. To clear his head. All Katya and Lawrence could assume was that his meeting hadn't gone well.

With no other option but to take his car and wait for Brodie to calm down, Katya headed back to his house. Which was how she ended up standing in the doorway of his living room, wondering what her parents were doing there.

By the looks of it, her mother was going through wedding magazines with Denise, while her father napped in the corner of a sofa. With his long legs stretched out in front of him, he had his arms folded over his chest, and if she wasn't mistaken, he was softly snoring.

He also still wore his funeral tartan.

"There she is." Her mother bounced to her feet when she spotted Katya. "That dress looks lovely on you." She nudged Katya's dad awake with the toe of her shoe. "Doesn't she look pretty in a dress? Much better than those jeans she lives in."

Her dad's eyes flew open. "I'm awake," he barked.

"The dress looks great." Denise came over to give Katya a much-needed hug. "Definitely prettier on you than on me. Now, tell me how the meeting went. I'd rather talk about that than the dress." She peered into the hallway. "Where's Brodie?"

"He needed a"—she made quotation marks in the air with her fingers—"walk to clear his head."

"Oh." Denise gave her a smile filled with pity. "It went well then."

"Sit down," her mother urged as she led Katya over to a sofa. "Tell us everything. Bain," she called, "be a darling, and make us some tea."

"I live to serve," Bain called back.

Whether that meant they were getting tea, Katya didn't know. She also wasn't sure why Bain wasn't at work with the rest of his brothers, and then her eyes landed on Denise.

"Please tell me you haven't been hanging out here alone with Bain."

"Nope, he only came home half an hour ago. Said he had some files to go through, and he might as well do it here." She preened. "He also said the view was better here than at the office."

"You're playing with fire," Katya warned. As usual, her words fell on deaf ears.

"Enough about Bain." Her mother stroked Katya's hair. "We're dying to know what happened with the lawyers."

Katya sank into the sofa with a sigh. "It didn't go well. I don't think there's any way to stop Catherine from getting her grubby hands on Ben's gift—even if we could afford a lengthy court battle to fight for it." She blinked back sudden tears. "I think we're going to lose the land."

"Oh, my wee darling." Her mother sat beside Katya and pulled her into a fierce hug. "I'm so sorry this is happening to you."

Katya sniffed, inhaling her mother's floral scent and finding comfort in it. "So am I."

Delia leaned away from her and brushed a stray tear from Katya's cheek. "This is horrible, and it's undoubtedly a setback, but it's nothing you two can't overcome together. That's the most important thing in all of this. At least you have Brodie."

Katya caught Denise's sympathetic smile and almost started crying all over again. At some point soon, she'd have to tell her parents she didn't have Brodie either. The news would devastate her mother.

Her father cleared his throat, appearing uncomfortable in the face of female emotion. "Do you want me to have a talk with Kitty?"

Katya held out a hand to him, which he readily took. "I appreciate the offer, Dad, I just don't think it'd make any difference." Plus, he was still sporting a black eye from his fight with Joe. It would be best if he didn't have to deal with a gunshot wound as well, and Catherine Baxter did delight in using her rifle against unwelcome guests.

Her dad squeezed her hand. "If you change your mind, let me know. Hell, I could even drag Joe along for backup. I'm sure we can put our differences aside for the greater good."

"Thanks, Dad."

To her surprise, Bain sauntered into the living room at that moment, carrying a tray full of mugs, a teapot, milk and sugar.

"You have a tray?" Katya was genuinely shocked. "And a teapot?"

"Of course not," her mother said. "I brought them with me."

"What else would you take on a visit to your daughter?" Bain said with a straight face.

"You know?" Her mother considered him. "I've never been able to tell when you're mocking me."

His smile could have charmed the pants off the queen. "Would I dare?"

To Katya's disgust, her mother blushed, and her father made a territorial growling noise. Bain just sauntered back out of the room, looking cocky as hell.

"Your mother has something she thought might cheer you up." Denise waggled her eyebrows at Katya, setting off all kinds of internal alarms.

"I almost forgot." Her mother reached down beside the sofa and pulled out the suitcase containing Natasha's wedding dress.

"You're giving it to me for the museum?" She didn't have the heart to tell her mother that, without Ben's land, there would be no museum.

"Don't be silly," her mother said. "I thought we'd try it on to see what alterations it needs. Denise is great with a needle and thread, and I'm not so bad myself. Between us, we can make you look a million dollars. This will be fun and will help take your mind off all the things out of your control. You'll see."

"Yes," Denise said solemnly, her eyes sparkling with mischief. "This will be fun." Then she mouthed *for us*.

THE LAST THING Brodie expected to find when he made it home was Katya standing on his living room coffee table, wearing a wedding dress, with Delia and Denise at her feet. Oh, and Fraser snoring on a couch.

"No!" Delia screeched as soon as she spotted him. "You aren't supposed to see the bride before the wedding."

"Um." Brodie was confused. "I hate to tell you, Delia, but that ship sailed long ago."

"Get your mind out of the gutter." She rushed over to smack his chest before trying to push him out of the room. "I meant the dress."

"Mum," Katya said with obvious long-suffering. "Let him come in and sit down. This isn't a normal wedding, and you know it. Plus, this is Brodie's house."

"Technically, this house belongs to Craig Wallace," Fraser said, his eyes still closed. "And he's no' looking after it properly. If I were you, son, I'd ask for a decorator to come in and spruce the place up a bit."

"I'm back to being son then?" Brodie asked the lump of a man on the couch. "I thought I was the loser who ruined your daughter's life."

Fraser opened one eye. "Can you no' be both?"

Savage logic—there was no arguing with it. "I'd like a minute alone to talk to Katya."

She moved to step down from the table, but her mother stopped her. "Not until I have that hem pinned up. I swear, your great-grandmother must have been six-foot tall. Either that or this dress dragged wherever she went. It's not like it has a train—though goodness knows there's enough material in the skirt to make one—it's just overly long."

"I'll put the dress back on when I've finished talking to Brodie," Katya said.

"No, you won't. I know you. You'll make a run for it and end up getting married in jeans again like you did last time."

A look of longing passed over Katya's face at the mere mention of her beloved jeans.

"How about"—Denise linked her arm through Delia's—"we all go have a nice cup of tea in the kitchen, and let Brodie and Katya talk in here?"

"Aye," Delia said slowly, "I guess that would work. Don't you dare do anything to damage that dress while I'm gone, Katya Jane Savage MacGregor. Fraser! Come along."

"I was comfy here," Fraser complained as he dragged himself to his feet. "Don't upset her," he warned Brodie as he passed.

"Don't move from that table," Delia called from the hallway.

Thankfully, Denise had the presence of mind to shut the door behind her. Then he was alone with Katya.

"Do you think they're done giving orders?" Katya glared at the closed door.

Brodie had other more important issues on his mind than Katya's parents. "We need to talk." He closed the distance between them.

"Great. Those four little words no one ever wants to hear."

"I've done some thinking."

"And there's another four...."

He shook his head at her. "Be serious. We need to discuss the situation with the land." And not get distracted by the sight of Katya in an ivory white dress that made her skin glow.

The neck wasn't as low as he would have liked, and it was a tad snug in parts, yet it still flowed over her like cream off the back of a spoon. His fingers itched to touch, to see how soft the material felt—especially where it cupped her breasts like gentle hands.

"Hey, eyes up here," she snapped.

"Why would I do that when the view down here is so good?"

"You're a pervert, do you know that?" She didn't sound particularly bothered by it either. "If you must know, it's a little snug in the chest area. I don't think Natasha had much up top."

"Poor old Tom, because I definitely appreciate a fuller figure on my woman." His hand reached up before he could stop it.

She smacked it away. "Mum will kill me if she comes back in here and finds dirty fingerprints on my boob."

Brodie looked at his hand. It seemed clean enough.

"Anyway," Katya grumped. "Are you ready to tell me what Catherine said to you at the lawyer's office, or do I need to beat it out of you?"

That was Katya's way of threatening to tickle him until he caved.

He took a step back, out of reach, and watched her smirk. "She offered to give me the land—if I agreed to divorce you and never speak to you again."

As he watched, her face turned the same color as her dress. "You accepted her offer, didn't you?"

Brodie stilled. "What makes you think that?"

Katya shook her head, visibly upset. "It's everything you wanted. You can build on the land without having to share it with me." She blinked rapidly and focused on the cornices at the top of the walls.

"It's a funny thing," Brodie said. "If you'd asked me a month ago what I wanted, I would have said exactly that."

Hesitantly, she turned to look at him. "And now?"

Brodie placed his hands on the sash tied around her waist. "Since then, I've learned that I don't exactly spend time considering what I want. I have a tendency to float along, believing everyone else's ideas for me are perfectly fine."

"It's because you're too easygoing," Katya said softly, her hands finding his shoulders.

With her on the coffee table, he was looking up at her for a change, and he couldn't miss those eyes softening.

"You used to tell me that all the time," he said.

"I was worried you were only doing things to make your family happy." She shrugged, although it was far from nonchalant. "I also worried you were doing stuff you didn't want to do just to make me happy."

His hands flexed on her waist. "Then when I didn't go along with your idea to travel the world, you thought I'd snapped and was telling you exactly what I wanted for a change. Kat, tell me you didn't really believe I was desperate to get rid of you?"

She swallowed, and he watched her throat bob. "I figured you'd gone along with the marriage because I'd wanted it, and when I wanted to travel, it gave you the perfect excuse to get out of being with me. It was the perfect excuse. I laid it all out for you. Practically gift wrapped on a plate."

"No," he whispered. "No, that's not it at all."

"After a while, I came to believe I'd used our fight as an excuse to run away," she confessed in her own whisper. "Maybe, it was me who wanted out?"

"How about," Brodie said, "we stop coming up with stories about what happened and agree we were too young to know what we were doing or why? How about we stop fighting and agree we still love each other?"

Her breath hitched.

"And," he added, "how about we put an end to this gulf between us and carry on from here together?"

"Brodie." Pain colored her voice and shone in her eyes. "That gulf is full of things we did that we can't take back. I'm not sure we can move on from that. We're different people now."

"Aye, we're adults now. We don't have to think with our hormones, we can engage our brains. We've wasted too much time, Kat, and I don't want to waste any more. Sure, we've changed, but do you know what?" He leaned closer to cup her cheek. "I like this new Katya. She's a little different from the one I knew, which isn't a bad thing. Down deep, she's still the girl I've always loved. She's smart and funny and sexy as hell. She pushes me to stop accepting the easy options in life and to take some risks. She makes me feel alive.

"I've been treading water for ten long years and didn't even know it until you came back into my life and threw me a lifeline. I'm holding on to that lifeline, Kat, and I'm not letting go this time. So, you can walk away. You can say it's too hard to start again, to build something better, something more mature than we ever had as kids, but it won't do you any good. This time, I won't stand by while you leave me. This time, I'll follow you wherever you go. Plus, somebody needs to make sure you don't get killed by a drug-running gang."

"If I end up crying like a girl, I'll punch your broken nose," she threatened, making him wisely ignore the tears on her cheeks. "I'm not sure I can trust like that again."

"Because I hurt you when I rejected you." He closed his eyes briefly before looking into hers. "I will regret that until the day I die, and I will spend my life trying to show you how sorry I am that I ever did that to you."

"I'm not looking for you to do penance forever."

"I'm Catholic, Kitten, it's what we do. One way or another, I'll earn your trust again and make you believe that I was never rejecting you. I was just being a selfish scared wee boy."

She stared into his eyes for the longest time before gently cupping his face. "We've lost so much time," she whispered. "Let people in that had no place between us."

He felt the ache in her words right to his soul, because it was his pain too. "Ten years is nothing compared to a lifetime."

"Yeah," she whispered. "I do still love you, even though you're a huge, big baby."

"I can live with that." He stroked his thumb over her bottom lip. "As long as you still love me."

"I'm an idiot, but I do."

"That's my girl." He cupped her head and brought her down so he could sip at her lips before kissing away the tears on her cheeks. "Marry me, Katya. Be my wife again," he whispered. "What do you say?"

"I'll say what I said the last time you asked." She smiled through the tears. "Aye, but I expect I'll regret it."

Brodie's smile was impossible to repress. "Lucky I find that romantic streak of yours so adorable."

"I'm sorry I left," she whispered against his lips. "I've always been sorry."

"Shh," he breathed. "We're drawing a line under the past and starting afresh. Okay?"

She nodded, her hands tightening their hold on his face. It was a bittersweet beginning. One tainted with the knowledge of everything they'd lost during their time apart. They were no longer each other's only lovers. Not their only kiss. Brodie had missed the excitement of watching Katya train to be a pilot. She'd missed him growing into a man you could count on. But there was nothing they could do about the choices they'd made in the past. All they could do was forgive themselves—and each other—and move on.

"I like this dress," he said between small, gentle kisses.

"Mum's determined we renew our vows."

"Then maybe we should."

She nipped his bottom lip. "Are you only saying that to make her happy?"

He cocked his head to the side and thought about it. "I don't think so, but that's going to be a hard habit to break." Plus, he wasn't sure it was purely habit. He suspected that wanting to please those around him was a big part of his personality. After all, if something really didn't matter that much to him, what was wrong with compromising on it?

"Don't worry," she said with a smile against his mouth. "I'll help you break it."

Brodie returned the smile, kissing her through it until the smile faded and the kiss took over. His hands slid around to the back of her dress, delighting in the silk beneath his fingertips—until they brushed over an area that wasn't soft at all. In fact, it felt...crinkly.

"Brodie, poking me in the back is not a turn on," Katya grumbled.

"I think there's something tucked into the dress."

She reached behind her and felt the sash. Her eyes went wide. "It feels like paper."

"Turn around," Brodie said, and she did so eagerly.

"Be careful," she ordered. "It's probably really old."

"Strange how I didn't think of that myself," he muttered

as he carefully removed a small, tightly folded piece of paper.

"What is it?" Katya, who wasn't known for her patience, swung back around as he unfolded it.

Eyes wide, he looked up from the paper. "It's a certificate of divorce."

37

———

April 1946

Scotland

If Tom thought it strange his fiancée wanted to wear a wedding dress she already owned, he hadn't said so.

"The women at the camp made it for me as a gift," Natasha had told him. "They had a sewing class at the displacement camp and someone found some parachutes. They said they would make beautiful wedding dresses, so that's what they made. This one was given to me."

He'd stroked a hand over her hair and pressed a kiss to her forehead. "Then it's good you have a dress to wear that means something to you. Although, another man would wonder why the women thought handing out wedding dresses was a good idea. Not me though." His grin was contagious. "Because, if I did, I'm sure my *combat-trained* wife would soon sort me out."

Ever since he'd discovered what she'd done in the war,

he'd been openly proud of her. In fact, there were moments when she had to remind him it was a secret that could get her sent back to the Soviet Union. If she hadn't, Tom would have shouted about her from the rooftops.

After explaining about the dress as best she could, she'd taken it to the local women's craft group and asked them to make some adjustments. Despite the dress being precious to her, she couldn't walk down the aisle to Tom wearing the same style as she had with Ben.

The women had been more than enthusiastic about helping her, and they'd speedily transformed her dress into something new. A sash now wrapped around the middle, circling her waist several times before draping down the back to the hem. The puff sleeves were gone, replaced with neat cap sleeves, while the boatneck had been transformed into a tasteful scoop, and they'd removed some of the fullness of the skirt to give her a sleeker, more sophisticated silhouette—although, they'd kept the length. It was as beautiful as the dress the women had made for her when she married Ben. But this one was different enough to be just for Tom.

A quiet rap at her bedroom door sent Natasha scurrying to answer it. She expected to find Betty McLeod, one of her bridesmaids, on the other side. Instead, she found Ben.

For a second, shock made it impossible to move or even think, then she found her voice. "Ben, what are you doing here? You're supposed to be in the church with Tom."

After the gunshot incident, Ben had sought help from a doctor in Glasgow who specialized in treating men who suffered from trauma after returning from the war. Ben didn't talk about his visits to the doctor, but over the weeks, he'd started to behave more like the man she'd grown to love—as a friend. He still had flashbacks, although giving up whisky had stopped the paranoid episodes, and he no longer believed he was being spied on. Not only that, he looked healthier and stronger too. Mainly due to his housekeeper never letting him skip a meal.

"I came to give you this." He handed her a folded piece of paper before tucking his hands into the pockets of his suit jacket. "It's important you have it before you walk down the aisle."

With trembling fingers, Natasha unfolded the paper. Her hand flew up to cover her mouth as she gasped. In her hand was a divorce certificate. She was no longer married to Ben Baxter.

"Ben," she whispered, tears welling in her eyes.

"Had things been different," he said softly, "I think we could have fallen in love. There was the potential for it to happen. Then you met Tom, and everyone could see you were meant to be together. You'll always be a dear friend to me. Probably the only person in the world who understands what I went through, but it's clear you were born to be loved by my best friend."

"I, I'm, I..." She wasn't sure what to say.

"It's okay, Tasha." Ben smiled. "There are no debts between us and never will be. I saved you in Germany, and you saved me in Scotland. Not only my life but my sanity— in more ways than you'll ever know." He took a deep breath as he stepped back from the doorway. "After the wedding, I'm going away for a wee while. Don't worry, it has nothing to do with you two, and I expect to be back well before you make me an uncle." He grinned.

"Where are you going?" Natasha wanted to hold him to her and keep him safe in Invertary.

"To Germany," he said wryly. "They need help with rebuilding, and I think going back will help me deal with the things that happened during the war. It's as though I need to be a part of the healing process over there in order to move on."

"Promise you won't stay away too long?" She blinked away tears.

"I promise." He gave her a shy smile. "Plus, there's a lassie here who needs a few years to grow up before she can cope with the likes of me. I'm no' an easy man."

No. He wasn't. But he was a courageous one. "Anne?" Natasha teased, knowing full well Ben had noticed the feelings his housekeeper had for him.

"None of your business." He winked at her. "Now, finish getting ready. I have to get to the church to make sure Tom doesn't bolt before you arrive."

"Don't even joke about that." She laughed, because she knew Tom would never abandon her.

As Ben walked away, he glanced back over his shoulder. "Tasha? The dress is perfect." And then he was gone.

Natasha closed her bedroom door softly before studying the divorce certificate again. Carefully, she folded it until it was small enough to tuck into the folds of the tight sash around her waist. She didn't want to leave it in her room or her luggage, where it could get lost. No, this document was precious, and Natasha wanted to keep it safe. After the wedding, she'd put it away in case she ever needed it.

Until then, she wanted to think only about her soon-to-be husband and the happy life that lay ahead of them.

38

———

By the time Brodie and Katya made it to the council meeting that evening, the old Presbyterian church's hall was jam-packed.

"This must be the daftest idea we've ever had," Katya hissed at him as they made their way to the two empty seats Brodie's brothers had saved for them right in the middle of the hall.

"I'm inclined to agree," Brodie said. "And that's saying a lot. Remember the time we freewheeled down a mountain on our bikes? That seemed like such a great idea when we were eight. We're lucky we didn't die."

"Luck had nothing to do with it." No, their journey toward the loch at breakneck speed had been slowed by fields of heather and several large bramble bushes. When they'd eventually limped home, they'd been scratched to hell and bleeding everywhere.

Spotting her mother sitting in a seat that put her directly under one of the overhead spotlights, Katya shook her head. Even in the middle of a crowd, Delia managed to find a way to shine.

Brodie waved at her mum. "Do you think she seeks out the dramatic spots, or do they find her?"

"Oh, she looks for them." In her *Streetcar Named Desire* look—fifties dress, pearls, perfectly coiffed hair, silk gloves, and a lace fan—Delia was dressed for drama tonight. "It's nice to see Dad finally out of mourning dress, though." Wearing green and yellow tartan, Fraser sat at his wife's side.

Smiling at Brodie's parents—positioned in the front row next to the women of Knit or Die, who had their knitting out—Katya took a seat beside Darach.

She bumped his arm with her shoulder. "How's it hanging?"

"I'm not talking to you." He continued to stare straight ahead, arms folded and a scowl on his face.

"Aw, come on, Darach, this isn't my fault." Mostly.

He glared down at her. "Of course, it's your fault. It's always your fault when you two are together. He's just the muscle for your master plans."

"To be fair," Katya felt the need to point out, "half the time, he comes up with ideas on his own."

"You're as bad as each other." Darach turned his grumpy face back to the front of the hall, where Dougal—the town's unofficial mayor—had his head together with the council secretary.

"Would it help if I promised to make it up to you?" She batted her lashes as he gave her the side-eye.

"How?"

"I'm working on that part," she said honestly.

"Aye, well, you can get back to me when you're done. Then we'll talk."

Bain leaned forward to look around Darach. The fool was grinning. "If it's any consolation, I completely forgive you, and I have no problem with talking to you."

"Sit your arse back," Darach snapped. "She's not going to put in a good word for you with Denise. That girl doesn't want you. Let it go."

"And another dream cruelly destroyed by my uncaring brothers," Bain said woefully as he leaned back into his seat.

Giving up on both of them, she glanced past Brodie to Conall and Kade. They smiled and gave her a thumbs-up, which made her laugh. Seemed she'd managed to upset only one brother this time.

A tap on her shoulder had Katya turning to find Denise. "Are you sure about this?"

Katya nodded. "I don't see any other option."

"Nor do I," Denise said softly.

"Order, order!" Dougal bellowed from the front of the hall, making Katya turn back around.

Brodie's hand immediately found hers and squeezed tight. When she smiled up at him, he pointed to the chairs near the far wall. Catherine Baxter sat next to her farm manager, looking most pleased with herself.

A sick, falling sensation had Katya rubbing her stomach, the urge to vomit strong. Fortunately, it passed. The woman mystified her. How could anyone allow themselves to become that bitter and twisted? Why would you want to live like that? And then it occurred to her—sometimes the only thing people had to hold on to was their hatred and anger. Sometimes they were too afraid of what they'd have without it that they never let it go.

Katya really didn't want to be like that. "I forgive you for everything that happened with us," she whispered to Brodie. "There's no need for penance. As far as I'm concerned it's done and forgotten."

"Tell you what"—his eyes sparkled with mischief— "throw in forgiveness for every stupid thing I'll do in the future, and we have a deal."

"Not on your life." *Bloody chancer.*

"Order!" Dougal boomed as he pounded the lectern with the wooden gavel, making the new young vicar beside him wince.

Behind him, Caroline McInnes—the town's unofficial secretary and the most organized woman Katya had ever met—got to her feet. She walked over to the lectern, took the gavel from Dougal, and leaned into the microphone. "The meeting is about to begin. Please be quiet."

There was immediate silence, which had Dougal glaring at the crowd.

"I'm not sure I can wait for the 'any more business' part of the agenda," Katya confessed. "My stomach's already doing somersaults."

"If it gets too bad, we'll interrupt and do our bit early," he whispered back.

Oh, Dougal would *not* like that. "Only if we have to."

"First item on the agenda," Dougal held up a piece of paper and read from it. "Kit—sorry, *Catherine* Baxter would like to discuss the condition of the road leading up to Baxter Farm. Catherine, the floor is yours." Dougal gestured to the microphone, set up on a stand facing the platform.

As Catherine strode over to the mic, Dougal took an old-fashioned stopwatch out of the pocket of his lime-green Harris Tweed waistcoat—which, for some reason, he'd teamed with a pink shirt. "I will be timing you," he told Catherine. "Please do not go over your allotted time."

Catherine hadn't changed out of her twinset and pearls, and the sight made Katya's blood boil. It took every ounce of strength she possessed not to erupt with rage at the woman who'd made it her mission to ruin Katya's life. Instead, she tried to concentrate on what Catherine was saying.

"As you're aware"—Catherine's sharp voice came over the speakers—"the private road up to Baxter Farm is owned by my family. In recent years, there has been a dramatic increase in traffic along that road—especially seeing as it now links up to the main road. The road wasn't designed for that much use and has become littered with potholes and debris. I would like to file a motion asking that council funds be used for repairs. I fail to see why I should foot the bill for what is now essentially a public road."

"I object!" Katya was on her feet before she'd even realized she intended to stand.

Catherine turned and smirked at her. "Well, you *are* quite objectionable."

In a panic, Katya glanced down at Brodie. "I couldn't wait," she hissed. "She annoys me."

"Fine." With a sigh, he stood beside her, holding her hand. He raised his voice and said, "Apparently, Katya objects."

There was a ripple of laughter from everyone but the American singer Josh McInnes, who was wolfing down popcorn and staring at them as though they were his own personal reality TV show.

Dougal leaned into the mic, which he didn't need in the first place because they could hear his voice in Glasgow on a normal day. "This isn't the way we do things. If you object to Catherine's proposal, file it with the council to be considered before the next meeting."

"That isn't what I object to," Katya said loudly.

"Then, for goodness' sake, what do you object to?"

Judging by the purple hue of his face, Dougal was fast losing patience.

"I object to Kitty Baxter as a whole."

This caused raucous laughter.

"Settle down, settle down," Dougal called but was ignored. He grabbed the gavel again and smacked it on the lectern. "I said order!" The gavel broke in two, and a piece flew past Caroline's head.

"Sorry, Vicar," Dougal said. "I'll replace it."

"I hope you're going to apologize to Caroline too," Josh McInnes said. "And FYI, my wife isn't as easy to replace, so maybe watch where you're throwing things in future."

"Sorry, Caroline," Dougal muttered.

"That's the third one this year," somebody commented from the crowd as the room started to quieten.

"You can't object to a person," Dougal told Katya. "Now, sit down and stop interrupting council business."

"Actually," Brodie piped up, "we have something to say to everyone, and we might as well do it now, seeing as Katya's stolen the floor anyway."

"This is ridiculous," Catherine said into the microphone. "My issue has been on this agenda for a month. Are you really going to let someone disrupt the order of things purely because they have 'something to say'? Are we going to pander to every child who needs attention?"

"I need my own microphone," Katya grumbled.

Like an answer to her prayer, a little old woman zoomed down the aisle on a mobility scooter. She wore a tartan muumuu, and a hairnet covered her practically bald hair.

"Here"—she thrust a mic at Katya—"you can use mine. I always bring my own because Dougal hogs the bloody thing."

Katya gaped as she took the mic from Betty McLeod's outstretched hand. "I thought you were dead."

"People keep saying that to me," the old woman grumbled. "There's plenty of life in this old duck yet." Then she zoomed away again, giving Catherine a one-fingered salute as she passed.

"I object," Catherine snapped. "I have the floor, and she can't have a microphone purely because she wants one."

The mayor threw up his hands. "You object, she objects, everybody objects."

"Dougal?" Katya called. "This will only take a minute, and then we'll leave the building, and you can get on with things." She took a deep breath. "Brodie and I are renewing our vows two weeks on Saturday at the Catholic church— sorry, Vicar—and everyone in town is invited."

There was a mixed reaction to her announcement. The people who knew they were in a fake relationship appeared confused. Those who didn't were excited. And Catherine Baxter looked disgusted.

Catherine grabbed the microphone off the stand and turned to face Katya. "If you think a fake ceremony will help your case with the judge, you're sorely mistaken."

Brodie took the mic from Katya's hand. Which was probably a good thing, as she was about to swear at Catherine. Over the PA system of a Presbyterian church.

"There are one or two things we need to clear up," Brodie said. "Some of you were told that Katya and I were faking our reunion to try to stop Kitty Baxter from taking back the land Ben gave us. That was true—the emphasis being on was. We're now genuinely together and would like you all to celebrate with us during another wedding ceremony." He flashed a boyish grin. "Seeing as we eloped last time, we feel we owe you a wedding anyway. Oh, and as the icing on the cake, you don't need to bring us any presents."

"This is ridiculous," Catherine said. "I'm telling you, this won't work. Look around you. Nobody believes you. You're only making fools of yourselves. And truthfully, it doesn't matter how far you take this, you don't have a hope in hell of keeping my land." Her smile was spiteful.

"We know," Brodie said, causing gasps from the crowd. "That's why we're returning the deed." He nodded to Conall, on the end of the row, who got up and took the piece of paper Brodie had passed down to him over to Catherine.

For once, Catherine Baxter had nothing to say.

Seeing their deed in Catherine's hand made Katya want to howl in pain at the injustice of it all. That land didn't belong to the Baxters—Ben had intended it for her and Brodie. He would have been disgusted at his daughter's behavior and what she'd turned into. Swallowing down her anger, Katya fought to let it go, knowing it would only eat her alive. And then she'd end up like Kitty.

"What about your plane?" Dougal asked. "And the tourist flights?"

Brodie returned the mic to Katya and let go of her hand to wrap his arm around her shoulders.

"We still plan to do that, but first..." She looked at Brodie, who nodded. "We're going away together after the wedding. There's a seven-seater World War Two seaplane we'd like to buy. Once we have that, we'll find a place for the museum and set up flying tours from the loch itself."

Brodie took the mic back. "We need the seaplane because Katya's *finally* realized that taking only one tourist up at a time isn't going to make us rich."

The crowd burst out laughing, and Katya gave Brodie a

look that she hoped made it clear payback was in his very near future.

"So that's it," Katya said as the laughter died down. "The land belongs to the Baxters again, we're getting married again, and we're off hunting planes...again."

"No," Brodie said, only for her ears. "Not again. This is our first time hunting together. And I have a feeling it won't be our last."

A warm feeling, originating from her heart, spread throughout her body and pushed out the resentment she felt toward Catherine. She might not know what the future held, but she knew it was going to be wonderful, because Brodie was by her side.

"Dougal," Katya said into the mic. "That was all we had to say. We're sorry for the interruption, and...eh...carry on."

A roar filled with laughter, shouting, and chatter filled the hall as Katya and Brodie squeezed out of their row and headed for the exit. As they left, Brodie signaled to Conall that it was time to hand over the other piece of paper they'd asked him to give Catherine. Conall nodded while Katya pushed through the doors and out into the warm summer evening.

As they stood in the street in front of the church, someone called out their names, and when they turned, they weren't at all surprised to find Catherine bearing down on them.

"Is it real?" She held up the document.

"Very," Brodie said. "We found it tucked in with Natasha's things."

"You should also know," Katya added, "that Ben and Natasha were never in love with each other and never had an affair. Ben was distant with his family because he was still dealing with the trauma he suffered in the war. That's why he spent time with Natasha. They spoke about the war and it helped him. He loved your mother."

Catherine gasped, clutching the divorce certificate to her chest.

Brodie tugged Katya into his body as if to shelter her. "We have boxes of letters, notebooks, and other information Katya's collected over the years. They detail what your father went through during the war and how he coped with the lingering trauma afterward."

Catherine swallowed hard. "May I...may I see those?"

"Sure," Brodie drawled. "They'll be in the museum when it opens."

Catherine blinked, looking confused. "When will that be?"

"Hard to tell." Katya shrugged. "We lost the land we planned to build it on, so I guess we'll just have to see what we can find when we return from plane hunting."

Catherine's mouth pursed. "I see. This is punishment for being mistaken about our families?"

"No." Katya felt suddenly weary. "Your punishment is knowing you made a woman's family suffer for decades when all she did was help your father deal with his PTSD. Now, if you don't mind, we have a wedding and a trip to plan."

They turned their backs on Catherine and started down the street toward the loch.

"I'll return the land," Catherine shouted after them.

"No, thanks," Brodie and Katya answered at the same time as they walked away.

At the bottom of the street, the water glistened in the evening sun.

"Do you think I could learn to fly?" Brodie asked as they walked hand in hand.

"I don't see why not." Katya grinned at him. "After all, they sent a monkey into space."

"Oh, you'll pay for that." Brodie tugged her to him.

She jerked out of his hold and was running before he could catch her. "Last one to the loch has to buy dinner," she shouted over her shoulder.

"You won't win this time," he called after her.

But Katya felt like she already had.

ABOUT JANET

I'm a Scot, living in New Zealand and married to a Dutch man. I write contemporary romance with a humorous bent – this is mainly due to the fact I have an odd sense of humour and can't keep it out of anything I do! If I wasn't a writer, I'd like to be Buffy the Vampire Slayer, or Indiana Jones. Unfortunately, both these roles have already been filled. Which may be a good thing as I have no fighting skills, wouldn't know a precious relic if it hit me in the face, and have an aversion to blood. When I'm not living in my head, I'm a mother to two kids, several pet sheep, one dog, four cats, three alpacas, two miniature horses, eight guinea pigs and an escape artist chicken.

I love to hang out with my readers in my Facebook group, so if you're up for it, come join us there.